Romeo's g   one finger   raised her   p gaze. Her stomach knotted at the savage determination on his face.

'They will never get their hands on you or our son. You have my word on this, Maisie.'

She shook her head, her insides growing colder by the second. 'But you can't guarantee that, can you? Or you wouldn't be here with six bodyguards in tow.'

'There's one way to ensure your safety,' he said, his gaze raking her face as if he wanted to pull the answer from her even before he'd asked the question.

'What's that?' she murmured.

'You will marry me. Then you and our son will know the protection of my name.'

Secret Heirs of Billionaires

There are some things money can't buy…

Living life at lightning pace, these magnates are no strangers to stakes at their highest. It seems they've got it all… That is until they find out that there's an unplanned item to add to their list of accomplishments!

Achieved:

1. Successful business empire

2. Beautiful women in their bed

3. *An heir to bear their name…?*

Though every billionaire needs to leave his legacy in safe hands, discovering a secret heir shakes up his carefully orchestrated plan in more ways than one!

Uncover their secrets in:

Unwrapping the Castelli Secret by Caitlin Crews
Brunetti's Secret Son by Maya Blake

Look out for more stories in
The Secret Heirs of Billionaires series in 2016!

millsandboon.co.uk

BRUNETTI'S SECRET SON

BY
MAYA BLAKE

Published in Great Britain 2015
by Mills & Boon, an imprint of Harlequin (UK) Limited,
Eton House, 18-24 Paradise Road, Richmond, Surrey, TW9 1SR

© 2015 Maya Blake

ISBN: 978-0-263-25090-9

Harlequin (UK) Limited's policy is to use papers that are natural,
renewable and recyclable products and made from wood grown in
sustainable forests. The logging and manufacturing processes conform
to the legal environmental regulations of the country of origin.

Printed and bound in Spain
by CPI, Barcelona

Maya Blake's hopes of becoming a writer were born when she picked up her first romance aged thirteen. Little did she know her dream would come true! Does she still pinch herself every now and then, to make sure it's not a dream? Yes, she does!

Feel free to pinch her too, via Twitter, Facebook or Goodreads! Happy reading!

Books by Maya Blake

Mills & Boon Modern Romance

Married for the Prince's Convenience
Innocent in His Diamonds
His Ultimate Prize
Marriage Made of Secrets
The Sinful Art of Revenge
The Price of Success

The Untameable Greeks

What the Greek's Money Can't Buy
What the Greek Can't Resist
What the Greek Wants Most

The 21st Century Gentleman's Club

The Ultimate Playboy

Visit the Author Profile page
at millsandboon.co.uk for more titles.

CHAPTER ONE

THE HIDEOUS MANSION was just as he'd recalled in his nightmares, the gaudy orange exterior clashing wildly with the massive blue shutters. The only thing that didn't quite gel with the picture before him was the blaze of the sun glinting off the grotesquely opulent marble statues guarding the entry gates.

Romeo Brunetti's last memory of this place had been in the chilling rain, his threadbare clothes sticking to his skin as he'd huddled in the bushes outside the gates. A part of him had prayed he wouldn't be discovered, the other more than a tiny bit hopeful that discovery would mean the end to all the suffering, the hunger, the harrowing pain of rejection that ate his thirteen-year-old body alive from morning to night. Back then he would've welcomed the beating his reluctant rescuer had received for daring to return Romeo to this place. Because the beating would have ended in oblivion, and the bitterness coursing through his veins like acid would have been no more.

Unfortunately, the fates had decreed otherwise. He'd hidden in the bushes, cold and near catatonic, until the ever-present hunger had forced him to move.

Romeo stared up at the spears clutched in the hands of the statues, recalling his father's loud-bellied boast of them being made of solid gold.

The man who'd called him a bastard and a waste of space to his face. Right before he'd instructed his minion to throw him out and make sure he never returned. That he didn't care whether the spawn of the whore he'd rutted with in an alleyway in Palermo lived or died, as long as he, Agostino

Fattore, the head of the ruling crime family, didn't have to see the boy's face again.

No…not his *father*.

The man didn't deserve that title.

Romeo's hands tightened on the steering wheel of his Ferrari and he wondered for the thousandth time why he'd bothered to come to this place. Why he'd let a letter he'd shredded in a fit of cold rage seconds after reading it compel him into going back on the oath he'd made to himself over two decades ago. He looked over to the right where the towering outer wall to the late Agostino Fattore's estate rose into the sky, and sure enough, the bush was exactly as he remembered it, its leafy branches spread out, offering the same false sanctuary.

For a wild moment, Romeo fought the strong urge to lunge out of the car and rip the bush out of the earth with his bare hands, tear every leaf and branch to shreds. Tightening his jaw, he finally lowered his window and punched in the code his memory had cynically retained.

As the gates creaked open, he questioned again why he was doing this. So what if the letter had hinted at something else? What could the man whose rejection had been brutally cold and complete have to offer him in death that he'd failed so abjectly to offer in life?

Because he needed answers.

He needed to know that the blood running through his veins didn't have an unknown stranglehold over him that would turn his life upside down when he least expected it.

That the two times in his life when he'd lost control to the point of not recognising himself would be the only times he would feel savagely unmoored.

No one but Romeo knew how much he regretted wasting the four years of his life after the bitter night he'd been here last, looking for acceptance anywhere and any way he could find it. More than hating the man whose blood ran through his veins, Romeo hated the years he'd spent trying to find a replacement for Agostino Fattore.

Giving himself permission to close his heart off at seventeen had been the best decision he'd ever made.

So why are you here? You're nothing like him.

He needed to be sure. Agostino might no longer be alive, but he needed to look into the heart of Fattore's legacy and reassure himself that the lost little boy who'd thought his world would end because of another's rejection was obliterated completely.

Impatient with himself for prevaricating, Romeo smashed his foot on the accelerator and grunted in satisfaction as the tyres squealed on the asphalt road leading to the courtyard. Unfolding himself from the driver's seat, he stalked up to the iron-studded double doors and slammed them open.

Striding into the chequer-tiled hallway, he glared at the giant antique chandelier above his head. If he had cared whether this house stood or fell, that monstrosity would have been the first thing in the incinerator. But he wasn't here to ponder the ugly tastes of a dead man. He was here to finally slay ghosts.

Ghosts that had lingered at the back of his consciousness since he was a child but that had been resurrected one night five years ago, in the arms of a woman who'd made him lose control.

He turned as slow feet shuffled in his direction, followed by firmer footholds that drew a grim smile from Romeo. So, the old order hadn't changed. Or maybe the strength of Romeo's anger had somehow transmitted to Fattore's former second in command, prompting the old man who approached to seek the protection of his bodyguards.

Lorenzo Carmine threw out his hands in greeting, but Romeo glimpsed the wariness in the old man's eyes. 'Welcome, *mio figlio*. Come, I have lunch waiting for us.'

Romeo tensed. 'I'm not your son and this meeting will not last beyond five minutes, so I suggest you tell me what you withheld in your letter right now and stop wasting my time.' He didn't bother to hide the sneer in his voice.

Lorenzo's pale grey eyes flared with a temper Romeo had witnessed the last time he was here. But along with it came the recognition that Romeo was no longer a frightened little boy incapable of defending himself. Slowly, his expression altered into a placid smile.

'You have to pardon me. My constitution requires that I strictly regulate my mealtimes or I suffer for it.'

Romeo turned towards the door, again regretting his decision to come here. He was wasting his time looking for answers in stone and concrete. He was wasting his time, full stop.

'Then by all means go and look after your constitution. Enjoy the rest of your days and don't bother contacting me again.' He stepped towards the door, a note of relief spiking through him at the thought of leaving this place.

'Your father left something for you. Something you will want to see.'

Romeo stopped. 'He was not my father and there's nothing he possesses in this life or the next that could possibly interest me.'

Lorenzo sighed. 'And yet you came all this way at my request. Or was it just to stick out your middle finger at an old man?'

Romeo's jaw clenched, hating that the question he'd been asking himself fell from the lips of a man who'd spent his whole life being nothing but a vicious thug. 'Just spit it out, Carmine,' he gritted out.

Lorenzo glanced at the nearer bodyguard and nodded. The beefy minder headed down the long hallway and disappeared.

'For the sake of my friend, your father, the Almighty rest his soul, I will go against my doctor's wishes.' The remaining guard fell into step behind Lorenzo, who indicated a room to their left.

From memory, Romeo knew it was the holding room for visitors, a garishly decorated antechamber that led to the receiving room, where his father had loved to hold court.

The old man shuffled to a throne-like armchair and sank heavily into it. Romeo chose to remain standing and curbed the need to pace like a caged animal.

Although he'd come through the desolation of his ragged past, he didn't care for the brutal reminders everywhere he looked. The corner of this room was where he'd crouched when his father's loud lambasting of a minion had led to gunshots and horrific screams the first time he'd been brought here. The gilt-framed sofa was where his father had forced him to sit and watch as he'd instructed his lieutenants to beat Paolo Giordano into a pulp.

He didn't especially care for the reminder that it was possibly because of Fattore's blood running through his veins that he'd almost taken the same violent path when, tired of living on the streets, he'd almost joined a terror-loving gang feared for their ruthlessness.

Sì, he should've stayed far away, in the warmth of his newest and most lavish by-invitation-only Caribbean resort.

His eyes narrowed as the second bodyguard returned with a large ornately carved antique box and handed it to Lorenzo. 'It's a good thing your father chose to keep an eye on you, wasn't it?' Lorenzo said.

'Scusi?' Romeo rasped in astonishment.

Lorenzo waved his hand. 'Your mother, the Almighty rest *her* unfortunate soul, attempted to do her best, but we all knew she didn't have what it took, eh?'

Romeo barely stopped his lips from curling. The subject of his mother was one he'd sealed under strict lock and key, then thrown into a vault the night he'd buried her five years ago.

The same night he'd let his guard down spectacularly with a woman whose face continued to haunt him when he least expected it. A woman who had, for the first time in a long time, made him want to feel the warmth of human emotion.

A tremor went through him at the memory, its deep and disturbing effect as potent, if not more so, than it'd been that night when he'd realised that his emotions weren't as clinical and icy as he'd imagined them to be.

He shut down that line of thought.

Maisie O'Connell had had no place in his life then, save as a means of achieving a few hours of oblivion, and she most certainly didn't have one now, in this cursed place. Like the bush outside this miscreation of a mansion, she represented a time in his life he wanted banished for all time.

Because it makes you uncomfortable…vulnerable even? Basta!

'You seem to be under the misapprehension that I'll indulge you in fond trips down potholed memory lanes. Be assured that I will not. If I remember correctly, *you* helped to throw me out of the gates when I was a child. Your exact words, presumably passed down from my father, were—*I see you again, you leave in a body bag.*'

Lorenzo shrugged. 'Those were hot-headed days. Look at you now. You've done very well for yourself despite your less than salubrious beginning.' A touch of malice flared in his eyes. 'None of us imagined a boy conceived in the gutter would rise to such esteem.'

Romeo shoved his hands in his pockets so he wouldn't do the unthinkable and strangle the old man where he sat. 'Then I guess it's a good thing I was intelligent enough to realise early on that whether you were born in the gutter or with a dozen golden spoons clutched in your fist, our lives are what we make them. Otherwise, who knows where I'd be today? In a mental institution, perhaps? Bemoaning my fate while rocking back and forth in a straitjacket?'

The old man laughed, or he attempted to. When the sound veered into a bone-jarring coughing spell, his body-

guards exchanged wary glances before one stepped forward
with a glass of water.

Lorenzo's violent refusal of help had the guard springing
back into his designated position. When the coughing fit
passed, Lorenzo opened the box and took out several papers.

'You were never going to go down without a fight. I saw
that in you even when you were a boy. But you'll do well to
remember where that intelligence comes from.'

'Are you really suggesting that I owe what I've made of
myself to you or the pathetic band of thugs you call a family?' he asked, incredulous.

Lorenzo waved him away. 'We'll discuss what you owe
in a bit. Your father meant to do this before he was tragically taken from us,' he muttered.

Romeo curbed the need to voice his suspicions that his
father's departure from this life hadn't been tragic at all;
that the boat explosion that had taken his life and those of
his wife and the two half-sisters Romeo had never been allowed to meet hadn't been accidental, but the target of a
carefully orchestrated assassination.

Instead, he watched Lorenzo pull out document after
document and lay them on the desk.

'The first order of business is this house. It's yours free
and clear from any financial obligations. All the lawyers
need is your signature to take possession. It comes with the
collection of cars, the horses and the three hundred acres
of land, of course.'

Astonishment rendered Romeo speechless.

'Then there are the businesses. They're not doing as well
as we'd hoped, and certainly not as well as your own businesses are doing. The Carmelo *famiglia* mistakenly believe
this is an excuse for them to start making moves on Fattore business, but I suspect that will all turn around once
our business has been brought under the umbrella of your
company, Brunetti International—'

Romeo laughed. 'You must be out of your mind if you

think I want any part of this blood-soaked legacy. I'd rather return to the gutter than claim a single brick of this house, or associate myself in any way with the Fattore name and everything it stands for.'

'You may despise the Fattore name, but do you think *Brunetti, son of a two-bit whore* has a better ring?' Lorenzo sneered.

It didn't, but in the bleak, terrible hellhole of his childhood it had been the better of two evils. Especially since that greater evil had warned him never to use the name *Fattore*.

'This is your legacy, no matter how much you try to deny it,' Lorenzo insisted.

'You can sit there and rewrite history until the walls crumble around you,' Romeo enunciated with a burning intensity he suspected would erupt the longer he spent in this house. 'But your five minutes have come and gone, old man. And this meeting is well and truly over. Any problems you have with your extortion business and territorial wars with the Carmelo family are yours to deal with.'

He made it to the door before Lorenzo spoke.

'Your father suspected that when the time came you would prove intransigent. So he asked me to give you this.'

For the second time, Romeo froze, his instincts screeching at him to keep walking, but his brain warning that to do as he so desperately wanted would be unwise.

Lorenzo held out a large manila envelope, which he slid across the desk with a smug look.

'I told you I'm not interested in anything bearing the Fattore name. Whatever is in that envelope—'

'Is of a more…personal nature and will interest you, *mio figlio*. I'm confident of it.'

Romeo abandoned the need to remind the old man not to call him son. Lorenzo was enjoying needling him a little too much, and Romeo was fast reaching boiling point.

Striding across the room, he snatched up the envelope and ripped it open. The first picture punched him in the gut, expelling a harsh breath. It showed him standing at his mother's graveside, the only attendee besides the priest, as Ariana Brunetti was laid to rest.

He flung the picture on the desk, his mouth twisting as the next picture showed him in funereal black, sitting at his hotel bar, staring into a glass of cognac.

'So Fattore had me followed for an afternoon five years ago. Perhaps he would've better profited using that time to tend his businesses.'

Lorenzo tented his fingers. 'Keep going. The best is yet to come.'

Dark premonition crawled up Romeo's spine as he flipped to the next photo. It showed him walking out of his hotel and down the street that led to the trendy cafés near the waterfront.

He froze at the next picture and stared at the image of himself. And her.

Maisie O'Connell—the woman with the angelic face and the tempting, sinful body. The combination, although enthralling enough, wasn't what had made her linger in his mind long after he'd moved on to other women, and other experiences.

Something had happened with her in that hotel room, above and beyond mind-obliterating sex. He'd walked away from her feeling broken, fighting a yearning that had terrified him for a long time, until he'd finally forced it back under control.

He had no intention of resurrecting those brief, unsettling hours. He was in control of his life. In control of the fleeting moments of emotion he allowed himself these days.

He threw down the pictures, not caring when they fanned out in a careless arc on the desk. Eyes narrowed at Lorenzo, he snapped, 'It's almost laughable that you think documenting my sex life would cause me anything but acute irritation. Irritation that might just push me into having this house torn to the ground and the whole estate turned into a car park.'

The old man reached across, shuffled through the pictures, then sat back again.

Exhaling, Romeo looked down and saw more pictures of the woman he'd shared his most memorable one-night stand with. But these were different. Taken in another country, judging from the street signs. Dublin, most likely, where Maisie had said she was from during one of the brief times they'd conversed in that electric night they'd spent together.

Still caught up in riotous emotions, he nudged the picture impatiently with his fingernail.

Maisie O'Connell, striding down a busy street in a business suit and high heels, her thick, glorious hair caught up in an elaborate bun. A vision far removed from the sexy little sundress and flip-flops she'd been wearing the first time Romeo had seen her outside a waterfront café in Palermo. Her hair had been loose then, hanging to her waist in a ripple of dark fire.

Romeo unveiled the next picture.

Maisie, hailing a taxi outside a clinic, her features slightly pale and drawn, her normally bright blue eyes dark with worry.

Maisie, sitting on a park bench, her face turned up to the sun, her hand resting on her belly.

Her very distended belly.

Romeo swallowed hard and picked up the last picture, his body suspended in shock as he brought it up to his face.

Maisie, pushing a pram down a quiet Dublin street, her mouth tilted in a postcard-perfect picture of maternal bliss as she reached into the stroller.

'*Madre di Dio*, what is the meaning of this?' he breathed, his voice cold enough to chill the whole mausoleum of a mansion.

'I will not insult your deductive powers by spelling it out for you,' Lorenzo answered.

Romeo flung the photo down, but he could not look away from them. Spreading his fingers through the glossy images, he found further evidence of surveillance. Apparently his father had decided to stop following Romeo and focus instead on the woman he'd slept with on the day of his mother's funeral. A woman whose goodness had threatened to seep into him, to threaten the foundations of his carefully barricaded emotions.

'If these images are supposed to paint some sort of picture, then you've wasted your time. Sexually active individuals have brief encounters and go on to have relationships and families all the time. Or so I'm told.'

He'd never indulged in a relationship. In fact, he actively discouraged his lovers from even entertaining a glimmer of the idea. Romeo suppressed a grim smile. He knew his attitude to relationships had earned him the amusingly caustic label of *Weekend Lover*. Not that he cared. Hell, if it spelled out his intentions before he even asked a woman out, then all the better.

Affection was never on the table, the faintest idea of love strictly and actively forbidden. His interactions were about sex. Nothing more.

'So you don't care to know the time span during which these pictures were taken?'

'Fattore must have had his own warped reason, I'm sure.'

Lorenzo continued to stare at him. 'Then you won't want to know that the woman gave her child an Italian name?'

Romeo snorted in disbelief. He hadn't told Maisie his surname. He'd been very careful in that regard because he hadn't wanted any association with either his mother or his father discovered, as tenuous as the connection could've been, seeing that he hadn't set foot in Sicily in over fifteen years.

'You two must have been desperate to clutch at so many straws. My suggestion to you would be to leave this woman alone to raise her child. She means nothing to me other than a brief dalliance. Whatever leverage you seek through her has no teeth.'

Lorenzo shook his balding grey head. 'Once you have calmed down and learnt a little of our ways, you'll realise that we don't tend to leave stones unturned. Or facts unchecked. Your father certainly wouldn't pin the future of his organisation, of his *famiglia*, on a whim. No, *mio figlio*, we checked and double-checked our facts. Three DNA tests by three different doctors confirmed it.'

'How did you come by samples for these tests?'

'Contrary to what you think of us, we're not bumbling idiots. A strand of hair or a discarded juice cup is all we need, and quite easy to come by.'

The gross violation that deed would've entailed turned his stomach and primitive anger swelled through him. 'You set your thugs loose on a little boy?'

'He's not just any little boy. Your woman gave birth exactly nine months after your encounter. And your son is very much a Fattore.'

CHAPTER TWO

MAISIE O'CONNELL FLIPPED the Closed sign to Open and enjoyed the tingle of excitement that never failed to come with that little action.

It had been a long, hard slog, but *Maisie's* was finally ticking over very nicely, was making a steady profit, in fact. Putting her beloved restaurant in the hands of a professional chef while she'd taken the intensive course in gourmet Italian cooking had paid off. The added feature in one of Dublin's top newspapers had given *Maisie's* the extra boost that had seen her bookings go from half full to booked solid a month in advance.

Picking up the glass-topped menu stand, she pushed open the door and positioned it for maximum effect on the pavement.

As she turned to go back in, a stretch limo with blacked-out windows rolled by and stopped two doors down from where she'd paused. Maisie eyed the car. Although it wasn't strange for luxury cars to pass through the quiet little village of Ranelagh, seeing as they were close to Dublin city centre, the presence of this car caused a different sort of tingle. Telling herself she was being too fanciful, she swiped a dishcloth over the surface of the menu stand and went back in. She checked on her kitchen and waitstaff of twelve, made sure preparations were under way for their first booking at midday, then went into her office.

She had roughly half an hour to get to grips with the restaurant's accounts before she had to be back in the kitchen. As she sat down, her gaze fell on the picture propped up on her desk. The pulse of love that fired to her heart made her breath catch. Reaching out, she traced the contours of her son's face, her own face breaking into a smile at the toothy, wide-eyed happiness reflected in his eyes.

Gianlucca. The reason for her existence. The reason the hard decisions she'd made five years ago had been worth every moment of heartache. Turning her back on the career she'd trained so hard for had not been easy. Certainly her parents had piled on enough guilt to make walking away feel like the betrayal they'd accused her of committing. Her own guilt for confirming their fears that the apple didn't fall far from the tree was bone-deep and would probably always be. She hadn't planned on getting pregnant as her mother had at twenty-four but she refused to let the guilt prevent her from loving or caring for her child.

She'd known from a very young age that her parents, had they been given a choice, would've remained childless. As hard as it'd been, she'd tried to accept that not everyone was built to nurture a child. Her parents certainly had found raising her a challenge, one they hadn't deemed as worthy as the academic careers they'd pursued relentlessly. She'd always known she came an indifferent second to her parents' academic ambitions.

But she'd wanted Gianlucca the moment she'd found out he was growing inside her.

There had been nothing she wanted more than providing the very best for her son.

She had given him the very best.

The tiny niggle of ever-present guilt threatened to push its way through, but she smashed it down. She'd done everything she could when she'd found out she was pregnant. Even going against her parents' intense disapproval to make that daunting trip back to Sicily. She'd tried.

Yes, but did you try hard enough?

She dropped her hand from the picture and resolutely opened the account books. Indulging in *might have beens* wouldn't get the chequebook balanced or the staff paid. She was content enough. More important, her son was happy.

Her gaze drifted back to the almost-four-year-old face that was already taking the shape of the man he would one day be. To the deep hazel-gold eyes that looked so much like his father's. Eyes that could sometimes make her believe he could see straight into her soul, just as the older pair had done to her that long afternoon and longer night in Palermo five years ago.

Romeo.

A portentous name if there ever was one. While her life hadn't ended in fatal tragedy like the famous story, meeting Romeo had significantly altered it, her son being the only bright thing that had emerged from encountering that dangerously sexy, but deeply enigmatic Italian with eyes that had reflected enough conflict to last him several lifetimes.

Enough.

She switched on her computer and had just activated the payroll system when a knock sounded on her door.

'Come in.'

Lacey, her young reservations manager, poked her head around the door, her eyes wide and brimming with interest. 'There's someone here to see you,' she stage-whispered.

Maisie suppressed a smile. Her young employee had a flair for the dramatic and saw conspiracies and high drama in the simplest situations.

'If it's someone else looking for a job, please tell them I'm not hiring anyone. Not till the summer season really kicks off…' She stopped speaking as Lacey shook her head frantically.

'I don't think he's looking for a job. Actually, no offence, Maisie, but he looks like he could buy this place a hundred times over.' Her eyes widened and she blushed, then bit her lip. 'Sorry, but he looks really, really rich, and really, really, *intense.*' Lacey's eyes boggled some more. 'And he came in a *limo*,' she whispered again, looking over her shoulder into the restaurant.

The tingling Maisie had experienced earlier returned full force. 'Did he give you a name?'

'No, he just asked if you were in and ordered me to come and get you.' Lacey glanced furtively over her shoulder again, as if expecting their visitor to materialise behind her. 'He's very...*full-on*.'

Recalling her own line of thoughts moments ago and the intensity of Romeo's personality, she shivered. Shaking it off, Maisie stood up and brushed her hands down the practical black skirt and pink shirt she'd chosen to wear today.

She'd left all that dangerous intensity back in Palermo. Or *it* had left her, seeing as she'd woken up alone the morning after, with only rumpled sheets and the trace of her lover's scent on the pillow as evidence that she hadn't imagined the whole encounter.

She was in Ranelagh, the serene village she'd chosen to build a life for herself and her son in, not the sultry decadence of Palermo and its dangerous residents.

No danger or intensity whatsoever welcome here.

'Okay, Lacey. I'll take care of it.' Lacey's head bobbed before she disappeared from the doorway.

Sucking in a breath and telling herself she was being silly to feel so apprehensive, Maisie stepped out from behind her desk. In her short but successful stint as a criminal lawyer, she'd faced her share of unsavoury and even dangerous characters.

Whatever unknown quantity faced her out there in her beloved restaurant, she could face it.

Maisie knew just how wrong she was even before the tall, broad-shouldered figure clad from head to toe in black turned around from his brooding inspection of his surroundings.

Outwardly, her body froze a few steps into the restaurant. But inside, her heart kicked into her stomach. *Hard.*

'Romeo.'

She realised she'd said the name rattling through her brain aloud when he turned slowly and pinned her with those brooding hazel-gold eyes. That impossibly rugged jaw she'd thought she'd blown out of all proportion tightened as his gaze raked her from head to toe and back again. His prominent, cut-glass cheekbones were more pronounced than she remembered and his hair was longer, wavier than it had been five years ago. But the man who stood a dozen paces away was no less dynamic, no less captivating than the man who'd sat across from her in the café that memorable day.

If anything, he commanded a more overpowering presence. Perhaps it was because they were so far away from the place they'd first met, or because her mind was turning itself inside out to decipher exactly why he was here. All the same she found herself bunching a fist against her heart as if that would stop its fierce pounding.

'I'm not certain whether to celebrate this moment or to condemn it,' he rasped in a tense, dark voice.

'How did you… How did you find me?'

One eyebrow spiked upwards. 'That is what you wish to know? How did I find you? Were you attempting to stay hidden, perhaps?' he enquired silkily.

'What?' Her brain grew fuzzier, her heart racing even faster at the ice in his tone. 'I'm not hiding. Why would I want to hide from anyone?'

He approached slowly, his eyes not leaving her face, nor his hands the deep pockets of his overcoat. Even though it was early June, the weather remained cool enough to require a coat, and he wore his as a dark lord wore a cape, with a flourish that demanded attention. 'We haven't seen each other in five years and your first request is to know how I found you. Pardon me if I find that curious.'

'What would you have me say?' She licked lips gone

dry as he took another step closer until she had to crane her neck to see his eyes.

Mesmeric, hypnotising eyes.

So like his son's.

The blood drained from her face and thinking became difficult. She'd imagined this scene countless times. Had imagined how she would say the words. How he would take it. How she would protect her son from even the slightest hint of rejection, the way she'd done when her parents had transmitted that same indifference they'd shown Maisie all her life to her beloved son.

But words wouldn't form in her brain. So she stared at him, her thoughts twisting and turning.

'*Hello*, perhaps? Or, *how have you been, Romeo*?'

She caught his chillingly mocking tone and stiffened.

'Why would I? I seem to recall waking up to find myself alone in a hotel suite rented by an anonymous stranger. You didn't bother to say goodbye then, so why should I bother to say hello now?' she replied.

His nostrils flared then and a memory struck through her jumbled thoughts. They'd been caught up in one of the few short bursts of conversation in his suite. She'd unwittingly let slip the fraught state of her relationship with her parents, how lonely and inconvenient she felt to them, as if she were an unwanted visitor sharing a house with them.

His nostrils had flared then, too, as he'd admonished her to be grateful she had parents at all—strangers or otherwise. That observation had rendered her silent and a little ashamed, not because she'd hated being chastised, but because she'd seen the naked agony in his eyes when he'd said that. As if the subject of parents was one that terrorised him.

Maisie pushed the memory away and struggled to stay calm when he finally released her from his stare and looked around.

'What do you do here when you're not dabbling in being a restaurateur?' he asked.

She bristled. 'I'm not dabbling. I own this restaurant. It's my career.'

'Really? I thought you were a high-powered lawyer.'

She frowned. Had she told him that in Palermo? Back then she'd been newly qualified and working on exciting cases. Back then her parents had finally, grudgingly, accepted her career choice. She would even go as far as to consider that for the first time in her life she'd achieved something they were proud of, even if they hadn't quite been able to show it in the warm, loving way she'd seen her friends' parents exhibit.

Of course, they hadn't been thrilled that she'd announced soon after that she was taking a whole month off to travel Europe.

Despite her having the full support of her bosses to take the time off, her parents had advised her against the trip. Their utter conviction that stepping off the career ladder, even briefly, would ruin her life had finally confirmed how much they rued bringing a child, bringing *her*, into their lives.

And once she'd returned and told them she was pregnant...

Her heart caught at their bitter disappointment when she'd finally revealed her news. Roberta O'Connell hadn't needed to spell out that she thought Maisie had ruined her life for ever. It'd been clear to see. And knowing that by definition they thought having *her* had been a mistake had been an ache she hadn't been able to dispel.

Maisie shook her head to dispel the memory. 'No, not any longer. I gave up practising four years ago,' she answered Romeo.

He frowned. 'Why would you give up the job you trained so hard for?'

So she *had* told him more than she thought. Because how else would he know? And why was he questioning her like this, probing her for answers he already knew? Was he trying to trip her up somehow?

She swallowed. 'My priorities changed,' she replied crisply and stepped back. 'Now if you were just passing through and stopped to catch up, I really must get on. My first customers will be here shortly and I need to make sure the kitchen's ready to start the day.'

'You think I came all this way simply *to catch up*?' He looked around again, as if searching for something. Or someone.

Apprehension flowed like excess adrenaline through her blood, making her dizzy for a moment.

Romeo couldn't know about Gianlucca. Because *she'd* searched for him to no avail. No one else knew who the father of her child was. The only people who she would've confessed Romeo's identity to—her parents—hadn't wanted to know after she'd confessed to the one-night stand. Which was just as well because Maisie wouldn't have liked to confess that she hadn't known the surname of the man who'd impregnated her.

Maisie had a hard time accepting the fact that the only time her mother had initiated a heart-to-heart conversation had been to tell her to abandon her child's welfare to childminders and nannies. That her son, once he was born, should be left to others to raise, so Maisie could focus fully and solely on her career. There'd even been an offer of a fully paid boarding school once he was a toddler! Despite her knowing her parents' views on hands-on parenting, it'd still been harrowing to hear her mother's words, to know that had her parents had the choice when she was born, they'd have abandoned *her* to the same fate.

'I really don't know what you're doing here. But like I said, I need to be getting on—'

She gasped when he caught her upper arms in a firm, implacable hold.

'Where is he, Maisie? *Where is my son?*' he demanded, his voice a cold, deadly blade.

Several things happened at once. The door to the kitchen burst open and Lacey rushed through, just as the front door swung inward and a party of four walked in. The scene stopped in almost comical freeze-frame. No one moved except for Romeo, whose eyes narrowed as they went from the door to Lacey and then to Maisie's face.

When shock continued to hold her tongue prisoner, Romeo's lips compressed. Glancing at Lacey's name badge, he jerked his head imperiously. 'Lacey, you're in charge of reservations, yes?'

Lacey nodded, her wide-eyed look returning full force.

'Then see to the customers, *per favore*. Your boss and I will be in her office.'

Romeo marched her into the small room and shut the door behind him with a precise movement that suggested he was suppressing the need to slam it. Maisie was conquering equally intense emotions.

She put the width of her desk between them, then glared at him.

'I don't know who you think you are, but you can't walk in here and start bossing my employees about—'

'Deflecting won't help this situation. You know why I'm here. So let's dispense with trivialities. *Tell me where he is.*' That last remark was said with icy brevity that hammered a warning straight to her blood.

'Why?' she fired back, potent fear beginning to crawl up her spine.

Astonishment lit through his golden eyes. '*Why?* Are you completely insane? Because I want to see him.'

'Again, why?' A cloud descended on his face and Maisie held up her hand when he opened his mouth, no doubt to once again question her sanity. 'Let's stop for a moment and think about this rationally. We had a one-night stand.' She couldn't help the high colour that rushed into her face at the so very telling term. 'After which you walked away without so much as a thank-you-ma'am note. You used me, then disappeared into the night. A month later, I found out I was pregnant. Fast-forward five years later, you walk in the door and demand to see my son.' Maisie raised her hand and ticked off her fingers. 'I don't know your background. I don't know whether that aura of danger about you is just for show or the real thing. Hell, I don't even know your *last name*. And you think I should just expose you to my child?'

Several emotions flitted across his face—astonishment, anger, a touch of vulnerability that set her nape tingling, then grudging respect before settling into implacable determination.

He stared at her for a time, before he exhaled sharply. 'If the child is mine—'

She laughed in disbelief. 'Let me get this straight. You came here without even being sure that the child you're so desperate to see is yours?'

He folded his arms across his massive chest, the movement bunching his shoulders into even wider relief. Maisie became acutely aware of the room shrinking, and the very air being sucked up by his overwhelming presence. 'Since I've never met him, I cannot be one hundred per cent sure that he's mine, hence the request to see him. A man in my position has to verify allegations of fatherhood.'

Her eyes widened. 'Allegations? *Plural?* Are you saying this isn't the first time you've left a woman in a hotel room and found out there have been consequences to your actions?' Maisie wasn't sure why that stung so much. Had she imagined herself somehow unique? That a man who *looked* like him, kissed and made love as he had, would have limited the experience to her and only her? 'And what do you mean, a man in your position?'

Her barrage of questions caused his eyes to narrow further. 'You don't know who I am?'

'Would I be asking if I did?' she threw back. 'If you want

any semblance of cooperation from me, I demand to know your full name.'

His jaw flexed. 'My name is Romeo Brunetti.' The way he said it, the way he waited, as if the pronouncement should be accompanied by a round of trumpets and the clash of cymbals, set her spine tingling. When she didn't speak, a curious light entered his eyes. 'That means nothing to you?'

She shrugged. 'Should it?'

He continued to stare at her for another minute, before he shook his head and started to pace the small space in front of her desk. 'Not at all. So now we have our long-overdue introductions out of the way.'

Maisie cleared her throat. 'Mr Brunetti, I—' She froze as he let out a stunned breath.

Her gaze flew to his face to find his gaze transfixed on the photo on her desk. 'Is this… Is this him?' he asked in a tight, ragged whisper.

When she nodded, he reached forward in a jerky movement, then stopped. Apprehension slid over his face. He fisted and then flexed his hand, before he slowly plucked up the frame. In another person, she would've been certain he was borderline terrified of a mere picture.

Terrified or dreading?

The reminder of the cold indifference her parents had felt about their grandson, about her, made her itch to snatch the photo from him, protect her son's image the way she fought every day to keep him from the rejection she'd been forced to live with her whole life.

She glanced at the picture clutched in Romeo's large hand.

It had been taken at Ranelagh Gardens on the first day of spring. Dressed in a smart shirt, jeans and bright blue woollen jumper, Gianlucca had looked a perfect picture of health and happiness, and Maisie hadn't been able to resist capturing his image.

She watched now as Romeo brought the picture up close

to his face, his features drawn tight, his breathing slow and controlled. After almost a minute of staring at the photo without a hint of emotion, he raised his hand and brushed his fingers over Gianlucca's cheek, almost in direct imitation of what Maisie herself had done a mere half hour ago.

'*Mio figlio*,' he murmured.

'I don't know what that means,' Maisie replied in a matching whisper.

He blinked and sucked in a deep, chest-filling breath. 'My son. It means my son.' He looked up, his gaze deeply accusing. '*He's my son*. And you kept him from me,' he snarled, his voice still not quite as steady as it'd been moments ago.

Maisie stumbled backwards, bumping into the chair behind her. 'I did nothing of the kind. And if you stopped to think about it for a moment, you'd realise how ridiculous that allegation is.'

He shoved a hand through his thick dark hair, dislodging any semblance of order it'd been in. He began to pace again, the photo clutched in his large hand. 'How old is he?' he demanded when he paused for a moment.

'He's four in three weeks.'

He resumed pacing in tight circles. 'Four years... *Dio mio*, four years I've been in the dark,' he muttered to himself, slashing his hand through his hair again.

'How *exactly* were you enlightened?' It was a question he hadn't yet addressed.

He froze, as if her question had thrown him. 'We'll get to that in a moment. First, please tell me his name and where he is.'

The urgency in his voice bled through to Maisie. She wanted to refuse. Wanted to rewind time and have this meeting not happen. Not because being given the chance to reveal her son's existence to his father wasn't what she wanted.

From the moment she'd found out she was pregnant, she'd known she would give her child every opportunity to know his father. She'd gone to Palermo during her first trimester with that exact reason in mind and had given up after two weeks with no success in tracing Romeo.

No, the reason Maisie wanted to rewind time and take a different course was because she knew, deep in her bones, that Romeo's presence wasn't just about wanting to get to know his son. There was a quiet hint of danger about him that set her fear radar alight. And he hadn't yet shown her that the prospect of a son filled him with joy. All he'd done so far was put an alpha claim on a child he didn't know.

A child she would lay her life down to protect.

'Why are you really here?'

His brows clamped together. 'I believe we've tackled that particular question.'

She shook her head. Something was seriously, desperately wrong. Something to do with her precious son.

'No, we haven't. And I absolutely refuse to tell you anything about him until you tell me what's going on.'

CHAPTER THREE

ROMEO STARED DOWN at the picture one more time, his heart turning over as eyes the exact shade as his own stared back at him. The child...*his son*...was laughing, pure joy radiating from his face as he posed, chubby arms outstretched, for the camera. A deep shudder rattled up from his toes, engulfing him in a sense of peculiar bewilderment. And fear. Bone-deep fear.

He couldn't be a father. Not him, with the upbringing he'd had, the twisted, harrowing paths his life had taken before he'd wrestled control of it. He wasn't equipped to care for a dog, never mind a child. And with the blood flowing through his veins...the blood of a thug and a vicious criminal...

Dio mio.

Lorenzo hadn't been lying after all. A single wave of impotent rage blanketed him to know that the two men he despised most had known of the existence of the boy before he did. And while a part of him knew levelling accusations of subterfuge on the woman standing before him was unfair, Romeo couldn't help but feel bitter resentment for being kept in the dark, even while he continued to flounder at the reality stabbing him in the chest.

He pushed the emotion aside and concentrated on the reality he *could* deal with—her continued denial of access. Because whether he was equipped to handle the prospect of fatherhood or not, she was at this moment behaving like an irrational person...a mother bear—a concept acutely alien to him.

Inhaling deep to keep his emotions under control, he

rubbed his thumb over the face of his son. 'I have only just discovered I have a child.' He stopped when she raised her eyebrow again to remind him of her unanswered question. 'Through…business associates who wished to get my attention—'

She shook her head, her long ponytail swinging. 'What on earth does that mean? Why would business associates want to use your child to get your attention?' High colour had flown into her cheeks, reminding him of another time, another place when her emotions had run equally passionate. 'What type of business are you involved in?' she voiced suspiciously.

So she didn't know who he was. Something vaguely resembling relief speared through him. When his business partnership with Zaccheo Giordano had become public knowledge five years ago, his world had exploded with fawning acolytes and women falling over themselves to get his attention. That attention had increased a hundredfold when he'd opened his first super-luxury resort off the coast of Tahiti, a feat he'd repeated soon after with five more, seeing him skyrocket onto the World's Richest list.

It was curiously refreshing not to have to deal with the instant personality change that accompanied recognition of his name. But not refreshing enough to know his response had triggered suspicion that could keep him from his reason for being here. Even though her instinct might yet prove correct.

He needed to frame his words carefully.

'You have nothing to fear from me.' He'd managed to lock down his control after that gut punch he'd received on seeing her again. From here on in, he would be operating from a place of cold, hard intelligence.

She shook her head again. 'Sorry, that's not good enough. You'll have to do better than that.' Her gaze went to the picture frame he held on to, a fierce light of protection and possession burning in her striking blue eyes.

'Tell me the exact nature of your business or this conversation ends now.'

Romeo almost laughed. She was seriously deluded if she thought her heated threats would in any way dissuade him from seeing his son, from verifying for himself that the child truly belonged to him.

'I'm the CEO and owner of Brunetti International,' he replied.

She frowned for a moment, then her features morphed into astonishment. 'Brunetti…those resorts you need to sell an organ or a limb before you can afford a night there?'

He made a dismissive gesture. 'We cater to people from all walks of life.'

She snorted. 'As long as they've sold their grandmothers to be able to afford your billionaire rates.'

Romeo pursed his lips. His wealth wasn't the subject under discussion here.

The fact that she seemed to be a rare species, a mother who stood like a lioness in protection of her child, a child whom he'd yet to be certain without a shadow of a doubt shared his DNA, should take precedence.

'You know who I am now. You'll also know from your previous career that information can be discovered if one digs deep enough. My business associates dug deep enough and they found you and my son.'

'My son.'

The sudden urge to snarl *our child* took him by surprise. He stared down at the picture, clutching at the fraying edges of his control when he began to feel off balance again. '*Per favore.* Please. Tell me his name.'

Her gaze went to the picture and her features softened immediately.

The look was one he'd witnessed before, in that hotel room five years ago. It was a look that had set so many alarm bells ringing inside his head that he'd withdrawn swiftly and decisively from it. He looked away because just as he'd had no room to accommodate *feelings* then, he had no room for them now.

'His name is Gianlucca. Gianlucca O'Connell.'

An irrational surge of displeasure threatened to floor him. *'O'Connell?'*

Again that challenging arch of her eyebrow. Back in Palermo he'd seen her passion, her fire, but that had been directed to the bedroom, and what they'd done to each other in bed. Seeing it in a different light didn't make it any less sexy. Yet the punch of heat to his libido took him by surprise. He'd grown so jaded by the overabundance of willing women that lately he'd lost interest in the chase. For the past three months, work had become his mistress, the only thing that fired his blood in any meaningful way.

'That *is* my name. Or did you expect me to call him Gianlucca Romeo?'

He gritted his teeth. 'Did you even make an effort to find me when you knew you carried my child?'

A look crossed her face, a mixture of pride and anger, and she raised her chin. 'Did you want to be found?' she fired back.

Knowing how well he'd covered his tracks, a wave of heat crawled up his neck. He'd succeeded more than in his wildest dreams. He'd walked away, having effectively smashed down any residual feelings of rejection, or the idea that he could be worthy of something more than the brain and brawn that had seen him through his harrowing childhood into the man he was today.

The hours of imagined softness, of imagined affection, had been an illusion brought on by his mother's passing. An illusion he'd almost given in to. An emotion he'd vowed then never to entertain even the merest hint of again.

'We'll address the subject of his surname at another time. But now we've established who I am, I'd like to know more about him. Please,' he added when her stance remained intransigent.

'All I know is your surname. I don't even know how old you are, never mind what sort of man you are.'

Romeo rounded the desk and watched her back away, but looking into her eyes he saw no sign of fear. Only stubbornness. Satisfied that she didn't fear him, he moved closer, watched her pupils dilate as a different sort of chemistry filled the air. Her sudden erratic breathing told him everything he needed to know.

'I'm thirty-five. And five years ago, you gave yourself to me without knowing anything more about me besides my first name.' He watched a blush wash up her throat into her face with more than a little fascination. 'You were in a foreign place, with a strange man, and yet you trusted your instinct enough to enter my hotel suite and stay for a whole night. And right now, even though your heart is racing, you don't fear me. Or you would've screamed for help by now.' He reached out and touched the pulse beating at her throat. Her soft, silky skin glided beneath his fingertips and blazing heat lanced his groin again. Curbing the feeling, he dropped his hand and stepped back. 'I don't mean you or the boy harm. I just wish to see him. I deal in facts and figures. I need visual evidence that he exists, and as accommodating as I'm willing to be, I won't be giving you a choice in the matter.'

She swallowed, her eyes boldly meeting and staying on his. 'Just so you know, I don't respond well to threats.'

'It wasn't a threat, *gattina*.' They both froze at the term that had unwittingly dropped from his lips. From the look on her face, Romeo knew she was remembering the first time he'd said it. Her nails had been embedded in his back, her claws transmitting the depth of her arousal as he'd sunk deep inside her. His little wildcat had been as crazy for him as he'd been for her. But that was then, a moment in time never to be repeated. 'I'm merely stating a fact.'

She opened her mouth to reply, then stopped as voices filled the restaurant. 'I have to go. This is our busiest afternoon slot. I can't leave Lacey on her own.'

Romeo told himself to be calm. 'I need an answer, Maisie.'

She stared at him for a long moment before her gaze dropped to the picture he held. She looked as if she wanted to snatch it from him but he held on tight. She finally looked back up. 'He goes to playgroup from eleven to three o'clock. I take him to the park afterwards if the weather's good.'

'Did you have plans to do that today?'

She slowly nodded. 'Yes.'

Blood rushed into his ears, nearly deafening him. He forced himself to think, to plot the best way he knew how. Because rushing blood and racing hearts were for fools. Fools who let emotion rule their existence.

'What park?' he rasped.

'Ranelagh Gardens. It's—'

'I will find it.'

She paled and her hands flew out in a bracing stance. 'You can't… Don't you think we need to discuss this a little more?'

Romeo carefully set down the picture, then took out his phone and captured an image of it. He stared down at his son's face on his phone screen, and the decision concreted in his mind. 'No, Maisie. There's nothing more to discuss. If he's mine, truly mine, then I intend to claim him.'

Maisie slowly sank into the chair after Romeo made a dramatic exit, taking all the oxygen and bristling vitality of the day with him. She raised her hand to her face and realised her fingers were shaking. Whether it was from the shock of seeing him again after convincing herself she would never set eyes on him again, or the indomitability of that last statement, she wasn't certain.

She sat there, her hand on her clammy forehead, her gaze

in the middle distance as she played back every word, every gesture, on a loop in her mind.

The sound of laughter finally broke through her racing thoughts. She really needed to walk the floor, make sure her customers were all right. But she found herself clicking on her laptop, typing in his name on her search engine.

The images that confronted her made her breath catch all over again. Whereas she hadn't given herself permission to linger on anywhere but Romeo's face while they'd been in her office, she leaned in close and perused each image. And there were plenty, it seemed. Pictures of him dressed in impeccable handmade suits, posing for a profile piece in some glossy business magazine; pictures of him opening his world-renowned resorts in Dubai and Bali; and many, many pictures of him with different women, all drop-dead gorgeous, all smiling at him as if he was their world, their every dream come true.

But the ones that caught Maisie's attention, the ones that made her heart lurch wildly, were of Romeo on a yacht with another man—the caption named him as Zaccheo Giordano—and a woman with two children. The children were Gianlucca's age, possibly a little older, and the pictures were a little grainy, most likely taken with a telephoto lens from a long distance.

He sat apart from the family, his expression as remote as an arctic floe. That lone-wolf look, the one that said approach with caution, froze her heart as she saw it replicated in each rigid, brooding picture that followed. Even when he smiled at the children, there was a distance that spoke of his unease.

Trembling, Maisie sat back from the desk, the large part of her that had been agitated at the thought of agreeing to a meeting between Romeo and her son escalating to alarming proportions.

She might not know how he felt about children generally, but if the pictures could be believed, Romeo Brunetti wasn't the warm and cuddly type.

Maisie gulped in the breath she hadn't been able to fully access while Romeo had been in the room and tried to think rationally. She'd tried to find Romeo five years ago to tell him that they'd created a child together. It was true that at the time she'd been reeling from her parents' further disappointment in her, and in hindsight she'd probably been seeking some sort of connection with her life suddenly in chaotic free fall. But even then, deep down, she'd known she couldn't keep the news to herself or abandon her baby to the care of strangers as her parents had wanted.

So in a way, this meeting had always been on the cards, albeit to be scheduled at a time of her choosing and without so much…pulse-destroying drama.

Or being confronted with the evidence that made her mothering instincts screech with the possibility that the father of her child might want him for reasons other than to cement a love-at-first-sight bond that would last a lifetime.

She clicked back to the information page and was in the middle of Romeo's worryingly brief biography when a knock announced Lacey's entrance.

'I need you, Maisie! A group of five just walked in. They don't have a booking but I don't think they'll take no for an answer.'

Maisie suppressed a sigh and closed her laptop with a guilty sense of relief that she didn't have to deal with Romeo's last words just yet.

'Okay, let's go and see what we can do, shall we?'

She pinned a smile on her face that felt a mile from genuine and left her office. For the next three hours, she pushed the fast-approaching father-and-son meeting to the back of her mind and immersed herself in the smooth running of the lunchtime service.

* * *

The walk to Gianlucca's nursery took less than ten minutes, but with her mind free of work issues, her heart began to race again at the impending meeting.

Every cell in her body urged her to snatch her son and take him far away.

But she'd never been the type to run, or bury her head in the sand.

She'd give Romeo the chance to spell out what he wished for, and if his parting remarks were anything to go by he would be demanding a presence in her son's life. She would hear him out, but nothing would make her accommodate visitation with her son until she was absolutely sure he would be safe with Romeo.

Her heart lurched at the thought that she'd have to part from him for a few hours maybe once or twice a week. Maybe a full weekend when he grew older. Her breath shuddered out, and she shook her head. She was getting ahead of herself. For all she knew, Romeo would take one look at Lucca, satisfy himself that he was his and ring-fence himself with money-grubbing lawyers to prevent any imagined claims.

But then, if that was what he intended, would he have taken the time to seek them out?

Whatever happened, her priority would remain ensuring her son's happiness. She stopped before the nursery door, unclenched her agitated fists and blinked eyes prickling with tears.

From the moment he'd been born, it'd been just the two of them. After the search for Romeo had proved futile, she'd settled into the idea that it would always be just the two of them.

The threat to that twosome made her insides quiver.

She brushed her tears away. By the time she was buzzed in, Maisie had composed herself.

'Mummy!' Gianlucca raced towards her, an effervescent bundle of energy that pulled a laugh from Maisie.

Enfolding him in her arms, she breathed his warm, toddler scent until he wriggled impatiently.

'Are we going to the park to see the ducks?' he asked eagerly, his striking hazel eyes—so like his father's it was uncanny—widened expectantly.

'Yes, I even brought some food for them,' she replied and smiled wider when he whooped and dashed off towards the door.

She spotted the limo the moment they turned into the square. Black and ominous, it sat outside the north entrance in front of an equally ominous SUV, both engines idling. Beside the limo, two men dressed in black and wearing shades stood, their watchful stance evidence that they were bodyguards.

Maisie tried not to let her imagination careen out of control. Romeo Brunetti was a billionaire and she'd dealt with enough unscrupulous characters during her stint as a lawyer to know the rich were often targets for greedy, sometimes dangerous criminals.

All the same, she clutched Gianlucca's hand tighter as they passed the car and entered the park. Gianlucca darted off for the duck pond, his favourite feature in the park, as soon as she handed him the bread she'd taken from the restaurant.

He was no more than a dozen paces away when a tingle danced on her nape. She glanced over her shoulder and watched Romeo enter the park, his gaze passing cursorily over her before it swung to Gianlucca.

Maisie's heart lurched, then thundered at the emotions that washed over his face. Wonder. Shock. Anxiety. And a fierce possessiveness that sent a huge dart of alarm through her.

But the most important emotion—love—was missing.

It didn't matter that it was perhaps irrational for her to

demand it of him, but the absence of that powerful emotion terrified her.

Enough to galvanise her into action when he walked forward, reached her and carried on going.

'Romeo!' She caught his arm when she sensed his intention.

'What?' He paused, but his gaze didn't waver from Gianlucca's excited form.

'Wait. Please,' she whispered fiercely when he strained against her hold.

He whirled to her, his nostrils flaring as he fought to control himself. 'Maisie.' His tone held a note of barely leashed warning.

Swallowing, she stood her ground. 'I know you want to meet him, but you can't just barge in looking like…' She stopped and bit her lip.

'Looking like what?'

'Like a charging bull on steroids. You'll frighten him.'

His face hardened and he breathed deep before spiking a hand through his hair. After another long glance at Gianlucca, he faced her. '*Bene*, what do you suggest?'

Maisie reached into her bag. 'Here, I brought one of these for you.'

He eyed her offering and his eyebrows shot up. 'A bag of dried bread?'

'He's feeding the ducks. It's his favourite thing to do. I thought you could…approach him that way.'

Romeo's eyes darkened to a burnished gold. Slowly, he reached out and took the offering. '*Grazie,*' he muttered with tight aloofness.

She held on when he started to turn away, silently admonishing herself for experiencing a tiny thrill of pleasure when his arm flexed beneath her fingers. 'Also, I'd prefer it if you didn't tell him who you are. We can have a longer discussion about where we go from here before anything happens.'

A dark look gleamed in his eyes, but he nodded. 'If that is what you wish.'

'It is.'

He nodded, then tensed as a trio of kids flew by on their way to the pond. 'I agree, perhaps this isn't the most appropriate venue for an introduction.'

A tight knot eased in Maisie's stomach and she realised a part of her had feared Romeo would only want to see his son from afar and decide he didn't want to know him. She had yet to decipher his true motives, but she would allow this brief meeting.

'Thank you.'

He merely inclined his head before his gaze swung back to Gianlucca. Knowing she couldn't postpone the meeting any longer, she fell into step beside Romeo.

Gianlucca threw the last of his bread into the waiting melee of ducks and swans and broke into a delighted laugh as they fought over the scraps. His laughter turned into a pout when the ducks swam off to greet the bread-throwing trio of kids. 'Mummy, more bread!' When Maisie remained silent, he turned and raced towards them. 'Please?' he added.

She glanced at Romeo and watched the frozen fascination on his face as Gianlucca reached them. She caught him before he barrelled into her and crouched in front of him. 'Wait a moment, Lucca. There's someone I want you to meet. This...this is Romeo Brunetti.'

Lucca tilted his head up and eyed the towering man before him. 'Are you Mummy's friend?'

Romeo's head bobbed once. 'Yes. Nice to meet you, Gianlucca.'

Gianlucca immediately slipped his hand into Romeo's and pumped with all his might. A visible tremble went through Romeo's body, and he made a strangled sound. Gianlucca heard it and stilled, his eyes darting from the giant man to his mother.

The overprotective mother in her wanted to scoop him up and cuddle him close, but Maisie forced herself to remain still. Her breath caught as Romeo sank into a crouch, still holding his son's hand, his eyes glistening with questions.

'I look forward to getting to know you, Gianlucca.'

Lucca nodded, then gasped as he saw what Romeo held in his other hand. 'Did you come to feed the ducks, too?'

Romeo nodded. '*Sì*…yes,' he amended and started to rise. His body bristled with a restlessness that made Maisie's pulse jump. 'That was my intention, but I'm not an expert, like you.'

'It's easy! Come on.' He tugged at Romeo's hand, his excitement at having another go at his favourite pastime vibrating through his little body.

Maisie stayed crouched, the residual apprehension clinging to her despite the sudden, throat-clogging tears. As meetings between father and son went, it had gone much easier than she could've hoped for. And yet, she couldn't move from where she crouched. Because, she realised, through all the scenarios she'd played in her mind, she'd never really thought beyond this moment. Oh, she'd loftily imagined dictating visitation terms and having them readily agreed to, and then going about raising her son with minimal interference.

But looking at Romeo as he gazed down at his son with an intense proprietary light in his eyes, Maisie realised she really had no clue what the future held. Her breath shuddered out as Romeo's words once again flashed through her brain.

There's nothing more to discuss. If he's mine, truly mine, then I intend to claim him.

She slowly rose and looked over her shoulder. Sure enough, the two black-clad bodyguards prowled a short distance away. About to turn away, Maisie froze as she spotted two more by the south gate. Two more guarded the west side of the park.

Heart in her throat, she approached the duck pond, where Romeo was throwing a piece of bread under her son's strict instruction.

His head swung towards her and his expression altered at whatever he read on her face. 'Something wrong?'

'I think I should be asking you that,' she hissed so Gianlucca wouldn't overhear, but she placed a protective hand on his tiny shoulder, ready to lay down her life for him if she needed to. 'Do you want to tell me why you have *six* bodyguards watching this park?' Her voice vibrated with the sudden fear and anger she couldn't disguise.

His face hardened and the arm he'd raised to throw another bite into the pond slowly lowered to his side. 'I think it's time to continue this conversation elsewhere.'

CHAPTER FOUR

ROMEO WATCHED SEVERAL expressions chase over her face.

'What does that mean?' she asked, her blue eyes narrowing before she cast another alarmed glance at the burly men guarding the park.

He followed her apprehensive gaze and indicated sharply at his men when he saw that other parents were beginning to notice their presence. The men melted into the shadows, but the look didn't dissipate from Maisie's face. When her hand tightened imperceptibly on Gianlucca's shoulder, Romeo's insides tightened.

'My hotel is ten minutes away. We'll talk there.' He tried not to let the irony of his statement cloud the occasion. He'd said similar words to her five years ago, an invitation that had ended with him reeling from the encounter.

That invitation had now brought him to this place, to his son. He had no doubt in his mind that the child was his. Just as he had no doubt that he would claim him, and protect him from whatever schemes Lorenzo had up his sleeves. Beyond that, he had no clue what his next move was. He didn't doubt, though, that he would find a way to triumph. He'd dragged himself from the tough streets of Palermo to the man he was today. He didn't intend to let anything stand in the way of what he desired.

He focused to find her shaking her head. 'I can't.'

Romeo's eyes narrowed as a hitherto thought occurred to him. 'You can't? Why not?' He realised then how careless he'd been. Because Lorenzo's pictures had shown only Maisie with his son, Romeo had concluded that she was unattached. But those pictures were four years old. A lot could have happened in that time. She could've taken another lover, a man who had perhaps become important enough to see himself as Gianlucca's father.

The very idea made him see red for one instant. 'Is there someone in your life?' He searched her fingers. They were ringless. But that didn't mean anything these days. 'A *lover*, perhaps?' The word shot from his mouth like a bullet.

Her eyes widened and she glanced down at Gianlucca, but he was engrossed in feeding the last of the bread to the ducks. 'I don't have a lover or a husband, or whatever the *au fait* term is nowadays.'

Romeo attributed the relief that poured through him to not having to deal with another tangent in this already fraught, woefully ill-planned situation. 'In that case there shouldn't be a problem in discussing this further at my hotel.'

'That wasn't why I refused to come with you. I have a life to get on with, Romeo. And Lucca has a schedule that I try to keep to so his day isn't disrupted, otherwise he gets cranky. I need to fix his dinner in half an hour and put him to bed so I can get back to the restaurant.'

He stiffened. 'You go to work after he's asleep?'

Her mouth compressed. 'Not every night, but yes. I live above the restaurant and my assistant manager lives in the flat next door. She looks after him on the nights I work.'

'That is unacceptable.'

Her eyes widened with outrage. 'Excuse me?' she hissed.

'From now on you will not leave him in the care of strangers.'

Hurt indignation slid across her face. 'If you knew me at all, you'd know leaving my son with some faceless stranger is the last thing I'd do! Bronagh isn't a stranger. She's my friend as well as my assistant. And how dare you tell me how to raise my son?'

He caught her shoulders and tugged her close so they wouldn't be overheard. 'He is *our* son,' he rasped into her ear. 'His safety and well-being have now become my concern as much as yours, *gattina*.' The endearment slipped out again, but he deemed it appropriate, so he didn't allow the tingle that accompanied the term to disturb him too much. 'Put your claws away and let's take him back to your flat. You'll feed him and put him to bed and then we'll talk, *sì*?'

He pulled back and looked down at her, noting her hectic colour and experiencing that same punch to his libido that had occurred earlier.

Dio, he needed this added complication like a bullet in the head.

He dropped his hand once she gave a grudging nod.

'Lucca, it's time to go,' she called out.

'One more minute!' came his son's belligerent reply.

A tight, reluctant smile curved Maisie's lips, drawing Romeo's attention to their pink plumpness. 'He has zero concept of time and yet that's his stock answer every time you try to get him away from something he loves doing.'

'I'll bear that in mind,' he answered.

He glanced at his son and that sucker-punch feeling slammed into him again. It'd first happened when Gianlucca had slid his hand into his. Romeo had no term for it. But it was alive within him, and swelling by the minute.

Unthinking questions crowded his mind. Like when had Gianlucca taken his first step? What had been his first word?

What was his favourite thing to do besides feeding greedy ducks?

He stood, stock-still, as a plan began to formulate at the back of his mind. A plan that was uncharacteristically outlandish.

But wasn't this whole situation outlandish in the extreme?

And hadn't he learned that sometimes it was better to fight fire with fire?

The idea took firmer root, embedding itself as the only

viable course available to him if he was to thwart the schemes of Lorenzo Carmine and Agostino Fattore.

The more Romeo thought about the plans the old men, in their bid to hang on to their fast-crumbling empire, had dared to lay out for him, the more rage threatened to overcome him. He'd tempered that rage with caution, not forgetting that a wounded animal was a dangerous animal. Fattore's lieutenant might be old, and his power weakened, but Romeo knew that some power was better than no power to people like Lorenzo. And they would hang on to it by every ruthless means available.

Romeo didn't intend to lower his guard where Lorenzo's wily nature was concerned. His newly discovered son's safety was paramount. But even if Lorenzo and the shadows of Romeo's past hadn't been hanging over him, he would still proceed with the plan now fully formed in his mind.

He followed Maisie as she approached and caught up Gianlucca's hand. 'Time to go, precious.' The moment he started to protest, she continued, 'Which do you prefer for your tea, fish fingers or spaghetti and meatballs?'

'Spaghetti balls,' the boy responded immediately, his mind adeptly steered in the direction of food, just as his mother had intended. He danced between them until they reached the gate.

Romeo noticed his men had slipped into the security SUV parked behind his limo and nodded at the driver who held the door open. He turned to help his son into the car and saw Maisie's frown.

'Do you happen to have a car seat in there?' she asked.

Romeo cursed silently. 'No.'

'In that case, we'll meet you back at the restaurant.' She turned and started walking down the street.

He shut the door and fell into step beside her. 'I'll walk back with you.'

She opened her mouth to protest but stopped when he

took his son's hand. The feel of the small palm against his tilted Romeo's world.

He hadn't known or expected this reality-changing situation when he'd walked into that mansion in Palermo yesterday. But Romeo was nothing if not a quick study. His ability to harness a situation to his advantage had saved his life more times on the street than he could recount. He wasn't in a fight-to-the-death match right now, but he still intended to emerge a winner.

Maisie's first priority when she'd decorated her flat was homey comfort, with soft furnishings and pleasant colours to make the place a safe and snug home for her son. But as she opened the door and walked through the short hallway that connected to the living room she couldn't help but see it through Romeo's eyes. The carpet was a little worn, one cushion stained with Lucca's hand paint. And suddenly, the yellow polka-dot curtains seemed a little too bright, like something a *girlie* girl would choose, instead of the sophisticated women Romeo Brunetti probably dated.

What did it matter?

She turned, prepared to show her pride in her home, and found him frozen in front of the framed picture collage above her TV stand. Twelve pictures documented various key stages of Lucca's life so far, from his scrunched-up hours-old face to his first Easter egg hunt two months ago.

Romeo stared at each one with an intensity that bordered on the fanatic. Then he reached out and traced his fingers over Lucca's first picture, the tremor in his hand hard to miss.

'I have digital copies…if you'd like them,' she ventured.

He turned. The naked emotion in his eyes momentarily stopped her breath.

'*Grazie*, but I don't think that would be necessary.'

Her heart stopped as the fear she hadn't wanted to fully

explore bloomed before her eyes. 'What does that mean?' she asked, although she risked him further exploiting the rejection he'd just handed her.

'It means there are more important things to discuss than which pictures of my son I would like copies of.'

Lucca chose that moment to announce his hunger.

Maisie glanced at Romeo, questions warring with anger inside her.

She didn't want to leave her son now that she knew Romeo was preparing to back away. Especially since there was also the outside threat evidenced by the bodyguards in the SUV that had crawled behind them as they'd walked back. He travelled with too much security for a garden-variety billionaire.

That knowledge struck fear into her heart that she couldn't dismiss.

'Go and make his meal, Maisie,' Romeo said.

The taut command in his voice jerked her spine straight.

'I'd rather take him into the kitchen with me.'

'Is that your normal routine?' he queried with narrowed eyes.

'No, normally he likes to watch his favourite children's TV show while I cook.'

Romeo gave a brisk nod. 'Go, then. I'll find a way of entertaining him,' he replied.

'What do you know about entertaining children?' she demanded fiercely.

His jaw clenched. 'Even rocket science has been mastered. Besides, you'll be in the next room. What could go wrong?'

Everything.

The word blasted through her head. She opened her mouth to say as much but saw Lucca staring with keen interest at them. The last thing she wanted was for her son to pick up the dangerous undercurrents in the room.

Romeo watched her for a minute, clench-jawed. 'Are there any other exits in the flat, besides the front door?'

Maisie frowned. 'There's a fire escape outside my bedroom.'

'Is it locked?'

'Yes.'

'Okay.' He strode out and she followed him into the hallway. She watched him lock and take out the key and return to her. 'Now you can be assured that I won't run off with him while your back is turned. I'll also keep conversation to a minimum so I don't inadvertently verbally abuse him. Are you satisfied?'

Her fingers curled around the key, and she refused to be intimidated. 'That works. I won't be long. The meatballs are already done... I just need to cook the pasta.'

Romeo nodded and looked to where Lucca knelt on the floor surrounded by a sea of Lego. He shrugged off his overcoat and draped it over the sofa. Maisie watched him advance towards Lucca, his steps slow and non-threatening, to crouch next to him.

Lucca looked up, smiled and immediately scooped up a handful of Lego and held it out to him.

Maisie backed out, fighting the tearing emotions rampaging through her. Admonishing herself to get her emotions under control, she rushed into the kitchen and set about boiling water for the spaghetti, all the while trying to dissect what the presence of the bodyguards meant.

Surely if Romeo was in some sort of trouble the Internet search would've picked it out? Or was she blowing things out of proportion? Was she wrong about billionaires travelling with that much security? She frowned at the total excess of it. And what about Romeo's explanation that his business associates had found Lucca? From her time as a lawyer, Maisie knew deep background checks had become par for the course during business deals, but from Romeo's expression in the park, she couldn't help feeling there was more.

Her heart hammered as horrific possibilities tumbled through her mind. The world was a dangerous place. Even in a picturesque haven like Ranelagh, she couldn't guarantee that she would always be able to keep Lucca safe.

She froze at the sink. Had she invited danger in by letting Romeo Brunetti through her front door? Or had he been right when he'd told her she'd instinctively trusted him in Palermo or she'd never have gone up to his suite that day?

She must have on some level, surely, or she'd never have given him her virginity so easily.

Stop!

The only way to find out what was going on was to talk to Romeo. That wouldn't happen unless she stopped dawdling and got on with it.

She fixed Lucca's meal and set it up in the dining nook attached to her kitchen. Seeing Romeo sprawled on his side on the living-room floor stopped her in her tracks. Between father and son, they'd built a giant castle and were debating where to station the knights, with Lucca in favour of ground sentry duty and Romeo advocating turret guards.

He sensed her watching and looked up. Again Maisie was struck by the determination on his face.

And again, he shuttered the look and handed the knight to Lucca.

Maisie cleared her throat before she could speak. 'Lucca, your food's ready.'

'One more minute!'

Romeo lifted an eyebrow and gave a mock shudder. 'Do you enjoy cold spaghetti, Gianlucca?'

Lucca shook his head. 'No, it tastes yucky.'

'Then I think you should eat yours now before it turns yucky, *si*?'

'See what?' Lucca asked, his eyes wide and enquiring.

Romeo reached out and hesitantly touched his son's hair. '*Si* means yes in Italian,' he said gruffly.

'Are you Ita…Itayan? Mummy said I'm half Itayan.'

Romeo's eyes flicked to Maisie for a moment, then returned to his son. 'Yes, she's right. She's also waiting for you to go eat your dinner.' A quiet, firm reminder that brought Lucca to his feet.

He whizzed past her and climbed into his seat at the small dining table. He barely waited for Maisie to tuck his bib into place before he was tearing into his spaghetti.

Romeo leaned against the doorjamb, a peculiar look on his face as he absorbed Lucca's every action.

Then he turned and looked at her, and her heart caught. Nothing could keep down the geyser of apprehension that exploded through her at what that absorbed look on Romeo's face meant for her and her son.

In that moment, Maisie knew that nothing she said or did would stop what was unravelling before her eyes. It didn't matter whether Romeo loved his son or not, he would do exactly as he'd said in her office this morning.

Romeo Brunetti had every intention of claiming his son.

Maisie entered the living room and paused to watch Romeo's broad frame as he looked out of the window at the street below. With the endless horrific thoughts that had been tumbling through her mind for the past three hours, she wondered if he was just pavement-watching or if there was some unseen danger lurking out there.

He turned and her breath caught at the intensity in his face, the dangerous vibe surrounding his body. Wanting to get this over with quickly, she walked further into the living room.

'He's out like a light. When he's worn out like that, he won't wake until morning.' Maisie wondered why she'd been dropping little morsels like this all evening. Then she realised it was because Romeo voraciously lapped up each titbit about his son.

Because a part of her hoped that, by doing so, she could get him to rethink whatever he was plotting for Lucca's future? Did she really think she could turn Romeo's fascination with their son into love?

Love couldn't be forced. Either it was there or it wasn't. Her parents had been incapable of it. They'd cared only for their academic pursuits and peer accolades. None of that love had spilled to her.

She balled her fists. She would rather Romeo absented himself completely than dangle fatherhood in front of her son, only to reject him later. 'You wanted to talk?' she ventured. The earlier they laid things out in the open, the quicker she could get back to the status quo.

Romeo nodded in that solemn way he sometimes did, then remained silent and still, his hands thrust into his pockets. He continued to watch her, dark hazel eyes tracking her as she straightened the cushions and packed away the toys.

Too soon she was done. Silence filled the room and her breath emerged in short pants as she became painfully aware that they were alone, that zing of awareness spreading wider in the room.

She realised she was fidgeting with her fingers and resolutely pulled them apart. 'I don't mean to hurry this along, but can we just get it over—'

'Sit down, Maisie.'

She wanted to refuse. Just on principle because she wouldn't be ordered about in her own home, but something in his face warned her she needed to sit for what was coming.

Heart slamming into her ribcage, she perched on the edge of the sofa. He took the other end, his large body turned towards her so their knees almost touched. Again awareness of just how big, how powerfully built he was, crowded her senses. Her gaze dropped to his hands, large with sleek fingers. She recalled how they'd made her feel, how the light dusting of hair on the back had triggered delicious shivers in her once upon a time.

A different tremble powered up her spine.

Maisie gave herself a silent shake. This wasn't the time to be falling into a pool of lust. She'd been there, done that, with this man. And look where it had got her.

Look where she was now, about to be given news she instinctively knew would be life-changing.

She glanced up at him. His hazel eyes probed, then raked her face, and his nostrils flared slightly, as if he, too, was finding it difficult to be seated so close to her without remembering what they'd done to each other on a hot September night in Palermo five years ago. His gaze dropped to her throat, her breasts, and she heard his short intake of breath.

'Romeo…'

He balled his fists on top of his thighs and his chest expanded in a long inhalation. 'You're right about the bodyguards. I normally only travel with two members of my security team.'

Her stomach hollowed out. 'Why…why the increase?'

'It's just a precaution at this stage.'

'What does that mean?' she demanded. 'Precaution against what?'

'It means neither you nor Gianlucca are in danger at the moment.'

'But you're expecting us to be at some point?' Her voice had risen with her escalating fear and the shaking had taken on a firmer hold.

He shook his head. 'You don't need to panic—'

'Oh, really? You tell me my son could be in danger and then tell me not to panic?' she blurted, all the different scenarios she'd talked herself out of tumbling back again. She brushed her hands over her arms as cold dread drowned her.

'I meant, there was no need to panic because I'll ensure your safety,' he said.

'Safety from what?' When he remained silent, she jumped to her feet and paced the small living room. 'I think you should start from the beginning, Romeo. Who are these people and what do they want with you? With our son?'

She froze. 'Are you involved in…in criminal activity?' she whispered in horror.

His mouth compressed and his face set into harsh, determined lines. 'No, I am not.'

The scathing force of the words prompted her to believe him. But the fear didn't dissipate. 'Please tell me what's going on.'

He rose, too, and paced opposite her. When his fists clenched and unclenched a few times, she approached. At the touch of her hand on his arm, he jerked, as if he'd been elsewhere.

As he stared down at her, his mouth compressed. 'My past isn't what you'd call a white-picket-fence fairy tale,' he said obliquely.

Maisie attempted a smile. 'Only the books I read to Lucca contain those. Real life is rarely that way.'

A grim smile crossed his lips. 'Unfortunately, mine was a little more dire than that.'

She kept quiet, mostly because she didn't know how to respond.

'The man whose blood runs through my veins was the head of a Sicilian organised crime family.'

She gasped, then stepped back as the import of the words sank in. 'You're a member of a Mafia gang?'

'No, I'm not.' Again that scathing denial.

'But your…your father is?'

'He wasn't my father. We just share the same DNA,' he bit out in a harsh tone that spoke of anger, bitterness and harrowing pain.

Maisie's eyes widened. As if aware of how he'd sounded, Romeo breathed deeply and slid his fingers through his hair. 'The abbreviated story is that I met him twice. Both times ended…badly. What I didn't know until yesterday was that he'd kept tabs on me all my life.'

'Why?' she demanded.

Romeo shrugged. 'Since I didn't know the man, I can

only guess it was some sort of power-trip thing to watch whether I failed or succeeded. Or it may have been for other reasons. I care very little about what his motives were.'

Maisie frowned. 'You talked about him in the past tense…because…'

'He and his family died in a yacht explosion a year ago.'

The rush of blood from her head made her light-headed. 'Was it an accident?' she asked, her lips numb.

His mouth pursed for a few seconds before he answered, 'Officially. But probably not.'

Her gasp brought his head up. Cursing under his breath, he strode to her and grasped her arms. 'I'm only going by what my gut tells me, Maisie. I don't have hard evidence to the contrary.'

'And your gut tells you he was assassinated?'

He nodded.

A million more questions crowded her brain, but she forced a nod. 'Go on.'

His hands moved to her shoulders, a firm glide that left a trail of awareness over her skin. 'I received a letter from his lawyers a month ago, summoning me to Palermo, which I ignored. I received a few more after that. The last one told me he'd left me something I needed to collect in person.' His mouth twisted. 'My curiosity got the better of me.'

'What was it?'

'His monstrosity of a mansion. Along with his plans for my future.'

Ice slithered down her spine. 'What plans?'

One hand moved to her neck and cupped her nape. The familiarity of that gesture thawed the ice a little, replacing her terror with a wave of warm awareness.

'He never had a son…not a legitimate one anyway. I think somewhere along the line he intended to contact me, bring me into the *family business*. He just never got the chance to. But he told his second in command about it. He was the one who asked the lawyers to contact me.'

'What does he want from you?'

'The *famiglia* is falling apart. They need a new injection of young blood, and an even greater need for an injection of financial support.'

'You have both.'

'But I intend to give them neither.'

Maisie stared at his granite-hard face, the deep grooves bracketing his mouth and the dark gold of his eyes, and the pennies finally tumbled into place. 'But if you don't intend to... Oh, my God. You think they mean to use Lucca to make you do what they want?' she rasped in a terror-stricken voice.

His grip tightened and one finger caught her chin and raised her face to his spear-sharp gaze. Her stomach knotted at the savage determination on his face. 'They will *never* get their hands on you or our son. You have my word on this, Maisie.'

She shook her head, her insides growing colder by the second. 'But you can't guarantee that, can you? Or you wouldn't be here with *six* bodyguards in tow.'

'There's one way to ensure your safety,' he said, his gaze raking her face as if he wanted to pull the answer from her even before he'd asked the question.

'What's that?' she murmured.

'You will marry me. Then you and our son will know the protection of my name.'

CHAPTER FIVE

SHE WENT HOT, then cold, then colder. Until she felt as brittle as chilled glass. Dumbly, she stared into those burnished gold eyes, sure she'd misheard him.

'What did you say?'

'The *famiglia* isn't as powerful as it once was, but I'm not willing to dismiss them out of hand, either. Marrying me will grant you and Lucca protection, which you could be vulnerable without.'

'No way. I can't…I can't just *marry* you! We know next to nothing about each other.'

A look curled through his eyes. 'Our circumstances aren't commonplace. Besides, we've already done things a little out of sequence, don't you think?'

She laughed, but the sound was more painful than she wanted it to be. 'This is far from a quaint little romantic caper.'

He nodded. '*Sì*, which is why I want to ensure I have all the bases covered for your protection.'

'Oh, God!'

'Maisie—'

'No.' She pulled out of his hold and backed away. 'This is preposterous. You have to find another way to protect Lucca.'

Golden eyes bored into hers. 'There's no other way. There's an unspoken code, *gattina*. They may be thugs, but they respect family. Marrying me means you and Lucca become off limits.'

'But it still won't be a cast-iron guarantee, will it?'

He shrugged. 'Nothing in life is guaranteed. I have no

intention of involving myself in that life, but there may be resistance. A temporary marriage is our best option.'

The cold pronunciation chilled her to the bone. She kept backing away until her shoulders nudged the window. Unrelenting, he prowled towards her.

'No way. I can't do it, Romeo. I just... I can't just fold up my life and uproot my son to live goodness knows where, looking over my shoulder every day!'

'Look!' He reached her, grasped her shoulders and turned her around, directing her gaze to the street, where his men maintained a watchful guard. 'Is this how you want Lucca to live? Surrounded by men in black carrying guns? Can you honestly say that you'll experience a moment of peace in the park, knowing that his life could be in danger from unknown elements at each second of the day?'

She shuddered. 'That's not fair, Romeo.'

His bitter laugh scoured her skin. 'Life's *never* fair, *gattina*,' he whispered in her ear. 'Believe me, I have firsthand experience in just how unfair life can be. That's why I want this for our son. He will bear my name, legitimately, and my protection.'

'But you *cannot* guarantee that, can you? Can't you just go to the authorities and tell them about this?'

He levelled a deep sigh. '*Sì*, I can. My lawyers have been apprised of what's going on. But, technically, Lorenzo hasn't committed a crime yet, just issued veiled threats. Even when he does, the wheels of justice don't always move fast, Maisie. You of all people should know that.'

Sadly, she knew that all too well. Nevertheless, she couldn't give what he was suggesting any room to grow. That a part of her wanted to let it grow deeply unnerved her. 'We can still—'

'We can do a lot of things.' He reached for her again, pinning her arms to her sides. 'None would be as effective as what I'm proposing. At the very least, it'll buy time until I can find another solution.'

She pulled away. She thought of her parents, of the frosty existence she'd lived with. Her parents' lack of warmth hadn't just been directed at her. They'd been equally frosty to each other. As she'd grown up, she'd realised that the only reason they'd married and stayed married had been because of her. A shiver of horror raked her from head to toe at the thought of placing herself in a similar arrangement. Lucca was sharp. It would be a matter of time before he sensed that his parents didn't love one another. The thought of what it would do to him made her recoil.

'Maisie—'

'No!' she cried. The part of her that hadn't been freaking out completely threw up its arms and buckled beneath the part that was exploding with hysteria. 'I won't do it! I won't—'

She gasped as strong arms clamped around her and she was hauled into his body.

'*Basta!* There's no need to get hysterical.'

She fought to free herself, but his arms tightened their hold on her. 'I'm not getting hysterical,' she lied. Inside, she was going out of her mind with information overload. And being this close to Romeo, feeling his taut, warm body against hers, wasn't helping, either. Planting her hands on his chest, she pushed. 'Let me go, Romeo!'

'Calm down, then I will.'

She stilled, then made the mistake of glancing up at him.

His eyes were molten, his lips parted slightly as he stared down at her. The look on his face morphed to replicate the dangerous sensations climbing through her.

'No…' she whispered.

'No,' he agreed roughly. And yet his head started to descend, his arms gathering her even closer until her breasts were pressed against his chest.

A second later, his hot, sensual mouth slanted over hers, and she was tumbled headlong into a different quagmire.

Only, this one contained no fear, no horror. Only an electrifying sizzle that rocked her from head to toe.

His tongue breached her mouth, his teeth biting along the way. Maisie whimpered as sensation engulfed her. She opened her mouth wider, her tongue darting out to meet his.

He groaned and pulled her closer. One hand fisted her hair, angled her head for a deeper penetration, while the other slid down her back to cup her bottom. He squeezed and yanked her into his hardening groin. As if a torch paper had been lit between them, Maisie scoured her hands over him, trailing his shoulders, his back, the trim hardness of his waist before her fingers dug into the tightness of his buttocks.

A rough sound exploded from his lips as he rocked against her pelvis, imprinting his erection against her belly in a clear demand that made her moan. Hunger she'd taught herself to bury suddenly reared up, urgent and demanding. When his hand cupped her breast and toyed with her nipple, Maisie wanted to scream, *Take me!*

But even that sound would have taken too much effort, drugged as she was by the power of his kisses. Her fingers trailed back up, curled into his hair as she gave herself over to the sensation drowning her.

'*Gattina*…my little wildcat,' he groaned once he'd lifted his head to trail kisses along her jaw.

Maisie moaned as he bit her earlobe. 'Romeo.' Her speech was slurred and the secret place between her legs lit on fire from wanting him. From wanting her hunger assuaged.

He recaptured her mouth and Maisie was certain she would die just from the pleasure overload.

'Mummy!'

They exploded apart, their breaths erratic and ragged as they stared at each other across the space between them.

Romeo looked dazed, hectic colour scouring his cheekbones, his golden eyes hot and brooding and alive with arousal. She suspected she wore the same look, if not worse.

'*Mummy!*'

She lurched, still dazed, towards the door leading out into the hallway.

'*Gattina.*'

She didn't want to hear that term, didn't want to be reminded that she'd behaved like a horny little hellcat with her son asleep two doors away. But she turned anyway, met that torrid, golden gaze.

'Fix your shirt,' he rasped throatily.

Maisie looked down at the gaping shirt exposing her chest. The buttons had come undone without her having the vaguest idea when it'd happened. Flushing, she shakily secured them and hurried to her son's room.

He sat up in bed, rubbing his eyes, his lower lip pouting. She sat and scooped him into her lap and hugged him close.

'Hey, precious. Did you have a bad dream?'

'Yes. It was the bad goblins.' His lip trembled and he tucked his head into her shoulder.

'It's okay now, baby. Mummy's here. I'll slay the silly goblins so they can't get you.'

He gave a sleepy little giggle and wriggled deeper into her embrace.

She sat there, minutes ticking by as she crooned to him, until he fell back asleep. Planting a gentle kiss on his forehead, she caught movement from the corner of her eye and looked up to see Romeo framed in the doorway.

With her emotions nowhere near calm, Maisie couldn't form a coherent thought, never mind form actual words, so she watched in silence as he came and crouched at the side of the bed, his hand trailing gently down Lucca's back.

When his eyes met hers, her breath strangled at the fierce determination brimming in the hazel depths.

'You will slay his imaginary goblins. But what about his real ones?' he murmured, his voice low and intense.

'Romeo—'

'*I* will take care of those. All you have to do is accept my name.'

The implications of what he was asking was no less daunting, no less grave than it'd been half an hour ago when he'd dropped the bombshell. While she'd never given much thought to a future beyond being a mother and owner of a business she loved, she'd also not written it off. But what Romeo was asking… The idea was too huge to even comprehend.

'It's not as monumental an undertaking as you think,' he said, reading her thoughts with an accuracy that terrified her. 'Think of it as a time-buying exercise.'

His gaze fell to Lucca's sleeping form. His hand moved, as if to touch him, but he placed it back down on the bed.

The telling gesture made Maisie's breath strangle in her chest. 'You care about him, don't you?' she murmured.

A look crossed his face, which he quickly blanked. 'I didn't know he existed until twenty-four hours ago. But he's mine, and I take care of what's mine.'

He looked up, the clear, deadly promise blazing for her to see. It shook her to the soul, seeing the promise she'd made to her son the moment he'd drawn breath visible on another person's face.

She opened her mouth to say yes, then felt a cold finger of dread. As much as she wanted to protect her son, she couldn't live with herself if she risked swapping Lucca's physical well-being for his emotional one.

His eyes narrowed, and she was sure he was reading her thoughts again. He gently scooped up Lucca and placed him back in bed, pulling the Lego-themed coverlet over his little body before he straightened.

'Let's finish this talk. Now.' His voice vibrated with low, commanding intensity.

His heavy, dominating presence crowded her as they re-entered the living room. Knowing what she had to say, she turned to face him.

'What's the problem?' he asked.

She threw out her arms. 'Where do you want me to start? Even if I wanted to say yes to what you're proposing, what happens with us?'

A dark frown clamped his forehead. 'Us?'

'Yes, us. You and me. We're virtual strangers. What makes you think we'd last a day under the same roof?'

He shrugged. 'I'm inclined to think if we both know what's at stake, we can make it work.'

And what was at stake was her son's welfare. This was all for Lucca. She was merely the extra passenger along for the ride. The current situation had only made the claiming more urgent. The kiss that had happened was just residual hormones from their last time. Nothing more.

Lucca was the reason Romeo was here in the first place. She didn't think for a second that saying no would send Romeo packing. Regardless of the *Mafia code* or a marriage of convenience, the man in front of her would claim his son. She knew it with a bone-deep certainty.

'Maisie.' Another hard command. She was beginning to recognise how he'd risen to his powerful status so quickly. He packed more imperious presence in his little finger than most men packed in their whole bodies.

'I don't know what to say…'

He waited.

'Before I agree, I need your assurance that you'll resolve this as quickly as possible.'

His nostrils flared, but he nodded. *'Sì.'*

'That you'll tell me if anything changes where protecting Lucca is concerned.'

'You have my word.'

She sucked in a breath, but the enormity of what she was contemplating weighed on her with crushing force. 'Okay… then I'll marry you.'

A golden light flared in his eyes, and he nodded once.

'I'll take care of the details. You don't need to worry about anything.'

With that, he strode to where he'd draped his coat over the sofa and shrugged into it. Surprise scythed through her.

'You're leaving?'

'I have a few phone calls to make. I'll be back in the morning.'

Maisie was still reeling from his words and from what she'd committed herself to hours later when she realised that sleep would remain elusive.

She was still awake at 6:00 a.m. when firm knuckles hammered on her door.

'Is there a particular reason you feel inclined to break down my door at the crack of dawn?'

Romeo raised an eyebrow at the scowl that greeted him from beneath the cloud of auburn hair.

'I would've called, but I didn't want the phone to wake Lucca.' He also hadn't wanted to give her a chance to back out of what he'd convinced her to agree to yesterday.

Nothing would get in the way of him claiming his son. Attempting to give the child who was a part of himself the one thing that was denied him—a chance to choose his own path, free from the stain of illegitimacy.

Romeo might not know or even believe in love. But he could grant Gianlucca the acceptance and security that was never given him.

And Maisie O'Connell wouldn't stand in his way.

But she could, and continued to, glare at him. 'I suppose I should thank you for that consideration.'

'You're not a morning person, I see.'

'Great observation.' She eyed the coffee and croissants in his hand before slicing him with those bright blue eyes again. 'Is one of those for me?' she asked in a gruff, sleep-husky voice.

It was then he noticed the shadows under her eyes. Perhaps he should've waited a little while longer before arriving. But he'd grown tired of pacing his hotel suite. And he hadn't been certain that her *yes* had been from a place of belief that they were doing the right thing. The more he'd paced, the more he'd been sure she would change her mind given any more thinking room.

Romeo intended to give her none.

It had become clear very early on that her devotion to Lucca was absolute. It had been the only thing that had made him leave last night.

That and the need to push his investigators harder to find something concrete he could use against Lorenzo.

'Is that a no?'

He focused to see Maisie sliding a hairband from her wrist. She caught it in her teeth, then gathered her heavy silky hair into a bunch at the back of her head. The action drew up her nightshirt, showing off her shapely thighs and legs. Heat trickled through him as his gaze trailed up to linger on her heavy, pert breasts, thrown into relief by the act of securing her hair.

She seemed to notice the thick layer of awareness that had fired up, and her eyes darkened a touch.

Reining in his libido and burying the recollection of how those breasts had felt in his hands last night, he held out the coffee. There would be no repeat of last night's lust-fuelled encounter. Romeo had no intention of letting sex clutter up his plans.

He of all people knew one moment of madness could destroy a life. It was the reason he existed. It was the reason his mother had spent years blaming him for destroying her life.

It's the reason your son's here.

He accepted that sound analysis, just as he'd accepted that now he knew of Lucca's existence, he would safeguard his upbringing with everything he possessed. He'd witnessed too many people fall through the cracks to leave his son's fate to miracles and chance.

His own existence had been proof that miracles didn't exist.

'Thank you,' Maisie murmured huskily, taking the proffered beverage before stepping back to let him in. He handed her the pastry and followed her into the kitchen. She placed the croissants on a plate but didn't make a move to touch them. 'It's a little too early for me.'

Again he experienced a tiny bout of guilt, then told himself there would be plenty of time for her to rest once he got them away from here.

Her gaze flicked to him, then darted away. But in that look Romeo caught the hesitation he'd been dreading. He gritted his teeth.

He didn't want to resort to plan B, but he would if necessary. 'Second thoughts are natural. As long as you keep your eye on the big picture.'

She bit her lip. 'I can't believe this is happening.'

'It's happening, *gattina*. We'll tell Lucca when he wakes up. Is there anyone else you wish to inform? Your parents?' He vaguely recalled her mentioning them in the intermittent burst of chatter that had preceded him inviting her to his suite that night in Palermo.

Her expression shuttered and she took a large gulp of coffee. 'My parents are no longer in the picture.' A bleak note of hurt threaded her voice. 'And even if they were, this wouldn't be the ideal scenario to present to them, would it? Their only child marrying the father of her child because the Mafia were issuing threats?' Her mouth twisted in mocking bitterness.

His eyes narrowed at the odd note in her voice. 'They wouldn't want you to do what is necessary to safeguard their grandson?'

Her gaze remained lowered and she crossed her arms around her middle in a gesture of self-preservation. 'I wouldn't know. Besides the odd birthday and Christmas card, I haven't spoken to them in four years.'

Four years. The same length of time as his son had been alive. Certain there was more to the story, he opened his mouth to ask. But her head snapped up and she flashed him a pursed-lip smile.

'How much time do I have to get my things in order? I'll need a few days at least to talk to... You're shaking your head. Why?' she enquired curtly.

'We're leaving this morning.'

'That's impossible. I have to pack and make sure I get the right person to look after the restaurant until...' She stopped and frowned. 'Will I be able to return any time soon?' Wide blue eyes stared at him with a mixture of resignation and sadness.

'Not for a while.'

'How long is a while?'

'A few weeks, a few months? It's probably best that you forget about this place for the time being.'

The sadness was replaced with a flash of anger. 'That's easy for you to say. You haven't spent the better part of two years working night and day to get a business off the ground.'

He allowed himself a small smile. 'I know a little bit about the hard work it takes to establish a business.'

She grimaced. 'But you don't know how it feels to do it on your own with no support from anyone else. The fear that comes from knowing that one failure could mean you have nothing to help you look after your child.' She shook her head, as if realising how much she'd revealed.

Romeo chose not to enlighten her about his personal relationship with fear and failure—of the rough, terrifying nights he'd spent on the streets when he was barely into his teens; of the desperate need for acceptance that had led him to contemplate, for a blessedly brief moment, whether he was truly his father's son.

He'd rejected and stumbled away from the gang initiation rites and earned himself a bullseye on his back for a while. But it hadn't stopped the fermenting thought that perhaps the life of a *Mafioso* was blueprinted in his blood.

That was a part of him he intended would never see the light of day.

But it was a thought he had never been able to shake off.

He downed the espresso and watched her struggle to get her emotions under control. 'Tell me what you need to do to expedite things.' He had spent most of the night putting things in place to remove her and Lucca as quickly as possible, but he had the feeling telling her that right now wouldn't go down well.

'I have to speak to Bronagh about assuming a full-time managerial position for starters. Then make sure the staff are taken care of.' She started to slide her hands through her hair, realised she'd caught it in a ponytail and switched to sliding the long tail through her fingers. 'I can't just up and leave.'

The need to get her and Lucca away from here, as quickly as possible, smashed through the civilised barrier he'd placed on himself so far. 'A Michelin-star chef will be here at nine to take over the day-to-day running of the restaurant. Once Lucca is awake, I have a team of movers waiting outside to pack your things. You can keep the apartment or I can arrange for it to be sold, that's your choice. We'll stop over in London, where we will be married at four this afternoon. After that we'll fly straight from London to my island in Hawaii.'

She'd stilled as he spoke, her eyes growing wider with each plan he laid out. 'But…we can't get married that quickly,' she blurted. 'We need a special licence and that takes—'

'It's taken care of.'

She shook her head. 'This is going too fast, Romeo.'

He folded his arms. 'The sooner this layer of protection

is in place, the sooner I can concentrate on dealing with Lorenzo.'

Apprehension crept into her eyes and he cursed under his breath.

She abandoned her coffee and folded her arms. Romeo willed his gaze to remain above her neckline, not to watch the tail of hair trail across her breasts with each breath she took. 'Do we at least have time to discuss what sort of marriage we're going to have?'

He tensed. 'Excuse me?'

'Well, this isn't going to be a traditional marriage, is it? As you said, we're only doing this to ensure Lucca's safety, so I presume the physical side of things won't be part of the marriage.'

Despite having told himself precisely the same thing after his control slipped last night, something moved through his belly that felt very much like rejection. He gritted his teeth.

'If that is what you wish, then it will be so.'

Her lashes swept down. 'Yes, that's what I want. I think you'll agree, sex tends to cause unnecessary confusion.' A flush crept up her neck and Romeo was struck by how innocent she looked.

'Sì, Lucca is the most important thing in all this.' Why did the words feel so hard to get out?

She gave a brisk nod. 'I'll go and get changed. He'll be waking up any minute now.' She started to walk towards the door, then stopped and turned with a grace that hinted at balletic training.

Romeo frowned. He knew next to nothing about the mother of his child. All he had were the basic facts produced by his private investigators. He'd been so focused on his son that he'd only requested information from Maisie's pregnancy to date.

He hadn't really paid attention to their random conversations five years ago. He'd gone seeking oblivion of the carnal nature and had fallen head first into a maelstrom of emotions he still had a hard time reliving. He'd tried afterwards to explain it away as his grief talking, but that hadn't quite rung true.

The idea that he'd been burying a lonely yearning that had chosen his mother's death to emerge had shaken him to the core.

It wasn't a place he wanted to visit ever again.

He mentally shrugged. He didn't *need* to know any more about Maisie, other than that she would continue to remain devoted and invested in keeping their son safe.

'I'd like to keep Bronagh as assistant manager. She's been a huge support and I don't want this new manager tossing her out after I'm gone, okay?'

'If that's what you need to put your mind at rest, then it will be done.'

She opened her mouth, as if she wanted to say more, but nodded and left.

His phone vibrated in his pocket. He pulled it out before it started to ring. Anger throbbed to life when he saw the familiar area code. Strolling out of the kitchen, he answered it.

'You may be used to not taking no for an answer, but if you want to have any dealings with me, you'll listen when I say I'll be in touch when I'm good and ready.'

'You have the benefit of youth on your side, Brunetti, but I'm reduced to counting the minutes.'

'Perhaps you should remember that before you test me any further,' he grated out.

Lorenzo gave a barking laugh. 'You think I don't know what you're up to? You may secure your *figlio* a layer of protection, but your legacy will still need to be claimed.'

Romeo's rage built. 'My legacy doesn't involve indulging a handful of geriatric old men, desperate to hang on to the old ways. I'm better at this game than you give me credit for. Being forced to live in the gutter has a way of bringing out a man's survival instincts.'

For the first time, Lorenzo seemed to falter. 'Brunetti...'

'Do not call me again. I'll be in touch when I'm ready.'
He hung up and turned at the sound of his son's laughter.

The sound moved through him, and he froze in place
for a second.

Gianlucca was his legacy. One he intended to guard with
his life, if necessary.

He swallowed and got himself under control just as his
son burst excitedly into the living room.

'Mummy says we're going on a plane today!'

'Yes, you're coming to live with me for a little while.'

'Do you have a big house?'

The corner of Romeo's mouth lifted. 'It's big enough for
my needs, yes.'

Lucca's head tilted pensively. 'Does it have a duck pond?'

'Not yet,' he replied, then gave in to the compulsion to
offer more; to make a little boy happy. 'But I will build one
for you.'

His eyes rounded. 'My very own duck pond?' he whispered in awe.

A peculiar stone lodged in Romeo's throat, making it
difficult to swallow. '*Sì*…yes. Your very own.'

A giant smile broke over his son's face. 'Wow! Can I also
have a bouncy castle?'

Romeo opened his mouth, but Maisie shook her head.
'We'll discuss it later.'

Lucca continued to beam. 'It's going to be the best adventure ever!'

Unable to speak on account of all the tectonic plates of
his reality shifting inside him, Romeo could only nod.

CHAPTER SIX

MAISIE FOUND OUT just how much of an adventure when she was ushered into an exclusive Mayfair boutique five hours later with a team of stylists. As per Romeo's imperious request, the shop had been shut so the attendants could focus solely on her. He sat in the large reception room, flipping through a document while keeping an eye on Lucca, who was getting his own special outfit for the wedding.

Wedding...

She was getting married. To the father of her child. The man she'd thought she'd never set eyes on again after waking up alone in a hotel room in Palermo. The dizzying turn of events threatened to flatten her. But as she'd taken to reminding herself in case any fanciful thoughts took over, all this was happening for the sake of her son.

This was a wedding in name only; it would *be* a marriage in name only. And once this whole business with Romeo's dark past was over with, she would resume her life.

All the same, she couldn't stop a bewildering shiver as the wedding dress she'd chosen was slipped over her head.

Made entirely of cream silk, the calf-length dress had the scoop-neck design both in the front and back, and lace sleeves covering her to the elbow. The material hugged her from bodice to thigh, with a slit at the back for ease of movement. It was simple, elegant and businesslike enough to not portray any of those fanciful thoughts that fleeted through her mind every time she so much as dropped her guard. Dress on, she slipped her feet into matching cream heels and moved to where a hair and make-up expert had been set up.

Maisie had lost the ability to keep up with how fast Romeo had moved once things were set in motion. There'd been no time to get sentimental once she'd summoned the staff, especially with Romeo's overwhelming presence at her side reassuring them that nothing would change in the running of the restaurant.

Her staff knew and respected Bronagh. It was that alone that had made temporarily stepping away from the place she'd poured her heart and muscle into bearable.

And then Romeo had floored her by inviting Bronagh to London to act as witness at their wedding.

The surprises had kept coming, with her first, brief trip in a private jet, hammering home to her just how powerful and influential the man she would be marrying shortly really was.

'There, I think you're set.'

Maisie refocused and examined the chic pinned-up hairstyle and subtle, immaculate make-up, and forced a smile. As much as she'd told herself this marriage wasn't real, she couldn't halt the horde of butterflies beating frantically in her belly. 'Thank you.'

'And I hope you don't mind, but we sent out for a bouquet. It seems a little wrong that a bride should get married without one, you know?' The owner of the boutique, an elegant, fortyish woman, said. 'Especially when you're marrying Romeo Brunetti.' The clear envy in her eyes and the awe in her voice echoed through Maisie.

She was saved from answering when the door opened and Bronagh entered holding a stunning cream-and-lilac rose arrangement bound with crystal-studded ribbon. 'I'd say this bouquet is the most gorgeous thing I've ever seen, but I think you take the prize for that, Maisie,' she said, her soft brown eyes widening as Maisie rose and she looked her over. 'You're going to knock that man of yours dead.' There was a faintly querying note in her voice, but the reason Maisie had become fast friends with Bronagh Davis was because she'd offered friendship without prying just when Maisie had needed that. And although the other woman had probably guessed that Romeo was Lucca's father—the similarities between them seemed to grow with each passing second—she hadn't questioned Maisie.

'You win all the points for flattery,' Maisie replied, surreptitiously rubbing her palms together to keep them from getting any more damp.

Bronagh smiled and handed over the bouquet. 'You can award me the points later. Your men are getting impatient, and from the way the older one is pacing, I wouldn't be surprised if he storms in here and claims you.'

The butterflies' wings flapped harder. Maisie swallowed down her absurd nervousness and any lingering sadness that indicated she wished this were real, that she were marrying a man she'd taken the time to meet, fall in love and ultimately join her life with.

That was a pipe dream she'd long ago abandoned, even before she'd been faced with an unplanned pregnancy and the sheer dedication she'd needed to take care of her child. She'd been exposed too many times to the ruthless indifference inherent in loveless relationships to believe that she would be the exception to the rule. The love she'd felt for Lucca the moment he was born had been a miraculous gift she intended to guard with everything she held dear. So she'd driven her energy into providing a home for her child, despite her parents' icy disapproval.

Maisie reminded herself that this situation wasn't in her control, that even in this she was putting Lucca's needs first.

Her needs didn't matter.

That particular thought took a steep dive when she emerged from the changing room and was confronted with Romeo Brunetti in a three-piece suit. Immaculate, imposingly masculine and utterly breathtaking, he was impossible to ignore. From the top of his neatly combed, wavy black hair, to the polished toes of his handmade shoes, he reeked irrefutable power and enough sexual magnetism to make kings quake and women swoon in his presence. And that look in his eyes…that brooding, almost formidable intensity that had made her tingle from head to toe the first time she'd seen him…

Yes. Maisie was reminded then how very needful she could be. And how some needs were impossible to suppress even with an iron will. She stared. Tried to pull her gaze away. Failed. And stared some more. At the back of her mind, a tiny voice said it was okay to stare because he was doing the same to her.

The look in his eyes was riveting, as if he were seeing her for the first time. A part of her thrilled at that look, the way it made her feel sexy and desirable…until she reminded herself that nothing would come of it. Nothing could.

Her attention was mercifully pulled away when Lucca rushed towards her. 'You look beautiful, Mummy!'

Her smile wobbled when she saw his own attire—a miniature one of his father's, right down to the buttoned-up waistcoat. 'So do you, my precious.'

Romeo seemed to unfreeze then from his stance. 'Come, the car's waiting.'

Everyone snapped to attention. Two guards appeared at the shop door and nodded. They exited and slid into the back of the limo and were driving the short distance to the register office at Marylebone when he reached into his jacket, pulled out a long, velvet box and handed it to her.

'What's this?' she blurted.

One corner of his mouth lifted. 'I thought your absence of jewellery should be addressed.'

Her hand went to her bare throat. 'I…I didn't think it was necessary.' Which, in hindsight, sounded a little foolish. She was marrying one of the world's richest men. Whether the marriage was real or not, she was about to be thrust into the limelight the proportions of which she was too afraid to imagine. The women Romeo had dated before were all raving beauties compared to her.

A flush rose in her face when his eyebrow quirked. 'You may not, but we don't wish to attract unnecessary gossip,' he murmured, his voice deep but low enough to keep Bronagh and Lucca, who sat on the far side of the limo, from over-hearing. 'Open it.'

Fingers shaking, she prised the box open and gasped. The three-layered collar necklace contained over two dozen diamonds in different cuts and sizes, the largest, teardrop gem placed in the middle. The stunning jewels, along with a pair of equally breathtaking earrings, sparkled in her trembling hand. Maisie realised her mouth was still open when Romeo plucked the necklace off its velvet bed and held it out.

'Turn around.'

Still stunned, she complied and suppressed a tremble when his warm fingers brushed her nape. She turned to-wards him to thank him and froze when he leaned forward to adjust the necklace so the large stone was resting just above her cleavage. The touch of those fingers…there… sent her blood pounding through her veins. She looked up and met dark hazel eyes. The knowing and hungry look reflecting back at her stopped whatever breath she'd been about to take. They stared at each other, that intense con-nection that seemed to fuse them together whenever they were close sizzling between them.

'Wow, that's stunning.'

Maisie jerked guiltily at Bronagh's awed compliment. Another blush crept into her face when she realised she'd momentarily forgotten that her friend and son were in the car. To cover up her embarrassment, she hastily reached for the earrings and clipped them on. Then exhaled in a rush when Romeo produced another ominous-sized box.

'Romeo…'

His eyes flashed a warning and she swallowed her ob-jection. This time he opened it. The large diamond-and-ruby engagement ring defied description. And probably defied any attempt to place a value on it. Silently, Maisie held out her left hand, absurdly bemused to take in the fact that between one heartbeat and the next she'd been draped in jewels that cost more than she would earn in a lifetime.

She smiled through further gasps from Bronagh and just willed herself to breathe. She might not have fully absorbed what she was letting herself in for publicly by agreeing to marry Romeo Brunetti the billionaire, instead of Romeo Brunetti, father of her child, but she'd faced tougher challenges and triumphed. She could do this.

The marriage ceremony itself was shockingly brief.

Whatever strings Romeo had pulled to secure a special licence had pressed home his importance. They were ushered into an oak-panelled room that reeked history and brevity. The registrar read out their commitments in a deep but hushed voice and announced that they were man and wife within twenty minutes of their arrival.

Romeo's kiss on her lips was swift and chaste, his hands dropping from her shoulders almost immediately. She told herself the wrench in her stomach was nerves as she followed him to the desk where their signatures formalised their union.

As she signed her name, Maisie reaffirmed that she was taking the necessary steps to keep her son safe. It was what kept her going through the lavish Mayfair meal with Bronagh, after which Bronagh was driven to the airport to catch a flight back to Dublin, and they were driven straight to a private airport south of London.

Unable to stand the thick silence in the car now that Lucca had fallen asleep, she cleared her throat.

'I didn't know Italians could marry in London without jumping through bureaucratic hoops.'

Romeo switched from looking out of the window. The brooding glance he sent her made her wish for a moment she'd let the silence continue. 'I've lived in London for over ten years. Other than two days ago, the last time I was in Italy was when you and I met.'

Surprise lifted her brows. 'I thought you were a resident. You seemed to know your way about where…where you were staying.'

His mouth twisted. 'I was, once upon a time. But in a much more inhospitable part.'

'Inhospitable?' she echoed.

That brooding gaze intensified. 'I wasn't always affluent, *gattina*. I can probably go as far as to say I'm the definition of *nouveau riche*. I know the streets where we met well because I used to walk there at night in the hope that I would find leftover food in bins or a tourist who was willing to part with a few euros for a quick shoe shine. Barring that, I would find an alleyway to sleep in for a night, but only for a night because inevitably I would be sent packing by the *polizia* and threatened with jail should I return.'

Maisie wasn't sure which was more unnerving—the harrowing account of his childhood or the cold, unfeeling way in which he recounted it. Either way, the stone-cold horror that had wedged in her stomach grew, until she was sure her insides were frozen with pain at imagining what he'd been through.

'You said you only met your father twice,' she murmured, unable to erase the bleak picture he drew in her mind, 'but what about your mother?'

Lucca stirred in his sleep, and Romeo's eyes shifted to his son before returning to hers. 'My mother is a subject I don't wish to discuss, especially on my wedding day.' His smile mocked the significance of the day.

But Maisie couldn't dismiss the subject as easily. 'And child services? Surely there was some support you could've sought?'

He blinked, his nostrils flaring slightly before he shrugged. 'The support is the same in Italy as it is in England. Some fall through the cracks. And if one tried hard enough to evade the clutches of a system that was inherently flawed, one could succeed.'

Despite catching his meaning, Maisie couldn't fathom why he would choose to live on the streets. 'How long did you sleep rough for?' she asked, her heart bleeding at the thought.

His mouth compressed in a cruel line. 'Two years until the authorities got fed up with hauling me away every other night. A do-gooder policewoman thought I would be better off in the foster system.' He gave a harsh, self-deprecating laugh. 'Unfortunately, she couldn't have been more wrong. Because then it was really driven home that my kind wouldn't be welcome in a normal, well-adjusted home.'

'Your kind?'

'The bastard children of violent criminals.'

Her hand flew to her mouth. 'Oh, God!'

Romeo's eyes once again flicked to his sleeping son and he shook his head. 'Don't worry, *gattina*. I got out the second I could. Now look at me.' He spread his hands in mock preen. And although his voice was even, Maisie saw the shadows of dark memory that blanketed his eyes and hardened his mouth. 'According to the media, I'm every woman's dream and every parent's ideal suitor for their wholesome daughter. Consider yourself lucky for bagging me.' His teeth barred in a mirthless smile.

'Romeo—'

He lunged close so quickly, filled every inch of her vision so spectacularly, her breath snagged in her chest. His fingers pressed against her mouth, forcibly rejecting any words she'd been about to utter. 'No, *gattina*. Save your warm-hearted sympathy and soft words for our son,' he rasped jaggedly. 'You be there for him when he scrapes his knee and when the goblins frighten him at night. I require no sympathy. I learnt to do without it long before I could walk.'

He sat back and for a full minute remained frozen. Then

his chest rose and fell in a single deep exhalation before he pressed a button next to his armrest. A laptop slid from a side compartment and flickered on. Strong fingers tapped the keys, flicking through pages of data with calm efficiency.

As if he hadn't just torn open his chest and shown her the raw wounds scarring his heart.

Romeo tapped another random key, stared unseeing at the stream of words and numbers filling the screen.

What in the name of heaven had he been thinking?

Had he not sworn only last night to keep his past locked in the vault where it belonged? Through all the voracious media attention that had exploded in his life once his first resort had achieved platinum-star status, he'd kept his past safely under wraps. Besides Zaccheo Giordano, the only man he considered a friend, and his wife, Eva, no one else knew about the desperately traumatising childhood he'd suffered. Many had tried to dig, only to accept the illusion that his secret past made him alluringly mysterious, and left it at that. Romeo had been more than glad to leave things at that.

So why had he just spilled his guts to Maisie O'Connell? And not only spilled his guts, but ripped off the emotion-free bandage he'd bound his memories with in the process?

He tried to think through it rationally; to decipher just what it was about this woman who let all the volatile, raw emotions overrun him.

Their meeting hadn't been accompanied by thunder and lightning. There'd been nothing remotely spectacular about it. To the contrary, he'd walked past her that night at the waterfront café in Palermo with every intention of continuing his solitary walk.

Lost in thoughts of bewildering grief and hoping the night air would clear his head, he'd walked for miles from the cemetery where Ariana Brunetti had found her last resting place. He'd barely taken in where he was headed, the

need to put distance between the mother whose only interest had been for herself and how much she could get for
selling her body, a visceral need.

When he'd finally reached the stone wall overlooking
the water, he'd stood lost and seriously contemplated scal-
ing the wall and swimming away from the city that bore
only harrowing memories. The sound of tourists drinking
away the night had finally impinged, and he'd had the brilliant idea of drowning his sorrows with whisky.

He'd walked past her, barely noticing her.

It was only as he'd ordered his third whisky that he'd
caught her staring. Even then, he'd dismissed her. He was
used to women staring at him. Women coming onto him
since he'd been old enough to shave.

But he'd caught her furtive glances, those bright blue
eyes darting his way when she thought he wasn't looking.
Romeo wasn't sure why he'd talked to her that night. Perhaps it'd been that lost look she'd been trying so hard to disguise. Or the fact that a group of male tourists had noticed
her and were placing bets on who would buy her the next
drink. Or the fact that his mother's last words to him had
left him raw, feeling as if his very skin had been peeled off.

You're just like him...just like him...

In the hours and days that had followed, he'd been able
to stop those words ringing in his head.

Having that drink in that café had been a last, desperate
attempt to drown out the words.

He'd raised his glass to her in a silent toast. She'd smiled
shyly and asked what he was toasting. He'd made some
smart remark or other he couldn't recall. He'd kicked out
the seat opposite in brusque invitation and she'd joined him.

Midnight had arrived and they'd walked to his hotel,
both of them very much aware of what would happen next.

He'd walked away the next day, even more exposed than
he'd ever been in his life.

But he'd pulled himself together, refusing to be the needy

shadow of a man who'd yearned for a kind word from the mother who'd rejected him all his life. And he'd succeeded.

Nothing should've prompted this puzzling and clever way Maisie had managed to slip under his guard not once, but twice. It was a weakness he couldn't, *wouldn't* abide.

He stole a glance from the corner of his eye and saw that she was gazing at the passing scenery, her fingers toying with her new rings.

He breathed a little easier, confident that moment of madness was behind him. That she was taking his advice and letting the temporary aberration pass.

'I'm sorry I dredged up bad memories for you,' she said suddenly.

Romeo shut the laptop with studied care, resisting the urge to rip the gadget out of its housing and throw it out of the window.

'Maisie—' he growled warningly.

'I know you don't want to talk about it now and I respect that. But I just wanted you to know, should you ever feel the need to talk, I'm here.'

For one shocking, ground-shaking moment, his black soul lifted at those words. He allowed himself to glimpse a day when he would unburden himself and feel whole, clean. The picture was so laughable, he shook his head in wonder at his own gall.

He was the son of a whore and a vicious thug. He'd contemplated hurting another human being just so he could join a gang…to gain respect through violence. Walking away, sick to his stomach, hadn't absolved him of the three days he'd worn the probation leathers and trawled the dark streets of Palermo, looking for a victim. He would never be clean, never be washed free of that stain. He hadn't bothered to try up until now. He never would.

'*Grazie*, but I can assure you that day will never come.'

CHAPTER SEVEN

THE BRUNETTI INTERNATIONAL RESORT MAUI was a tropical oasis that had been created with heaven itself in mind. Or at least that was what the brochure stated.

Maisie had silently rolled her eyes when she read the claim.

Looking around her as they alighted from the seaplane, she accepted the statement hadn't been an exaggeration. A long, sugar-sanded beach stretched for a half mile before it curved around an outcrop of rock that looked perfect for diving.

From the beach, the land rose gently, swaying palm trees blending with the increasingly denser vegetation Maisie had spotted from the plane before they'd landed.

She knew the resort housed six koa-wood-and-stone mansions, each large and luxurious enough to cater to the most demanding guest, with the largest, a twelve-bedroom sprawling architect's dream, sitting on top of a hill in the centre of the island.

From the brochure she'd read she also knew that the mansion had been booked for the next three years and that guests paid a king's ransom for the privilege.

She had been admiring the stunning architecture of the resort when her eyes had grown heavy. Jerking awake, she'd found her shoes had been taken off, her seat reclined and a pillow tucked under her head. She'd looked up from the soft cashmere throw keeping her warm to find Lucca and Romeo at the dining table, tucking into a meal. Or rather, Lucca had been eating and chattering away, with his father watching him with that silent intensity and awe that had struck a peculiar ache in Maisie's chest.

Romeo had looked up then, locked gazes with her before being diverted by their son. Unlike in the car when his emotions had bubbled just beneath his skin, he'd looked cool and remote, very much the powerful, in-control billionaire. He'd looked untouchable, and Maisie believed he meant for the moment in the car never to happen again. Whatever had prompted him to reveal a horrific chapter of his past had been resealed in an impenetrable fortress, never to be revisited again.

She'd berated herself for feeling mournful, for experiencing his pain as acutely as if it were her own. She had no right to it, no right to pry or feel strangely bereft when he'd shut her out and refocused his attention on Lucca.

Her parents had tried to drill into her that her brain was her most valuable asset, but Maisie had known that wasn't true. With the birth of her child, she'd known love was the greatest gift she could give, and receive. Same as she knew that Romeo, like her parents, didn't have a need for it. He believed in protecting his son, much as her own parents had provided a roof over her head and put clothes on her back. But, like them, he had nothing more to give.

And while she couldn't turn her compassion off at will, she needed to guard against overexposure of the emotion that had drawn her to Romeo in the first place. His grief and misery that night had been like a beacon. She'd wanted to comfort him, grant him reprieve from the shackles that bound him.

The result had been waking up alone, and returning home weeks later, pregnant. She would do well to remember that.

'Are you coming?'

She jumped at Romeo's prompt and realised she'd stopped at the bottom of the stone steps leading up from the beach.

'Yes, of course.' She smiled at the six white-uniformed staff ready to unload their luggage and followed Romeo up to the buggy parked on the pavement. He lowered an excited Lucca onto the seat and fastened his seat belt before turning to her.

'Would you like a quick tour now or later?' he asked coolly.

'Now would be great, thanks.'

He nodded and started the buggy. When Lucca wriggled excitedly, Romeo slowed down and touched his son's arm. 'Sit still, *bambino*, or you'll have to walk all the way back to the house.'

Lucca looked round. 'Where's the house?' he asked.

Romeo pointed up the hill to a large villa whose glass cathedral-like dome dominated the hilltop. 'All the way up there.'

Lucca immediately stilled, his eyes rounding as he stared up at Romeo. 'I'll be still.'

Romeo looked over at her, a small smile playing on his lips before he tentatively ruffled Lucca's hair. '*Bene*…that means good in Italian.'

'*Bene,*' Lucca repeated, intoning the syllables in near perfect match of his father's accent.

Maisie looked around and realised two things. That the brochure hadn't done enough justice to the description of Hana Island. And also that only two of the mansions that Romeo drove past looked occupied.

'But I thought this place was fully booked for years in advance?'

'It was…until yesterday when I cancelled half of the bookings.'

'Why?'

'Because I wanted to guarantee our privacy. The two families who are staying here have been fully vetted and have signed confidentiality agreements. The others were a little more testy, so I compensated them for their trouble and sent them to another resort. Complimentary, of course.'

Maisie looked around as they headed up the hill. The whole place was the very epitome of paradise. But then paradise had contained a poisonous snake.

'Surely you don't think…'

He sent her a warning look. She bit her lip and waited until he'd stopped the buggy in front of a large set of double doors made of polished koa wood and released Lucca's seat belt. When Lucca scampered off towards the house, he turned to her.

'No, I don't think we'll have any trouble here, but I took the necessary precautions nevertheless.'

She looked around the lush paradise. 'But we can't stay here for ever, Romeo.'

His jaw flexed. 'We'll remain here until I find a way to fix this. Besides, the world thinks we're on our honeymoon, so why not enjoy the time off?' He glanced over to where Lucca was examining a spray of giant bright orange flowers. 'I can't imagine you've had any downtime since he was born.'

Maisie smiled reluctantly. 'I don't imagine I'll be getting any until he's at least eighteen.'

He watched her with a quizzical look. 'But it will be a relief not to be burdened with him 24/7, *sì*?' There was a hard bite to his tone that set her nerves on edge.

She frowned. 'I don't consider him a burden,' she retorted.

'Was he the reason you switched careers?' he enquired.

'Well…yes, but—'

'Pursuing a career in criminal law to operating a restaurant in a quaint little village is quite a change.'

'It was a choice I made both for Lucca and myself.'

He nodded. 'You've proved you're capable of adapting. So adjusting to our new situation shouldn't be a big problem.'

She looked around. 'I'm not built to lie about sipping cocktails. I need a challenge, even with Lucca around.'

'Then we will find other challenges for you.'

'Thank you. Now, is this interview of my mothering skills and commitment over? I'd like to get out of these travelling clothes.'

He continued to stare at her in that direct, invasive way of his, as if trying to see beneath her words to any truth she was hiding.

After several minutes he nodded and alighted from the buggy.

Double doors swung open and two women came forward, one an older Tongan native and a younger girl who approached Lucca with a smile. Maisie noticed she walked with a slight limp.

'This is Emily. She'll be helping you look after Lucca. And Mahina is our housekeeper.

Maisie managed to keep a smile on her face throughout the introductions and the tour of Romeo's mansion. She even managed to make the right noises when she saw the Olympic-sized pool and the hot tub, and the man-made cave that opened up into a private waterfall complete with pool at the back of the property.

She smiled through giving Lucca a quick wash, with a helpful Emily unpacking his clothes. When the girl offered to take him away for a glass of juice, Maisie forced a nod, welcoming the opportunity to find Romeo and give him a piece of her mind.

After searching fruitlessly upstairs and knocking on over a dozen doors, she finally found him in a large, airy room converted to a study, with rows of books covering one wall, and an imposing desk and chair fronting a floor-to-ceiling glass window.

She shut the door behind her after his imperious directive to come in and stalked to where he sat, master and commander of his empire.

'How dare you hire a nanny without consulting me,' she fired at him when he looked up from the document he was perusing.

His brows clamped for a second before he rose and rounded the desk. Maisie forced herself not to step back from the broad-shouldered magnificence of his physique. He'd also changed from the suit he wore to travel, into a turquoise polo shirt and a pair of white linen trousers, into which he shoved his hands. 'I didn't think you would object.'

'Why? Because I'm so eager to be lightened of the *burden* of caring for my son?'

'Because I'm told every mother needs a break every now and then.'

'And who, pray tell, enlightened you of this fact? It can't have been your mother, since I'm guessing she wasn't a contender for mother of the year?'

His cold tensing confirmed she'd gone too far. 'We seem to be straying away from the issue under discussion. You slept for less than an hour on the plane and I'm sure you didn't have much sleep the night before. The jet lag will kick in very hard shortly.' He shrugged. 'I thought you would welcome the help.'

She told herself not to soften at his consideration. 'Is that all she is—temporary help?' she pressed.

'No. She helps around the resort when needed, but she's the only one with childcare training.'

She shook her head. 'Romeo—'

Narrowed eyes studied her closely. 'What exactly is the problem here?'

'The problem is you made a decision about Lucca's care without consulting me.'

He exhaled with a rush of irritation. 'This is an adjustment for all of us, Lucca included. Some decisions will have to be made with or without your input.'

'No, I don't accept that. Not when it comes to my son.'

He shrugged. 'Okay, you can use Emily when you see

fit, or not at all. I'll leave that decision up to you. But you can't control every moment of his life, Maisie.'

Cold anger robbed her of breath for a moment. Then the words came tumbling out. 'You've known him for what, two days? And you dare to say that to me?'

His eyes turned a burnished gold. 'Is it my fault that I didn't know of his existence before then?'

'Well, it's not mine! Had you bothered to stick around the morning after—'

'For what purpose? Exchange false promises of hooking up again? Or perhaps you wanted compliments on what a great night we shared?'

An angry flush replaced the cold rage. 'I don't know why you're being so vile! And pardon me if I didn't know the right etiquette for the morning after one-night stands. That was my first and last experience. But I certainly didn't think I'd wake up alone with no trace of the man I'd spent the night with. Or that you'd instruct the concierge not to divulge any information as to your identity. If you want to be angry at anyone, be angry at yourself, because despite that deplorable behaviour, despite you leaving me there to do the walk of shame on my own, I still went back to look for you when I found out I was pregnant.'

His face froze in a mask of surprise. 'You did what?'

'I went back. I used savings I would've been better off investing for my unborn child to pay for a two-week stay in that exorbitant hotel. I walked the streets of Palermo every day and visited every café I could find for a fortnight.' She laughed. 'I drank enough decaf lattes to float a cruise ship, all in the hope that I might find you. Do you know how many hits there are for *Romeo of Palermo* on the Internet?'

He shook his head slowly, as if in a daze.

'Well, I won't bore you with figures. Let's just say tracking every one of them down would've taken me years. I didn't speak the language, so either I was laughed off or every enquiry was met with a blank look. So, yes, I gave up after two weeks and decided my time would be better spent planning a safe and comfortable future for my son. So don't you dare tell me I won't be consulted about each and every decision where he's concerned. And don't you dare make me feel bad about the consequences of something that we both did *consensually*.'

A red flush scoured his cheekbones before he inhaled deeply. Whirling about, he strode to the window and gazed out at the spectacular view.

When she was convinced the silence would stretch for ever, she approached and stood next to him. 'Are you going to say something?' she ventured in a quieter voice once several more minutes had passed.

He slanted a glance at her. 'It is not often I'm surprised. But you have surprised me, *gattina*,' he rasped.

'Because I've shown that underneath that auburn hair I have a temper?' she half joked.

A flicker of a smile ghosted over his lips. 'That wasn't a surprise. I'm very much aware of the depths of your passion.'

She reddened and glanced away before she was tempted to read a different meaning to his words. 'What, then?'

'What you did…' He paused and shook his head. 'No other person I know would've done that. And you're right. After the way I left, you had every right to write me off. And I did make sure that I would not be easy to find.'

'That's an understatement. Do you do that often? Erase your presence so thoroughly your conquests can never find you?' she asked before she could stop herself.

'Not in such direct terms. There is usually an understanding of the transient nature of my liaisons.'

'Oh…right.' That told her.

'That night was different for me, too, in many ways.'

She wanted to ask, but that bleak, haunted look was back in his eyes again, along with that do-not-disturb force field that told her she would risk emotional electrocution if she so much as raised an eyebrow in inquiry. To her surprise, he continued.

'It had been a trying day, one I didn't wish to face even though I knew it was coming.'

'Yeah, we all have days like that.'

He looked at her, his gaze brushing her face, her throat, her body, before turning his attention to the window again. 'But you came back, despite feeling the sting of rejection and perhaps a lot aggrieved?' he asked.

'I put myself in my child's shoes and knew that I needed to give him a chance to know his father. But I guess a part of me was terrified that I couldn't do this on my own and was in some way looking for support.' She shrugged. 'The moment I got back to Dublin, I accepted that I was in this alone. Then Lucca was born, and with each day that passed the fear receded. I was no longer alone. I had him.'

His stare returned, stayed longer this time. 'You're no longer alone where his care is concerned.'

She raised her eyebrows. 'But you don't agree that I should be consulted on all things?'

A steely look entered his eyes. 'I'll grant you a healthy debate about the major issues that concern him. And you can attempt to tear me to pieces on the minor ones.'

'So in other words, we'll argue about everything?'

The corner of his mouth lifted. 'Only because you seem to thrive on arguments.'

Her mouth curved in answer. 'Be warned, I never stop until I get my way.'

His eyes dropped to her mouth, and a heated channel forged between them. Her breath shallowed, her heart racing as she read the look loud and clear.

Desire thickened in her veins, her core throbbing until she yearned to squeeze her thighs together to alleviate the ache.

'Perhaps I will let you win on occasion,' he murmured,

his voice husky and deep. When his gaze dropped to linger on her breasts, a light tremble went through her.

She was thinking it was wise to move away before she did something foolish, like rise on tiptoe and taste his mouth, when a knock sounded on the door.

'Yes?' he answered, his eyes still on her.

Emily entered with Lucca, who smiled broadly when he saw her. 'Lucca wants to go for a swim. I wanted to check with you that it was all right to take him,' Emily said.

Romeo eyed Maisie with one brow quirked.

She lifted her chin. 'I'll take him,' she answered. When his eyes narrowed, she sighed. 'We'll *both* take him?' she amended.

The corner of his mouth twitched. *'Grazie,'* he murmured.

Maisie nodded. 'Okay. I'll go and change.'

Romeo strode forward and caught Lucca up in his arms. 'We'll meet you by the pool.'

In her room, Maisie fingered her sensible one-piece suit, replaying the conversation with Romeo in her mind. He'd been surprised that she'd returned to look for him, more than surprised, in fact. Stunned. That she would want to do the right thing.

Again she found herself wondering just how damaging his relationship with his mother had been. He'd called her a whore in the car. Had he meant that *literally*? She shuddered. Why else would a child call his mother by such a derogatory term?

It was clear that Romeo Brunetti had huge skeletons in his closet. And she was treading on dangerous ground in being so interested in uncovering them. That he'd taken such drastic steps to disconnect himself from her after their single night together should warn her that he didn't want any entanglements that didn't involve his son. She would do well to remember that. Along with remembering that theirs would in no way be a physical merger. No matter how heatedly he looked at her. No matter how much her blood thrilled to insane sexual possibilities each time he was within touching distance.

There would come a time when she'd have to walk away with her son after all this was done.

She would be better off if she made sure to walk away with her heart intact.

Romeo noticed her cooler demeanour the moment she came down the terrace steps and walked through the leafy archway dividing the extensive barbecue and entertainment area from the pool. And it had nothing to do with the military-issue swimming suit she wore, or the tight knot she'd pulled her hair into at the top of her head.

Her gaze, when it skated over him, was wary. As if between the time they'd spoken in his study and her changing, she'd withdrawn into herself.

Had she somehow guessed at his true intention towards his son when this problem with Lorenzo was over?

No, there was no way she could know. He quashed the voice in his head that prompted him to recall Maisie's uncanny intuitiveness. She'd known just how to delve beneath his skin and burrow to the heart of his need that night five years ago.

She'd given him passion and compassion in abundance, two emotions that had been seriously lacking in his life up till then. She'd made him *believe* and *hope*, for a few blissful hours, until dawn and reality had come crashing in. For a while he'd resented her for those feelings. Until he'd realised the fault wasn't hers. It was him, daring to believe in mirages and miracles.

He watched her drop her sunglasses on the table and walk to the edge of the pool, her smile guarded as she observed Lucca's antics. For the first time in his life, Romeo experienced the need to enquire as to a woman's feelings. The unsettled feelings that had slashed through him in the car returned and grew as he watched her swim to the other end of the pool and stay there.

Normally, when the women he dated began exhibiting contrary attitudes, it was a prelude to them asking for *more*. Of his time. Of a commitment. It was the reason he'd drastically reduced his dating span from a few weeks to the odd weekend.

He had nothing more to offer a woman besides a good time in bed and a very generous parting gift come Monday morning.

So what did Maisie's attitude mean?

She had his ring on her finger. Albeit temporarily, and for the sake of their son. But she also had him here, far from civilisation should they choose, and as exclusive as resorts came. And if and when she chose to alter the terms of their non-physical relationship to a physical one, he was more than willing to negotiate.

So what was wrong?

'Faster, faster!' Lucca urged as he rode on Romeo's back. 'Mummy, let's race.' He held out his arms to his mother. Maisie smiled and swam towards them, but she still avoided Romeo's gaze. And kept a conspicuous distance between them as they splashed from one end of the pool to the other.

Eventually, he took a tired and protesting Lucca out of the water. Maisie followed them out and dried him, before taking him indoors. When she returned and perched on her lounger with that same air of withdrawal, he narrowed his eyes.

'I don't like mixed signals,' he snapped.

Her head jerked towards him. 'What?'

'You were fine when you left the study. Something has obviously happened between then and now. What is it?'

'Nothing. I just took a little time to think, that's all.'

Something tightened in his chest, but he forced out the question. 'And what did thinking produce?'

She flashed a bright, false smile. 'I concluded that you're

right. Lucca and I have never had a holiday. This will be good for him…for all of us. As long as I can find something to keep me busy at times, I won't stand in your way about the small things.'

He heard the words and processed them as the half-truth they were. Then sat back and formulated how to get the full truth out of her.

CHAPTER EIGHT

'WE'RE HEADING OUT to choose a venue for a duck pond. You said you'd join us.' Romeo used a tone that made it clear his request wasn't up for debate. His annoyance the past few days had grown into a simmering anger. Albeit that anger was directed more at himself for the unaccustomed feeling of *caring* so much.

But some of it was directed at the woman who raised her head from her video conversation with her friend in Dublin and looked at him with a blank stare.

He'd been on the receiving end of that stare every time he walked into a room, just as every time he came within touching distance she found a way to move away. He'd thought she would be happy when he'd arranged for her to work with the chef at the resort restaurant a few hours each day to keep her skills sharp. She'd been pleased and his chef had sung her praises, but Maisie continued to be aloof.

Enough was enough. He wanted that distance gone.

The voice that suggested he might live to regret closing that distance was ruthlessly suppressed. He strolled further into the room and stopped in front of her, arms folded. 'Our son is waiting.'

Satisfaction burst through him when her eyes lit up with rebellious fire.

'Um…sorry, Bronagh, I have to go. I'll be in touch again at the end of the week.' She smiled and signed off, then glared up at him. 'Was there any need to be so rude?'

'Perhaps you should ask yourself the same question.'

A frown marred the light, golden hue of her skin, the result of enjoying the Hawaiian sun. 'What on earth are you talking about?'

'You've called your friend three times since we got here. You don't think she'd be offended that you're micromanaging her from a distance?'

Her eyes widened. 'Of course not, we discussed me calling her before I left Dublin.'

'Every other day?'

'Maybe not, but—'

'What percentage of your call involved discussing the restaurant?'

She bit her lip and flushed bright red. 'That still doesn't excuse your rudely interrupting me.'

'I'm only doing what you asked, *gattina*, and reminding you that you said you'd come with us to view the site. If you've changed your mind, all you have to do is say so. Lucca would be disappointed, of course, but...' Romeo shrugged.

She frowned and checked the clock on the laptop. 'I haven't changed my mind. I just didn't realise what the time was, that's all.' She looked at him and her gaze swung away almost immediately. 'I...I'll be right there.'

He narrowed his eyes when she remained seated. 'Is there a problem I should know about?' he grated, realising he was reaching the end of a hitherto unknown rope of patience.

'No.' Her lower lip protruded in an annoyed action so reminiscent of their son that he almost laughed. But his annoyance was far greater than his mirth. And it grew the longer she remained seated.

'Do I need to eject you from that chair?' he asked softly.

Her loose, waist-length hair slid over her shoulders as she swivelled her chair sideways. 'I only meant that I'd meet you outside after I get changed.'

He assessed her blue vest top. 'There's nothing wrong with what you're wearing.'

Her colour rose higher. 'Not the top maybe, but the shorts aren't appropriate for going outside.'

Romeo's legs moved of their own accord, skirting the desk to where she sat. 'Stand up.'

She threw him another of those highly annoyed looks but reluctantly stood.

He nearly swallowed his tongue.

The bright pink hot pants moulded her hips like a second skin and ended a scant inch below where the material met between her thighs. Instant arousal like nothing he'd ever experienced before battered him so hard, he was sure his insides had been rearranged in the process.

'Che diavolo,' he managed to squeeze out when he dragged his gaze from that triangle of temptation between her thighs and the silky smooth length of her shapely legs to her bare feet and up again.

'Don't blame me,' she muttered with husky accusation. 'It's not my fault your personal shoppers got my size wrong. If you'd let me go with them like I suggested, none of this would've happened.'

He met her impossibly blue eyes with a stunned exhalation. 'Are you telling me *all* your clothes are too small?'

He'd had a new wardrobe organised for Maisie and Lucca when it had become apparent that she'd packed clothes suitable for an Irish summer, not the tropical Hawaiian heat. And he for one had been tired of Maisie's ugly swimsuit after seeing it a second time.

She lifted her hand to fiddle with her hair and a glimpse of her toned midriff sent his temperature soaring another thousand degrees. 'They're a size smaller than I'd normally prefer.'

'And you didn't say something because?' He was aware his voice was uneven, hell, *strangled*, and that continuing to stand this close to her while she was dressed like a naughty cheerleader was an immensely bad idea, but his feet refused to move anywhere but closer, the need to slide his fingers between her legs, test the heat of those hot pants, almost overpowering.

'Would I have sounded anything but a diva if I'd demanded they send everything back?'

Since he knew every single one of the women he'd dated before would've made exactly that demand, and more, he allowed himself a smile. 'You're my wife. You're well within your rights to demand anything you want, as often as you want.'

She seemed to grow unsteady, her hand reaching out blindly for the sturdiness of the desk. But her gaze didn't move from his, an action for which he felt almost elated. Romeo couldn't take in how much he'd missed looking into her eyes until that moment. Which was absurd, but unshakeably true.

'It's okay, it's not a big deal. I can get away with most of the tops and dresses, and I'd planned to only wear the shorts indoors.' She licked her lips and laughed a touch nervously. 'Besides, I can stand to lose a pound or ten.'

'*Nothing* about your body requires adjustment,' he growled.

She was perfect. And she was blushing in the full-bodied way again that was pure combustion to his libido.

His eyes dropped to where she was winding one leg around the other, her toes brushing her opposite insole. Hunger clawed through him.

Madre di Dio!

'Go. Change if you must. We'll be waiting out front,' he forced out before the unbearable need pounding through him overcame his better judgement and he bent her over the desk.

She nodded and backed away, turning to hurry out of the door. When he was sure she was out of earshot, he let out a thick, frustrated groan, the sight of her delicious backside seeming to tattoo itself in his mind.

He was nowhere near calm when she emerged in a strapless lilac sundress and flip-flops. Luckily for him, his son's presence served as enough of a deterrent for his out-of-control libido.

Ten minutes later, it became clear she'd gone back to not fully engaging with him, busying herself with fussing over Lucca and avoiding his eyes when he looked her way.

Gritting his teeth, he focused on delivering them to the first duck-pond scouting location.

They toured three sites before arriving at the perfect place for a duck pond. Well within sight of the villa, the area was flat and clear of trees, within full view of the beach. Not that Lucca would ever be alone, but Romeo was satisfied the security posted at various points around the island would have a perfect view of where Maisie and his son were at all times.

The head of the three-man construction crew he'd hired spread out the blueprint on a portable table and began discussing design and schedules, with Lucca merrily pointing out where he wanted his rocks and fountain situated.

Leaving them to it, Romeo strolled to where Maisie stood several feet away, her gaze on the beach a quarter of a mile below.

Her head jerked up as he neared, and she inhaled sharply at the force of his stare, her eyes widening before she attempted to avert her head. He caught her chin and held her still.

'You want to tell me what's going on?'

That blank stare again. 'Sorry, I don't know what you mean.'

'I thought we agreed to make this work,' he rasped.

'We are.'

'You call *this* making it work?' he blazed under his breath.

'Romeo, why are you annoyed with me?'

His low mocking laughter grated. 'I suppose I should be gratified that you've noticed that I am annoyed.'

She pulled her chin from his hand. 'If it's about me for-getting about the time of the duck-pond visit—'

'Don't do that, *gattina*. It's beneath you,' he cut across her.

'I don't know what you want me to do. I'm here for Lucca. Isn't that what we both ultimately want?' Her voice pulsed with something he couldn't put his finger on.

No, he wanted to say. *I want you to stop shutting me out.*

He stepped closer and her delicate apple shampoo and sunflower perfume washed over his senses. 'What he needs is parents who exchange more than a greeting and a "pass the salt" when they're in the same room. I may not know enough about little boys yet, but I know he'll pick up the tension between us if we don't clear the air.'

She shook her head. 'But there *is* nothing to clear.'

He begged to differ. About to demand the truth, he looked deeper into her eyes and finally got *why* the atmo-sphere between them had altered so drastically.

'*Dio*, how could I have missed this?' he muttered almost to himself.

Panic flared in her eyes, darkening the striking blue to an alluring navy. He allowed himself a smile, a little less unsettled now he knew the root cause of her frostiness.

'We'll take this up again tonight, when Lucca is in bed.'

'I have nothing to take up with you,' she blurted.

'Then you can enjoy your meal and listen to me talk.'

Enjoying the heated suspicion in her eyes, he turned and strode back to join the group. The final design of the pond was agreed, an ecstatic Lucca skipping back to the buggy.

Back at the villa, he watched Maisie rush away with an excuse of rustling up a snack for their son. Romeo curbed a smile, satisfied now that he knew what the problem was of fixing it. He was pussyfooting his way through the un-familiar landscape of being a father. The tension between him and Maisie stood to jeopardise that. The unnecessary argument in his study this afternoon had proved that. It needed to be resolved. And by midnight, the situation between them *would* be rectified, with results he was sure would please them both.

He picked up his son and hurled him in the air, his heart tumbling over when he received a shriek of delight in return.

'Again!' Lucca urged.

Romeo's smile widened and he complied.

He'd never relied on luck to achieve his goals, but with a tiny bit of luck he'd get his son's mother shrieking those same words to him by the time he was done with her.

Maisie inspected the multitude of new dresses in her wardrobe and finally selected a bronze-coloured cotton shift with a crossover bodice tie. She knew she was risking being late, but ever since her conversation with Romeo earlier she'd been dreading the seven-thirty dinner he'd asked Mahina to prepare.

To say she was terrified of that sudden light that had dawned in his eyes after he'd demanded to know what was going on would be an understatement. And that self-assured smile he'd worn from then on had been an even more ominous sign that whatever he intended to discuss with her tonight would be something she might not be able to deny him.

She tied the knot beneath the bodice of the dress and shakily clipped her hair into a loose knot at her nape. The sleeveless design of the dress would ensure she remained cool in the sometimes sultry evening heat.

And if all hell broke loose, there was also the swimming pool to jump into. She gave a short hysterical giggle and slipped her feet into open-toed platform heels.

Knowing she couldn't linger any longer, she hurried to Lucca's room and checked on him, smiling at Emily, who was folding laundry in the walk-in closet, before making her way to the terrace.

The light from fat candles giving off evocative scents blended with solar lamps dotted around the garden and pool.

Next to the table set out for two, a tall silver ice bucket held a bottle of champagne. Romeo was nowhere in sight.

Before she could breathe a sigh of relief from the nerves churning her stomach, she sensed him behind her and turned.

He was dressed in black trousers and a fitted black shirt, his sleeves rolled back to reveal bronzed forearms and a sleek watch. With a few buttons opened at his throat, it was impossible to miss the light wisps of hair or the strong neck and the rugged jaw thrown into relief by all that black. That image of a dark lord, master of all he surveyed, sprang into her mind again.

Maisie swallowed and willed her hormones to stop careening through her bloodstream. But even at this early stage in the night, she knew it would be an uphill battle to continue fighting the need that whistled through her with the ominous sound of a pressure cooker reaching explosion point.

'There you are,' he murmured in a deep, hypnotic voice. 'I was beginning to think I'd been stood up.'

'I wasn't aware this was a date,' she replied feebly. The setting sun, the soft Hawaiian music playing from hidden speakers…the way he looked at her, all pointed to this being all about the two of them and nothing to do with their son.

She took a tiny step back as he came towards her, all dark and brooding. His eyes told her he knew what she was fighting. And the calculating gleam told her he intended to make sure she would lose.

'Come, sit down.'

He walked past her, trailing an earthy scent of spicy sandalwood and his own potent musk that drew her like a supercharged bee to pollen, and pulled out a chair.

With a feeling of walking towards her doom, Maisie approached and took her seat, then gasped when his fingers trailed the back of her neck.

'You must be more careful in the sun, *gattina*. You have mild sunburn right here.'

She shivered and touched the slightly sore spot, berating herself for being disappointed because his touch had been for an impersonal reason. 'September in Palermo was the hottest weather I'd encountered before Hawaii. I think I might need a stronger sunscreen.'

He sat opposite her, his gaze thoughtful as it rested on her face.

As Mahina served their first course, she held her breath, knowing questions were coming from Romeo.

As soon as the housekeeper left, he asked, 'You never took holidays abroad when you were younger?'

She shook her head. 'There was never time for holidays. Or any free time for that matter. Dedication to my studies seven days a week from kindergarten till I graduated from law school saw to that.'

His eyes narrowed. 'Your parents demanded this of you?'

'Yes.'

When she didn't elaborate further, he pressed. 'Tell me about them.'

'I thought our pasts were out of bounds?'

Reaching for the chilling bottle, he poured her a drink before serving himself. 'They are, but I seem to have shared a lot of mine with you without meaning to. I think it's time we address the imbalance.'

Looking away from him for a moment, she contemplated the last of the lingering orange-and-purple sunset and the stars already beginning to make an appearance.

She didn't want to talk about her parents, or the single-minded ambition that drove them and had made her childhood an endless drudge of trying, and failing, to please them.

And yet, she found herself nodding.

CHAPTER NINE

SHE PICKED UP her fork and tasted the exotic fruit and prawn salad, and busied herself with chewing while pushing her food around on her plate as she struggled to find the right words.

'My parents knew very early on that I wasn't academically gifted as they were—they're both Fulbright scholars and prize academic excellence above everything else.'

'Including you?' he asked astutely.

She swallowed and answered without looking up. 'Including me. I was an accident, who turned even more burdensome when I was unable to fulfil my full potential in their eyes.' When he didn't respond, she risked a glance.

His face was set in a carefully blank expression, but she glimpsed a look in his eyes, a *kinship*, that made her throat clog.

Clearing it, she continued. 'To say they were stunned their genius hadn't been replicated in me was an understatement. I was five when they made me take my first IQ test. They refused to believe the result. I took one every year until I was fifteen, when they finally accepted that I wouldn't be anything more than slightly above average.'

She sipped her champagne, let it wash away the bitter knowledge that she would always be a disappointment in her parents' eyes.

'Did they stop pushing you at this point?' he enquired sharply after helping himself to the last morsel on his plate.

Her mouth twisted. 'On the contrary. They pushed me harder with the belief that as long as they continued to polish me I would turn into the diamond they wanted instead of the unacceptable cubic zirconia.'

'I disagree with that description of yourself, and the assessment that you're average, but go on,' he encouraged, lounging back, all drop-dead-gorgeous danger, to nurse his drink as their first course was cleared away.

She shrugged. 'There's nothing much to add to that. They were indifferent to everything in my life besides my academic achievements, such as they were. When I told them I wanted to be a lawyer, they grudgingly accepted my decision, then immediately started pulling strings for me to be hired by one of the Magic Circle law firms in the country. When I told them I was taking three months off and then returning to take a position at a firm in Dublin, our relationship strained even more.'

'But you didn't back down?'

She laughed bitterly. 'It's hard being an average child of two geniuses, who hadn't wanted a child in the first place. I guess I'd reached a point where I'd had enough.' She'd wanted to lash out, rebel against the oppressive weight of her parents' indifference. Palermo had been her moment of rebellion. And while she would never regret having Lucca, she was beginning to be afraid that the one man she'd rebelled with had set a benchmark for all other men to come. And that each and every one of them would be found wanting.

She drank some more, felt the bubbles buzz through her veins and loosen her tongue. She even managed a less strained smile when Mahina delivered their second course.

'I presume that three-month vacation included your stop in Palermo?' he asked when they were alone again.

With the unburdening of her past came an unexpected increase in appetite. Or it could've been the alcohol.

Shrugging inwardly, Maisie tucked into the grilled mahi mahi and gave an appreciative moan. 'Yes. I'd always been fascinated with all things Italian.' She paused, glanced at him and saw the mildly mocking brow he lifted in her direction. Flushing, she returned her attention to her plate. 'I had some money saved from when I worked part-time at uni, and toured the whole of Italy. Palermo was my third stop.'

'And did your relationship improve once you resumed your career?' he asked. His questions weren't prying, as she supposed hers had been. He seemed to be interested in her life, her past, and not just as a means of passing time at the dinner table.

So she found herself recounting the one painful event in her life she'd sworn never to revisit again. 'Not once they found out I was pregnant by a man whose last name I didn't even know. Both my mother and father came from broken homes. They were estranged from their parents by the time I grew up. I know they hadn't planned on getting married, but they did because my mother fell pregnant with me. When I in turn got pregnant, the confirmation that the apple truly didn't fall far from the tree was too much for them to stomach.' The words fell from her lips in sharp bursts, the pain she'd smothered away in her heart rising to stab her once again.

She chanced a glance at Romeo and saw that he had frozen, his face a taut, forbidding mask.

'So they severed ties with you?' he asked in a chilling voice.

'Not exactly. But they had views on how to bring up Lucca that I didn't welcome.'

'What views?'

'They wanted me to put him in the care of nannies to start, and then boarding school when he was four—'

Romeo's curse stemmed the flow of her narrative. 'So he wouldn't get in the way of your career?' he bit out.

'Yes,' she replied, her throat painful with the admission that no matter what she achieved, she wouldn't be worthy in her parents' eyes.

His breath hissed out in pure rage. *'Madonna mia,'* he sliced out, his nostrils flaring as he struggled to control himself. 'Did you consider it?' he asked with a narrow-eyed stare.

'No. I gave up my job, enrolled in a gourmet cooking course, then moved to Ranelagh to open the restaurant.'

A morose silence fell over the table, their half-eaten meal growing cold as the sharp cries of cicadas pierced the night.

'This wasn't how I planned this evening unfolding,' Romeo said several minutes later after he'd refilled her glass.

Maisie laughed self-deprecatingly, that buzz in her veins somehow making the pain throbbing in her chest sharper. She was sure it was light-headedness that made her enquire breezily, 'So how had you planned this evening going, then?'

He didn't answer for a long time. Then he stood, tall, imposing, breathtaking. 'Come, we'll walk on the beach for a while.' He grabbed his glass and the half-finished bottle in one hand and held out his other. 'Let the night air wash away unpalatable memories.'

Maisie knew she ought to refuse, that the alcohol swirling through her bloodstream would inhibit any rational decisions she needed to make.

And yet she found herself sliding her hand into his, rising to her feet and discarding her shoes when he instructed her to.

The walk to the beach was lazy, the sultry night air and soft ukulele-threaded music emerging from hidden speakers seeming to slow everything down to a heavy, sensual, irresistible tempo.

He let go of her hand when they reached the sand, filled their glasses with the last of the champagne, then walked a few feet away to dispose of the bottle.

Toes curling in the warm sand, she strolled to the water's edge, laughing softly when the cool water splashed over her feet.

For a single moment, Maisie dared to wonder how it

would be to be in this place with the man of her dreams under different circumstances; if she'd been on a real honeymoon, not a desperate attempt to thwart a wizened old thug's threats.

The path her parents had set her on as a child hadn't left much room for dreaming. She'd been too busy trying to earn their love, to make herself worthy of their acceptance, to entertain such flights of fancy.

But she was a grown woman now, and surely there was nothing wrong with letting her imagination run wild for a few minutes, in letting her senses be overwhelmed by this beautiful place, this breathtaking man beside her?

She drained her second glass and didn't protest when Romeo took it away, then returned to stand behind her. Her breath shuddered out when he slid his hands over her shoulders and started a gentle massage of the tension-knotted muscles.

'What are you doing, Romeo?' she asked shakily after several minutes, when she started to melt beneath the warm kneading.

'You're tense. Why?'

'Probably because you're touching me.'

'You were tense before I touched you. Did I do something to make you this way?'

She released a single bark of laughter. 'The whole world doesn't revolve around you, Romeo.'

'Perhaps not, but if there's a problem going on with you it needs to be addressed, do you not agree?' He turned her around, looked into her face and frowned. 'Are you bored? Do you require more challenges?'

'No, I'm finding the lessons with Chef Sylvain illuminating and Mahina is teaching me a few Tongan recipes that will come in handy when I return to Ranelagh.'

His mouth compressed but he nodded. 'But you're not happy. Don't deny it.'

She tried to step out of his hypnotising sphere, but he held her by the elbows.

'This afternoon you thought you knew what ailed me.'

His gaze sharpened, then he gave a wry smile. 'Maybe it was my own need talking.'

'What…what need?'

'The need that claws beneath my skin, threatens to eat me alive…'

She made a barely audible sound when he pulled the clip from her hair and the heavy knot tumbled over her shoulders. Strong fingers slid through her hair in slow, sensual caresses. Maisie realised her dream was sliding dangerously into a yearning for reality that would be hard to push back in a bottle should she set it free.

But still she stayed, moaning softly when his mouth brushed the sensitive and tender spot below her ear. Light kisses traced along her jaw, down her neck to the pulse hammering at her throat. Desire pounded her, making her limbs heavy and the need to maintain that distance she'd been struggling to achieve melt away.

He spun her into his arms, and she gasped at the voracious hunger stamped on his face.

'Romeo…'

His kiss stopped whatever feeble attempt she'd been scrambling for to save herself from the unstoppable freight train of sexual fury that hurtled towards her. But as he took control of her mouth, control of her body, Maisie knew she would welcome being taken over, being flattened by the sheer force of his hunger, as long as it satisfied hers.

And it would.

From searing memory, she knew Romeo was an unselfish lover. If anything, he achieved a deeper level of arousal by piling on her pleasure, taking her to the very brink of sexual release and burning with her as they both fell.

He would give her everything her body desperately craved. And more.

But what happened next? What of tomorrow?

The questions began like small, icy kernels at the back of her mind. Then loomed, snowballed, until she pushed at his chest, desperate to free herself of this illusion.

'Stop!'

He raised his head immediately but didn't release her. 'You want me. Don't bother denying it,' he lashed out at her, his body vibrating with the tension that would surely explode at any moment.

His gaze dropped to her lips when she licked them, savouring the taste of him to pathetically add to her collection of memories.

'Yes, I do. But I won't let you use me to scratch an itch that only stems out of being thrown together more than anything else.'

He cursed under his breath. 'What's that supposed to mean?'

'It means we have a thing for each other, I won't deny that. But it's meaningless. Just a brand of chemistry that will probably go away if we ignore it. I'm not going to experiment on something cheap and tawdry just because we both happen to have time on our hands. I have more self-worth than that.'

He dropped his hands and took a single step back, but his dark gold eyes stayed on her. Accusing. Condemning. 'We took marriage vows. I think that elevates anything that happens between us well above cheap and tawdry.'

'Please don't do that. Don't rewrite the script on what the end goal is here. We only got married because of Lucca. And we agreed there would be no physical manifestation of those vows. Don't change the terms now.'

He laughed mockingly. 'You talk to me about changing the terms when you can't be in the same room as me or have a simple conversation without your pulse jumping all over the place?'

Heat suffused her face, along with anger. 'So you thought

you'd take pity on your sexually frustrated wife and do something about it?' she threw at him. 'How very stoic of you.'

'If I recall, leaving the physical side out of the marriage was your decision. I merely agreed because you seemed strongly wedded to the idea, pun intended. There's no shame in requesting a renegotiation.'

'I'm not requesting anything! All this...' she waved her hand at the sandy beach, the jaw-droppingly gorgeous moonlight and the discarded champagne bottle and glasses '...was your doing. Some sort of attempt at seduction, perhaps?'

He fisted his hair and then released it with a Latin flourish that made her belly quiver against her will.

'Only because I thought it wise to tackle the situation before one of us exploded,' he growled, his cheekbones hollowing out as he glared at her.

'Well, consider it tackled. I'll endeavour to keep my *desires* under better control from now on.'

The tension in his body was so palpable, she could almost reach out and touch it.

'You do realise there are millions of married couples who actually have sex with each other? Why not us?'

A shiver went through her, but she still managed to lift her chin and face that challenge head-on. 'Because I'm not built to have emotionless sex,' she flamed at him, at the end of her tether. 'And I'm damn sure you know that, Romeo. So stop. Please...just stop!'

Burnished gold eyes gleamed with such intensity, Maisie feared she might have poked the lion one too many times. For several seconds he just stared at her, hands on hips, his gaze probing to her very soul.

A heavy sigh depressed his chest, then he nodded solemnly. 'I will stop if you want me to. But I think we both know it won't be that easy, *gattina*. Come and find me when you change your mind.'

CHAPTER TEN

SHE MADE IT through the next seven days. Even went as far as to pat herself on the back for her stellar performance. Even when her body threatened resistance and advocated surrender at every turn, Maisie ground her teeth and sallied forth.

She looked into Romeo's eyes when he addressed her; didn't move away when he approached to discuss whatever was on his mind, or dance away as she normally would've when they took turns teaching Lucca to swim.

Even when she began to suspect that Romeo was deliberately testing her resolve by standing too close when they watched a particularly stunning sunset, or when his fingers lingered a touch too long when he passed her a plate of fruit at the breakfast table.

In those times she forced herself to remember how transient this situation was. And that the end might come sooner rather than later. He'd opened up when she'd heard him having a heated phone call two nights after their escapade on the beach.

Lorenzo had finally come out and demanded a cash settlement to restore the *famiglia's* dwindling power. Romeo had flatly refused.

The old man had retreated.

Whether that was merely a distraction tactic was something Romeo was investigating, but so far they had nothing concrete to indict him with. But if it proved not to be, then Lucca could be well out of danger before his fourth birthday next week. They hadn't discussed what would happen afterwards and she'd presumed Romeo would want access to his son, but Maisie couldn't see the man who'd been labelled the Weekend Lover, the same man who'd walked away from her so definitely five years ago, wanting to remain tied down through a marriage licence.

Her heart lurched painfully and she turned from watching Romeo and Lucca splashing on the other side of the pool. She thought of her little flat in Ranelagh and immediately hated herself for thinking it would be dull and dreary compared to this brilliant paradise. Compared to living under the same roof as Romeo.

Ranelagh was her home. One she was proud of.

She'd survived putting Romeo behind her five years ago. As painful as it'd been, she'd survived walking away from parents who would never love her the way she knew parents should love their child.

She would get through this when the time came.

'Is this your new way of attempting to tune me out? Staring out to sea and hoping you'll be turned into a mermaid?' His low voice seared along her nerve endings, starting that infernal flame that would only build the longer he stayed close.

She looked around and saw Emily walking off with a tired Lucca. Once they'd settled into a routine, Maisie had come round to the idea of letting Emily help with Lucca. They got on well, and Maisie could indulge in honing her culinary skills without guilt.

Bracing herself, she met Romeo's dark hazel eyes, the blazing sexual fire he no longer attempted to hide evident in his return stare.

'How very arrogant of you to assume my every thought revolves around you,' she replied coolly, although cool was the last thing she felt when he was this close, his arms braced on either side of the pool wall, caging her in.

'When I'm with you, like this, I guarantee that every one of mine revolves around you,' he supplied in a whispered breath.

Maisie suppressed a shiver. 'If you're trying to get me to crawl into your bed like a pathetic little sex slave, forget it.'

'There's nothing remotely pathetic about you, *gattina*. When you *do* crawl into my bed, I imagine you'll be a fierce little warrior woman.' He moved closer, his warm, chiselled torso sliding against her back in the water. 'Don't make me wait too long, though.'

Her fingers clung to the edge of the pool, her knuckles turning white with the effort. 'Or what?' she whispered fiercely. Daringly.

'Or your wildcat ways will be met with a much more predatory force than would be wise for either of us,' he breathed.

'Romeo, don't.'

It was then she felt the barely leashed dominance of his whole body. His powerful erection nudged her bottom, its hard and thick promise making her shut her eyes and bite back the helpless, hungry moan that rose to her lips.

'You think sex between us will be emotionless?' he queried in a harsh whisper.

She shook her head. 'What else can it be?'

'It wasn't five years ago. You had enough passion for both of us, and more. And I gave you what you needed. This time, we're husband and wife. You can let it count for something or you can let the transient nature of our situation stop you from demanding what you want. What we both want. Think about that, Maisie.'

The next second, he was swimming away, hauling himself out of the water like an arrogant god. He didn't look her way again as he towelled off and entered the villa.

Maisie stayed put, fighting the need to surrender with every last atom in her body, fiercely resisting the knowledge that the uphill battle with herself where Romeo was concerned was only just starting. And that this time, she risked losing more than just her dignity.

* * *

As Romeo had instructed all week, they dined outside, between sunset and when the stars came out. She kept the conversation on safe topics, determined to stay away from the
bombshell he'd placed between them at the pool.

We're husband and wife.

The yearning those words triggered in her was something she didn't want to dwell on.

'The builders assure me the work will be done by the
weekend. Which is just as well because I think our son has
reached the point where we'll wake up one morning and
find him down there finishing the pond with his own two
hands.' The words were delivered with a bracing amount
of amused dread.

Maisie laughed. 'I think poor Emily's at her wits' end,
too, with reassuring him the pond will be ready by his birthday. If he decides to finish it on his own, I think she might
help him, just for the sake of achieving some peace.'

Romeo smiled, and his face was transformed from
brooding sexiness to heart-stopping so fast her heart took
a dizzy dive. 'I suppose it's a blessing then he's managed
to twist her around his fingers so soon. I can foresee a time
when she adores him as much as we do.'

He froze suddenly and his breath caught. The eyes that
met hers held stunned shock and when he reached for his
red wine, she saw how his hand trembled.

She laid her hand over his as a lump rose in her throat.
'It's okay to admit you love your son, Romeo,' she said gently. 'In fact, I think it's time you told him as much, and that
you're his father.'

The shock dissipated, replaced by the customary brooding. He eyed her with a mildly disparaging look. 'So was
this some sort of test?'

She jerked her hand away. 'Excuse me?'

'To see how I fared in the fatherhood stakes before offering your permission to let him know I'm his father?' he tagged on.

'Of course not,' she replied, the barb stinging deep and painfully. 'You really think so little of me? Or of yourself?' she added, because she sensed some of that pointed remark was directed at himself.

A fleeting expression flashed across his face, almost like regret. Then his features tightened. 'Why would you think any more of me or my fathering skills? You know enough about my background to know I have no experience in this. That my own childhood has left scars I'll never be able to erase. Scars that could manifest in unpredictable ways somewhere down the line.'

She frowned. 'What do you mean?'

His mouth pursed for so long she thought he wouldn't answer. 'You know I lived on the streets. What you don't know is that I joined a gang a few years after that. One that even the authorities feared to tackle.'

Unease climbed into her throat. 'Why?'

'Because I wanted to fit in, *somewhere*.'

The raw vulnerability caught at her heart. 'And did you?'

He exhaled harshly. 'Not after I refused to perform the initiation rites.'

'Which were?'

Her heart froze as he enunciated what he'd been asked to do. Silence settled over their table, until he raised his head.

'You see why fatherhood isn't a job I'm to be trusted to settle into easily.'

Maisie's heart squeezed at the pain in his voice. 'But you walked away. You chose to walk away instead of hurting another human being.'

'That doesn't mean I'm equipped to handle this!'

'You're fighting Lorenzo instead of giving in to threats and extortion. You swore to protect Lucca within hours of meeting him. You've done nothing but care for him since we got here. Doesn't that tell you something? Love makes you vulnerable sometimes, but it doesn't make you weak.'

His mouth twisted, but the pain in his eyes dissipated a little. 'I wouldn't know. Lucca's young now, adorable and easy to handle. Who's to say what will come later, and how well we'll handle it?' His voice was thin and a touch bleak, holding echoes of his past.

Her hands clenched on the pristine white tablecloth. 'Stop borrowing trouble, Romeo. You've done well so far. Let's just take it one day at a time. And if you're not ready to tell Lucca that you're his father, then we'll wait.'

A muscle flexed in this jaw. 'I wanted to tell him who I was the first moment I knew he was mine.'

The touch of frost inside her melted. 'Fine. Tomorrow, then, or the day after. Whenever you're ready.'

His mouth compressed for several seconds. Then he nodded. *'Bene.'*

Maisie swallowed and nodded in return. She started to reach for her water glass, but he caught her hand in his.

'I'm sorry for not handling this better.'

The remaining frost was replaced by dizzying warmth. 'It's okay. I muddle through motherhood every day.' She smiled.

He raised her hand to his lips and kissed the soft skin. 'You've done an admirable job, *gattina.*'

Heat unfurled in her stomach, wending its way through her body when he continued to caress her with his mouth.

She cleared her throat and forced herself to say something before she crumbled beneath the smouldering onslaught. 'And you've had more experience than I think you're letting on.'

His eyebrows rose.

'There was a picture of you in the paper, on a yacht with two little boys,' she pried gently.

A look crossed his face, a facsimile of the one he wore whenever he interacted with his son. 'Rafa and Carlo are

Zaccheo's twin sons, and my godsons.' He shrugged. 'At least that's what it says on paper. I don't really have much interaction with them.'

'Zaccheo is your ex-business partner?'

He hesitated for a moment, then nodded. '*Sì*, but he is more than that.'

'In what way?'

Hazel eyes darkened a touch. 'Our pasts were intertwined for a brief time during which we formed an unlikely bond.' His tone suggested he wouldn't elaborate, but as she had before, Maisie couldn't help but pry, her need to know this man inside and out a yearning that wouldn't go away.

'Before or after you lived on the streets?'

'Before. Zaccheo's parents took me in for a while, but that situation could never be anything but temporary because my presence in their lives was not their choice.'

He turned her hand over, his fingers tracing her palm in slow, lazy circles. It wasn't a sensual move, even though there was plenty of that arcing between them. It was a grounding touch that sought, and received, a connection.

'Are you ever going to tell me what happened with your mother?' she murmured.

He froze immediately. 'I don't consider the subject suitable dinner conversation.'

She sighed. 'Then I guess, since dinner is over, I should retire to bed.'

'So you can tuck yourself into your cool sheets and congratulate yourself for escaping this needless torture you insist on putting us both through?' he grated at her, a different, more dangerous brooding taking over his face. She also detected a vulnerability that made her wonder whether there was something more going on here than she was aware of.

She slowly pulled her hand away. 'It's not needless.'

His mouth twisted. 'I suppose it's something that you don't deny it's torturous.' He caught up his glass and drained the last of his wine. The precision with which he set down the exquisite crystal made her think he would very much like to launch it across the terrace floor and watch it shatter in a million pieces.

He shoved his chair back and stood. 'Perhaps I'll take a leaf out of your book and live in denial for a while. I'm sure there's an urgent business decision I need to make somewhere in my company. Sleep well, *gattina*,' he said mockingly, before striding off in the direction of his study.

She knew the mocking command would have the opposite effect even before she undressed and slid into bed two hours later after giving up the pretence of reading.

Tossing and turning, Maisie tried rationalising and re-affirming her decisions. When by the thousandth time her own reasoning sounded mockingly hollow, she gave up. Frustrated, she yanked back the sheets and sat up. The hot-pink silk negligee she wore felt sticky on her skin, but the warm night air was inviting, a great way to empty her thoughts of the disturbing feeling that her resistance was crumbling.

Tugging the silk over her head, she went into her dressing room and rummaged through the drawer containing her new selection of swimwear. When her fingers closed over an as-yet-unworn set, she pulled out the string bikini she'd looked at and immediately discarded when her wardrobe had arrived. Of all the swimwear that had been delivered, this was the most daring. The cups of the top part of the black-and-orange set barely covered half her breasts and the matching panties were made of nothing more than three pieces of string, leaving very little to the imagination.

Making a face, she set it aside. Then glanced back at it. The little thrill of naughtiness surged higher the longer she eyed the garment.

She was tired of being sensible. Especially at one o'clock in the morning. Deciding to add a little bit of spice to her illicit swim, she quickly donned the bikini and threw a white linen tunic over it.

The villa was quiet, and she breathed a sigh of relief as she passed Romeo's empty study.

The path to the waterfall was softly lit by garden lamps. Snagging a towel from the stack near the swimming pool, she skirted the villa and hurried through the short tunnel and cave that opened into the stunning rock pool. Disrobing, Maisie dived into the pool, submerging for several seconds, hoping the heavenly cool water would wash away her turbulent thoughts.

The strong compulsion to make the most of what she had *now* before it was taken away from her wouldn't dissipate. On the contrary it grew stronger the harder she willed it away, the harder she swam from one end of the pool to the other.

Finally, wrung out emotionally and physically, she perched on the rock beneath the waterfall, leaning her head back to catch the edge of the cascading water, and sighed at the delicious sting of the warm water on her face.

'You insist you have no illusions of pursuing a life as a mermaid, and yet here you are again.'

She jerked at the sound of Romeo's voice and nearly fell into the water. Righting herself, she stared at his imposing, braced-legged stance at the opposite end of the pool. And swallowed hard.

He was dressed, like her, for swimming, his trunks hugging thick, hair-dusted thighs. But whereas she'd worn a tunic, he only wore a towel around his neck. Her breath strangled and died in her lungs, her pulse racing at the sheer magnificence of him.

She was doomed.

She knew it even before he dropped into the pool and swam lazily towards her. Halfway, he ducked under the water, struck out in a powerful crawl and emerged at her feet. Hands braced on either side of her thighs, he stared wordlessly at her, his gaze intense, broodingly ravenous. Maisie stared down at his breathtaking face, the droplets of water glistening on his skin in the moonlight like tiny diamonds.

Raw sexual energy leapt where their skin connected, firing arousal so strong she could almost touch it.

'Did sleep elude you, as it did me, *gattina*?' he enquired with a husky rasp after an endless throb of silence.

She nodded dumbly, her fingers reaching out of their own accord to trace his eyebrow, his cheekbones. His jaw.

'Have you grown tired of fighting the inevitable?' he pressed.

Her blood roared in her ears, drowning out her every resistant thought. 'I've grown tired of fighting you.'

The gleam in his eyes dimmed for a moment. 'It's not me you've been fighting, but yourself. If nothing else, be true to yourself about that, before this goes any further,' he growled, his stare telling her he wouldn't accept anything but her agreement.

And he was right.

She had been fighting this purely for her own self-preservation. How could she not? The consequences should he reject her a second time would be even more devastating than before. She knew it deep in her soul. With the passage of time her feelings towards him were changing, morphing into something deeper, stronger, that she couldn't seem to control.

The movement of the water jerked him a tiny fraction. The result was a slide of her fingers across his hot, beautiful skin, bringing her to the here and now, to the almighty need pounding through her blood.

'I'm tired of fighting,' she whispered raggedly.

'Then surrender,' he urged thickly. 'Just let this be.' His hands moved, sliding over her thighs to capture her knees. Tugging them open, he surged closer, his eyes so fierce and intense they seemed aflame from within. 'I can't stand another night of wanting you and being denied. Of imagining the many ways of having you, without going out of my mind. Surrender, *gattina*. Surrender now.'

Desire, wild and unfettered, wrenched through her, rendering the last of her resistance useless. Her fingers speared into his wet hair, using her hold to tilt his face up to hers.

Bending, she took his mouth in a greedy kiss, intent on gorging herself on a feast she'd stalwartly denied herself but couldn't resist another moment longer.

Somewhere down the line the devastation would be great. When she was back in her role of single mother far away in Ranelagh, her shredded emotions would have time to mourn, to berate her for her choices.

But here…now, in this heavenly place with this man who put the very gods to shame, she would live in the moment. She would just…*live*. As she had that night in Palermo, she would give as much of herself as she could and take what Romeo offered.

She groaned when he moved her closer to the edge of the rock and deepened the kiss, taking over her surrender with the terrifyingly intoxicating thrust of his tongue and the thrilling power of his body.

The waterfall pounded with elemental force behind her, but it was nothing compared to the demanding power of Romeo's kiss. He kissed her as if he'd hungered for her for aeons. As if he couldn't get enough of her.

Being wanted like that was like a drug to her senses. After years of bleak, icy indifference, it was a drug she craved more of with each passing second.

So she protested with a loud whimper when he pulled away. Before she could reach for him, he planted a hand on her belly, pressed her back till she was flat on the rock. He picked up her legs and swung them onto the rock before surging out of the water to join her.

For a long, taut moment, he stared down at her, his gaze

sizzling over her from top to toe. Then he prowled over her, his hands braced on either side of her head.

'I've often imagined you like this, spread over this rock like a pagan sacrifice for me to feast on, to pleasure until neither of us can move. Now here you are, wearing this wisp of clothing meant to tempt even the holiest of saints,' he breathed, triumph blazing through his golden eyes.

'It's a good thing you're not a saint, then, isn't it?' she managed, then watched a wicked smile curl his lips.

'*Sì*, it's a very good thing. Because no saint should be allowed to see you like this. Or allowed to do this.' He flicked his tongue over the wet material of her bikini top, then, with a deep groan, he shoved the material aside with his teeth and repeated the action several times, before pulling her nipple into his mouth.

Her back arched off the rock with a cry that was indeed pagan, thick arousal firing straight between her legs. He suckled long and hard, his groans matching hers as sensation cascaded through her.

'*Dio mio,*' he muttered when he lifted his head. He speared her with an almost shocked expression before he looked down at her exposed breasts. '*Dio mio, gattina,* you're intoxicating. I want to devour every inch of you.' Impatiently, he tugged at the bikini strings, pulling them away to bare her body to him.

A drop of water splashed onto her neglected nipple. With another wicked smile, he licked at it, then trailed his hot mouth down her torso to the line of her bikini bottom. Unable to keep her hands at her sides, Maisie speared her fingers in his hair, holding him to her quivering belly when he nipped her flesh in tiny, erotic bites.

By the time he released the ties and pulled away her meagre covering, she'd skated into pure delirium, compelled by a force beyond her control. She raised her head and met his gaze a second before he tasted the centre of her.

'Oh, God!' The force of her need jerked through her, then

set in motion a series of undulations he was only too glad to
follow. When her eyes started to roll shut, he pulled away.

'No, watch me, *gattina*. Watch me enjoy you the way
I've been dying to do.'

The eroticism of the request pushed her closer to the
edge. Panting, she nodded and kept her gaze on him as
he lapped at her, his tongue executing wicked circles that
cracked open a previously untapped well of pleasure.

'Romeo,' she groaned raggedly, the rush of feeling almost
too much to bear. 'Please…I can't take any more.'

'You can.' Opening her wider, he altered the pressure of
his tongue, his hypnotic gaze telling her she was under his
control, to do with as he pleased.

When she began to thrash, he simply laid a hand on her
belly and continued his assault. And with each kiss, he grew
just as possessed with the red-hot fire consuming them.

'Now, Maisie,' he growled against her swollen flesh an
eternity later.

With an agonised cry, she let go, her whole body con-
vulsing with a release so powerful, she lost all sense of
space and time.

CHAPTER ELEVEN

SHE OPENED HER EYES to find him sprawled next to her, his fingers tracing her mouth as he stared down at her, a peculiar expression simmering in his eyes.

'What?'

He kissed her, her earthy taste on his lips and the reason for it making her blush. When he raised his head, that look still lingered.

'You returned home from Palermo pregnant.' His hand trailed from her neck to her belly and stayed there while his eyes held her prisoner.

'Is there a pointed question in there somewhere?' she murmured, her heartbeat still thundering loud enough to compete with the sound of the waterfall. 'I'm on the Pill now if that's what you're asking. It helps regulate my period.'

'It's not, but that's good to know.' His hand continued to wreak havoc on her. 'You changed careers and forged another life for yourself all alone. Did you at any point seek another man's bed to alleviate your loneliness?' he asked thickly.

She knew how weak and pathetic responding in the positive would make her look. But she couldn't lie. Not when she'd just experienced an incredible earth-moving event.

She threaded her fingers through his wet hair. 'I was alone, not lonely. But no, Romeo. You were the last man I slept with.'

His chest moved in a deep inhalation and his eyes filled once again with that primitive, razor-sharp hunger that threatened to obliterate her.

The hand on her belly trailed to her thighs, his fingers

digging into her skin in an urgent caress as his head dropped to hers once more. Falling into the kiss, Maisie gladly let sensation take over again, moaning when her hand trailed over taut muscle and bone to finally close on his steely length.

She caressed him as he'd once hoarsely instructed her to, a thrill coursing through her when he groaned brokenly against her lips.

All too soon, he was rolling on the condom he'd plucked from his trunks. Bearing her back, he parted her thighs and hooked his arms under her knees.

He stared deep into her eyes and thrust home in one smooth lunge.

'Oh!'

His growl of male satisfaction reverberated to her very soul. Her fingers speared into his hair as he began to pleasure her with long, slow strokes, each one pulling a groan from her that only seemed to turn him on harder.

He kissed her mouth, her throat, her nipples, with a hunger that grew with each penetration, until she was sure he wouldn't stop until she was completely ravished.

'You're mine. Say it,' he demanded gutturally, when her world began to fracture.

'Romeo…'

'I want to hear it, Maisie.' He slid deep and stopped, the harsh, primitive request demanding a response.

Something shifted inside her, a deep and profound knowledge sliding home that once she admitted this there would be no going back. That she would be giving herself over to him completely, body and soul.

He angled his hips, the move a blatant demonstration that he had all the power, that he controlled every fibre of her being.

'I…' She groaned when he moved again, delivering that subtle thrust that sent her to the very edge of consciousness.

'Tell me!'

'I'm yours…yours. Please…' Her nails dug into his back, and she surged up to take his mouth with hers. 'Please, Romeo. I'm yours…take me,' she whispered brokenly.

Romeo moved, his senses roaring from the words, from her tight and wet heat, from the touch of her hands on his skin. He couldn't get enough. He wanted more. All of her, holding absolutely nothing back. He reared back so he could look into her eyes, to see for himself that she meant it, that she belonged to him completely.

Her eyes met his, the raw pleasure coursing through her shining in the stunning blue depths. There was no fight, no holding back, just a beautiful surrender that cracked something hard and heavy in his chest, bringing in the light and abating the tortured, weighted-down bitterness for the first time in his life.

The sense that he could fly free, that he could find even deeper and truer oblivion in her arms than he had their first time in Palermo, slashed across his consciousness, making his thrusts less measured, the need to achieve that transcendental plane a call to his very soul.

He looked down at her, saw her eyes grow dazed and dark as her bliss encroached. Letting go of her legs, he speared his fingers into her hair and kissed her.

'Now, *gattina mia*,' he croaked, knowing he was at the edge of surrender himself.

'Yes, oh, yes,' she replied. Then she was thrashing beneath him, her sex clamping around his in a series of convulsions that sent him over the edge.

With a loud roar, Romeo flew, barely able to keep from crushing her as he found a release so powerful, had he believed in heaven he would've been certain he'd truly found it in that moment.

He came back down to the touch of her hands trailing up and down his back, her mouth moving against his throat in a benediction of soft kisses.

Again another blaze of memory slashed across his mind,

a sense of déjà vu throwing him back five years, to his hotel suite in Palermo. The feeling that he was raw and exposed, that the woman beneath him wasn't one he could bed and discard, pounding through him. Romeo was certain it was why he'd left as he had the next morning, ensuring he left no trace of himself behind.

Because after mere hours with her, he'd instinctively known that Maisie O'Connell had the power to burrow under his skin, unearth tortured truths and hidden desires he wanted no man or woman to unveil. He'd listened abstractedly as she'd spilled her hopes and dreams and had wanted nothing more than to tell her he'd arrived in Palermo the week before, hoping that for once in his life the woman who'd given birth to him would look at him with any feeling other than hate. That he'd spent a week by his mother's bedside, hoping for a morsel of affection, or regret for the way she'd callously discarded him.

He'd somehow managed to keep his tortured thoughts to himself, but he could tell she'd sensed them, and she'd soothed his soul with the same soft kisses and caresses she gifted him with now.

Then, as now, she'd given herself completely, despite not knowing any more than his first name.

The need to unburden completely powered through him now, but he held himself back. She knew about his father partly through the need to furnish her with information about Lorenzo's plans and partly because he'd let down his guard. But his mother was a different story.

The secret shame that clawed through him had never abated, despite the years he'd spent in bitterness. After he'd buried his mother, he'd bricked away the pain, secure in the knowledge that she no longer had the power to hurt him with her rejection. He'd only ever felt those foundations crumble with Maisie. And her power over him wasn't one he felt comfortable with. It spoke to a weakness he wasn't ready to face.

Shoving his unsettling thoughts back in the vault, he stared down and allowed himself to bask in her soft smile. The sex he could more than deal with, even if it came with a brief exposure of his soul. The benefits were worth it. More rewarding than securing the best business deal.

'Should I be afraid of that smug smile you're wearing right now?' she asked, her voice slightly dazed and heavy with spent bliss.

Arousal spiked again, the magic of her body transporting him into pleasure with blinding speed. Replacing the condom, he expertly reversed their positions, lying back to take in her goddess-like beauty.

With her long, wet hair plastered to her golden skin, she truly looked like a wanton mermaid.

'*Sì*, you're about to make another of my fantasies come true.' He cupped her heavy breasts, played his thumbs over the stiff peaks and felt her body quicken to his touch. He grew harder, need lashing through him as he watched her accept, then revel in, her new position.

She tested the rhythm, quickly found one pleasing to them both and commenced a dance that had them gasping and groaning within minutes.

He reached between them and found her heated centre. Playing his fingers expertly over her, he watched her throw back her head, her nails digging into his chest as she screamed her release.

He followed gladly, eager to experience that piece of heaven again. Eager to leave behind hopes and yearnings that would never be fulfilled. He'd refused to wish after seeing each fragile desire turn to dust before his eyes as a child.

But Maisie in his arms, in his bed, was an achievable goal. One he intended to hang on to for as long as he could.

Maisie awoke slowly, her senses grappling with the strange bed she slept in and the warm, solid body tangled around hers. Vague memories of being carried from the waterfall slid through her mind. She stirred and the heaviness of satiation moved through her limbs, bringing back wild and more vivid memories of last night.

Opening her eyes to brilliant sunshine, she forced herself not to panic as the full realisation of what had happened reared up like a giant billboard in front of her.

She'd given herself to Romeo. Not just her body, but her heart, her soul. She'd known right from the start that giving herself to him this time round would be her undoing. Heck, she'd told him as much!

Just as she'd suspected when she'd promised she was his, she'd been making a declaration that went beyond sex. Each decision she'd taken when it came to her child and his father had been made from her heart. She just hadn't been brave enough to admit it to herself. But now she knew.

She was in love with Romeo Brunetti.

Had probably fallen in love with him the moment she'd sat down across from him that day in Palermo.

Her stomach clenched even as her heart accepted the deep, abiding truth. He was the reason she'd never paid another man any attention, had embraced motherhood without much of a thought for finding a father figure for her son. Deep down she'd known no one could come close to Romeo so she hadn't even tried to replace him.

And now… She breathed deep as her eyes fell on her wedding rings. Now, she could do nothing but brace herself for the agony to come. And it would come. Loving Romeo was her greatest risk and would bring the greatest consequence. Of that, she was certain.

'*Buon giorno, gattina.*' Strong fingers brushed her hair from her face and drew her back against the warm sheets. 'What troubles you so much that you wake me with the power of your thoughts?' he asked, his eyes probing hers with the sharpness of a scalpel.

'Everything and nothing,' she replied obliquely, desperately hoping to buy more time to compose herself.

'An answer guaranteed to send a man into fits of puzzlement. Or the nearest jewellery store.'

'Is that how you usually placate your other women?' she asked, a sensation moving through her that she deciphered as deep jealousy.

Intense eyes narrowed. 'I wasn't aware you needed placating. Perhaps you should tell me where I've misstepped?'

She glanced away. 'I don't. You haven't. Sorry, I was prying again.'

Warm fingers captured her chin, a thoughtful look in his eyes. 'I guess it's only fair, since I questioned you about past liaisons.'

She shook her head, perversely wanting to know, but also desperate to live in denial. If only for a while longer. She chose the latter. 'I don't need a biography of your past conquests. I know enough to get that you have a healthy sexual appetite.' A blush suffused her face and he slanted her a wicked grin.

'Is that what concerns you?'

She shook her head, but she couldn't tell him, of course. Because that would be tantamount to shoving her heart underneath the wheels of a Sherman tank. So she went for the next best thing. 'Why did you bring me to your bedroom? I wasn't expecting to wake up here.'

The smile left his face and that dark brooding look returned. 'Why do you think?' His voice pulsed with an emotion she couldn't name.

She pulled her lower lip into her mouth. 'I thought last night was just…' She paused. 'I meant it when I said I don't want this to get complicated.'

Too late.

But that didn't mean she couldn't salvage a little bit of dignity from the dire situation. Guard her heart from more pulverising down the road.

'So *your* itch has been scratched and you're ready to put

it all behind you?' he queried in a dark, dangerous voice, throwing her own words back in her face.

'I didn't expect it to last beyond last night. Isn't that your record?'

'I see we're back to past conquests again.'

'Romeo—'

'No, you listen. Last night barely dented the depth of my need. And if you're truthful, you'll admit the same. I brought you to my bed because this is where you belong. You can protest as much as you want and we can go back to circling each other until we drive each other insane, or you can choose to admit your feelings and take what you want.'

She opened her mouth, intent on denying everything he'd said. On doing *the right thing*. Getting up, walking back to her own room. To her painfully lonely bed. And more nights filled with the vicious ache of wanting him.

But the words died in her throat. Denying herself suddenly felt like the opposite of *the right thing*. As if saying the words out loud would be like slicing a knife into her arms and opening her veins. Sure, there was a life of desolation waiting for her once she walked away from him, but there was no need to start the torture *now*.

She stared up at him, at the vitality of the body caging hers, the need blazing in his eyes, and resolved to just *be* for now.

'Will you stay?' he pressed.

Slowly, she nodded. 'Yes, I will.'

He proceeded to show her the true meaning of good morning. And she gave herself over to the incandescent sensation.

She was still smiling four mornings later, even as she studiously ignored the tiny voice that called her ten kinds of a fool.

They rose, showered together, their hands and lips revelling in the newness of just being together without tension. Oh, the sexual tension was ever-present. It barely left them alone and Maisie was beginning to doubt it ever would. But there was an ease between them that tugged at her heart when Romeo smiled at her and walked her to her room so she could get dressed.

He lounged in the doorway of her dressing room, his eyes wickedly intent on her body as she pulled on panties and a bra, and slid her white shift dress over her head.

After slipping her feet into heeled sandals, she took his outstretched hand and they left the room.

'Are you sure?' she asked him.

He nodded, although his throat moved in a hard swallow. 'Yes, it's time to tell him.'

As they reached the stairs, she glanced at him and was shocked to see that, for the first time since she'd known him, Romeo looked nervous. Vulnerable.

'Are you okay?' she asked as they descended the stairs and headed towards the kitchen, where Lucca could be heard chattering away to Mahina and Emily.

Romeo gave a strangled laugh. 'It's not every day I tell an almost-four-year-old boy I'm his *papà*.'

Her hand closed on his and drew him to a stop. Standing on tiptoe, she offered what she'd intended to be a supportive kiss.

His hands locked on her hips, and he slammed her back against the wall to deepen the kiss. He kissed her as if trying to draw sustenance from her. By the time they pulled apart several minutes later, they were both breathing hard. His eyes were needy pools, searching and a little lost.

She placed her hand on his cheek, her heart melting when he cupped it and pressed it deeper into his skin. 'You'll be fine. He adores you as much as you do him.'

His head dipped as if he wasn't quite sure how to deal with the alien feeling of being the object of a child's adoration. *'Grazie,'* he finally murmured. When he raised his head, the confident, virile man had slid back. 'Let's do this.'

He tugged her after him, and they entered the kitchen together.

Ten minutes later, in the privacy of Romeo's study, Lucca stared at his father from the safety of his perch on his mother's lap. Then his gaze moved to her face and back to Romeo's, his eyes wide, hazel saucers. 'You're my daddy?' he asked in hushed awe.

Romeo's throat moved several times before he could speak. '*Sì*, I am your *papà*,' he intoned in a deep, moving voice.

Lucca tilted his head to one side, then shook his head. 'Not *papà*…*daddy*. I want you to be a *daddy*.'

A telltale sheen covered Romeo's eyes and he blinked rapidly before he nodded. '*Va bene*, I will be a daddy.'

Lucca launched himself off her lap and threw his arms around his father. Romeo's strong arms gathered the chubby body to him, his eyes closing on a depth of feeling that made Maisie's eyes fill with helpless tears. Father and son stayed locked for an eternity. Or as much as a toddler could stand until impatience set in.

When he was lowered to his feet, Lucca stared up at his father. 'Can I tell Emily?'

Romeo nodded. 'You can tell whomever you wish.'

Lucca started to race out of the door but then stopped suddenly. 'I wished very, very hard for a daddy,' he said solemnly. 'And it came true!'

Romeo looked stricken for several long seconds. Then he shook his head, as if denying whatever thought had crossed his mind. 'I'm glad for you, *bel bambino*.'

After watching Lucca run off, Romeo turned to her and pulled her to her feet. Seeing her tears, he gently wiped them away and planted a soft kiss on her lips. '*Grazie, il mio dolce.*'

Swallowing the lump in her throat, she smiled. 'I told you it'd be a piece of cake,' she said.

His blinding answering smile lit her up from the inside,

starting a shaky weakness that made her lower her gaze in case he read the depth of emotions moving through her. 'Perhaps I should listen to you more,' he suggested with a quirked brow.

'Perhaps I should get that in writing,' she answered.

He was still chuckling when they trailed their son. The announcement turned into an impromptu celebration with pancakes and juice, after which they got down to the urgent business of planning Lucca's heavily duck-pond-themed birthday party.

Finding out that the Giordano family would be joining them on the island in two days, along with the guests staying at the villas, and that Romeo was expected to host a dinner party, Maisie felt a rush of panic.

The only party she'd thrown so far had involved a cake, sandwiches and screaming kids in a playgroup's ball pit.

She was nowhere near sophisticated enough to handle a houseful of billionaires. She tried to pin a smile on her face as Romeo's eyes narrowed at her from across the kitchen island.

'What's wrong?' he asked as soon as they were alone.

'Nothing...' she started to say, then blurted, 'I've never thrown a dinner party before. Or a birthday party for a billionaire's son for that matter.'

He frowned. 'He's still the son you raised from birth. As for the party, everything's taken care of. I have caterers flying in from Honolulu to assist the chefs who cater for the island guests.'

Somehow her anxiety only escalated. 'Oh, so you don't really need me at all, do you?'

His frown deepened. 'Of course I need you. What's this really about?'

On some level, Maisie knew she was reacting to a deeper anxiety, one that stemmed from the knowledge that Romeo's life was so smoothly coordinated, aside from her role in his bed, he didn't need her for much else. Even Lucca would be extremely well taken care of by Emily and Mahina, should Maisie suddenly find herself rubbed out of the picture.

'Maisie?' he growled warningly.

She shrugged. 'I guess I'm feeling a little surplus to requirements.' Not to mention suddenly aware of her precarious position of temporary wife. 'I barely do anything for Lucca any more besides eat breakfast and sometimes lunch with him. Other times, he'd rather play with Emily or hang out with you.'

He took her by the arms. 'You've had him to yourself for almost four years. It's understandable the small separation on occasion would feel strange. And that separation was probably more pronounced because you were avoiding *me*,' he pointed out. 'But if you want me to prove that you're not surplus to requirements, just say the word, and I'll oblige you.'

She looked into eyes darkening into burnished gold and a blaze sparked through her. But alongside it rose a wave of desolation. Sex with Romeo was out of this world. Each experience felt as if she were touching the stars. But it was *just sex* for him. It would never be anything more.

So when he gathered her close and kissed her, she responded with a lingering taste of sadness that made tears brim behind her closed eyes.

His phone rang just when she thought the tears would spill and betray her, and she breathed a sigh of relief. He pulled it from his pocket and checked the screen. Frowning, he looked at her. 'Sorry, it's Zaccheo. I have to take it.'

Waving him away, she hurriedly escaped the sunlit living room. Her first thought was to find Lucca. She found him in the playroom and pulled him into a close embrace. When he demanded she read his favourite story, she obliged.

She was on the fifth read when Romeo entered the room.

She jerked upright at the volcanic fury on his face. 'What's wrong?'

'Zaccheo and Eva are arriving tomorrow.'

A day earlier than planned. 'Why?'

'Because they've been pulled into this insane situation in Palermo. It's time to end this before it gets out of hand.'

CHAPTER TWELVE

HER FIRST IMPRESSION of Zaccheo Giordano drove home the understanding of why the two powerful men were friends.

He carried himself with the same ruthless energy as Romeo, albeit with a little less brooding intensity. That energy was exhibited clearly when he stepped from the buggy and clasped Romeo's hand in an unsmiling, yet moving greeting.

His intensity lessened dramatically when he helped his heavily pregnant wife up the short steps into the wide villa entranceway.

Eva Giordano was gorgeous in a pocket-Venus, burst-of-energy way that drew interested eyes to her wild tumble of blonde hair and sharply contrasting dark eyebrows and darkly ringed green eyes.

Despite the strong evidence of love between them, Maisie sensed a tension between her and Zaccheo, which was explained once introductions had been made and Romeo was hugging Eva.

'I'm sorry we had to descend on you prematurely, but it was either *we all* came here or *we all* went to Palermo.' She cast an irritated look at her husband. 'The vote was eventually unanimous that we come here, since I refused to be left behind while Caveman over here went off to tackle Carmelo and Lorenzo on his own.'

Zaccheo muttered under his breath about intransigent women and helped corral his twin sons when they escaped their nanny and started fighting over who was better suited to drive the buggy.

Eva turned from greeting Romeo and her gaze fell on

Lucca. 'Oh, hello there, beautiful boy.' Her wide smile seemed to enchant her husband, who lost his growly look and came to stand beside her, one hand gently caressing her swollen belly.

The look of pure, blazing love that passed between them caused Maisie's heart to drop in misery into her belly. But she managed a smile and coaxed a shy Lucca from behind her. Within minutes he and the Giordano boys were exploring the new toy room Romeo had installed for him.

Mahina served drinks on the terrace and the tension mounted again the moment she left.

'What exactly did Carmelo want from you?' Romeo asked tersely, once Zaccheo had apprised them of the threat from Palermo's other crime lord.

'His ridiculous demands are the same as Lorenzo's to you. They're both terrified one would attain more power than the other. But he had the nerve to threaten my family. I cannot allow that to stand.'

Eva rolled her eyes. 'You realise how much like a bad gangster movie actor you sound?' When his eyes narrowed, she continued, completely unfazed. 'You have a veritable army guarding me and the boys when you're not around, and Carmelo's claims of you owing him allegiance because your father was a one-time lieutenant of his before he switched sides to Romeo's father is flimsy at best. How do we even know that's true?' She looked at Romeo. 'Besides, I know you two have enough dirt on the man to send him to jail for a long time.'

Romeo shook his head. 'I've talked to the lawyers about it. It's all circumstantial without hard evidence. I only witnessed Zaccheo's father being beaten.' He sent his friend a look of grim-faced sympathy, to which Zaccheo nodded. 'He was still alive when I was thrown out of Fattore's mansion. We need irrefutable evidence of blood on Lorenzo's hands.'

'So, what's the alternative?' Eva exclaimed. 'A duel at dawn beneath Mount Etna?'

Romeo's jaw clenched but he didn't refute Eva's outlandish claim. Maisie's stomach hollowed out, both at the news Romeo had just delivered and his intent expression.

'You're not thinking of going back to Palermo, are you?' she demanded in a shocked whisper.

His eyes when they met hers were hard, implacable, with no trace of the gentleness they'd held yesterday before Zaccheo's phone call. 'It's the only option. I won't entertain the idea of my son living in fear.'

Zaccheo nodded in grim agreement and captured his wife's hand when she began to protest.

Maisie struggled not to feel excluded and even more miserable as Romeo proceeded to converse to the couple, switching to Italian when the debate got heated.

Once or twice, she spotted Eva's probing glance and fixed a smile on her face, answering her questions about the island and the villa when she switched back to English.

When Eva yawned loudly and started to droop, Zaccheo stood and ushered her inside.

Knowing she wouldn't be able to sit and make small talk while her insides were shredding with the knowledge that Romeo had room in his heart only for his son, and not her, she jumped to her feet.

'I'll go see if the boys are okay.'

He caught her hand and stopped her. 'You're upset because I intend to confront Lorenzo?'

'Does my opinion matter enough for you to change your mind? I thought you were pursuing a different route other than direct confrontation.'

His jaw flexed. 'I suspected his mellowed stance was all a bluff. Just as I suspect, this is nothing more than an extortion scheme, probably concocted between him and Carmelo. The timing is a little too synchronised. Whatever it is, I need to end it once and for all.'

She tried to pull away but he held on. 'Since your mind's made up, there's no need for my opinion, is there?'

'*Gattina*—'

'Don't call me that.' The blurted plea rushed out before she could stop it.

He gave a hiss of frustration. 'You suddenly have a problem with the name?'

'No, only your use of it when you're trying to put me back in your little box marked *Handled*.'

His mouth twisted. 'Even if such a box existed, the physical and psychological scratch marks you leave on me would point to an abject failure in my task.'

She tugged at her hand again until he freed her. 'And you'll continue to fail. Because I won't be put in a box and labelled as to what I need to be. Never again.'

A new tension stilled his body. 'You think that's what I've been doing to you?'

'What have you been doing, if not knocking down my every objection in a bid to get your way since you found out about Lucca?' she threw back.

'He's my son. There was never a doubt that I would claim him. You knew that. Did you think I wouldn't do everything in my power to give him everything that had been denied me?' he demanded.

'No, but what sort of mother would I have been if I'd wilfully turned my back on the one thing you led me to believe would save our son.'

His nostrils flared. 'You believe that's no longer true?'

'I went along with this marriage because it would protect us while you found a *business* solution to this problem. Now you tell me you're planning some sort of vendetta-settling and I'm left asking myself whether this marriage was worth the aggravation I put myself through in the first place if the outcome is going to be a different one! Would I not have been better off in Ranelagh, alone with my son while you carelessly diced with death?'

A searing wave of shock washed over his face before his eyes, mouth and jaw hardened in a look of pure bitterness.

'So you regret this marriage?' he demanded in a low, icy voice.

'Tell me the truth, Romeo. Was marrying me really necessary?'

His jaw clenched for a long time before he bit out, 'Yes.'

'To save Lucca from Lorenzo or to give him your name?'

Her heart threatened to beat itself out of existence, and her limbs felt frozen and useless as she stared at him.

'At the time, the two weren't mutually exclusive.'

'So you didn't exaggerate one to get the other?'

He jerked upright and strode to the edge of the terrace, his movements erratic. For several minutes he said nothing, and slowly his balled fists loosened.

Then he turned. 'You're right. I should've thought this through a little longer, given myself better options.'

Maisie's agonised gasp was barely audible, but it seemed to open a new set of floodgates, bringing fresh waves of pain. She knew she was a fool then for expecting him to tell her their marriage wasn't a mistake. That it was more than just a means to ensure Lucca's safety. That however it'd started out, it was worth holding on to, worth salvaging.

Hearing his words brought home to her just how foolish she'd been to hope. Just like five years ago, Romeo had made a mistake with her. One he regretted. Only this time, he'd told her so to her face rather than let his absence speak for him.

Footsteps preceded Zaccheo's reappearance on the terrace and brought a jagged but final end to the conversation. Catching the other man's narrow-eyed, assessing glance, she pinned a smile on her face. 'I'm going to check on the boys.'

She stumbled blindly indoors, operating on automatic rather than with any sense of purpose, as she headed for the toy room. Reaching the doorway, she saw that Emily and the Giordano nanny had readied the boys for bed.

Forcing her feet to move, she went to her son and brushed her fingers over his hair. He looked up for a moment, his deep hazel eyes connecting with hers in a wide, loving look before he was distracted by one of his new best friends.

Feeling lost, cast adrift in a merciless ocean, Maisie wandered back out, trying hard not to buckle under the realisation that she'd sped up her exit from Romeo's life with that last tirade. Because surely telling the man who'd married you for the sake of his son that you'd rather not be married to him was a request to be freed the moment the necessity became obsolete?

Pain ripped through her heart as she entered her bedroom. How could it look so bleak and lonely after just a few short nights spent away from it? How could her heart shred so badly at the thought that she wouldn't spend another night in Romeo's bed?

A broken moan, much like a manifestation of grief, poured out of her throat as she sank onto the side of her bed.

Her shame at the knowledge that she would shed her dignity for another night in Romeo's bed bit deep as she lay back and sobbed into her pillow. She would go back on her word, on the promise she'd made after distancing herself from her parents' continued disapproval never to contort herself into another's expectations of her. She would put herself in a box labelled *desperate and willing to beg for Romeo's love* if she had the faintest glimpse that he returned a sliver of what she felt for him.

The sickening feeling of how far she would go triggered harder sobs, until her head throbbed and her body was wrung out. Still the pain came, washing over her in waves as the sun slid low and she knew she had to get up and dress for dinner.

Over and over as she showered, she saw his face, felt his silence like a final, doomed slash across her heart and wondered how she would face him across the dinner table. For a moment she wished for the man who had brushed her feelings aside and taken control. But she shook her head.

They'd gone past that this afternoon. There was no hiding from the glaring knowledge that Romeo didn't love her and never would. That his only interest was for his son.

Her only choice was to muddle through the next few days, and leave the island when Romeo did. If he was intent on having his son guarded by a security detail, he could do so in Ranelagh. She wouldn't be able to bear staying here, cocooned in a fool's paradise. She would confront reality head-on, put one foot in front of the other until she learned to live with the pain.

Shutting off the shower, she dressed in an ensemble appropriate for entertainment, applied enough make-up to disguise the puffiness under her eyes and left her room.

She encountered Eva emerging from her own suite and pinned a smile on her face.

'Oh, good, were you going to check on Lucca? We can share story time and be done in half the time,' Eva said with an engaging grin.

They entered the large guest suite where the children had been relocated after Lucca refused to be parted from his new friends and took turns reading until all three fell asleep.

In the living room, they found the men sipping whiskies. Romeo crossed to the drinks cabinet and returned with a mineral water for Eva and a glass of champagne for her, which he handed over with a rigidly blank look on his face.

Her breath caught painfully and she looked away as Eva smiled and patted the bump covered by her stunning jade-green gown. 'Sorry I conked out on you earlier. These two kept me up during the flight with their incessant kicking.'

Maisie's eyes widened. 'You're having another set of twins?'

Eva grinned. 'Turns out twins run in both our families. My great-grandmother was a twin, and Zaccheo's mother told him his grandfather was a twin, too. Something to be thankful for, since he's determined to not stop knocking me up until he has a full football team. That means I get to do this *only* half a dozen times.'

Zaccheo broke off his muffled conversation with Romeo and strolled over to his wife. 'You know you love carrying my children, *dolcezza*.'

'Yeah, keep telling yourself that, champ. After these two I'm taking an extended leave of absence from getting pregnant.'

Zaccheo lifted a brow. 'As long as it's merely a leave and not a resignation.'

Eva rolled her eyes but curled into his side when he sat down next to her.

The conversation turned to children. Romeo maintained brooding silence throughout, and only offered brusque opinions when Eva forced him into the conversation. Zaccheo seemed perfectly at ease with Romeo's mood, but Maisie couldn't help her breath catching whenever Romeo slid her an icy glance.

The tense atmosphere continued through dinner, the men chatting about business and Eva attempting to engage Maisie in general conversation. She couldn't remember because she was concentrating on keeping the sob at the back of her throat whenever she looked at Romeo.

And how pathetic was that? To know she'd been nothing more than a plaything in his bed while he got to know his son, and yet still feel as if her world were caving in on itself every time she remembered that in a handful of days she would walk away from him for ever.

'Oh, for goodness' sake. Can we sort this thing out once and for all? Can't you see how distressed this is all making Maisie?'

Her head jerked up at Eva's sharp retort to find the other woman glaring at her husband.

Zaccheo turned to her with one brow tilted. 'Don't get yourself worked up, *dolcezza*. Everything's under control.'

Eva snorted. 'God, you men can be so blind at times! Can't you see we're tearing ourselves apart here? Tell them, Maisie.'

Both sets of male eyes turned towards her, one grimly amused and the other as icily brooding as they'd been all evening.

Painfully pulling her gaze from Romeo's, she pursed her lips. 'Sorry, it seems I no longer have a vote.' Not that she ever did. Or ever would.

Eva sighed heavily and pulled her fingers through her wild, curly blonde hair. 'What do we have to do to get through to you two?' she demanded, exasperated.

'Eva, *mia*, I won't have you this distressed,' Zaccheo all but growled.

'Then stop this stupid cavemen course of action.' She threw her napkin down, winced when her babies also made their thoughts known about the effect her distress was having on them. Zaccheo started to rise, but she waved him away. 'I'm fine. I think Maisie and I will go for a walk, leave you two to ponder the wisdom of your ideas.'

The excuse to be out of Romeo's oppressive presence was too great to turn down. Rising, she took the arm Eva held out after kicking off her shoes. Following her, Maisie kicked off her shoes, too, and they headed outside.

'I hear there's a stunning waterfall here somewhere. I'd love to see it.'

Maisie stumbled to a halt. 'Um…do you mind if we don't?' she pleaded raggedly, unable to bear the thought of returning to where she and Romeo had made love. She knew she'd given herself away when Eva's eyes widened.

'Of course,' she murmured softly. 'We'll go down to the beach instead.'

They walked in silence for a while, taking in the lush vegetation gleaming under strung-out lights, and the view of a night-lit Maui in the distance, before Eva glanced at her. 'You'll have to take the bull by the horns at some point, you know. Men are obtusely blind sometimes—even the cleverest, billion-dollar-empire-commanding ones can fail to see what's right in front of their faces.'

Maisie shook her head. 'It's not like that between Romeo and me,' she painfully explained.

'Maybe not, but the pain you are feeling right now, I've been there. It took weeks before I came to my senses, and I didn't have a toddler to contend with during that time. You and Romeo—there's something there.' She stopped Maisie when she opened her mouth to deny it. 'You had his child four years ago, and he married you within two days of seeing you again.'

'Because of Lucca.'

Eva pursed her lips. 'I married Zaccheo because I thought I didn't have a choice. But deep down, I knew I did. Things happen for a reason, but it's the endgame that matters. Fighting for what you want even when you think everything's hopeless.'

'I don't *think* it's hopeless. I know it is,' she stressed.

Eva looked as if she wanted to argue the point, but her lashes swept over her lovely green eyes and she nodded. 'Okay. I'm sorry for prying. I'll let the matter drop, except to say I've never seen Romeo like this before. Sure, he has that sexy brooding thing going on most of the time, but never like this, not even five years ago, when his mo—' She stopped, visibly pursing her lips to prevent her indiscretion.

Maisie's chest tightened. 'Something bad happened to bring him to Palermo then, didn't it?' It went to show how much she didn't know about Romeo.

'I can only say a bad chapter of his life came to an end. But he wasn't as affected as he is now.'

Maisie shook her head. 'This is all about Lucca,' she insisted as they reached the beach.

Eva nodded, a sage smile curving her lips, before she pulled up the skirt to her elegant gown. 'Okay. Now I'm probably going to ruin my dress, but since my husband refuses to allow me to swim in the ocean until our sons are born, but he happens to be annoying me a lot right now, I'm damn well going for a quick dip.'

Maisie gave a smile that barely lifted the corners of her mouth. 'You know he can see you from the villa, right?'

Eva gave a stubborn, cheeky smile. 'I'll be out before he gets here.'

Maisie didn't think it was wise to stand in her way. The waters weren't especially deep for half a mile or so, but she kept an eye on her, trying not to think about what Eva had said.

Because it wasn't a subject worth pursuing. Romeo had made himself more than clear. And if he'd looked shocked, it was because he probably hadn't thought she would confront him about it.

After a few minutes, tired of the agony replaying through her soul, Maisie adjusted her clothing and waded into the warm, inviting water.

CHAPTER THIRTEEN

ROMEO DIDN'T LOOK UP from the fireplace when his friend joined him, but he accepted the glass containing a double shot of whisky Zaccheo held out to him.

'Tell me your wife drives you half as crazy as mine does me,' Zaccheo growled.

Romeo downed half the glass's content and stared into the remaining amber liquid. 'She's not my wife,' he growled.

'That ring on your finger and the misery on your face tell a different story, *mio fratello*,' Zaccheo challenged with a grim chuckle.

Romeo's chest squeezed at the term. Although he'd only connected with Zaccheo for a brief month when they were children, he'd never forgotten the boy whose life had touched his. Rediscovering that bond of brotherhood as an adult had made Romeo believe he wasn't truly alone in this world. But lately, he'd discovered there were various forms of loneliness.

A loneliness of the heart, for instance…

Zaccheo's hand of friendship might have conquered a small part of his soul, but he was finding out, much to his emerging horror, that it would never be enough. Not like what he'd been secretly hoping for a few weeks.

'The ring is meaningless. She doesn't want to be married to me,' he snapped and downed the rest of the drink. A replacement arrived seconds later, and he took it, his fingers tightening around the cold glass. The platinum-and-gold wedding ring in question caught the light, winking mockingly, and a deep urge to smash the glass moved through him.

Before he could give in to it, Zaccheo replied, 'Before you tear the place to pieces, perhaps you should listen to what your woman has to say.'

'She's already said her piece. And I heard her loud and clear.' Although he wished he hadn't. He wished he hadn't stopped her on the terrace in the first place, that he'd postponed the moment of complete rejection for a while longer.

Why? So he could continue to live in this fool's paradise?

'I've learned to my cost that there's a difference between listening and hearing.'

Romeo's mouth twisted. 'You sound like a damn agony-aunt talk-show host. A very bad one.'

'Mock all you want. You'll learn the difference soon enough.'

Used to Zaccheo providing solid, formidable opinions when needed, Romeo wondered whether his friend was going soft in the head. A glance at him as he strolled to the window to look down at the beach where his wife and Maisie had headed proved otherwise. The ruthless man was behind those strong features.

Zaccheo turned towards him. 'What are we going to do about Palermo? We need to resolve it soon before my wife decides she doesn't want to be married to me any more, either.' The mocking tone belied the brutal intent in his face.

Romeo shook his head. 'Fattore's absurd demands started all of this. Eva's right. You need to be with her and the boys in New York. I'll handle Lorenzo and Carmelo.'

The old man was what had set all this in motion. And while he was grateful for having his son in his life, he couldn't let the nuisance carry on any longer.

The need to teach Fattore's ex-lieutenant a salutary lesson charged through him and he rolled his tense shoulders. 'I should've gone with my instincts and cut Lorenzo off at the knees much sooner, instead of entertaining his foolishness.'

'You needed time to find out what he was capable of.'

'And now I have.'

His phone buzzed and he looked at the screen. Speak of the devil.

'Lorenzo.' His blood boiled as he put his phone on speaker. 'You've saved me the trouble of a phone call.'

'*Bene.* You have good news for me, I hope.'

'I don't deal in hope, old man. Never have,' Romeo snarled.

Zaccheo gave a grim smile and sipped his whisky.

'Whether you like it or not, you have blood ties to this family. Your father left it to you. You can't just turn your back on it.'

Romeo exhaled through the need to punch something. He managed to suppress his rage and frustration and glanced at Zaccheo.

The man he considered his only friend also wore an expression of quiet rage. Romeo knew Zaccheo had learned a thing or two about seeking retribution from his wrongful imprisonment several years ago. Just as he knew the threat against his sons would need to be answered.

But he also knew getting dragged into a Mafia war wasn't what either of them wanted. What he wanted was to be done with this in a single, definitive way.

He hardened his voice so there would be no mistaking his intent.

'You've insisted on shoving my parentage down my throat every chance you got to suit your needs. Well, you got your wish. I'll be in Palermo in seventy-two hours. I promise, you won't like the news I deliver.'

He ended the call and threw the phone on the sofa. About to down his drink, he noticed Zaccheo's rising tension as he stared at the beach far below. In a split second, his friend's disbelieving expression turned into bewilderment. '*Madre di Dio*, is that…? Are they…?'

Romeo followed his gaze, and horror swept through him. 'Yes, they're swimming in the ocean,' he supplied grimly.

And Maisie was further out, almost at the point where the ocean floor dipped dangerously.

'*Porca miseria*, only my wife would decide to swim in the Pacific Ocean fully clothed and at five months pregnant with twins.' He sprinted towards the door with Romeo fast on his heels.

They reached the beach in minutes, with Zaccheo a few feet ahead of him, just as Eva waded ashore. Romeo didn't have to guess that she was exhausted, despite the sheer exhilaration on her face.

Exhilaration that turned into wary apprehension when she spotted her husband's thunderous look. She put out her hands. 'Zaccheo—'

'Not a single word, *dolcezza*, if you know what's good for you,' he sliced at her, before scooping her into his arms and striding off the beach.

Romeo rushed past them, toeing off his socks and shoes. He'd discarded his jacket and shirt as they raced from the villa. He dived into the water, striking out for the lone figure a quarter of a mile away.

He reached Maisie in minutes. And she had the audacity to look at him with a puzzled expression.

'What are you doing out here? Is Eva all right?' she asked.

'What the hell do you think you're doing?' he snapped.

'I thought it was obvious.' She searched the beach, her face turning anxious. 'Is—'

'*Sì*, Eva is fine,' he reassured impatiently. 'Although I've no idea what she was thinking, going for a swim in her condition.'

'She's a strong swimmer, and I was right beside her until she decided to head back. Then I made sure I kept an eye on her.'

'From here, close to where the currents swirl dangerously?' he accused. He couldn't see below the water, but he could see the neckline of her gown and knew how long her dress was, and how hopelessly inept she would've been at saving herself had she been caught in a rip current.

Her mouth twisted as she treaded water. 'Did I not mention I was regional champion swimmer? It was one of the many *almost* talents my parents tried and failed to turn me into. Sadly, I never made it to nationals. One of my many, *many* failures, I guess.' The bitterness in her voice caught him in the raw, threatened to rip open a place he didn't want touched. Especially not since her declaration this afternoon.

'So you thought you'd add one more tick to this imaginary quota by wearing a dress that adds at least twenty pounds to your body weight when it's soaking wet?' he snarled, all the alien feelings that had been bubbling through him since their conversation on the terrace this afternoon rising to the edge.

She looked away from him, and he could've sworn she blushed before her face tightened with deep unhappiness. 'Not exactly.'

He caught hold of her shoulders and pointed her towards the beach. 'Swim back now.'

Her chin rose mutinously. 'Or what?'

Despite the dark emotions swirling through him...the searing agony of knowing that ultimately this woman didn't want him, the knife-edge of arousal lanced him at the fire in her eyes. 'You swim back under your own steam or I drag you back. Those are the only two choices available to you.'

'Romeo—'

'Now,' he interrupted her, unable to believe how like heaven and how very much like hell it felt to hear his name on her lips. 'You may be in a hurry to end this marriage, but it won't be through you carelessly drowning yourself.'

Her mouth dropped open in stunned shock, and he wanted to believe tears filled her eyes, but she turned abruptly and struck out towards shore before he could be certain, her strokes surprisingly swift and strong considering what she wore. He waited until she was a few dozen feet away before he followed.

She was wading waist deep by the time he passed her a few metres from shore. Heading for the cabana where fresh supplies of towels were stocked, he grabbed two and stalked back.

'You had no right to say that to me!'

Romeo looked up and stopped dead. 'What the hell are you wearing? Where's the rest of your dress? And I had no right to say what?' he tagged on abstractedly, unable to tear his eyes away from her body.

'To say that I'd deliberately drown myself.'

'I didn't say you'd do it deliberately, but I didn't think you'd be that careless, either. Although from the look of you, I was wrong in my assumption.'

The bottom part of her dress was missing, leaving her clad in a scrap of wet white lace that brought a growl straining from his chest. And with the top part wet and plastered to her skin, Romeo wondered how long he would last on his own two feet before the strength of need pounding through him buckled his knees.

Under the lights strung out between the palm trees, he watched heat crawl up her face. Although it was a fraction of the fire lighting through his veins. 'Care to tell me what happened to the rest of your dress?' he asked, his voice thick and alien to his own ears.

She waved at the sand near the steps. 'The skirt's over there. The top and bottom are joined by a zip,' she supplied. 'See, I wasn't as stupid as you imagined,' she added bitterly. 'Nor did I plan on risking drowning, either accidentally or deliberately. Amongst other things, I love my son too much to do that.'

Romeo wanted to ask what those other things were, whether it could include him, but for the first time in his life he stepped back from the need to know, his mind clasping on the fact that she hadn't corrected him on the need to end their marriage. Weariness moved through him, parts of him he didn't want to acknowledge feeling brutalised, as if he'd gone ten rounds with an unseen opponent and emerged the loser.

'Are you going to stand there all night or will you hand me one of those towels?' she asked in a low, tense voice.

He started to hand it to her, then stopped. Moving closer, he stared into her eyes, darker now with whatever emotions swirled through her. 'You're not a failure.'

'What?' she croaked, her face raised to his.

'In the water, you said you'd failed at many things.'

'Oh.' Her eyes darkened further and tears brimmed her eyes. 'I have. I failed to get my parents to love me, for instance.'

Her naked pain slashed him hard, despite thinking he'd steeled himself adequately against further unsettling emotion. 'That is *their* fault, not yours. I've learned the hard way that, with the best will in the world, you can't get someone to love you if they're incapable of it.'

Her eyes widened, questions swimming in her eyes. Questions he felt too raw to answer right then. He shook his head and briskly rubbed the towel in her hair. 'You're a huge success at the things you're passionate about.'

Her eyelids swept down, hiding her expression from him. Her laugh was hollow as she tried to take the towel from him. 'I wish I could agree, but sadly the evidence states otherwise. For one thing, you insist on calling what we have a marriage, but has it really been? Or have I just been the body to warm your bed while you burrow your way into your son's life? The woman you didn't trust enough to let her know how much legitimising your son means to you.'

His arms dropped. 'Maisie—'

'Don't, Romeo. I don't want to hear your slick excuses. The moment you found out about Lucca, you wanted him, regardless of who stood in your way. You scooped me up for the ride because that was the easiest option for you.'

He stepped behind her, and his gaze was dragged help-lessly over her body, down the enticing line of her spine to the twin dimples at the top of her buttocks, and the allur-ing globes below, perfectly framed by the wet lace caress-ing her skin.

'Easy? You think any of this has been easy?' He shook his head in self-disgust. 'I'm stumbling round in the dark, pretending I've got my head screwed on straight when the reality is that I'm terrified I'll irrevocably mess up a four-year-old boy's life. And, believe me, I'm perfectly equipped to do it. Whereas you know the answer to every question he asks. You know what he wants before he does. So yes, I exploited your devotion to him to help me get to know my flesh and blood. Condemn me for that, but believe me, *none* of this has been easy for me,' he rasped.

Her head fell forward with a defeated sigh. He told him-self to remember that she intended to walk away, take away the only thing resembling a true family he'd ever known. She was the reason he couldn't take a full breath without wondering if his organs were functioning properly. Some-how, she'd taught him to hope again, to dare to dream. And she'd smashed that dream with a handful of words.

Romeo *tried* to remember that.

But he couldn't help it. He lowered his head and brushed his lips against the top of her spine, where the wet hair had parted to reveal her creamy skin.

She made a sound, part arousal, part wary animal, but he was too far gone to heed the latter. The thought of her leaving, of never being able to do this again, scattered his thoughts to a million pieces, until only one thing mattered.

Here and now.

'Maisie.' He heard the rough plea in his voice. He dropped the towel and trailed his mouth over her shoul-ders, down her back, anxiety hurrying his movements. She shuddered under his touch.

'Romeo, please…'

He dropped to his knees and spun her around. '*Tesoro mio*, don't deny me this. Don't deny *us* this.' He wanted to say more, bare himself with words that were locked deep, but it was as if the language he needed to express himself was suddenly alien to him. But he could show her. He *would* show her.

He held her hips and kissed her soft belly, where his son had nestled, warm and loved. She gave a soft moan. Empowered, he deepened the caress, his tongue tasting her intoxicating skin. When she swayed and her hands clutched his shoulders, he groaned.

Roughly pulling her panties to one side, he fastened his mouth to her sex, caressing her with his tongue as he lapped at her.

'Romeo!'

He drowned beneath the heady sensation, of his wildcat digging her fingers into his skin. He dared to entertain the thought that there might be a way through this landmine that threatened to destabilise his world. He went harder, desperate to bring her pleasure, unashamed to hope it brought him something *more*, something lasting.

She gave another cry and shattered in his arms, her head dropping forward as she shuddered. Rising, he caught her in his arms, saw the dazed but almost resigned look in her eyes, and his stomach hollowed.

Ignoring the look, he carried her to the steps and helped her with the skirt. Then, covering her top half with the towel, he swung her into his arms and headed for the villa.

'I can walk, Romeo,' she said in a small, tight voice.

'I believe I'm living up to my caveman reputation.'

'You're performing to the wrong audience. You don't need to prove anything to me.'

He glanced down at her tear-stained face and his chest tightened. 'Do I not?'

She shook her head, but her eyes refused to meet his. 'I think we understand each other perfectly.'

He wanted to rail at her that he didn't understand; that he'd thought their moment at the waterfall, *before* they'd made love, had started something they could build on. Her mutinous expression stopped him.

Besides, he was beginning to think they communicated much better using a different language.

Entering the villa, he headed for the stairs and his bedroom. The moment she raised her head and looked around, she scrambled from his arms.

Romeo set her down and shut the door.

'Why have you brought me here?' she demanded.

The accusation in her eyes ripped through him but he forced himself not to react to it. Reaching for the towel, he tugged it from her, then he pulled her close.

'Answer me, Romeo…'

'Shh, *gattina*, just let this be.' Another rough plea he was unashamed of, even though it threw him back to another time, another place, pleading in a much younger but equally desperate voice.

It was the night his mother had packed his meagre belongings in a tattered bag and told him she was sending him to his thug of a father.

Disturbed by the memories that seemed intent on flooding in, he sealed his mouth to Maisie's, searching for her unique balm that soothed his soul.

His heart leapt when she didn't push him away, but then she wasn't responding, either. Groaning in frustration, he pushed his fingers into her hair, desperate to stem the alarm rising through him that he was fighting a losing battle.

Eventually, she tore her mouth away. 'Please stop. I don't want this.'

He raised his head, the landmine seeming to spread like an ocean before him. 'This?' he intoned starkly.

Her eyes slid past his, to a point beyond his shoulder. 'You. I don't want you.'

Acrid bitterness filled him, along with the sharp barbs

of memory, but still he pushed. 'That's a lie. I proved it once, I can prove it again and as many times as you need to face the truth.'

She shook her head wearily. 'That was just the sex talking. Nothing more.'

'So you mean you don't want me, the man?' Why did that feel so damn agonising to say?

Her gaze remained averted for another minute before meeting his eyes. 'You're an amazing father, and I'm sure you'll offer Lucca support and opportunities in life I can only dream of. But I can't stay with you. After our guests leave, I'm returning to Ireland with Lucca. I'm sorry, but this…this was a mistake.'

She started to take her rings off. He lunged for her hands, stopped the action before he fully realised he'd moved. 'You will not take off your ring!' The snarled command stemmed from deep within his soul.

Her blue eyes reflected pain, enough to hammer home just how much being here, being with him, was costing her. How could he not have seen that? How could he have entertained the idea that they could attempt a proper marriage?

'I can't…'

'I know my opinion matters very little to you, but think of our son. It's his birthday tomorrow. Are you this determined to throw a shadow over the occasion?'

Her face lost a trace of colour. 'Of course not.'

'Then wait. For his sake.'

Her head dipped and she pushed the rings slowly back on her finger. He forced himself to drop her hands, move away.

'I'll see you in the morning,' she murmured.

He didn't respond. He was struggling to find even the simplest explanation of what was going on inside him. He heard the door shut and paced to the window. In the reflection behind him, he saw the bed they'd risen from this morning and wondered at how much he hated the idea of sleeping in it now.

Undressing, he entered the shower and let the water beat over his head. It wouldn't drown out her words, her face.

I can't stay with you.

His bitter laughter rose above the pounding cascade.

At least those words had been less harsh than the ones his mother had thrown at him before she'd left him on Agostino Fattore's doorstep.

At least this time he wouldn't starve. Or live rough.

And yet he found himself bypassing the bed when he left the bathroom, and collapsing onto the sofa in his private living room. And when he was still awake when the orange streaked the horizon, he'd almost convinced himself the pain ripping through him wasn't worse than it'd been when he was a child.

The performance Maisie gave the next day was award-worthy. At some point while she was smiling and taking pictures of her son at what had been dubbed *The Best Birthday Party Ever*, she half hysterically toyed with contacting her parents and telling them they should've tried enrolling her into acting school.

Because she was able to stand next to Romeo as he helped an ecstatic Lucca cut the ribbon that officially unveiled his duck pond. Then look into his eyes and smile as they helped their son release the fifty balloons tied to the sturdy bridge in the middle of the pond. She even managed a laugh as two necking swans were immediately named Maisie and Romeo. She didn't crumble into a pain-ravaged heap when Lucca insisted his father kiss his mother to celebrate the naming.

And she certainly aced the small talk with the grown-ups while the kids took turns at the duck-feed dispenser.

Once the birthday-cake candles had been blown, the cake devoured, the children tucked in bed, she retired to her suite, showered and got ready for the dinner party.

She stood by Romeo's side as they greeted the two couples Romeo had trusted to remain on the island. Then calling on her skills as a restaurant owner, she supervised the caterers, made sure each guest was looked after, while avoiding being too close to Romeo for longer than a few minutes.

Luckily, Eva, and the phenomenon of carrying a second set of twins, quickly became the centre of attention and, seeming to have made up with her husband, engaged everyone with her effervescent personality.

As soon as the last guest left, Maisie headed for the door.

Romeo blocked her path. She stopped, her heart pounding.

'Well done on the dinner party,' he muttered.

She tried to avert her gaze, to stop absorbing every expression and contour of his face. But she couldn't look away.

'Thank you,' she replied.

He stared at her for another long moment, then he stepped away. 'Goodnight.'

She couldn't respond because her heart had lodged itself in her throat. Hurrying away, she gave in to the insane urge to glance over her shoulder. Romeo was watching her.

She tried to tell herself she didn't yearn for him to follow. By the time she got to her room and shut the door behind her, she knew she was lying to herself.

CHAPTER FOURTEEN

THEY LEFT THE ISLAND two days later, with a distraught Lucca heartbroken at having to leave his beloved ducks. Although he was slightly appeased at the thought of returning to his old pond at Ranelagh Gardens, Maisie knew there would be more tears when he found out his father wouldn't be staying.

The thought troubled her as she played with Lucca during the long flight. A couple of times, she'd attempted to start a conversation with Romeo about scheduling visits, but he'd given her a stony look and a crisp, 'We'll discuss it later,' after which he'd promptly returned to his endless phone calls.

That he was returning to Palermo had become clear during a particularly heated conversation.

Her heart flipped over hard at the thought of him returning to the place that had given him such a rough start in life.

He looked up then, and their eyes connected. For a moment, she thought she saw a flare of pain mingled with hope. But his expression hardened and his gaze veered away. This time, her heart bypassed the somersault stage and went straight for cracking right down the middle.

She was still trying to hold herself together when he took a break to eat and play with Lucca. He stopped by her armchair on the way back to where he'd set up his office and looked down at her.

'I have a team childproofing my London apartment and another scouting for a place in Dublin. Emily will be flying out to help take care of Lucca when he's with me. Is that acceptable to you?'

As she stared up at his grim face, her heart broke all over

again. Slowly, she nodded. 'I won't keep him away from you. I just need a reasonable heads-up when you're coming to see him, so I can arrange it with the playgroup.'

His mouth compressed and he nodded. '*Bene*, it will be done.' He walked away to the far side of the plane and didn't speak to her again until they landed.

As predicted, Lucca turned hysterical at the idea of his father leaving. Maisie watched, a stone lodged in her throat, as Romeo hugged him on the tarmac and reassured him that his absence wouldn't be a long one. After several minutes, Lucca calmed down and Romeo strode to where she stood.

He handed Lucca over, his hand lingering on his son before his jaw clenched. 'I'll be in touch in the next few days, a week at the most, to arrange a time to see him. And I'll call him tonight.'

'Um…sure.'

With another look at his son, Romeo turned and walked back into his plane.

Maisie stood frozen, her mind reeling at the thought that her marriage was ending right then and there, on a painfully bright summer's day in Dublin.

She clutched Lucca closer as he whimpered at his departing father. Romeo disappeared, and Lucca began to weep.

Forcing herself to move, she strapped him into his seat in the sleek car waiting for them, then buckled herself in next to him.

The sun was still shining when they pulled up outside her restaurant despite it being evening. Unable to face going in, she waved at a gawping Lacey and went straight up to her apartment. Her heart sank when a knock came at the door less than an hour later.

She opened it to Bronagh, who was trying hard to pretend she wasn't shocked to see her.

'I've just put Lucca down for the night. Do you want to come in for a cup of tea?' Maisie offered.

'Tea is great, but *you* look like you need something stronger.' Bronagh held out a bottle of red wine, the concern she was trying to hide finally breaking through.

By her third glass, Maisie had broken down and spilled every last pathetically needy feeling.

'So...what are you going to do?' Bronagh asked when Maisie stopped to toss back another fortifying gulp of wine.

Maisie looked up. 'Oh, please don't worry that I'm going to take over again at the restaurant. To be honest, I could do with the break.'

Bronagh shook her head. 'That wasn't what I meant. What are you going to do about Romeo?'

Maisie frowned. 'What do you mean? It's over.'

'You really think so? From what you said he didn't *have* to marry you. This is the twenty-first century and he's rich enough to afford a dozen armies to protect you and Lucca if he wanted to without putting a ring on your finger.' She nodded to Maisie's hand. 'And you're still wearing your wedding rings. Is he still wearing his?'

Maisie nodded abstractedly and frowned at the sparkling rings. 'What are you saying?'

Bronagh shrugged. 'That things seem awfully *unresolved* for two people hell-bent on chucking in the towel so quickly.'

'I'm not...I wasn't... He only wants sex.' She blushed and drank some more wine.

'Of course he does. Sex is the easiest way to hide deeper emotion, that's why it's called angry sex, rebound sex, make-up sex...need I go on?'

Miserably, Maisie shook her head.

Bronagh laid a gentle hand on her arm. 'You haven't known a lot of love in your life, but then neither has he. One of you has to be brave enough to scratch beneath the surface.'

'Why do I have to do the scratching?' Maisie blurted. 'Just because he thinks I'm a wildcat in bed doesn't mean... *God!* I can't believe I just said that.'

Bronagh laughed and rose. 'I think the jet lag and wine are doing their job. Get some sleep. I'll take the monitor with me when I go downstairs in case Lucca wakes up.'

Maisie hugged her friend, her thoughts rioting as she prepared for bed. When she lay wide awake three hours later, she wasn't surprised.

Bronagh's words raced through her mind.

While she didn't think she'd misinterpreted her conversations with Romeo, was it possible she'd blinded herself to a different possibility?

Could she guide Romeo into loving her? He might have been devoid of love before he'd arrived on her doorstep three weeks ago, but Maisie had seen what he felt for his son. And Romeo hadn't rejected the love that poured from Lucca. Surely he couldn't rule it out of his life for ever?

Turning over, she exhaled slowly, careful not to let too much hope take root.

When Romeo arrived on Saturday, she would try to broach the subject, see if there was a glimmer of anything worth pursuing.

Except Romeo didn't come on Saturday. He sent Emily and a team of bodyguards after calling with his apologies. He'd established a routine with Lucca where they videocalled for half an hour in the morning and half an hour in the evening. His greetings to Maisie when she connected his calls were cool and courteous. Any attempt at a conversation was quickly curbed with a demand for his son.

By the time he cancelled on Saturday, she knew, once again, she'd been foolish to hope. Yet she couldn't bring herself to take off her wedding rings. Nor could she find the strength to tell Lucca that, no, Mummy and Daddy would never live together again.

Admitting to herself that she was burying her head in the sand didn't stop her from doing exactly that. She helped out in the restaurant when she could, but even there she knew she wasn't on her full game, so she kept her presence to a minimum.

And then Romeo stopped calling.

For the first two days, she didn't have time to worry because she had her hands full controlling Lucca's misery-fuelled tantrums.

By the third day she was debating whether to call him. She talked herself out of it for half a day before dialling his number. It went straight to voicemail. Leaving a garbled message guaranteed to make her sound like a lunatic, she sat back, her stomach churning.

When he hadn't called by evening, she marched downstairs and strode across the road to where one of his guards was stationed.

'Have you heard from your boss?'

The thickset man frowned. 'My boss is across the road.' He indicated another heavily muscled man wearing wrap-around shades.

She sighed, exasperated. 'I mean your boss's boss. Mr Brunetti.'

'Oh. Sorry, miss, I don't have his number.'

'It's not miss, it's Mrs...Brunetti.' She waved her rings, unnecessarily, then cringed inside. 'I need to speak to Mr Brunetti.'

The man snapped to attention, then quickly strode over to his boss. The hushed conversation ensued and Wraparound Shades approached.

'I'm sorry, Mrs Brunetti, but Mr Brunetti requested that his whereabouts not be disclosed.'

Panic flared through her belly. 'Why?'

A shrug. 'He didn't say. I'm sorry.'

Maisie raced back upstairs, her heart crashing wildly against her ribs. She tried Emily's number and got a message to say she was on sabbatical in Hawaii.

She spent the night pacing her living room, alternating

between leaving a message and hitting Romeo's video-call button. Both went unanswered.

By mid-morning she was frantic. And angry. And miserable. For herself and for her son. But mostly, she was angry with Romeo.

Yanking her front door open, she faced the head bodyguard, arms folded. 'I'm about to buy a round-the-world plane ticket and drag my four-year-old to go and look for his missing father. I'm assuming your job includes accompanying us on trips abroad?'

He nodded warily.

'Good, then consider this your heads-up. We're leaving in an hour. I intend on starting in…oh, I don't know… Outer Mongolia?'

His eyes widened.

'Or perhaps you can save us all a wasted journey and tell me what country I should start in.'

The man swallowed, shifted from foot to foot. Maisie glared harder. 'You should start in Italy.'

The relief she'd expected never materialised. If Romeo was in Italy, then… 'Specifically in Palermo?'

Another wary nod.

She raced back to her flat and opened her laptop. The restaurant was closed today, and Bronagh had issued a standing babysitting assistance.

After debating whether to take Lucca with her, she decided against it, called Bronagh to tell her to pick up Lucca from nursery and booked a solo ticket.

Until she knew where Romeo was and the reason for his silence, she wasn't risking taking their son to Palermo.

After flying in Romeo's private jet, her cramped economy seat felt like torture. She emerged from the flight hot, sweaty and filled with even more panic when she realised she had no idea where to start looking for Romeo.

The last time she'd done this she hadn't been in possession of a last name.

This time the last name was one that held such power and prestige that, in her state of dishevelled hair and worn jeans, she would probably achieve the same results as last time. Laughter and ridicule.

Hailing a taxi to a three-star hotel, she quickly texted Bronagh to say she'd arrived, then showered, changed into a blue cotton dress and clipped her hair at her nape. Smoothing on lip gloss, she froze for a second when she realised it was the same dress she'd worn the night she'd met Romeo.

Hand shaking, she capped the tube and grabbed her bag.

The weather was much hotter in July than it had been the last time she was here, and a sheen of sweat covered her arms by the time she made it to Giuseppe's.

Heart thumping, she sat at a table and ordered a *limoncello*. Sipping the cool drink more for something to do than anything else, she tried to think through what she'd say to the only person who could give her answers as to Romeo's whereabouts—Lorenzo Carmine.

Whether the old man would actually answer her questions was a bridge she'd cross when she came to it. According to the article she'd found online, Lorenzo lived in a mansion once belonging to Agostino Fattore, a man whose picture bore a strong resemblance to Romeo, once you dragged your gaze from the skin-crawling cruelty in his eyes.

Her fingers curled around her glass, her stomach churning in horror at what the man she loved had suffered. Was probably still suffering…

Shutting her eyes, she dropped her head into her hands and breathed in deep. She wouldn't think the worst. She would get her chance to tell Romeo exactly how she felt.

All of it. With nothing held back.

Firming her jaw, she opened her eyes and jerked upright in shock.

He was pulling back the chair at the adjacent table. Sunglasses obscured his eyes and the direction of his gaze suggested he wasn't looking at her, but Maisie knew Romeo had seen her.

Her body's sizzling awareness was too strong to be anything but a reaction to his direct scrutiny.

A judder shook its way up from her toes as she stared at him, relief pounding through her to see him in one piece. Hungrily her eyes roved over him. His cheekbones looked a little more prominent, and his mouth a lot grimmer, but there was no mistaking the powerful aura emanating from him or his masculine grace when he curled elegant fingers around the tiny espresso cup the waiter slid onto his table a few minutes later.

He picked up the beverage, knocked it back in one greedy gulp, then stood, extracted a ten-euro note from his pocket and placed it on the table.

She sat poised in her chair unable to believe he would just leave without speaking to her.

Then his arrogant head turned her way. Heat sizzled over her skin, far hotter than the sun's rays as she stared back at him. His hands clenched into fists, then released.

Without a word, he strode onto the pavement leading away from the waterfront.

Maisie grabbed her handbag and raced after him. Everything about his quick strides and tense shoulders suggested he didn't want to be disturbed. But she hadn't come all this way to be turned away.

He turned into a vaguely familiar street five minutes later. When she recognised it, she froze, her pulse tripling its beat as she read the name of the hotel.

She jerked into motion when Romeo disappeared inside. By the time she entered the jaw-dropping interior of the marble-floored atrium, he was gone. She bit her lip and looked around the plush surroundings, wondering whether she would receive the same humiliating reception as she had last time.

'Signora Brunetti!' A sharply dressed man hurried towards her, his hand proffered in greeting.

'Um, yes?'

'I was asked this morning to look out for you and inform you that the room you seek is Penthouse One.'

'Ah…thank you.'

'*Prego.* If you'll come with me, I'll personally access the private lift for you.'

He escorted her to the lift, inserted the key and pressed the button, before stepping back with a respectful bow.

Clutching her bag against her chest, Maisie willed her pulse to stop racing. But it was no use. Now that she'd seen that Romeo was unharmed, every ounce of adrenaline was churning towards the emotional undertaking she was about to perform.

Should that fail…

Her knees buckled and she sagged against the gilt-edged mirrored walls as the lift doors opened. Sucking in a deep breath, she forced one foot in front of the other. The pristine white doors and gold-encrusted knobs loomed large and imposing in front of her.

Lifting a hand, she knocked.

CHAPTER FIFTEEN

HE OPENED THE DOOR after the third round of knocking. And said nothing. Bleak hazel eyes drilled into hers, seething emotions vibrating in the thick silence.

Maisie cleared her throat.

'You haven't called in four d-days. Our son is miserable without you,' she stammered when she eventually found her brain.

Romeo's face twisted with agonised bitterness and regret, before it resettled into stark blankness. 'I'll make it up to him. My business in Palermo took longer than I thought. I have a month-long business commitment in London starting next week. Once I'm settled, Emily will resume coordinating with you on visiting schedules. I'll also have my team provide you with useful numbers including my pilot's so you don't have to rely on commercial travel. There's a car waiting for you downstairs right now. My plane will take you back home. Have a safe trip back. *Arrivederci.*'

He shut the door in her face.

Her mouth dropped open in shock for several seconds before, temper flaring, she slapped her open palm repeatedly on the door. When he yanked it open, his face was a mask that covered a multitude of emotions. Emotions he was hell-bent on keeping from her.

'I came all this way and that's all you have to say to me?'

He shoved his hands deep into his pockets. 'What more is there to say? You've made it more than clear our son is the only subject on the table when it comes to you and me.'

'That's not true,' she replied.

His jaw worked. 'Dammit, what the hell do you want from me, Maisie?' he demanded gutturally.

'For starters, why did you tell the concierge my name with the instructions to let me up when I arrived?'

'Because you're the mother of my child, and still my wife—at least until one of us decides to do something about it. And also because I have security watching over you and Lucca twenty-four hours a day. I was told the moment you bought a plane ticket to Sicily. I thought I'd save you the trouble of an awkward enquiry at the front desk when you eventually got here.' The thinly veiled mockery made her skin sting.

Nervously, she shifted on her feet. 'Well…okay. I'm here. So are you going to let me in?' she asked with a fast-dwindling bravado.

He raised an eyebrow. 'Are you sure you want to come in? Surely this room holds bad memories for you.'

She looked over his shoulder and caught sight of the mixture of opulent and beautiful antique and modern furniture, some of which they'd appreciated up close and personal with their naked bodies. 'They weren't all bad,' she murmured huskily. 'In fact, the night before the morning after was quite spectacular. One of the best nights of my life.'

He froze, his hazel eyes flaring a bright gold before a cloud descended on his face. 'What a shame it is then that your worst was finding yourself married to me.' His voice leaked a gravel roughness coated with pain and her heart squeezed.

'Don't put words in my mouth, Romeo. I said I didn't want to be married to you. I didn't say it was because I hated the idea. Or you.'

Tension filled his body. 'What did you mean?' he asked raggedly.

'Are you going to let me in?'

He jerked backwards, his hand rigid around the doorknob. His warmth seemed to reach out to her as she passed him, his scent filling her starving senses so headily, she almost broke down and plastered herself against him.

The suite was just as she remembered. The luxurious gold-and-cream-striped sofa stood in the same place she'd first made love with Romeo. She dropped her handbag on it, her fingers helplessly trailing over the exquisite design as memories flooded her.

Unable to resist, she touched the glass-topped console table set between two floor-to-ceiling windows, then the entertainment centre, where Romeo had played *Pagliacci's* mournful theme tunes while he'd feasted on her.

'Do you wish me to leave you alone to reminisce?' he enquired tightly.

She turned to find him frozen against the closed door, his arms folded. He wasn't as calm as he appeared, a muscle flicking in his jaw as he watched her.

'Why are you standing over there, Romeo? Are you afraid of me?' she challenged, even though her heart banged hard against her ribs.

A harsh laugh barked from him, then his face seemed to crumple before he sliced his fingers through his hair. '*Sì*, I'm afraid. I'm terrified of what I feel when I'm around you. And even more terrified of my emotions when I'm not.'

The naked vulnerability in that announcement strangled her breath. The room took on a brightness that made her blink hard. Then she realised the brightness was her heart lifting from the gloom, hope rising fast and hard, against her will.

'What are you saying, Romeo?' She couldn't allow room for misinterpretation. The stakes were higher than ever this time.

He exhaled. Deep and long and shakily, his massive chest quaking beneath his black shirt. 'I mean, I love you, Maisie. Of course, I could be mistaken because I really don't know what love is. But I feel a ravaging emptiness every second of every day that I have to survive without you. I thought I knew what it felt to contemplate a hopeless future until the day you told me you regretted marrying me.' He shook his head and surged away from the door.

Striding to the window, he stared down into the street. 'I haven't been able to function since that moment. You're all I think about, all I crave…' Another juddering breath. 'Is that love? This feeling of desperate hopelessness?' he intoned bleakly.

Maisie moved until she was a few feet from him, desperate to touch him. 'I don't know, Romeo. Do you feel the same ache when you imagine us being together instead of apart? Or is it different, better?' she whispered.

His head dropped forward, his forehead resting against the cool glass as a tremble moved through his body. '*Per favore*…please, *gattina*, why are you doing this?' he groaned roughly. 'Why are you here?'

Maisie swallowed. 'I needed to see that you're all right. That Lorenzo—'

'Lorenzo is no longer an issue. The *famiglia* are abandoning his sinking ship. We have a witness who'll testify to what happened to Zaccheo's father after my father threw me out that night. Lorenzo is now facing a murder charge. Our combined testimony will put him away for good.'

She gasped. 'Why did he attack Zaccheo's father?'

'Paolo Giordano had the task of disposing of me after my mother left me on my father's doorstep. My father didn't want me, so Paolo took me home. Unfortunately, his wife was less than enthusiastic about having another mouth to feed. Paolo had the audacity to offend my father by trying to return me to him after a month. My father set Lorenzo on him.' He stopped, distant memories glazing his eyes before he shook them off. 'I made a statement to the chief of police two days ago. He issued warrants for Lorenzo's arrest. The case may collapse or it may not. Either way, Lorenzo is going to spend some time in prison before the case goes to trial. He'll know better than to come after me or mine again.'

'So, that was how you ended up on the streets? Because your mother didn't want you?'

'She was a high-class prostitute. Getting pregnant with me put a huge obstacle in her chosen career. When I became too much for her, she drove me to a house I'd never visited before, told me it was my father's house and drove away.'

'Did you see her again?'

He closed his eyes for a split second. 'Not until I stayed with her for a week, here in Palermo, five years ago.'

'The week we met?'

He nodded. 'She called, finally. After years of silence, she called me. I'd kept tabs on her over the years and knew when she fell on particularly hard times. I found ways to send her money without her knowing it came from me. I didn't want her contacting me because I was rich. I wanted her to do it because I was her son and she wanted to see me.' He shook his head, bitterness and pain warring over his face. 'The week before she died, she finally called. I was elated.'

'What happened?'

'She wanted the use of my credit card. She wasn't interested in who I was or whether I could afford it. She had a fast-growing brain tumour and didn't have long to live. She wanted to die in style. I checked her into the presidential suite at the Four Seasons. And I stayed with her, hoping that she'd show me, in some small way, that she'd regretted giving me away. She didn't. I held her hand until she passed away and all she did was curse me for looking like my father.

'So, you see, I don't know if this living, breathing thing inside me is love, or if it's a twisted need to cling to something that's damaged because I've touched it.'

The words wrenched at her soul. 'Please don't say that.'

He turned to face her, and his eyes were deep dark pools of pain. 'That day we met was the first time I accepted that hope was a useless emotion. That love didn't exist. Not for people like me.'

'Romeo…'

'It's okay, *gattina*. I know you don't love me.' His shoulders drooped in weary, agonised defeat. 'I'll make sure the divorce is fast and the settlement more than generous.'

Her breath shook. 'I don't want a divorce or your money, Romeo.'

A sound of a wounded animal seared from his throat. She took the final step and placed her left hand on his chest. 'If I did, I would've taken off my wedding ring the moment we left Hawaii.'

His gaze fell on her ring and his eyes flared bright, and then dimmed almost immediately. As if a light had gone off inside.

'We can't stay married simply for the sake of Lucca. I won't be responsible for bringing unhappiness to your life.'

'Then bring happiness. Love me. Be with me.'

His eyes slowly rose, connected with hers. 'But on the island, you said—'

'I said I didn't want to be married because I couldn't bear the thought of loving you and not having you love me back.'

His eyes widened and he jerked upright, his strong arms closing on her shoulders. *'Che cosa?'*

Tears brimmed her eyes. 'I love you, Romeo. I've loved you since the night we spent in this room. I've been miserable without you and I really don't want a divorce, if you don't mind,' she pleaded in a wobbly voice.

'I don't mind,' he responded, his face and voice dazed. 'If you let me, I intend to not mind for at least a dozen lifetimes.'

That bright light ripped through her senses once again. This time she embraced it. Revelled in its warmth. 'Good, because that's how long it'll take for me to show you how much you mean to me, too.'

'*Dio mio, gattina...*' His voice held humble worship, a touching vulnerability that made her cup his face.

'Hold me, Romeo. Kiss me. I've missed you so much.'

With a groan, he sealed his lips to hers.

Three hours later, she dragged her head from his chest and the soothing sound of his heartbeat. 'Are you ready to video-call with Lucca?'

Romeo raised his head and kissed her mouth. 'Hmm, I think I've finally come up with something that'll make him forgive me for not being in touch these past few days.'

'Oh, what's that?'

'A promise of a brother or sister.'

Maisie's heart leapt. She planted a kiss of her own on his willing lips. 'I think you just elevated yourself to *Best Father Ever* status.'

Romeo laughed and set up his laptop after Maisie alerted Bronagh to the incoming call.

Seconds later, the screen filled with their son's beautiful face. 'Mummy! Daddy, when are you coming home?' he demanded plaintively.

Romeo exchanged glances with her. 'We will be there by the time you wake up tomorrow, *bel raggazo.*'

'Okay! I've been learning some Itayan words, Daddy.' He gazed keenly into the screen.

Romeo's hand found hers, and he pressed it to his chest. 'Tell me,' he invited softly.

'*Ti amo, Papà,*' he said haltingly, then his face widened in a proud smile. 'It means, I love you, Daddy.'

Beneath her hand, Romeo's heart lurched, then raced wildly. His throat worked for several moments, before he spoke. 'That is exactly right, and I...' His eyes connected with hers, and tears brimming in hers, she nodded in encouragement. 'I love you, too.'

They rang off several minutes later, and Romeo took her in his arms and just held her. Somewhere in the suite, a mournful opera started.

'Why do you listen to those things? They're so sad.'

He hugged her closer. 'It was a reminder that hope was a futile emotion, that everything dies in the end. But now it'll be a reminder that even in the bleakest moments, the voices of heaven can still be heard.'

She raised her head and stared deep into his soul, her heart turning over. 'I love you, Romeo.'

He kissed her, accepting her love.

He hadn't said he loved her after that first time. But she didn't mind, because she felt it in every touch, every look, and knew he would get around to saying it again eventually, when their world grew less shaky with the depth of emotion rocking them.

When he raised his head, his eyes shone with a brightness that seared her with happiness, right to her very fingertips.

'I see you got away with not being taken to task by Lucca.'

He laughed. 'But I still intend to keep my promise to him and provide him with a brother or sister. Soon,' he stated with serious intent.

She traced his mouth with her fingers. 'Soon. I can think of nothing I want more than another baby with you.'

He gently turned her around and caressed her belly with both hands. Then his strong arms slid around her, swaying her to the sound of angels' voices.

'You're my beginning and my end, *il mio cuore*. My everything.'

EPILOGUE

Three years later

'WHO CAME UP with the brilliant idea that it'd be fun to pack seven hyperactive kids and two overachieving fathers onto a yacht for a vacation?' Eva grumbled as she chased after her ten-month-old daughter crawling at top speed towards the boat's chrome railing. Baby Donatella Giordano immediately screeched in protest at her thwarted bid for freedom.

Maisie grinned, raising her face to the dazzling Mediterranean sunshine. 'You think there would've been any stopping Romeo or Zaccheo once they co-bought the super-yacht they'd been drooling over for a year?'

Eva walked across the wide marble-tiled second-floor deck of the stunning vessel to join Maisie, her white bikini accentuating her tanned skin beautifully. Sitting down, she bounced Donatella on her lap until she quieted. 'It's a beautiful boat, but I haven't been able to sleep a wink from worrying that one of the boys will throw themselves overboard just for the sheer hell of it.'

'Romeo assures me that's impossible. Trust me, I grilled him for hours on that very subject before I agreed to bring Lucca and Marcelo.'

Two-year-old Marcelo glanced up at the mention of his name and grinned from where he splashed in the shallow pool with the second set of Giordano twins, Gianni and Angelo.

Eva kissed the top of her baby's head and sighed happily.

'It's good to see them relax, though, isn't it? I just wish they wouldn't relax so...*vigorously.*'

Maisie laughed and glanced to the side as two power-ful Jet Skis whizzed by, trailed by excited cheers and urges to *go faster.*

Romeo's jet carried Lucca and Zaccheo's his oldest sons.

As they made a final turn past the boat, Romeo's gaze met hers. The contact was brief, but the love blazing in his eyes snagged Maisie's breath. Her heart raced as the over-whelming love, which incredibly grew stronger every day, pounded through her blood. She reached up and touched lips that still tingled from when they'd made love hours ago. Then her hand drifted down to her flat belly, and the surprise that would bring another smile of joy to her hus-band's face.

'Since Romeo hasn't crowed about it, I'm guessing he doesn't know yet?' Eva asked, glancing pointedly at Maisie's stomach.

Maisie gasped. 'No, he doesn't, but how...?'

'Please. You've been positively glowing since you stepped aboard the *Dolcezza Gattina* yesterday. I'm guess-ing you didn't get a chance to tell him because Zaccheo mo-nopolised his attention until the early hours?'

Maisie snorted. 'He didn't come to bed until five this morning.' Whereupon he'd woken her and made love to her until she'd been too exhausted to move. By the time she'd woken again, he'd been up with their children. 'I'll tell him tonight.'

'Tell me what, *amore mio*?'

Maisie jumped guiltily at the deep voice that heralded her husband's arrival.

Romeo climbed the last step and headed straight for her. This close, his tight, lean physique, damp from the ocean's spray, was even more arresting. 'If I told you now, it wouldn't be a surprise, would it?' she finally said when she could speak past the wondrous reality that this gorgeous, incredible man belonged to her.

After kissing his younger son, he lowered his body onto her lounger and braced his hands on either side of her hips, caging her in. Outside the unique cocoon that wrapped itself around them whenever they were this close, Maisie peripherally saw Zaccheo greet his wife with a kiss; heard the staff attend to the children.

But she only had eyes for the man who stared down at her with an intensity that hadn't abated since the first moment they'd set eyes on each other.

'Is there any reason it needs to wait till tonight?' he asked with a thick rasp that spoke of other urgent desires.

She scrambled for a sound reason, but in the end couldn't find one. 'No.'

'Bene.' He stood and held out his hand. 'Come.'

Her excitement ratcheted another notch, but she paused as she stood. 'The children…'

His fingers tightened around hers. 'Emily has everything in hand.'

Romeo led his wife to the master suite and shut the door behind them.

Surprise or not, he would've found a way to bring her here at the first opportunity. Because he couldn't get enough of her. Of her love, her devotion to him, to their family. Of everything.

He pulled her bikini-clad body close now and exhaled with happiness when her arms slid around his neck.

'I love you.' She sighed against him.

He shuddered hard, those three words never ceasing to move him. *'Ti amo anch'io,'* he replied gruffly. 'I'm so thankful you made that journey to Palermo three years ago.'

'So am I, but I'd like to think you would've found your way to me sooner or later. You just needed to put your ghosts to rest.'

He nodded. The ghosts *had* finally been slain. Lorenzo Carmine had been found guilty of murder and jailed, never to breathe free air again. The rest of the *famiglia* had scattered to the wind, bringing an end to Agostino Fattore's poisoned legacy.

Romeo had resisted the urge to raze the Fattore mansion to the ground, instead renovating it with Maisie's help and donating it to the local orphanage.

From the trauma of his childhood and the bleak landscape he'd anticipated his future being, he was now submerged in love and happiness so profound, it scared him sometimes. Not enough that he would fail to hang on to it with both hands.

He pulled his wife closer. 'So, about my surprise?' he pressed as he tugged at the strings of her bikini.

Breathtaking blue eyes met his as she captured his hand, kissed his palm, then laid it gently over her stomach.

His heart stopped, then raced with pure bliss. 'Another baby?' he murmured in awe.

Maisie nodded, tears filling her eyes.

Dropping to his knees, he kissed her belly, and the miracle nestled within. *'Ciao, bella bambina,'* he whispered.

She smiled. 'You're so sure it's a girl this time?'

'I'm certain. She'll be as beautiful as her mother. And she will go a little way to balancing out the testosterone you find so challenging.'

She laughed as he scooped her up and tumbled her into bed.

Laughter ceased, and desire took over. They expressed their love in the gentle kisses and furnace-hot lovemaking.

A few hours later, they dressed and joined their children and the Giordanos around the large dinner table.

Their news was greeted with hugs and kisses, after which Zaccheo raised his glass.

'To family,' he toasted, glancing at every face around the table until finally resting lovingly on his wife. 'And to love.'

'*Sì*, to family,' Romeo echoed. Then his gaze found Maisie's. 'To my for ever,' he murmured for her ears alone.

* * * * *

You can read Zaccheo's story in
A MARRIAGE FIT FOR A SINNER
Available now!

'You feel naked?' Talos asked evenly.

He, more than anyone, knew how the imagination could run amok—how the fear of the unknown could be so much worse than reality. He also knew how he could help Amalie take the first step to overcome it.

'Yes,' she whispered.

The strange distance Amalie had seen settle over him dissipated. His attention on her was focused and strong.

'Then there is only one solution. You must *be* naked.'

'What…?'

But her solitary word hardly made it past her vocal cords. Talos had leant forward and pulled his shoes and socks off.

What was he doing?

His hands went to his shirt. Before she could comprehend what she was seeing, he'd deftly undone all the buttons.

'What are you doing?'

He got to his feet.

If she hadn't already pressed herself against the wall she would have taken a step back. She would have turned and run.

But there was nowhere for her to run *to*—not without getting past him first.

TALOS CLAIMS
HIS VIRGIN

BY
MICHELLE SMART

Published in Great Britain 2015
by Mills & Boon, an imprint of Harlequin (UK) Limited,
Eton House, 18-24 Paradise Road, Richmond, Surrey, TW9 1SR

© 2015 Michelle Smart

ISBN: 978-0-263-25090-9

Harlequin (UK) Limited's policy is to use papers that are natural,
renewable and recyclable products and made from wood grown in
sustainable forests. The logging and manufacturing processes conform
to the legal environmental regulations of the country of origin.

Printed and bound in Spain
by CPI, Barcelona

Michelle Smart's love affair with books started when she was a baby, when she would cuddle them in her cot. A voracious reader of all genres, she found her love of romance established when she stumbled across her first Mills & Boon book at the age of twelve. She's been reading (and writing) them ever since. Michelle lives in Northamptonshire with her husband and two young Smarties.

Books by Michelle Smart

Mills & Boon Modern Romance

The Russian's Ultimatum
The Rings That Bind
The Perfect Cazorla Wife

Society Weddings

The Greek's Pregnant Bride

The Irresistible Sicilians

What a Sicilian Husband Wants
The Sicilian's Unexpected Duty
Taming the Notorious Sicilian

Visit the Author Profile page
at millsandboon.co.uk for more titles.

This book is dedicated to Amalie,
who's been on this journey with me every step of the way.
xxx

CHAPTER ONE

TALOS KALLIAKIS DIPPED his head and rubbed the nape of his neck. The consultant's words had cut through to his marrow.

Looking back up to stare at his two brothers, he read the sorrow on their faces.

Astraeus Kalliakis—the King of Agon, their grandfather—was dying.

Helios, the eldest of the three brothers and heir to the throne, folded his arms and took a visible deep breath before breaking the silence. 'We need to bring the Jubilee celebrations forward.'

The whole of Agon was gearing up to celebrate Astraeus's fifty years on the throne. Everything was planned for the end of summer, six months away. The consultant oncologist had said in no uncertain terms he wouldn't last that long.

Talos cleared his throat before speaking. His vocal cords had never felt so raw. 'I suggest we concentrate on the Jubilee Gala and cancel the rest of the celebrations—they're all superfluous. Let's make the gala a true celebration of his life.'

'Agreed,' said Theseus, the middle brother, nodding. 'We should set the date for April—three months from now. It will be a push, but between us and the courtiers we can do it and do it well.'

Any later and there was every possibility their grandfather would not be there for it. Two months of intense chemotherapy would buy him time and shrink the tumours riddling his organs. But they would not cure him. It was too late for that.

Two months later

Talos Kalliakis headed through the back of the theatre that housed the Orchestre National de Paris, noting the faded, peeling wallpaper, the threadbare carpet that had to be older than his thirty-three years, the water-stained ceiling... No wonder the building was on the verge of being condemned. Of all the orchestral homes he'd visited in the past two months, the facilities here were by far the worst.

But he wasn't here for the facilities. He'd come here on a whim, when he'd been left disappointed by the violinists from all of France's other major orchestras, as he'd been left underwhelmed by those from the major orchestras of Greece, Italy, Spain and England.

Time was running out.

What he had assumed would be a simple task had turned into a marathon of endurance.

All he wanted to find was that one special musician, someone who could stroke a bow over the bridge of their violin and make his heart soar the way his grandmother had when she'd been alive. He would never claim to have a musical ear, but he was certain that when he heard it he would know.

The chosen violinist would be rewarded with the honour of playing his grandmother's final composition, accompanied by his or her own orchestra, at his grandfather's Jubilee Gala.

At that moment approximately a dozen Orchestre National de Paris violinists were lining up, ready to audition for him.

He just wanted it to be over.

The weak, impatient part of himself told him to settle

on *anyone*. Everyone who had auditioned for him thus far had been professional, note-perfect, the sounds coming from their wooden instruments a delight to anyone's ear. But they hadn't been a delight to his heart, and for once in his life he knew he had to select the right person based on his heart, not his head.

For his grandfather's Jubilee Gala he wouldn't—couldn't—accept anything or anyone but the best. His grandfather deserved no less. His grandmother's memory deserved no less.

Flanked by the orchestra directors, an assistant and his own translator, they turned single file down a particularly narrow corridor. It was like being in an indoor, dank version of the glorious maze in the Agon palace gardens.

The violinists were lined up backstage; the rest of the musicians sat in the auditorium. He would already be seated at the front of the auditorium himself if roadworks hadn't forced his driver to detour to the back of the theatre rather than drop him at the front.

His mind filled with the dozen other things he needed to be getting on with that he'd had to let slip these past two months. A qualified lawyer, he oversaw all sales, mergers and buyouts with regard to the business empire he'd forged with his two brothers. He didn't *always* use his legal skills to get his own way.

Theseus, the middle Kalliakis brother, had identified an internet start-up seeking investment. If projections were correct, they would quadruple their investment in less than two months. Talos, though, had suspicions about the owners...

His thoughts about unscrupulous techies were cut away when a faint sound drifted out of a door to his left.

He paused, raising a hand in a request for silence.

His ears strained and he rested his head against the door.

There it was.

The only piece of classical music he knew by name.

A lump formed in his throat—a lump that grew with each passing beat.

Wanting to hear more clearly, but not wanting to disturb the violinist, he turned the handle carefully and pressed the door open.

An inch was enough to bring the solemn yet haunting music to life.

His chest filled, bittersweet memories engulfing him.

He'd been seven years old when his parents had died. The nights that had followed, before his brothers had been flown back from their English boarding school—he'd been only a year away from joining them there—had left him inconsolable.

Queen Rhea Kalliakis, the grandmother he'd adored, had soothed him the only way she knew how. She'd come into his room, sat on the edge of his bed and played the 'Méditation' from Jules Massenet's *Thaïs*.

He hadn't thought about this particular piece of music for over twenty-five years.

The tempo was different from the way his grandmother had played it, slower, but the effect was the same. Painful and yet soothing, like balm on a wound, seeping through his skin to heal him from the inside out.

This one had it—the special, elusive *it*.

'That is the one,' he said, addressing the orchestra directors collectively. His translator made the translation in French for them.

The sharp-faced woman to his left looked at him with a searching expression, as if judging whether he was serious, until her eyes lit up and, in her excitement, she flung the door open.

There, in the corner of the room, her violin still under her chin but her bow flailing in her right hand, stood a tall, lithe girl—woman. She had the distinct look of a rabbit caught in the headlights of a speeding car.

* * *

It was those eyes.

She had never seen anything like them before, nor such intensity.

The way they had fixed on her... Like lasers. Trapping her.

Amalie shivered to think of them.

She shivered again when she stepped out of the theatre exit and into the slushy car park. Keeping a firm grip on her violin case—she really needed to get the strap fixed—she tugged her red-and-grey striped beanie hat over her ears.

A long black car with darkened windows entered the car park and crunched its way through the snow to pull up beside her.

The back door opened and a giant got out.

It took a beat before her brain comprehended that it wasn't a giant but Talos Kalliakis.

Intense, striking eyes—were they brown?—fixed on her for the second time in an hour. The effect was as terrifying and giddying the second time around. More so.

When the door of the practice room had swung open and she'd seen all those faces staring at her she'd wanted to shrink into a corner. She hadn't signed up for the audition, but had been told to attend in case the orchestra as a whole was needed. She'd happily hidden away from the action in the room behind the auditorium; there, but not actually present.

Those eyes...

They had rested on her for so long she'd felt as if she'd been stuck in a time capsule. Then they had moved from her face and, without a *bonjour* or *au revoir*, he'd disappeared.

There hadn't been time for her to appreciate the sheer size of the man.

She was tall for a woman—five foot eight. But Talos

towered over her, a mass of height and muscle that not even his winter attire could hide.

Her mouth ran dry.

He wore his thick ebony hair slightly too long, messy at the front and curling over the collar of his long black trench coat. Dark stubble, also thick, abounded over his square jawline.

Despite the expensive cut of his clothing, right down to what were clearly handmade shoes, he had a feral air about him, as if he should be swinging through vines in a jungle whilst simultaneously banging his chest.

He looked dangerous. Wildly dangerous. The scar on his right eyebrow, which seemed to divide it into two, only added to this sense.

He also looked full of purpose.

He took the few steps towards her with long strides, an outstretched hand and an unsmiling face. 'Amalie Cartwright, it is a pleasure to meet you,' he said in perfect English.

How did he know she was bilingual?

God but the man was *enormous*. He had to be a good six and a half feet. Easily.

Swallowing frantically to moisten her mouth, Amalie switched her violin case to her left hand and extended her right to him. It was immediately engulfed in his strong, darkly bronzed hand. It was like being consumed by a giant paw. Even through the wool of her gloves she could feel the heat from his uncovered hand.

'Monsieur Kalliakis,' she murmured in response.

She tugged her hand free and hugged it around her violin case.

'I require your attention. Please, get in the car,' he said.

I require your attention? If she hadn't been so unsettled by him and the deepness of his voice—a low bass both throaty and rich that matched his appearance perfectly— she would have been tempted to laugh at his formality.

With a start she remembered he was a prince. Royalty. Should she curtsey or something? He'd disappeared from the practice room before they could be formally introduced.

She cleared her throat and took a tiny step back. 'My apologies, *monsieur*, but I don't believe there is anything for us to discuss.'

'I assure you there is. Get in the car. It is too cold to have this discussion out here.'

He spoke as only a man used to throwing his weight around could.

'Is this about the solo? I did explain to your assistant earlier that I have a prior engagement for the gala weekend and won't be able to attend. My apologies if the message never reached you.'

The assistant, a middle-aged man with an air of implacability about him, had been unable to hide his shock when she'd said she couldn't do it. The orchestra directors had simply stared at her with pleading eyes.

'The message did reach me—which is why I turned back from the airport and returned here, so I could discuss the matter with you directly.'

His displeasure was obvious, as if it were *her* fault his plans had been ruined.

'You will need to cancel your engagement. I wish for you to play at my grandfather's gala.'

'I wish I could as well,' she lied. A lifetime of dealing with forceful personalities had prepared her well for this moment. No personality came more forceful than her mother's. 'But, no. It is not something I can get out of.'

His brow furrowed in the manner of someone who had never had the word *no* uttered within his earshot. 'You *do* realise who my grandfather is and what a huge opportunity this is for your career?'

'Yes, he is the King of Agon—and I do understand what a great honour it is to be selected to play for him—'

'*And* the majority of the world's great statesmen who will be there—'

'But there are many other violinists in this orchestra,' she continued, speaking over him as if he had not just interrupted. 'If you audition them, as you had planned, you will find most are far more talented than me.'

Of *course* she knew what a huge event the gala was going to be. Her fellow musicians had spoken about little else for weeks. Every orchestra in Europe had been alerted to the fact that Prince Talos Kalliakis was searching for a solo violinist. When it had been confirmed yesterday that he was coming to audition the violinists at the Orchestre National de Paris there had been an immediate mass exodus as every female musician in the orchestra had headed to Paris's beauty parlours for highlights and waxing and all other manner of preening.

The three Princes of Agon were considered Europe's most eligible bachelors. *And* the most handsome.

Amalie had known she wouldn't audition, so hadn't bothered to join the exodus.

If she'd known for a second that Talos had been listening at the door to her practice she would have hit as many bum notes as she could without sounding like a screeching cat.

There was no way—*no way in the world*—she could stand on the stage at the Jubilee Gala and play for the world. No way. She couldn't. The mere thought of it was enough to bring her out in a cold sweat.

The chill of the wind was picking up. She scrunched her toes inside her cold boots, which were getting wetter by the second as the icy snow seeped through the tiny seams and spread to her socks. The back of Talos's car looked very snug and warm. Not that she would find out for herself. The chill in his eyes perfectly matched the weather whipping around them.

'Excuse me, *monsieur*, but I need to go home. We have

a concert tonight and I have to be back here in a few hours. Good luck finding your soloist.'

The hardness of his features softened by the slightest of margins, but his eyes—she'd been right, they *were* brown: a light, almost transparent brown, with the blackest of rims—remained hard.

'We will talk again on Monday, *despinis*. Until then I suggest you think hard about what you are giving up by refusing to take the solo.'

'Monday is our day off. I will be in on Tuesday, if you wish to speak to me then, but there will be nothing for us to talk about.'

He inclined his head. 'We shall see. Oh—and when we next meet you may address me by my formal title: Your Highness.'

This time her lips tugged into a smile—one she had no control over. 'But, *monsieur*, this is France. A republic. Even when we had a royal family, male heirs to the throne were addressed by the title of "Monsieur", so I am addressing you correctly. And I feel I should remind you of what happened to those who boasted of having royal blood—they had their heads chopped off.'

Amalie took her seat on the stage, in the second row from the back, nicely encased amongst the orchestra's other second violins. Exactly where she liked to be. Hidden from the spotlight.

While she waited for Sebastien Cassel, their guest conductor, to make his indication for them to start she felt a prickling on her skin.

Casting her eyes out into the auditorium, she saw the projected ticket sales had been correct. She doubted they were even at half capacity.

How much longer could this go on?

Paris was a city of culture. It had accommodated and celebrated its orchestras for centuries. But the other orchestras weren't housed in a flea pit like the Théâtre de la Musique; a glorified music hall. Once, it had been full of pomp and glory. Years of neglect and underinvestment had left it teetering perilously, almost into the red.

A large figure in the stalls to her right, in the most expensive seats in the house, made her blink and look twice. Even as she squinted to focus more clearly the thumping of her heart told her who the figure was and explained the prickling sensation on her skin.

Immediately her thoughts flickered to Prince Talos. There was something about that man and the danger he exuded that made her want to run faster than if a thousand spotlights had been aimed at her. His breathtaking physical power, that gorgeous face with the scar slashing through the eyebrow, the voice that had made her blood thicken into treacle…

Juliette, the violinist she sat next to, dug a sharp elbow into her side.

Sebastien was peering at them, his baton raised.

Amalie forced her eyes to the score before her and positioned herself, praying for her fingers to work.

Being at the back of the eighty-strong number of musicians usually made her feel invisible—just another head in the crowd, with the spotlight well and truly away from her. She couldn't bear having the spotlight pointed at her, had actively avoided it since the age of twelve. More than that: she had cowered from it.

She couldn't see him clearly—indeed, she didn't even know for certain that it *was* him sitting in the stalls—but she couldn't shake the feeling that someone in the audience had their eyes fixed firmly on *her*.

Talos watched the evening unfold. The orchestra was a professional unit and played with a panache even the most musically illiterate could appreciate.

But he wasn't there to listen.

Once the concert had finished he had a meeting with the owner of this ramshackle building.

He'd originally planned to take his jet back to Agon and visit his grandfather, relieved that his two-month search for a violinist was over. Amalie Cartwright's belligerence had put paid to that.

Looking at her now, the fingers of her left hand flying over the strings of her violin, he could not believe her rudeness. Her thin, pretty face, with a sprinkling of freckles over the bridge of her straight nose, gave the illusion of someone dainty, fragile, an image compounded by a form so slender one could be forgiven for worrying about her being blown over in a breeze. She had the elegance so many Parisian women came by with seemingly no effort. He'd seen that earlier, even when her rich brown hair had been hidden under the hat she'd worn to keep the chill in the air at bay.

But looks could be deceiving.

She'd dismissed performing the solo at his grandfather's gala and, by extension, had insulted the Kalliakis name. And her jibe about the French royal family having their heads removed had been a step too far.

Amalie Cartwright *would* take the solo. He would make sure of it.

And what Talos Kalliakis wanted, he got. Always.

CHAPTER TWO

AMALIE BURIED HER HEAD under the pillow and ignored the ringing of her doorbell. She wasn't expecting any visitors or a delivery. Her French mother wouldn't dream of turning up unannounced so early in the morning—anything earlier than midday she considered to be the middle of the night—and her English father was on tour in South America. Whoever it was could come back another time.

Whoever it was clearly had no intention of coming back another time.

The ringing continued, now accompanied by the banging of fists.

Cursing in English and French, she scrambled out of bed, shrugged a thick robe over her pyjama-clad body and, still cursing, hurried down the stairs to open the front door.

'Good morning, *despinis.*'

And with those words Talos Kalliakis brushed past her and entered her home.

'What the…? Excuse me—you can't just let yourself in,' she said, rushing after him while he swept through her narrow house as if he owned it.

'I told you I would be speaking with you today.'

His tone was neutral, as if he were oblivious to her natural shock and anger.

'And I told *you* this is my day off. I would like you to leave.'

He stepped into the kitchen. 'After we have spoken.'

To reiterate his point he set his briefcase on the floor, removed his long black trench coat, which he placed on the back of a chair at her small kitchen table, and sat himself down.

'What are you doing? I didn't invite you in—if you want to speak to me you will have to wait until tomorrow.'

He waved a dismissive hand. 'I will take ten minutes of your time and then I will leave. What we need to discuss will not take long.'

Amalie bit into her cheek and forced her mind to calm. Panicked thinking would not help. 'This is my home and you are trespassing. Leave now or I will call the police.'

He didn't need to know that her mobile phone was currently atop her bedside table.

'Call them.' He shrugged his huge shoulders, the linen of his black shirt rippling with the movement. 'By the time they get here we will have concluded our conversation.'

She eyed him warily, afraid to blink, and rubbed her hands up her arms, backing away, trapping herself against the wall. What could she use as a weapon?

This man was a stranger and the most physically imposing man she had met in her life. The scar that slashed through his eyebrow only compounded the danger he oozed. If he were to…

She wouldn't be able to defend herself using her own strength. It would be like a field mouse fighting a panther.

His top lip curved with distaste. 'You have no need to worry for your safety—I am not an animal. I am here to talk, not to assault you.'

Would the panther *tell* the field mouse he intended to eat her? Of course not. He would insist it was the last thing on his mind and then, when the little field mouse got close enough…*snap!*

Staring into his striking eyes, she saw that, although cold, they contained no threat. A tiny fraction of her fear vanished.

This man would not harm her. Not physically, at any rate.

She dropped her gaze and rubbed her eyes, which had become sore from all that non-blinking.

'Okay. Ten minutes. But you should have called first. You didn't have to barge your way into my home when I was still sleeping.'

An awareness crept through her bones. While he was freshly showered, shaved—minimal stubble today—and dressed, *she* was in old cotton pyjamas and a dressing gown, and suffering from a severe case of bed hair. Talk about putting her at an immediate disadvantage.

He looked at his watch. 'It is ten a.m. A reasonable time to call on someone on a Monday morning.'

To her utter mortification, she could feel her skin heat. It might not be his problem that she'd had hardly any sleep, but it was certainly his fault.

No matter how hard she'd tried to block him from her mind, every time she'd closed her eyes his face had swum into her vision. Two nights of his arrogant face—there, right behind her eyelids. His arrogant, *handsome* face. Shockingly, devilishly handsome.

'This is my day off, *monsieur*. How I choose to spend it is my business.' Her mouth had run so dry her words came out as a croak. 'I need a coffee.'

'I take mine black.'

She didn't answer, just stepped to the other side of the kitchen and pressed the button on the coffee machine she had set before she went to bed. It kicked into action.

'Have you thought any more about the solo?' he asked as she removed two mugs from the mug tree.

'I told you—there's nothing for me to think about. I'm busy that weekend.' She heaped a spoonful of sugar into one of the mugs.

'I was afraid that would be your answer.'

His tone was akin to a teacher disappointed with his star pupil's exam results. Something about his tone made the hairs on her arms rise in warning.

Water started to drip through the filter and into the pot, drip by hot drip, the aroma of fresh coffee filling the air.

'I am going to appeal to your better nature,' Talos said, staring at Amalie, whose attention was still held by the slowly falling coffee.

She turned her head a touch. 'Oh?'

'My grandmother was a composer and musician.'

A short pause. 'Rhea Kalliakis...'

'You have heard of her?'

'I doubt there's a violinist alive who hasn't. She composed the most beautiful pieces.'

A sharp pang ran through him to know that this woman appreciated his grandmother's talents. Amalie couldn't know it, but her simple appreciation only served to harden his resolve that she was the perfect musician for the role. She was the *only* musician.

'She completed her final composition two days before her death.'

She turned from the coffee pot to face him.

Amalie Cartwright had the most beautiful almond-shaped eyes, he noted, not for the first time. The colour reminded him of the green sapphire ring his mother had worn.

That ring now lay in the Agon palace safe, where it had rested for the past twenty-six years, waiting for the day when Helios selected a suitable bride to take guardianship of it. After their grandfather's diagnosis, that day would be coming much sooner than Helios had wanted or expected. Helios needed to marry and produce an heir.

The last time Talos had seen the ring his mother had been fighting off his father. Two hours later the pair of them had been dead.

He cast his mind away from that cataclysmic night and back to the present. Back to Amalie Cartwright—the one person who could do justice to Rhea Kalliakis's final composition and with it, bring comfort to a dying man. A dying *king*.

'Is that the piece you wish to have played at your grand-father's gala?'

'Yes. In the five years since her death we have kept the score secure and allowed no one to play it. Now we—my brothers and I—believe it is the right time for the world to hear it. And at what better occasion than my grandfa-ther's Jubilee Gala? I believe *you* are the person to play it.'

He deliberately made no mention of his grandfather's diagnosis. No news of his condition had been released to the public at large and nor would it be until after the gala—by decree from King Astraeus, his grandfather, himself.

Amalie poured the freshly brewed coffee into the mugs, added milk to her own, then brought them to the table and took the seat opposite him.

'I think it is a wonderful thing you are doing,' she said, speaking in measured tones. 'There isn't another violin-ist alive who wouldn't be honoured to be called upon to do it. But I am sorry, *monsieur*, that person cannot be me.'

'Why not?'

'I told you. I have a prior engagement.'

He fixed her with his stare. 'I will double the appear-ance fee. Twenty thousand euros.'

'No.'

'Fifty thousand. And that's my final offer.'

'No.'

Talos knew his stare could be intimidating, more so than his sheer physicality. He'd performed this stare numerous times in front of a mirror, looking to see what it was that others saw, but had never recognised what it might be. Whatever it was, one throw of that look was enough to en-sure he got his own way. The only people immune to it were his brothers and grandparents. Indeed, whenever his grand-mother had seen him 'pull that face', as she had referred to it, she'd clipped his ear—but only hard enough to sting.

He missed her every day.

But apart from those members of his family he had never met anyone immune to his stare. Until now.

From Amalie there was not so much as a flicker, just a shake of her head and her long hair, which was in dire need of a good brush, falling into her eyes. She swiped it away.

Talos sighed, shook his head regretfully and rubbed his chin, making a great show of disappointment.

Amalie cradled her mug and took a sip of the hot coffee, willing her nerves to stay hidden from his piercing gaze.

All her life she'd had to deal with huge personalities and even huger egos. It had taught her the importance of keeping her emotions tucked away. If the enemy—and at that very moment Talos *was* an enemy to her, she could feel it—detected any weakness then they would pounce. Never make it easy for them. Never give them the advantage.

She had never found it so hard to remain passive. *Never.* Not since she'd been twelve and the nerves she'd fought so hard to contain had taken control of her. The fear and humiliation she'd experienced on that occasion felt as strong today as they had then.

But there was something about this man that *did* things to her; to her mind, to her senses. Inside her belly, a cauldron bubbled.

Talos reached for his briefcase, and for one tiny moment she thought she had won and that he would leave. Except then he placed it on the table and opened it.

'I have tried appealing to your better nature. I have tried appealing to your greed. I have given you numerous chances to accept the easy way…' He removed a sheaf of papers and held them up for her to see. 'These are the deeds to the Théâtre de la Musique. You are welcome to read through them. You will see they confirm me as the new owner.'

Stunned into silence, all Amalie could do was shake her head.

'Would you like to read them?'

She continued shaking her head, staring from the documents in his hand to his unsmiling face.

'How is it possible?' she whispered, trying to comprehend what this could mean—for her, for the orchestra…

'I put my offer in on Saturday evening. The purchase was completed an hour ago.'

'But how is this possible?' she repeated. 'This is *France*. The home of bureaucracy and red tape.'

'Money and power talk.'

He placed the deeds back in his briefcase and leaned forward, bringing his face to within inches of hers. Any closer and she'd be able to feel his breath on her face. 'I am a prince. I have money—a lot of it—and I have power. A lot of it. You would be wise to remember that.'

Then he leant back in his chair and drank his coffee, all the while his laser eyes burned into her.

She squeezed her mug, suddenly terrified to lose her grip on it. The implications were forming an orderly queue in her brain.

'Now I am the owner of the theatre I am wondering what I will do with the building and the orchestra it houses. You see, the previous owner was so struck with greed at the amount I offered he made no stipulations for the sale…' He drained the last of his coffee and pushed his mug away so it rested against hers. 'Take the solo, *despinis*, and I will throw so much money at the theatre the crowds will come flocking back and your orchestra will be the toast of Paris. Refuse and I will turn it into a hotel.'

The jostling in her brain stopped. The implications came loud and clear, with clanging bells and ringing sirens.

'You're blackmailing me,' she said starkly. 'You're actually trying to *blackmail* me.'

He shrugged indifferently and pushed his chair back. 'Call it what you will.'

'I call it blackmail. And blackmail is illegal.'

'Tell it to the police.' He displayed his white teeth. 'However, before you call them I should advise you that I have diplomatic immunity.'

'That is *low*.'

'I can and will go even lower. You see, little songbird, I have the power to ensure you never play the violin professionally again. I can blacken your name, and the names of all those you play with, so that no orchestra—not even a provincial amateur one—would touch you.'

The bubbling cauldron moved from her belly to her head, her brain feeling as if it were boiling with poison. Never had she felt such hate towards another human.

'Get out of my house.'

'Worry not, little songbird, I am ready to leave now.' He looked at his watch. 'I will return in six hours. You can give me your considered answer then.'

Her *considered answer*?

He was threatening to destroy her career, and the careers of her friends and colleagues, and he wanted her *considered answer*?

The cauldron toppled, sending a surge of fire pulsing through her, bringing her to her feet and to his side. Even with him seated and Amalie on her feet the physical imbalance between them was all too apparent. Fear and anger collided in her and she grabbed his arm, as if the force of her will could drag him to his feet and out of her home.

'I said get out of my house!' she shouted, pulling at him, uncaring that holding his arm was akin to holding a steel boulder. 'I don't care if you're a stupid prince *or* about your stupid diplomatic immunity—get *out*!'

With reflexes that would put a cat to shame, Talos yanked her wrists together and pinned the pair of them inside one of his giant hands.

'So you *do* have fire under that pale skin,' he murmured. 'I did wonder.'

'Let go of me right now,' she demanded, panic puls-

ing through her which only increased when he twisted—
pirouetted—her around to sit on his lap, keeping a firm
hold on her wrists.

Instinct made her lift her leg and kick back at him. The
heel of her bare foot connected with his shin, the pain lancing through her immediate.

For Talos, she might as well have been a toddler doing
their worst. He gave absolutely no reaction to her kick other
than to wrap his free arm around her waist to secure her to
him, ensnaring her even more effectively.

'I feel that hurt you more than it did me,' he said, holding her trapped hands up to examine them. 'Such elegant
fingers… Now, are you going to be a good girl and behave
yourself if I let you go?'

'If you call me a good girl again I'll…'

'What? Kick me again?'

She bucked, but it was a futile gesture. It was like being
trapped in steel.

Except it wasn't steel. It was solid man. And his fingers
were digging not unpleasantly into the side of her waist.

'You're scaring me.' It was part truth. *Something* was
scaring her. Terrifying her.

'I know, and I apologise. I will let you go when you assure me that you have your emotions under control and
will not lash out at me again.'

Strangely, the deep, rough timbre of his voice had the
desired effect, calming her enough to stop her struggling
against him.

Clamping her lips together, she forced herself to breathe,
and as she did so she inhaled a darkly masculine scent.
His scent.

She swallowed the moisture that filled her mouth, suddenly aware of his breath, hot in her hair. Every one of her
senses was heightened.

She couldn't choke another breath in. Her heart was
beating so hard she could hear it echo in her ears. And in

the silence that ensued she felt Talos's huge form stiffen too, from the strong thighs she was sat upon to the giant hands holding her in their snare.

She could no longer hear or feel his breath.

The only sound in her ears was the thrumming of her blood.

And then he released her hands and pushed her to her feet.

On legs that trembled, she shot to the other side of the kitchen.

Now she could breathe, but her breaths were ragged, her chest hurting with the exertion.

For his part, Talos calmly shrugged his muscular arms into his trench coat, wrapped his navy scarf around his neck and clasped his briefcase.

'Six hours, *despinis*. I will respect your decision—but know that should your answer continue to be negative the consequences will be real and immediate.'

Amalie's phone vibrated.

She pounced on it. *'Maman?'*

'Chérie, I have found out some things.'

That was typical of her mother—getting straight to the point. There didn't exist a sliver of silence that her mother's voice couldn't fill.

'I could not reach Pierre directly.'

She sounded put out—as if Pierre Gaskin should have been holding on to his phone on the remote chance that Colette Barthez, the most famous classical singer in the world, deigned to call him.

'But I spoke to his charming assistant, who told me he arrived late to the office this morning, gave every employee five hundred euros and said he was taking the next three months off. He was last seen setting his satnav to take him to Charles de Gaulle,' she added, referring to France's largest airport.

'So it looks as if he *has* sold it, then,' Amalie murmured.

Only two weeks ago Pierre Gaskin—the owner or, as she now firmly believed, the *former* owner of the Théâtre de la Musique—had been struggling to pay the heating bill for the place.

'It looks that way, *chérie*. So tell me,' her mother went on, '*why* has Prince Talos brought the theatre? I didn't know he was a patron of the arts.'

'No idea,' she answered, her skin prickling at the mention of his name. She kneaded her brow, aware that this must be something like her tenth lie of the weekend.

What a mess.

She hadn't told her mother anything of what had happened that weekend—she didn't have the strength to handle *her* reaction on top of everything else—had only asked her to use her contacts to see if there was any truth that the theatre had been sold to Talos Kalliakis.

Now she had the answer.

Talos hadn't been bluffing. But then she hadn't really thought he had been, had turned to her mother only out of a futile sense of having to do *something* rather than any real hope.

'I knew his father, Prince Lelantos…'

Her mother's voice took on a dreamlike quality. It was a sound Amalie recognised, having been her mother's confidante of the heart since the age of twelve.

'I sang for him once. He was such a…' she scrambled for the right word '…*man*!'

'*Maman*, I need to go now.'

'Of course, *chérie*. If you meet Prince Talos again, send him my regards.'

'I will.'

Turning her phone off and placing it on the table, Amalie drew her hands down her face.

There was only one thing left that she could do. She was going to have to tell Talos Kalliakis the truth.

CHAPTER THREE

WHEN TALOS PUNCHED his finger to the bell of Amalie's front door he knew she must have been waiting for him. She pulled the door open before his hand was back by his side.

She stared at him impassively, as if what had occurred between them earlier had never happened. As if she hadn't lost her calm veneer.

Without a word being exchanged, he followed her into the kitchen.

On the table lay a tray of pastries and two plates. A pot of coffee had just finished percolating. Amalie was dressed for her part, having donned a pair of black jeans that hugged her slender frame and a silver scoop-necked top. Her straight dark hair had been brushed back into a loose bun at the nape of her slender neck. She wore no make-up, and the freckles across her nose were vivid in the harsh light beaming from above them.

It was clear to him that she had seen reason. And why on earth would she not? She was a professional musician. He shouldn't have to resort to blackmail.

Time was running out. For the gala. For his grandfather. The chemotherapy he was undergoing had weakened him badly. There were days when he couldn't leave his bed— barely had the strength to retch into a bucket. Other days Talos found him in good spirits, happy to sit outside and enjoy the Agon sunshine in the sprawling palace gardens.

Talos remembered again that he had planned to return home after the auditions on Saturday and spend the rest of the weekend with his grandfather. Instead he'd been compelled to force through—and quickly—the purchase of that awful Parisian building. And for what? Because the only professional violinist he'd found capable of doing justice to his grandmother's final composition was playing hardball.

No one played hardball with Talos Kalliakis. *No one.* To find this slender thing standing up to him…

But she had seen reason. That was all that mattered now.

He allowed himself a smile at his victory, and sat in the chair he'd vacated only six hours before.

Defeat had never crossed his mind. It was regrettable that he'd had to resort to blackmail to get his own way but time was of the essence. The Jubilee was only a month away. There was still time for her to learn the piece to performance standard and for her orchestra to learn the accompanying music. He wanted them note-perfect before they took to the palace stage.

Amalie's arm brushed against his as she placed a mug in front of him. He found his attention caught by her fingers, as it had been earlier, when he'd had them trapped in his hand. It was the nails at the end of those long, elegant fingers that had really struck him. The nails of her left hand were short and blunt. The nails of her right hand were much longer and shapely. He'd puzzled over those nails all day… over what they reminded him of.

He'd also puzzled over the reaction that had swept through him when he'd pinned her to his lap after her anger had rushed to the surface.

Talos was a man who enjoyed the company of beautiful women. And beautiful women liked *him*. Women he didn't know would catch his eye and hold it for a beat too long. When they learned who he was their gazes would stay fixed, suggestion and invitation ringing from them.

Never had he met a woman who so obviously disliked him. Never had he met anyone—man or woman—outside his immediate family who would deny him anything he wanted.

Amalie Cartwright was a pretty woman in her own unique way. The defiant attitude she'd displayed towards him infuriated and intrigued him in equal measure.

What, he wondered, would it be like to light the fire he'd glimpsed that morning in a more intimate setting?

What would it take to twist that fire and anger into passion?

He had felt the shift in her when her whole body had stilled and her breath had shortened and then stopped. The same time his own breath had stopped. One moment he'd been staring at her fingers with bemusement, the next his body had been filled with an awareness so strong it had knocked the air out of him.

He'd never experienced a reaction like it.

And now, watching her take the same seat as she had that morning, he could feel that awareness stirring within him again.

The following month held infinite possibilities...

'Monsieur,' she said once she had settled herself down and placed her green gaze on him, 'earlier you appealed to my better nature—'

'Which you disregarded,' he interjected.

She bowed her head in acknowledgement. 'I had my reasons, which I am going to share with you in the hope of appealing to *your* better nature.'

He regarded her carefully but kept silent, waiting for her to speak her mind. Surely she wasn't trying another angle to turn the solo down?

'I'm sorry but I lied to you—I do not have a prior engagement on the gala weekend.' She gnawed on her bottom lip before continuing. 'I suffer from stage fright.'

The idea was so ludicrous Talos shook his head in disbelief and laughed.

'You?' he said, not bothering to hide his incredulity. 'You—the daughter of Colette Barthez and Julian Cartwright—suffer from *stage fright*?'

'You know who I am?'

'I know exactly who you are.' He folded his arms, his brief, incredulous mirth evaporating. 'I made it my business to know.'

He caught a flash of truculence in those green eyes, the first sign that the calm façade she wore was nothing but a front.

'Your French mother is the most successful mezzo-soprano in the world. I admit I hadn't heard of your father before today, but I understand he is a famous English violinist. I also learned that your father once played at Carnegie Hall with my grandmother, when he was first establishing himself.'

He leaned forward to rest his chin on his hands.

'*You* were a noted child prodigy until the age of twelve, when your parents removed you from the spotlight so you could concentrate on your education. You became a professional musician at the age of twenty, when you joined the ranks of the Orchestre National de Paris as a second violin—a position you still hold five years on.'

She shrugged, but her face remained taut. 'What you have described is something any person with access to the internet could find out in thirty seconds. My parents didn't remove me from the spotlight because of my education—that is what my mother told the press, because she couldn't bear the shame of having a daughter unable to perform in public.'

'If you are "unable to perform in public", how do you explain the fact that you *perform in public* at least once a week with your orchestra?'

'I'm a second violin. I sit at the back of the orchestra. We have an average of eighty musicians playing at any given performance. The audience's eyes are not on me but on the collective orchestra. It's two different things. If I play at your grandfather's gala everyone's eyes will be on *me* and I will freeze. It will bring humiliation to me, to my mother—and to your grandfather. Is that what you want? To have the world's eyes witness your star performer frozen on stage, unable to play a note?'

The only person who wouldn't be ashamed of her was her father. She might have referred to it as a joint decision by her parents, but in truth it had been her father who'd gone against her mother's wishes and pulled her out of the spotlight. He'd been the one to assure her that it was okay to play just for the love of the music, even if it was only in the privacy of her own bedroom.

Talos's eyes narrowed, a shrewd expression emanating from them. 'How do I know you aren't lying to me right now?'

'I…'

'By your own admission you lied about being busy on the gala weekend.'

'It was a lie of necessity.'

'No lie is necessary. If you can't handle eyes on you when you play, how were you able to join the orchestra in the first place?'

'It was a blind audition. Everyone who applied had to play behind a screen so there could be no bias. And, before you ask, of course I practise and rehearse amongst my colleagues, But that is a world away from standing up on a stage and feeling hundreds of eyes staring at you.'

He shook his head slowly, his light brown eyes unreadable. 'I am in two minds here. Either you are speaking the truth or you are telling another lie.'

'I am speaking the truth. You need to find another soloist.'

'I think not. Nerves and stage fright are things that can be overcome, but finding another soloist who can do justice to my grandmother's final composition is a different matter.'

Never mind that time had almost run out. He could spend the rest of his life searching and not find anyone whose playing touched him the way Amalie's had in those few minutes he had listened to her.

Talos had never settled for second best in his life and he wasn't about to start now.

'What do you know about my island?' he asked her.

She looked confused at the change of direction. 'Not much. It's near Crete, isn't it?'

'Crete is our nearest neighbour. Like the Cretans, we are descended from the Minoans. Throughout the centuries Agon has been attacked by the Romans, the Ottomans and the Venetians—to name a few. We repelled them all. Only the Venetians managed to occupy us, and just for a short period. My people, under the leadership of the warrior Ares Patakis, of whom I am a direct descendent, rose against the occupiers and expelled them from our land. No other nation has occupied our shores since. History tells our story. Agonites will not be oppressed or repressed. We will fight until our last breath for our freedom.'

He paused to take a sip of his coffee. He had to hand it to her: she had excellent taste.

'You are probably wondering why I am telling you all this,' he said.

'I *am* trying to understand the relevance,' she admitted thoughtfully.

'It is to give you an awareness of the stock that I, my family and our people come from. We are fighters. There isn't an Agonite alive who would back down in the face of adversity. Stage fright? Nerves? Those are issues to be fought and conquered. And with my help you *will* conquer them.'

Amalie could imagine it only too well. Talos Kalliakis ready for battle, stripped to nothing but iron battle gear, spear in hand. He would be at the front of any fight.

It was her bad fortune that he had chosen to fight *her*.

But her stage fright *wasn't* a fight. It was just a part of her, something she had long ago accepted.

Her life was nice and cosy. Simple. No drama, no histrionics. She refused to allow the tempestuousness of her childhood seep its way into her adult life.

'I have arranged with your directors for you to come to Agon in a couple of days and to stay until the gala. Your orchestra will start rehearsals immediately and fly out a week before the gala so you can rehearse with them.'

Her pledge to be amiable evaporated. 'Excuse me, but you've done what?'

'It will give you a month in Agon to acclimatise…'

'I don't need to acclimatise. Agon is hardly the middle of a desert.'

'It will also give you a month to prepare yourself perfectly for the solo,' he continued, ignoring her interruption, although his eyes flashed another warning at her. 'No distractions.'

'But…'

'Your stage fright is something that *will* be overcome,' he said, with all the assurance of a man who had never been struck with anything as weak as nerves. 'I will see to it personally.'

He stopped speaking, leaving a pause she knew she was supposed to fill, but all she could think was how badly she wanted to throw something at him, to curse this hateful man who was attempting to destroy the comfortable, quiet life she had made for herself away from the spotlight.

'*Despinis?*'

She looked up to find those laser eyes striking through her again, as if he could reach right in and see what she was thinking.

'Do you accept the solo?' His voice hardened to granite. 'Or do I have to make one hundred musicians redundant? Do I have to destroy one hundred careers, including your own? Have no doubt—I will do it. I will destroy you all.'

She closed her eyes and breathed deeply, trying to extinguish the panic clawing at her throat.

She believed him. This was no idle threat. He *could* destroy her career. She had no idea how he would do it, she knew only that he could.

If she didn't loathe him so much she would wonder why he was prepared to take such dark measures to get her agreement. As it was, she couldn't give a flying viola as to his reasons.

If she didn't comply he would take away the only thing she could do.

But how could she agree to do it? The last time she'd performed solo she'd been surrounded by her parents' arty friends—musicians, actors, writers, singers. She'd humiliated herself and her mother in front of every one of them. How could she stand on a stage with dignitaries and heads of state watching her and not be shredded by the same nerves? That was if she even made it on to the stage.

The one time she'd tried after the awful incident had left her hospitalised. And what she remembered most clearly about that dreadful time was her father's fury at her mother for forcing her. He'd accused her of selfishness and of using their only child as a toy.

A lump formed in Amalie's throat as she recalled them separating mere weeks later, her father gaining primary custody of her.

She was lucky, though. If times got really hard she knew she could rely on both her parents to bail her out. She would never go hungry. She would never lose her home. Her colleagues weren't all so fortunate. Not many of them were blessed with wealthy parents.

She thought of kindly Juliette, who was seven months pregnant with her third child. Of Louis, who only last week had booked a bank-breaking holiday with his family to Australia. Grumbling Giles, who moaned every month when his mortgage payment was taken from his account…

All those musicians, all those office workers…

All unaware that their jobs, security and reputations hung in the balance.

She stared at Talos, willing him to feel every ounce of her hate.

'Yes, I'll come. But the consequences are something *you* will have to live with.'

Amalie gazed out of the window and got her first glimpse of Agon. As the plane made its descent she stared transfixed as golden beaches emerged alongside swathes of green, high mountains and built-up areas of pristine white buildings... And then they touched down, bouncing along the runway before coming to a final smooth stop.

Keeping a firm grip on her violin, she followed her fellow business-class passengers out and down the metal stairs. After the slushy iciness of Paris in March, the temperate heat was a welcome delight.

From the economy section bounded excited children and frazzled parents, there to take advantage of the sunshine Agon was blessed with, where spring and summer came earlier than to its nearest neighbour, Crete. She hadn't considered that she would be going to an island famed as a holiday destination for families and historical buffs alike. In her head she'd thought of Agon as a prison—as dark and dangerous as the man who had summoned her there.

Amalie had travelled to over thirty countries in her life, but never had she been in an airport as fresh and welcoming as the one in Agon. Going through Arrivals was quick; her luggage arriving on the conveyor belt even quicker.

A man waited in the exit lounge, holding up her name on a specially laminated board. Polite introductions out of the way, he took the trolley holding her luggage from her and led the way out to a long, black car parked in what was clearly the prime space of the whole car park.

Everything was proceeding exactly as had been stated in the clipped email Talos's private secretary had sent to her the day before. It had contained a detailed itinerary, from the time a car would be collecting her from her house all the way through to her estimated time of arrival at the villa that would be her home for the next month.

As the chauffeur navigated the roads she was able to take further stock of the island. Other than expecting it to be as dangerous as the youngest of its princes, she'd had no preconceptions. She was glad. Talos Kalliakis might be a demon sent to her from Hades, but his island was stunning.

Mementoes of Agon's early Greek heritage were everywhere, from the architecture to the road signs in the same common language. But Agon was now a sovereign island, autonomous in its rule. The thing that struck her most starkly was how clean everything was, from the well-maintained roads to the buildings and homes they drove past. When they went past a harbour she craned her neck to look more closely at the rows of white yachts stationed there—some of them as large as cruise liners.

Soon they were away from the town and winding higher into the hills and mountains. Her mouth dropped open when she caught her first glimpse of the palace, standing proudly on a hill much in the same way as the ancient Greeks had built their most sacred monuments. Enormous and sprawling, it had a Middle Eastern flavour to it, as if it had been built for a great sultan centuries ago.

But it wasn't to the palace that she was headed. No sooner had it left her sight than the chauffeur slowed down, pausing while a wrought-iron gate inched open, then drove up to a villa so large it could have been a hotel. Up the drive he took them, and then round to the back of the villa's grounds, travelling for another mile until he came to a much smaller dwelling at the edge of the extensive villa's garden—a generously sized white stone cottage.

An elderly man, with a shock of white hair flapping in the breeze above a large bald spot, came out of the front door to greet them.

'Good evening, *despinis*,' he said warmly. 'I am Kostas.'

Explaining that he ran the main villa for His Highness Prince Talos, he showed her around the cottage that would be her home for the month. The small kitchen was well stocked and a daily delivery of fresh fruit, breads and dairy products would be brought to her. If she wished to eat her meals in the main villa she only had to pick up the phone and let them know; likewise if she wished to have meals delivered to the cottage.

'The villa has a gym, a swimming pool, and spa facilities you are welcome to use whenever you wish,' he said before he left. 'There are also a number of cars you can use if you wish to travel anywhere, or we can arrange for a driver to take you.'

So Talos didn't intend to keep her prisoner in the cottage? That was handy to know.

She'd envisaged him collecting her from the airport, locking her in a cold dungeon and refusing to let her out until she was note-perfect with his grandmother's composition and all her demons had been banished.

Thinking about it sent a tremor racing up her spine.

She wondered what great psychiatrist Talos would employ to 'fix' her. She would laugh if the whole thing didn't terrify her so much. Whoever he employed had better get a move on. She had exactly four weeks and two days until she had to stand on the stage for the King of Agon's Jubilee Gala. In those thirty days she had to learn an entirely new composition, her orchestra had to learn the accompanying score, and she had to overcome the nerves that had paralysed her for over half her lifetime.

CHAPTER FOUR

THE MORNING CAME, crisp and blue. After a quick shower Amalie donned her favourite black jeans and a plum shirt, then made herself a simple breakfast, which she took out to eat on her private veranda. As she ate yogurt and honey, and sipped at strong coffee—she'd been delighted to find a brand-new state-of-the-art coffee machine, with enough pods to last her a year—she relaxed into a wicker chair and let the cool breeze brush over her. After all the bustle of Paris it felt wonderful to simply *be*.

If she closed off her mind she could forget why she was there…pretend she was on some kind of holiday.

Her tranquillity didn't last long.

After going back inside to try another of the coffee-machine pods—this time opting for the mocha—she came back onto the veranda to find Talos sitting on her vacated chair, helping himself to the cubes of melon she'd cut up.

'Good morning, little songbird,' he said with a flash of straight white teeth.

Today he was dressed casually, in baggy khaki canvas trousers, black boots and a long-sleeved V-necked grey top. He was unshaven and his hair looked as if it had been tamed with little more than the palm of a hand. As she leaned over the table to place her mug down she caught his freshly showered scent.

'Is that for me?' he asked, nodding at the mug in her shaking hand.

She shrugged, affecting nonchalance at his unexpected appearance. 'If you don't mind sharing my germs.'

'I'm sure a beautiful woman like you doesn't have anything so nasty as germs.'

She raised a suspicious eyebrow, shivering as his deep bass voice reverberated through her skin, before turning back into the cottage, glad of an excuse to escape for a moment and gather herself. Placing a new pod in the machine, she willed her racing heart to still.

He'd startled her with his presence, that was all. She'd received an email from his private secretary the evening before, while eating the light evening meal she'd prepared for herself, stating that the score would be brought to her at the cottage mid-morning. There had been nothing mentioned about the Prince himself bothering to join her. Indeed, once she'd realised she wasn't staying in the palace she'd hoped not to see him again.

When she went back outside he was cradling the mug, an expression of distaste wrinkling his face. 'What *is* this?'

'Mocha.'

'It is disgusting.'

'Don't drink it, then.'

'I won't.' He placed it on the table and gave it a shove with his fingers to move it away from him. He nodded at her fresh cup. 'What's that one?'

'Mocha—to replace the one you kidnapped. If you want something different, the coffee machine's in the kitchen.' The contract she'd signed had said nothing about making coffee for him.

That evil contract...

She dragged her thoughts away before her brain could rage anew. If she allowed herself to fume over the unfairness, her wits would be dulled, and she already knew to her bitter cost that she needed her wits about her when dealing with this man.

As she sat herself in the vacant chair, unsubtly moving it away from his side, Talos reached for an apple from the plate of fruit she'd brought out with her. Removing a stumpy metal object from his trouser pocket, he pressed a button on the side and a blade at least five inches long unfolded. The snap it made jolted her.

Talos noticed her flinch. 'Does my knife bother you?'

'Not at all. Did you get that little thing when you were a Boy Scout?'

Her dismissive tone grated on him more than it should have. *She* grated on him more than she should.

'This little thing?' He swivelled the chair, narrowed his eyes and flicked his wrist. The knife sliced through the air, landing point-first in the cherry tree standing a good ten feet from them, embedding itself in the trunk.

He didn't bother hiding his satisfaction. 'That *little thing* was a present from my grandfather when I graduated from Sandhurst.'

'I'm impressed,' she said flatly. 'I always thought Sandhurst was for gentlemen.'

Was that yet *another* insult?

'Was there a reason you came to see me other than to massacre a defenceless tree?' she asked.

He got to his feet. 'I've brought the score to you.'

He strode to the cherry tree, gripped the handle of the knife and pulled it out. This knife was a badge of honour—the mark of becoming a man, a replacement for the Swiss Army penknife each Kalliakis prince had been given on his tenth birthday. There was an apple tree in the palace gardens whose trunk still bore the scars of the three young Princes' attempts at target practice two decades before.

Back at the table, aware of wary sapphire eyes watching his every movement, he wiped the blade on his trousers, then picked up his selected apple and proceeded to peel it, as had been his intention when he'd first removed the knife from his pocket. The trick was to peel it in one single movement before the white of the inside started to brown—a relic from his childhood, when his father would peel an apple before slicing it and eating the chunks, and something he in turn had learned from *his* father. Of course Talos's father hadn't lived long enough to see any of his sons master it.

Carrying a knife was a habit all the Kalliakis men shared. Talos had no idea what had compelled him to throw it at the tree.

Had he been trying to get a rise out of her?

Never had he been in the company of anyone, let alone a woman, to whom his presence was so clearly unwelcome. People wanted his company. They sought it, they yearned to keep it. No one treated him with indifference.

And yet this woman did.

Other than that spark of fire in her home, when he'd played his trump card, she'd remained cool and poised in all their dealings, her body language giving nothing away. Only now, as he pushed the large binder that contained the solo towards her, did she show any emotion, her eyes flickering, her breath sharpening.

'Is this it?' she asked, opening the binder to peer at what lay inside.

'You look as if you're afraid to touch it.'

'I've never held anything made by a royal hand.'

He studied her, curiosity driving through him. 'You look respectfully towards a sheet of music, yet show no respect towards me, a prince of this land.'

'Respect is earned, *monsieur*, and you have done nothing to earn mine.'

Why wasn't she scared of him?

'On this island our people respect the royal family. It comes as automatically as breathing.'

'Did you use brute force to gain it? Or do you prefer simple blackmail?'

'Five hundred years ago it was considered treason to show insolence towards a member of the Agon royal family.'

'If that law were still in force now I bet your subjects' numbers would be zero.'

'The law was brought in by the senate, out of gratitude to my family for keeping this island safe from our enemies. My ancestors were the ones to abolish it.'

'I bet your subjects partied long into the night when it was abolished.'

'Do not underestimate the people of this island, *despinis*,' he said, his ire rising at her flippant attitude. 'Agonites are not and never will be subjects. This is not a dictatorship. The Kalliakis family members remain the island's figure-heads by overwhelming popular consent. Our blood is their blood—their blood is our blood. They will celebrate my grandfather's Jubilee Gala with as much enthusiasm as if they were attending a party for their own grandfather.'

Her pale cheeks were tinged with a light pinkness. She swallowed. 'I didn't mean to insult your family, *monsieur*.'

He bowed his head in acceptance of her apology.

'Only you.'

'Only me?'

Her sapphire eyes sparked, but there was no light in them. 'I only meant to insult *you*.'

'If the palace dungeons hadn't been turned into a tourist attraction I would have you thrown into them.'

'And it's comments like that which make me happy to in-sult you. You blackmail me into coming here, you threaten my career and the careers of my friends, and you make me sign a contract including a penalty for my not performing at your grandfather's gala: the immediate disbandment of the Orchestre National de Paris... So, yes, I will happily take any opportunity I can to insult you.'

He stretched out his long legs and ran his fingers through his hair. 'It's comments like that which make me wonder...'

Her face scrunched up in a question.

'You see, little songbird, I wonder how a woman who professes to have stage fright so bad she cannot stand on a stage and play the instrument she was born to play has the nerve to show such disrespect to me. Do I not frighten you?'

She paused a beat before answering. 'You are certainly imposing.'

'That is not an answer.'

'The only thing that frightens me is the thought of standing on the stage for your grandfather's gala.' A lie, she knew, but Amalie would sooner stand on the stage naked than admit that she was *terrified* of him. Or terrified of something about him. The darkness. *His* darkness.

'Then I suggest you start learning the music for it.' He rose to his feet, his dark features set in an impenetrable mask. 'I will collect you at seven this evening and you can fill me in on your feelings for it.'

'Collect me for what?'

'Your first session in overcoming your stage fright.'

'Right.'

She bit her lip. Strangely, she'd envisaged Talos bringing an army of shrinks to *her*. That was what her mother had done during Amalie's scheduled visits after her parents' divorce. Anything would have been better than Colette Barthez's daughter being photographed at the door of a psychiatrist's office. The press wouldn't have been able to do anything with the pictures, or print any story about it, her mother had seen to that, but secrets had a way of not remaining secret once more people knew about them.

'Wear something sporty.'

'Sporty?' she asked blankly.

'I'm taking you to my gym.'

She rubbed at an eyebrow. 'I'm confused. Why would we see a shrink at your gym?'

'I never said anything about a shrink.'

'You did.'

'No, little songbird, I said *I* would help you overcome your stage fright.'

'I didn't think you meant it literally.' For the first time in her life she understood what *aghast* meant. *She* was aghast. 'You don't really mean that *you're* planning to fix me?'

He gazed down at her, unsmiling. 'Have you undertaken professional help before?'

'My mother wheeled out every psychiatrist she could get in France and England.'

'And none of them were able to help you.' It was a statement, not a question. 'You have a huge amount of spirit in your blood. It is a matter of harnessing it to your advantage. I will teach you to fight through your nerves and conquer them.'

'But…'

'Seven o'clock. Be ready.'

He strode away, his huge form relaxed. Too relaxed. So relaxed it infuriated her even more, turning her fear and anger up to a boil. Without thinking, she reached for a piece of discarded apple core and threw it at him. Unbelievably, it hit the back of his neck.

He turned around slowly, then crouched down to pick up the offending weapon, which he looked at briefly before fixing his eyes on her. Even with the distance between them the darkness in those eyes was unmistakable. As was the danger.

Amalie gulped in air, her lungs closing around it and refusing to let go.

Do I not frighten you…?

Frightened didn't even begin to describe the terror racing through her blood at that moment—a terror that increased with each long step he took back towards her.

Fighting with everything she possessed to keep herself collected, she refused to turn away from his black gaze.

It wasn't until he loomed over her, his stare piercing right through her, that she felt rather than saw the swirl flickering in it.

'You should be careful, little songbird. A lesser man than me might take the throwing of an apple core as some kind of mating ritual.'

His deep, rough voice was pitched low with an underlying playfulness that scared her almost more than anything else.

The thing that terrified her the most was the beating of her heart, so loud she was certain he must be able to hear it. Not the staccato beat of terror but the raging thrum of awareness.

He was so close she could see the individual stalks of stubble across his strong jawline, the flare of his nostrils, and the silver hue of the scar lancing his eyebrow. Her hand rose, as if a magnet had burrowed under her skin and was being drawn to reach up and touch his face...

Before she'd raised it more than a couple of inches, Talos leaned closer and whispered directly into her ear. 'I think I *do* frighten you. But not in the same way I frighten others.'

With that enigmatic comment he straightened, stepped away from her, nodded a goodbye, and then headed back to his villa.

Only when he was a good fifteen paces away did her lungs relax enough to expel the stale air, and the remnants of his woody, musky smell took its place, hitting her right in the sinuses, then spreading through her as if her body was consuming it.

If Amalie's long-sleeved white top that covered her bottom and her dark blue leggings strayed too far from the 'sporty' brief he'd given her, Talos made no mention of it when she opened her door to him at precisely seven that evening. He did, however, stare at the flat canvas shoes on her feet.

'Do you not have any proper trainers?'

'No.'

He gave a sound like a grunt.

'I'm not really into exercise,' she admitted.

'You are for the next thirty days.'

'I find it boring.'

'That's because you're not doing it right.'

It was like arguing with a plank. Except a plank would be more responsive to her argument.

But a plank wouldn't evoke such an immediate reaction within her. Or prevent her lungs from working properly.

For his part, Talos was dressed in dark grey sports pants that fitted his long, muscular legs perfectly, and a black T-shirt that stretched across his chest, showcasing his broad warrior-like athleticism.

The stubble she remembered from the morning was even thicker now...

It was like gazing at a pure shot of testosterone. The femininity right in her core responded to it, a slow ache burning in her belly, her heart racing to a thrum with one look.

He walked her to his car; a black Maserati that even in the dusk of early evening gleamed. She stepped into the passenger side, the scent of leather filling her senses.

She'd never known anyone fill the interior of a car the way Talos did. Beside him she felt strangely fragile, as if she were made of porcelain rather than flesh and blood.

She blinked the strange thought away and knotted her fingers together, silently praying the journey would be short.

'How did you find the composition?' he asked after a few minutes of silence.

'Beautiful.'

It was the only word she could summon. For five hours she had worked her way through the piece, bar by bar, section by section. She was a long way from mastering it, or understanding all its intricacies, but already the underlying melody had made itself known and had her hooked.

'You are certain you will be ready to perform it in a month's time?'

Opportunity suddenly presented itself to her gift-wrapped. 'A composition of this complexity could take me *months* to master. You would do far better to employ a soloist who can get a quicker handle on it.'

He was silent for a moment, and when he spoke there was an amused tinge to his voice. 'You don't give up, do you?'

'I don't know what you mean.'

'Oh, I think you do. I remind you, *despinis*, that you signed a contract.'

'And *you* said you would get me help.'

'I said I would help you and that is what I am doing.'

He brought the car to a stop at the front of a large cream building and faced her. Even in the dark she could see the menace on his features.

'I will accept no excuses. You *will* learn the composition and you *will* play it at the gala and you *will* do it justice. If you fail in any of those conditions then I will impose the contracted penalty.'

He didn't have to elaborate any further. The 'contracted penalty' meant turning the theatre into a hotel and causing the disbandment of the orchestra. That penalty loomed large in her mind: the threat to ruin every member of the orchestra's reputation…her own most especially.

'Understand, though,' he continued, 'that I am a man of my word. I said I would ensure that you are mentally fit to get on the stage and play, and that is what I will do. Starting now.'

He got out of the car and opened the boot, pulling out a black sports bag. 'Follow me.'

Not having any choice, she followed him into the building.

The first thing that hit her was the smell.

She'd never been in a men's locker room before, but this was *exactly* what she'd imagined it would smell like: sweat and testosterone.

The second thing to hit her was the noise.

The third thing was the sight of a man with a flat nose,

standing behind the reception desk at the entrance, spotting Talos and getting straight to his feet, a huge grin spreading over his face.

The two men greeted each other with bumped fists and a babble of Greek that ended with Talos giving the man a hearty slap on the back before indicating to Amalie to follow him. As they walked away she couldn't help but notice the blatant adoration on the flat-nosed man's face. Not a romantic adoration—she'd witnessed *that* enough times from her mother to know what it looked like—but more a look of reverence.

Past the reception area, they slipped through a door and entered the most enormous room.

Silently she took it all in: the square ring in the corner, the huge blue mats laid out in a square in another, the punching bags dangling at seemingly random places...

'Is this a *boxing* gym?'

He raised a hefty shoulder. 'I've boxed since my childhood.'

'I can't *box*!'

He gazed down at her hands. 'No. You can't. Throwing a punch at even the softest target has the danger of breaking a finger.'

She hadn't thought of that—had been too busy thinking that she'd never hit anyone or anything in her life and had always considered boxing to be the most barbaric of sports. It was fitting to learn that it was Talos's sport of choice. Her encounters with him were the closest she'd ever come to actually hitting someone.

He pointed to the corner with the blue mats. A tall, athletic blonde woman was chatting to a handful of men and women, all decked out in proper sports gear. 'That is Melina, one of the instructors here. I've signed you up for her kickboxing workout.'

Amalie sighed. 'How is enduring a kickboxing workout supposed to make me mentally fit for the stage?'

Without warning he placed his hands on her shoulders and twisted her around, so her back was to him. His thumbs pressed into the spot between her shoulder blades.

'You are rife with tension,' he said.

'Of course I am. I'm here under duress.'

She tried to duck out from his hold but his grip was too strong. *He* was too strong. His thumbs felt huge as they pressed up the nape of her neck. And warm. And surprisingly gentle, despite the strength behind them.

'The workout will help relieve tension and fire up your endorphins.' He laughed—a deep rumble that vibrated through her pores—and released his hold on her. 'All you will do is kick and punch into the air. If it helps, you can pretend I'm standing in front of you, receiving it all.'

She turned back to face him. 'That *will* help.'

The glimmer of humour left him. 'Your aggression needs an outlet.'

'I'm not aggressive!' At least she never had been before. Talos brought something out in her that, while not violent in the sense she'd always associated aggression with, made her feel as if a ferocity had been awoken within her, one that only reared up when she was with him. Or thinking about him. Or dreaming about him...

This workout might just prove to be a blessing after all.

'Maybe not, but the tension you have within you comes from somewhere...'

'That'll be from being here with you,' she grumbled.

'And once you have learned to expel it your mind will be calmer.'

'What about my body? I haven't exercised in for ever.'

His eyes swept up and down her body, taking in every part of her. It felt like a critical assessment of her physique and she squirmed under it. She waited for his verbal assessment but it never came.

'I will introduce you to Melina,' he said, striding away to the growing crowd around the instructor.

Melina's eyes gleamed when she spotted Talos, then narrowed slightly when she caught sight of Amalie, hanging back a little behind him.

Introductions were made and then Talos left them to it, heading to the ring in the corner, where a sparring bout had just started between two teenage boys. After a quick conversation with their trainer, Simeon, he left the main hall and went into the adjoining gym to start his own workout. He might spar later with Simeon, but first he wanted to warm his body up and get his muscles moving.

It felt as if it had been an age since he'd worked out, although it had only been one day.

Moving through the equipment, following the routine that had served him well since his army days, he found his concentration levels weren't as sharp as usual. Through the glass wall dividing the gym from the main hall he could see the kickboxing workout underway, and noted how Amalie had placed herself at the back of the pack, how self-conscious her movements were.

He didn't usually enjoy using the treadmill, but today he stayed on it for longer than normal, watching her. The warm-up was over and the session had begun in earnest. As the session progressed her movements went from tentative to a little less so. He could see the concentration on her face as she tried to copy what everyone around her was doing—the way she pivoted on the heel of her left foot before throwing an imaginary hook, the way she put her fists by her face, shifted her weight to her right foot, then brought her left knee up to her chest before kicking out.

She had an excellent centre of gravity, he noted. And for someone who professed to never exercise, her body was delectable, the leggings and long T-shirt she wore showing off her slender form to perfection.

She must have sensed his eyes upon her, for suddenly her gaze was on him, a scowl forming on her pretty face.

He didn't normally find a woman's anger cute, but with Amalie it was like being glared at by a harmless kitten.

Harmless kitten or not, the jabs and kicks she gave from that moment on brought to mind the image of a wildcat. She cut through the air with one particularly vicious right hook and he knew with deep certainty that it was *his* face she'd imagined her fist connecting with.

He reached for his towel and wiped his brow, inhaling deeply, trying to control the burn seeping through him. Watching Amalie work out had a strange hypnotic quality to it—as if she had magical powers pulling his attention to her.

It was time to take his attention elsewhere.

He was at the punching bags when her workout finished. He kept his focus on the bag before him, aware of her approach.

He would have been aware of her even if she hadn't cleared her throat to announce her presence by his side. Tendrils of sensation prickled his skin, and when he turned his attention from the punching bag to her, saw the dampness of her hair and the heightened colour of her cheeks, all he could think about was how she would look under the flames of passion.

'What did you think?' he asked.

Something resembling a smile spread across her face. 'Once I focused and imagined all my punches connecting with your face and all my kicks hitting your abdomen, it was great.'

He laughed. 'And how do you feel now?'

She considered the question, her lips pouting. 'I feel… *good.*'

'Is this the point where I say I told you so?'

She rolled her eyes. 'Are we going to be here much longer? Only I could really do with a shower. And something to eat.'

An image flashed into his mind of her standing naked under hot running water.

'There are showers here, with everything you need.'

'But then I'll have to change back into these sweaty things.'

'We have a selection of gym wear on sale too—I *did* say you would need suitable clothes to work out in. Choose some—and get yourself a decent pair of training shoes.'

'I haven't got any money on me.'

'Not a problem.' He looked over her head and beckoned someone.

A slight young girl of no more than sixteen appeared. Talos said something to her, then addressed Amalie again. 'This is Tessa. She will take you to our clothes store and then show you where the ladies' showers are. I'll meet you upstairs in the café when you're done.'

As soon as they'd headed off he focused back on the punching bag, trying to put aside the images of her naked that insisted on staying at the forefront of his mind.

He threw a particularly hard upper cut at the bag.

This was a singularly unique position he'd put himself in.

Amalie was incredibly desirable. He couldn't pinpoint what exactly it was, but it was as if she had some kind of aura that seeped into his skin and set a charge off inside him. Everything felt so much more heightened. He felt an awareness not only of *her* but also the chemical components that were making *him* feel off the scale. Put simply: being with her made him feel as sexy as hell.

Under any other circumstances he wouldn't hesitate to seduce her. Just imagining those long limbs wrapped around him put him on the path to arousal.

Her awareness of him was strong too—as starkly obvious as her loathing. Lust and loathing… An explosive combination.

But these were not normal circumstances. He had to get

her mentally prepared to take on the biggest solo of her life. It was the whole reason she was there. Something told him she wasn't the type of woman to go for the casual affairs he insisted on. Throwing sex into the mix could be like throwing a match into a situation that was already combustible.

He threw one last punch, then took a seat on the bench and, breathing heavily, undid the wraps around his hands, which he always put on even if only sparring with the punching bag. Experience had taught him how brittle the bones in the human hand were. The pain of breakage was negligible, but unless the hand was rested enough to allow the bones to heal it wouldn't set properly, and the boxer would be unable to punch at full power.

Resting a broken hand was as frustrating as desiring a beautiful woman, knowing she desired you too, but knowing you couldn't ever act on it.

CHAPTER FIVE

DESPITE THE LATENESS of the evening, the café upstairs was busy. Amalie had found a small table against the wall, where she could wait for Talos. Aware of the curious glances being thrown her way she pretended to examine the menu.

Testosterone abounded in the café. The vast majority of the patrons were male, all of them muscular, a fair few displaying broken noses and scarred faces. But their muscular physiques were dwarfed when Talos entered the room.

He spotted her immediately, and as he made his way over people stopped him to shake hands or bump fists.

She was glad his attention was taken, if only for a few moments. She pressed a hand to her chest and inhaled as much air into her tight lungs as she could get. The green sports pants and matching T-shirt she'd taken from the gym's sports clothing outlet suddenly felt very close against her skin. Constricting.

He'd changed into a pair of tight-fitting black jeans and a navy blue T-shirt, and had his sports bag slung over his shoulder.

He was a mountain man, and whatever he wore only emphasised his muscularity. Whether he was in a business suit, workout gear or something casual, she couldn't shake the feeling that he would be equally at home with nothing but a loin cloth wrapped around his waist.

'I thought subjects were supposed to kneel before royalty,' she said when he finally joined her.

A smirk appeared on his lips. 'If you want to get on your knees before me, I won't complain.'

She glared at him.

He settled his huge frame onto the chair opposite her. 'You have to admit your comment was an open invitation.'

'Only to someone with a dirty mind…' she said, but her voice trailed into a mumble as the imagery his comment provoked, startling and vivid, sent a pulse searing through her blood strong enough to make her entire face burn.

The fresh scent of his shower gel and the woody musk of his aftershave played under her nose, filling her senses. He still hadn't shaved, his stubble thick and covering his jawline in its entirety.

Certain she'd handed him another gold-plated open invitation, she cast her eyes down before he had a chance to read what was in them.

Instead of the expected quip, he asked in an amused tone, 'What would you like to order?'

As he spoke, he folded his arms onto the table, his biceps bulging with the motion. She should have stayed looking at his face.

Since when did blatant machismo testosterone do it for her?

The male musicians she worked with—especially her fellow violinists—were, on the whole, sensitive creatures physically *and* emotionally. There were always exceptions to the rule, such as Philippe, one of the Orchestre National de Paris's trombone players. Philippe was blond, buff and handsome, and he flirted openly with any woman who caught his eye. He was rumoured to have bedded half the female musicians in the orchestra.

But not Amalie, who found his overt masculinity a complete turn-off. The few boyfriends *she'd* had had been slight, unthreatening men, with gentle natures and a deep appreciation of music. Their evenings together had been spent discussing all things to do with music and the arts in general, with the bedroom not even an afterthought.

So why did Talos, whose physique and masculinity were ten times as potent as anything Philippe could even dream of having, make her feel all hot and squidgy just to look at him? None of her boyfriends had made her feel like he did—as if she wanted nothing more than to rip his clothes off.

'I don't read Greek,' she answered, dragging her vocal cords into working order. 'I wouldn't know what to choose.'

'We don't serve traditional Greek fare here,' he said. 'It's mostly high-carb and high-protein foods like pasta and steak.'

'Do they have burgers?'

He grinned.

'What's so funny?'

'After a hard workout I go for a burger every time.'

'With cheese?'

'It's not right without the cheese.'

'And chips?'

'It wouldn't be a complete meal without them.'

'Cheeseburger and chips for me, then, please.'

'Drink?'

'Coke?'

His sensuous lips widened into a full-blown grin that was as sinful as the food she wanted. 'Two cheeseburgers and chips, and two Cokes coming up.'

He got up from his seat, walked to the counter, fist-bumped the teenage boy working there and gave their order.

'It won't take long,' he said when he sat back at the table.

'Good. I am *starving*.'

'I'm not surprised after that workout you did.'

'It doesn't help that I forgot to have any dinner before we left.'

'How can you *forget* a meal?' He looked at her as if she'd confessed to forgetting to put her underwear on.

She shrugged. 'It happens. If I'm concentrating and lost in the music it is easy for me to forget.'

'It's no wonder you're a slip of thing.'

'I make up for it,' she said defensively. 'I might not eat at regular times, but I always eat.'

He eyed her, his look contemplative. Before he could say whatever was on his mind their food was brought over by yet another teenager.

'That *was* quick,' Amalie marvelled. Her famished belly rumbled loudly as she looked at the heaped plate. She didn't think she'd ever seen so many chips on a plate, or a burger of such epic proportions.

'We run a tight ship here.'

'That's not the first time you've said "we",' she said, picking up a thick golden chip that was so hot she dropped it back onto the plate. 'Are you involved in this place somehow?'

'This is my gym.'

She gazed at him, trying to stop her face wrinkling in puzzlement. 'But you have a gym in your villa.'

'And there's one at the palace too.' He picked up his burger and bit into it, devouring almost a quarter in one huge mouthful.

She shook her head. 'So why this place too?'

He swallowed, his light brown eyes on hers. 'This is a boxing gym. Sparring is no fun when you're on your own.'

'So you bought a gym so you could have some company?'

'There were a lot of reasons.'

'Do you run it?'

'I employ a manager. Enough questions—eat before your food gets cold.'

'Okay, but do me a favour and never tell my mother what I'm about to eat.'

His brow furrowed. 'Why? Would she disapprove?'

Amalie had already bitten into a chip, possibly the crisp-est and yet fluffiest chip she had ever tasted. She chewed, then swallowed it down with some Coke before answering. 'My mother is a gastronomy snob. She considers any food with English or American origin to be tantamount to eating out of a rubbish bin.'

'Yet she married an Englishman.'

'That's true,' she agreed, casting her eyes down. Her parents had been divorced for half her lifetime, yet the guilt still had the power to catch her unawares.

Talos picked up on an inflection in her tone. 'Was it a bad divorce?'

'Not at all. It was very civilised.'

'But traumatic for you?'

'It wasn't the easiest of experiences,' she conceded, before picking up her burger and taking a small bite.

It was with some satisfaction that he saw her eyes widen and her nod of approval.

'That is *good*,' she enthused when her mouth was clear.

'Maybe not the gastronomical heights your mother would approve of, but still high-quality,' he agreed.

'I think this might be the best burger I've ever had.'

'You mean you've eaten a burger *before*?' he asked, feigning surprise. 'Your mother will be shocked.'

'I hide all my convenience food when I know she's coming over.'

He grinned and took another bite of his burger. The workout had clearly done Amalie the world of good; most of her primness had been sweated out of her. She almost looked relaxed.

They ate in silence for a few minutes. It gratified him to see her eat so heartily; he had imagined from her slender frame and self-confessed lack of exercise that she would eat like a sparrow.

He tried to imagine eating with another woman here and came up blank.

In normal life this gym was his sanctuary—not somewhere he would bring a date, even if his date liked to work out. For the same reason he refused to make overtures to any of the women who worked here. Regardless of the fact that most of his female staff were, like the majority of his employees, teenagers, and so automatically off limits, he didn't want the messiness that inevitably came about when he ended a relationship to spill into his sanctuary.

Melina, his kickboxing instructor, had blatantly flirted with him when she'd first started work here and—despite her being in her mid-twenties, and attractive to boot—he'd frozen out all her innuendoes until she'd got the message.

The endorphins released during a vigorous workout always made him crave sex, but he disciplined himself with the iron will Kalliakis men were famed for. Except for his father. The Kalliakis iron will had skipped a generation with Lelantos…Lelantos had been weak and venal—a man who had allowed his strong libido and equally great temper to control him.

It *killed* Talos to know that of the three Kalliakis Princes, he was the most like their father.

The difference was that he had learned to control his appetites *and* the volatile temperament that came with it. Boxing had taught him to harness it.

Tonight, though, the endorphins seemed to have exploded within him, and the primal urge to sate himself in a willing woman's arms was stronger than ever. And not just any woman. *This* woman.

Theos, just watching Amalie eat made him feel like throwing her over his shoulder, carrying her to the nearest empty room and taking her wildly.

'Do you consider yourself French or English?' he asked, wrenching his mind away from matters carnal. He needed to concentrate on getting her mentally fit to play at his grandfather's gala, not be imagining ripping her clothes off with his teeth.

'Both. Why?'

'You speak English with a slight accent. It made me curious.'

'I suppose French is my first language. I grew up bilingual, but I've never lived full-time in England. My father's always kept a home there, but when I was a child we used it more for holidays and parties than anything else.'

'Was that because of your mother's influence?'

'I assume so. My mother definitely wore the trousers in that marriage.' A slight smile, almost sad, played at the corners of her lips.

'I have heard that she's a forceful woman.'

He'd heard many stories about Colette Barthez, not many of them complimentary. It was strange to think that the woman before him—a woman who tried desperately to fade into the background—was a child from the loins of the biggest diva on the planet. He had to assume she took after her father who, he'd learned, was regarded as a quintessential Englishman, with a dry humour and calm manner.

Amalie chewed on a chip, disliking the implication in his words and the way he'd delivered them. She, better than anyone, knew just how 'forceful' her mother could be in getting her own way, but that didn't stop her loving her and despising the people who would put her down.

'You don't become the most successful and famous mezzo-soprano in the world without having a strong will and a thick hide. If she were a man she would be celebrated.'

The scarred eyebrow rose in question.

She shook her head and pushed her plate to the side. 'She sold out Carnegie Hall and the Royal Albert Hall three nights in a row last year, but every article written about those concerts just *had* to mention her three ex-husbands, numerous lovers and so-called diva demands.'

The black scarred brow drew forward. 'That must be very hurtful for her to read,' he said, his tone careful.

'If it was the French media it would devastate her, but

in France she's revered and treated as a national icon. With the rest of the world's press, so long as they aren't criticising her voice or performance, she doesn't care—she truly does have the hide of a rhinoceros.'

But not when it came to love. When it came to affairs of the heart, her mother felt things deeply. Bored lovers had the power to shatter her.

'But they upset *you*?' he said, a shrewdness in his eyes.

'No one wants to read salacious stories about their mother,' she muttered, reaching for one more chip and popping it in her mouth before she could unloosen her tongue any further.

Her family and personal life were none of his concern, but she felt so protective when it came to her mother, who was passionate, funny, loving, predatory, egotistical and a complete one-off. She drove her up the wall, but Amalie adored her.

'That is true,' Talos agreed. 'My family also live under the spotlight. There are occasions when it can burn.'

She leaned back in her chair and stared at him through narrowed eyes. 'If you know how much the spotlight can burn, why would you push me back under it when you know it hurts me so much?'

'Because you were born to play under it,' he replied, his deep bass voice no-nonsense.

And yet she detected a whisper of warmth in those light brown eyes she hadn't seen before.

'It is my job to put you back under it without you gaining any new scars.'

'But the scars I already have haven't healed.'

There was no point in shying away from it. She'd seen enough psychologists in her early teens to know that she'd been scarred, and that it was those scars still preventing her from stepping onto a stage and performing with eyes upon her.

'Then I will heal them for you.'

A shiver ran through her as an image of his mouth drifting across her skin skittered into her mind, shockingly vivid… Talos healing her in the most erotic manner. It sent a pulse of heat deep into her abdomen.

She blinked rapidly, to dispel the unbidden image, and was grateful when another member of the gym chose that moment to come over to their table and chat with him.

Passion was something she'd always avoided. After her parents' divorce she'd spent her weekend and holiday visitations watching her mother bounce from lover to lover, marrying two of them for good measure, engulfed in desire's heady flames, trying to recapture the magic of her first marriage. Watching her get burned so many times had been pain itself. The guilt of knowing she was responsible for her mother's heartache—and her father's—had only added to it.

Her father had never brought another woman home, let alone remarried. Though he would always deny it with a sad smile, the torch he carried for her mother was too bright to extinguish.

If it hadn't been for that horrendous incident in front of her parents and their friends and its aftermath, when their child prodigy could no longer perform like the dancing seal she'd become, her parents would still be together today—she was certain of it. On the occasions when they were forced together, Amalie would watch them skirt around each other; her mother showing off her latest lover with something close to flamboyant desperation, her father accepting this behaviour with a wistful stoicism.

Amalie *liked* her quiet, orderly, passionless life. It was safe.

Talos Kalliakis made her feel anything but safe.

Talos rapped loudly on the cottage door for the second time, blowing out a breath of exasperated air. Just as he was about to try the handle and let himself in the door swung open and there Amalie stood, violin in hand and a look of startled apology on her face.

'Is it that time already?' she said, standing aside to let him through. 'Sorry, I lost track of time.'

He followed her through to the cosy living room. The baby grand piano sat in the corner, covered with sheets of paper and an old-fashioned tape recorder. Next to it stood a music stand.

She looked what could only be described as lively—as if she had springs under her feet. In the four days she'd been in Agon he'd never seen her like this.

'Would you mind if I give the workout a miss tonight?' she asked, her green sapphire eyes vibrant and shining. 'I've reached an understanding with the score and I want to solidify it in my mind before I lose the moment.'

'You are making headway?' It amused him to hear her discussing the score as if it were a living entity.

'Something has clicked today. I've made a recording of the piano accompaniment—I am so grateful your grandmother wrote an accompaniment for the piano as well as for a full orchestra—and playing along to it is making all the pieces come together.'

'Are you ready to play it for me?'

Her eyes rounded in horror. 'Absolutely *not*.'

'You're going to have to play it for me soon,' he reminded her. The countdown was on, the gala only three weeks and six days away.

'Let me master the composition before we discuss that.'

He eyed her contemplatively. 'You have until Friday.'

She'd accompanied him to his gym three nights in a row, her workouts intense and focused. Wanting her concentration to be used in figuring out the score, he'd deliberately steered any small talk between them away from the personal. Other than chauffeuring her to and from the gym, he'd left her to it.

A dart of panic shot from her eyes. 'I won't be ready by Friday.'

'Friday will give us three weeks to get you performance-ready. I know nothing of music. It makes no difference to me if you make mistakes at this early stage; I won't notice them. What concerns me is getting you used to playing solo in front of people again. We need to work on that as much as you need to work on the score itself.'

A mutinous expression flashed over her face before her features relaxed a touch and she nodded.

'You can have tonight off, but tomorrow you go back to the gym.'

'Has anyone ever told you that you're a slave-driving ogre?'

'No one has dared.'

She rolled her eyes. 'I want to get on—you can leave now.'

'And no one has ever dared tell me when I should leave before.'

'You must be getting old, because your memory is failing—I've told you to leave before, at my home in Paris when you barged your way in.'

'Ah, yes. I distinctly remember you tried using physical force to expel me.'

His loins tightened as memories of her soft, lithe body splayed on his lap while he controlled the flare of fire and passion that had exploded out of her assailed him anew. He cast a long, appreciative look up and down her body, taking in the short black skirt over sheer black tights and the short-sleeved viridian-green shirt unbuttoned to display a hint of cleavage...

'Would you like to use force to expel me now?'

She cuddled her violin to her chest as if for protection and took a step back.

'Imagine how fit all those workouts will make you,' he purred in a deliberately sensual tone, enjoying the colour heightening her cheekbones. 'Next time you choose to fight me with your body you might have a chance of overpowering me.'

'We both know I could train twenty-four hours a day, every day for a decade, and still not be strong enough to overpower you.'

'If you would like to put that theory into practice you only have to say.' He dropped his voice and stared straight into her almond eyes. *Theos*, she was temptation itself. 'I'm not averse to a beautiful woman trying to dominate me. Something tells me the results would be explosive.'

Other than the colour on her face, she showed no reaction. For the briefest of moments Talos wondered if his assumption that the attraction he felt for her was mutual was wrong—then he saw her swallow and swipe a lock of hair from her forehead.

'Enjoy your music,' he said, stepping out of the room with one last grin.

As he shut the cottage front door behind him he ruefully conceded that trying to get a rise out of the beautiful musician living in his guest house had served no purpose other than to fuel the chemistry swirling between them.

He would need an extra-long workout to expel the energy fizzing in his veins.

CHAPTER SIX

AMALIE DID SOMETHING SACRILEGIOUS. In a fit of temper, she threw the precious score onto the floor.

Immediately she felt wretched. It wasn't the poor score's fault that all the good feelings that had grown throughout the day had vanished. It was the composer's rotten grandson who had caused that with his rotten innuendoes.

Focus, Amalie, she told herself sternly.

But it was hard to focus on the sheets of wonderful music before her when all she could think about was wrestling Talos's clothes off him and seeing for herself if he was as divine naked as he was when clothed.

That body…

It would be hard. Every inch of it. But what would his skin feel like? Would it be hard too? Or would it be smooth? How would it feel against her own skin?

Focus!

It was none of her business what Talos Kalliakis's skin felt like, or how hard his body was, or to discover if it was true that the size of a man's feet was proportionate to the size of his…

Focus!

Talos had enormous feet. And enormous hands…

He also had a smile that churned her belly into soft butter.

'Stop it!' This time she shouted the words aloud and clenched her fists.

She'd woken that morning with a sense of dread that the gala was now less than four weeks away. If she didn't master the composition, then it didn't matter what tricks Talos had up his sleeve to get her performing onstage— she would be humiliated regardless. Right at that moment all that mattered was the composition.

Sitting herself on the floor, she hitched her skirt to the top of her thighs, crossed her legs and closed her eyes. There she sat for a few minutes, concentrating on nothing but her breathing—a technique taught to her by her father, who had confessed in a conspiratorial manner that it was the breathing technique her mother had learnt when she'd been in labour with Amalie. By all accounts her mother had ignored the midwife's advice and demanded more drugs.

The thought brought a smile to her face and pulled her out of the trance-like state she'd slipped into.

The edginess that had consumed her since Talos's brief visit had subsided a little, enough for her to put the sheets of music back onto her stand and press 'play' on the tape recorder.

As she waited for the backing music to begin she couldn't help thinking she *should* have gone for a work-out, which would have cleared her angst so much better than any meditation technique.

She nestled her violin under her chin and as the first notes of the accompaniment played out she counted the beats and began to play.

Soon she was immersed in the music, so much so that when a loud rap on the front door echoed through to the living room she had to physically pull herself out of it. A quick glance at her watch showed she'd been playing for two and a half hours.

She yanked the door open just as Talos raised his knuckles for another rap.

'Have you never heard the word *patience* before?' she scolded.

He grinned and held up a large cardboard box, the motion causing a warm waft of scent to emit from it. 'I'm too hungry for patience, little songbird. I bring us food.'

Us?

The divine smell triggered something in her belly, making it rumble loudly. With a start she realised she'd forgotten to eat the tray of food a member of his villa's staff had brought to the cottage for her earlier that evening.

Since their first trip to his gym, lunch and dinner had been brought to her on Talos's orders. She knew it was only the fear that she would become anaemic or something, and faint from hunger onstage, that prompted him to do it, rather than any regard for *her*, but his concern touched her nonetheless.

The tray from earlier was still on the dining table, untouched. A warm, almost fluffy feeling trickled through her blood that he'd noticed.

Hesitating for only a moment, she let him in and headed to the kitchen, grabbed a couple of plates and some cutlery, and took them through to the dining area of the living room.

What was she supposed to do? Insist that he leave when he'd gone to the trouble of bringing her food, just because she kept having erotic thoughts about him? It would be incredibly rude. He might have used blackmail to get her here, but since then he'd treated her decently. He'd treated her well. Thoughtfully. She wasn't a prisoner, as she'd feared she would be, but had his whole household staff at her disposal for whatever she wanted or needed.

More than any of that, she would be spending a *lot* more time with him in the coming weeks. She had to get used to feeling off-centre when she was with him. She *had* to. She refused to become a gibbering idiot in his presence.

Talos held aloft a bottle of rosé retsina. 'Glasses?'

Once they were settled at the table, Talos busy removing the foil lids of the dozen boxes spread out before them, she said, 'I didn't think there would be any takeaways open on a Sunday night.'

One of the chattier members of Talos's staff had warned her yesterday to get anything she needed on Saturday, as the island mostly shut down on a Sunday.

'There aren't—I got the chefs at the palace to cook for us.'

Oh, yes. He was a prince. In Paris his royalty was something she'd been acutely aware of. Here, in the relaxed atmosphere of Agon, it was an easy thing to forget.

'And they have proper takeaway boxes to hand?'

'The palace kitchens are ten times the size of this cottage and cater for all eventualities,' he answered lightly, pouring the retsina.

'Didn't you go to the gym?' He'd showered and changed into a pair of black chinos and a dark blue polo shirt since he'd turned up at the cottage earlier, so he'd clearly done his workout, but she couldn't see how he'd have had time to go the gym *and* the palace in the short time he'd been gone.

'As you weren't doing the kickboxing class I worked out at the palace gym. It gave me a chance to catch up with my brothers and my grandfather.'

That would be the King and the two other Kalliakis Princes.

'I thought you went to your gym every night?'

'I work out every night, but not always at the gym. I try and make it there a couple of times a week when I'm in the country.'

'Have you been putting yourself out for *me*, then?'

'You're my current project,' he said with a wolfish grin. 'As long as I get you on that stage for the gala I don't care if I have to be inconvenienced.'

That was right. She was his pet project. She had to remember that anything nice he did was with an ulterior motive and not for *her*.

She took a sip of retsina, expecting to grimace at the

taste, which she'd always found rather harsh. It was surprisingly mellow—like an expensive white wine but with that unmistakable resinous tang.

'You approve?' he asked.

She nodded.

'Good. It is our island's vintage.'

'Do you make it?'

'No—we rent out our land to a producer who makes it under the island's own label.'

The food looked and tasted as divine as its aroma. Amalie happily dived into *kleftiko*—the most tender slow-cooked lamb on the bone she'd ever eaten—and its accompanying *yemista*—stuffed baked tomatoes and peppers—eating as much as she could fit into her stomach. She hadn't realised how hungry she was.

As during their shared meal at his gym, Talos ate heartily. When he'd finished wolfing down every last scrap on his plate, and emptying the takeaway boxes of every last morsel, he stuck his fork into the few leftovers on her plate.

'For a prince, you don't behave in a very regal fashion,' she observed drily.

'How is a prince supposed to behave?'

She considered, before answering, 'Regally?'

He burst into laughter—a deep, booming sound that filled the small cottage. 'I leave the regal behaviour to my brothers.'

'How do you get away with that?'

'They're the heir and the spare.' He raised a hefty shoulder into a shrug. 'Helios will take over the throne when my grandfather...'

Here, his words faltered—just a light falter, that anyone who wasn't observing him closely would likely have missed. But she *was* observing him closely—was unable to tear her eyes away from him. It wasn't just the magnetic sex appeal he oozed. The more time she spent with him, the more he fascinated her. The man behind the magnetism.

'When the day comes,' he finished smoothly. 'Theseus has been groomed for the role too, for the remote eventuality that something untoward should happen to Helios.' He must have caught her shock at his unemotional analysis because he added, 'No one knows what's around the corner. Our father was heir to the throne, but life threw a curveball at him when he was only a couple of years older than I am now.'

The car crash. The tragedy that had befallen the Kalliakis family a quarter of a century before, leaving the three young Princes orphaned. Looking at the huge man sitting opposite her, she found it was almost impossible to imagine Talos as a small child. But he had been once, and had suffered the most horrendous thing that could happen to any child: the death of not one but both parents.

The sudden temptation to cover his giant hand and whisper her sympathies was smothered by the equally sudden hard warning in his eyes—a look impossible to misinterpret. *I do not want your sympathies. This subject is not open to discussion.*

Instead she said, 'Did your brothers get favourable treatment?'

He relaxed back immediately into a grin. 'Not at all. *I* got all the preferential treatment. I was the happy accident. I was raised without any expectations—a prince in a kingdom where the most that is expected of me is to protect my brothers if ever the need arises. Even my name denotes that. In ancient mythology Talos was a giant man of bronze. There are a number of differing myths about him, but the common theme is that he was a protector.'

Goosebumps broke out over her flesh.

Something told her this big brute of a man would be a fierce protector—and not simply because of his physique.

Cross him or those he loved and you would know about it.

She cleared her throat. 'Aren't older siblings supposed to protect the youngest, not the other way round?'

His smile broadened. 'Usually. But I was such a large newborn my parents knew my role would be to protect my brothers from anyone who would do harm to them or our lands.'

'And have you had to do much in the way of protection?' she asked.

'When I was a child it seemed my role was to protect them from each other,' he said with another laugh. 'They used to fight constantly. We all did.'

'Do you get on now?'

'We all still fight, but nowadays it is only verbally. We are brothers, and we get on and work well together. We protect each other. That said, they are both big enough and ugly enough to take care of themselves.'

Amalie felt a pang of envy. She would have loved a sibling of her own. Any kind of playmate would have been wonderful. Anything would have been better than a childhood spent travelling the world with her parents on their various tours, educational tutors in tow, the only child in a world full of adults.

'Even so, aren't princes supposed to travel with a retinue of protectors at all times? And have lots of flunkeys?' In Paris he'd arrived at her home alone both times. And the only staff he'd brought to the Théâtre de la Musique had been clerical.

'It would take a very brave person to take me on—don't you think, little songbird?'

She felt her cheeks turn scarlet. She wished he would stop addressing her as *little songbird*—hated the rush of warmth that flushed through her whenever he called her it. Instinct told her that to acknowledge it would be like waving a red flag to a bull.

'Helios always travels with protection—Theseus less so.' Something sparked in his eyes, as if he were asking a question of himself. 'If you would like to see me behave in a more regal fashion you can accompany me to the ball at the palace next weekend.'

'What ball?'

'It's something Helios is hosting—a private pre-gala celebration. There will be royal flunkeys and footmen everywhere, princes and princesses from around the world—and I, little songbird, will be in my most princely attire.'

'And you want me to go with you?' Was he asking her to go as his *date*?

'It will give me a chance to show you how princely I really am,' he teased.

'If it's such a formal affair, why haven't you already got someone to take with you?'

'If I took anyone else she would take it as a sign that I was serious about her and expect me to drop to one knee.'

'Do I take it that means you're not enamoured of the thought of marriage?'

Disgust crossed his face, as if she'd suggested he dunk his head into a vat of slime.

'You're a *prince*. Aren't you supposed to marry and produce heirs?'

'Helios will produce all the heirs Agon needs. Theseus will marry and produce some more as backup. Leaving me free to continue my bachelor lifestyle for eternity.'

'The eternal playboy?'

'I dislike that term,' he said, his eyes narrowing. 'It implies a certain disrespect towards women.'

She had to laugh. 'Don't tell me you're a feminist?'

'My grandmother was the strongest person I've ever known. If I was to disrespect any woman or make judgements on the basis of her gender I am certain my grandmother would hunt me down in my dreams to give me a dressing-down.'

'She sounds like a formidable woman.'

Talos nodded. Without his grandmother's loving but steely influence—especially when he'd hit his teenage years and gone completely off the rails—he knew he wouldn't be half the man he was today.

'She was a pillar of strength,' he said, raising his glass of retsina. 'And I think she would approve of you playing her final composition.'

She made a snorting sound. 'Why would you think that?'

'Because you have the same steel core she had.'

Amalie's eyes widened, and then she frowned, a V forming in the centre of her brow. 'I can't perform in front of people. *My* core is made of blancmange.'

'But, little songbird, you are the only person other than my family who dares stand up to me.'

Even now she was disagreeing with him.

For the first time he understood why Theseus had taken a two-year sabbatical after he'd completed his time at Sandhurst. The travelling part he'd always understood, but Theseus's insistence on travelling under an assumed name had been something he'd never got. Talos was proud to be a Kalliakis—proud of their family reputation as fighters, proud of his nation's people and culture. He saw himself as a protector of their proud island and had seen Theseus's insistence at disguising his identity as a snub to the Kalliakis name.

Now he understood how it must have felt for his brother to be treated as someone…*normal.* Theseus had shared many of his tales about the personal freedom he'd found in his time away, but only now did Talos understand why it had been such a special time for him.

Amalie was the first person since childhood to treat him like a normal person. She had no qualms about disagreeing with him on any subject. As he thought back over the past few days he realised that she simply didn't pander to him. He could be *anyone.*

Which meant that when she smiled at him—which, admittedly, was rarely—it was because she meant it. When those stunning green eyes became stark, their pupils enlarged, showing her desire for him—little tells she would hate to know he recognised—it was for *him*.

He'd never bedded a woman and been one hundred per cent certain whether she was in his arms out of desire for him or the aphrodisiac quality of his title. It had never bothered him—indeed, the idea that he could bed any woman he chose held an aphrodisiac quality of its own—but the mistrust had always been there, unacknowledged yet simmering away in the depths of his consciousness.

If he were to make love to Amalie there was no question that her responses would be authentic. If she made love to him it would be for *him*.

The temptation to lean over the table, cup that beautiful heart-shaped chin in his hand and taste those delectable lips was so strong he dug his toes into his boots to keep his feet grounded to the floor.

Theos, it was a temptation that grew harder to resist the more time he spent with her. His will power and control were legendary, and yet he was having to remind himself of all the reasons he had to hone them to greater strengths when with this woman.

Making love to Amalie could be disastrous. He was supposed to be getting her fit to play at his grandfather's gala, not plotting to get those lithe limbs wrapped around his waist...

He looked at his watch and got sharply to his feet. 'I need to head back. I'm flying to New York in the morning but I'll be back Thursday evening. I'll get Kostas to take you to Natalia's—she'll make a ball dress for you.'

'I haven't agreed to come,' she protested.

'I am a prince of the land, little songbird,' he answered with a grin. 'If you defy my wishes I will have you locked in the palace dungeons.'

'You've already said the dungeons are only a tourist attraction.'

He winked at her. 'It will take me two minutes to appropriate the keys for them.'

He laughed at the scowl she bestowed upon him.

'I'll see myself out. *Kali nýchta*, little songbird.'

He might not have any intention of acting on the absurdly strong chemistry growing between them, but he could damn well enjoy her company for one evening of entertainment.

CHAPTER SEVEN

A LOUD RAP on the front door broke Amalie out of the spell she was under.

She froze, violin under her chin, bow bouncing lightly on the E string. There was only one person she knew who so vividly announced his presence with just a knock on the door.

The five days of peace without Talos had come to an end. He'd returned to Agon the previous evening but she'd had a lucky escape in that he hadn't bothered with her. That hadn't stopped her spending the entire evening at his gym, looking over her shoulder, waiting for him to appear. And that sinking feeling when she'd been driven back to the cottage without him having made an appearance had *not* been disappointment.

'Hello, little songbird,' he said now, with a lazy smile on his face, the mid-afternoon sun shining down on him, enveloping him in a hazy, warm aura that made her stomach flip left, right and centre. 'Have you missed me?'

'Like a migraine,' she answered with a roll of her eyes, turning back into the cottage and leaving him to shut the door and follow her in, his low laughter at her quip reverberating through her.

'Have you had a good week?' he asked, stepping into the living room.

'It's been very peaceful, thank you. And yours?'

'Incredibly boring.'

'That'll teach you to be a lawyer.'

Today he actually looked lawyerly. Well, more like Tarzan dressed up as a lawyer, the crisp white shirt, open at the neck, rippling over his muscular chest, and charcoal trousers emphasising the length and power of his thighs. No matter what he wore he would still emit enough testosterone to fill a dozen buckets.

'It's a living,' he said, deadpan.

She couldn't help it. She laughed. She doubted Talos Kalliakis had needed to work a single day in his life.

'What does a man have to do to get a coffee round here?' he asked.

'Go to the kitchen and work the coffee machine.'

'But I am royalty. I shouldn't be expected to make my own coffee.'

'I'll have a mocha while you're there,' she said, only just stopping herself throwing a wink at him.

His irreverence was contagious.

His nose wrinkled. 'I have serious doubts about your taste, knowing you drink that muck.'

She had serious doubts about her taste too. Always she'd steered herself in the direction of safe, dependable men, those with whom she could have a nice, safe, dependable life.

There was nothing *safe* about Talos.

That little fact didn't stop her thinking about him constantly.

It didn't stop her heart from hammering at a *prestissimo* pace by virtue of just being under the same roof as him.

Luckily he took himself off to the kitchen, allowing her a few minutes to compose herself. When he returned, carrying their coffees, she'd put her violin away and sat herself in an armchair.

He placed their cups on the table and sprawled onto the sofa. 'I hear you've been going to the gym every day.'

'I was under orders, remember?'

He grinned. 'Melina thinks it is a shame you can't actually fight someone in a kickboxing match.'

Likely Melina would volunteer herself for that honour. Whilst not unfriendly, there was a definite coolness in the instructor's attitude towards her.

'I enjoy it,' she admitted.

The atmosphere at Talos's gym was different from anything she'd experienced before. There was a real collective feel about it, with everyone there prepared to help everyone else. Yes, there were some big egos, but it was a different kind of egotism from the sort she was used to in the classical music world—earthier, somehow. Considering she was one of the only women there, she never felt threatened, and she didn't think it was because everyone knew she was Talos's guest. The atmosphere of the gym itself engendered respect in all its patrons.

'Good. And how are you getting on with the score?'

'Well…I think.'

He quirked his scarred brow. 'You *think*?'

'I have no way of knowing if I'm playing it as your grandmother intended.'

'How do you mean?'

'My interpretation of the tempo she played it at might be different from her interpretation.'

He shrugged. 'You played the "Méditation" from *Thaïs* at a slower tempo than she played it, but it sounded equally beautiful.'

Talos noted the colour flush over her face, the flash of embarrassed pride that darted from her eyes.

He sat forward and rested his arms on his thighs. 'It is time for you to play for me.'

Her colour faded as quickly as it had appeared. She seemed to cower in her seat.

'I did say I would listen to you play today.'

She brightened. 'I've recorded myself playing it. You can listen to that.'

He cocked his head and sighed theatrically. 'I can see

that working well at the gala—we'll introduce our star soloist and wheel on a tape recorder with a wig.'

She spluttered a sound of nervous laughter.

He softened his voice, wanting to put her at ease. 'It is only you and me. It doesn't matter how many mistakes you make—all that matters is that today you play for me.'

There were three weeks and one day until the gala.

Judging by the terror vibrating off Amalie's frame, he would need every one of them.

He'd spent the four days in New York getting as much work done as he could, organising his staff and generally ensuring that he'd need to do minimal travelling until the gala was over. The business was being neglected by all three Kalliakis princes but what alternative did they have? All of them wanted to spend as much time with their grandfather as they could, to be there when he was having a good spell and craving their company. They were fortunate that their staff were the best of the best and could run much of the business with minimum input from them.

This trip away had been different from any other. He was always impatient to spend as much time on Agon as he could, but during this trip he'd found himself thinking of home far more frequently than normal. Thinking of *her* in his little guest cottage. He'd arrived back early yesterday evening and the temptation to pay her an immediate visit had shocked him with its intensity.

He'd resisted and headed to the palace. There, he'd shared a meal with his brothers, both of whom had been in foul tempers and had declined to answer any questions about their respective bad moods. Both had excused themselves the moment they'd finished eating. Shrugging his shoulders at their odd behaviour, Talos had sought out his grandfather, spending a pleasant couple of hours playing chess with him until a sudden bout of tiredness had forced his grandfather to call a halt.

It unnerved him how quickly his grandfather could fall

into exhaustion—one minute sitting upright, laughing, holding a conversation; the next his chin drooping, his eyes struggling to stay open, his speech slurring...

Talos could feel the time ebbing away. He could see it too. He'd only been four days in New York and his grandfather had lost even more weight, the large, vital man now a shadow of his former self.

The woman before him had the power to make his grandfather's last days the sweetest they could be. She could bring his beloved Rhea's final composition to life. She was the only person in the world who could do it justice.

He watched Amalie struggle for composure, feeling a strange tugging in his chest when she visibly forced herself to her feet and over to the baby grand piano, where she'd left her violin.

Not looking at him, she removed it from its case and fiddled with the strings, tuning them as his grandmother had always done before playing for him.

Moving her music stand behind the piano, as if she were using the piano for protection, she arranged the sheets of music until she was satisfied with how they stood, then rested her violin under her chin.

About to hit the first note, she halted, bow upright, and stared at him. 'I've almost memorised it. I won't need the sheet music when I do the gala.'

It was the first time he'd heard her utter her intentions to actually perform at the gala. He wondered if she was aware of what she'd just given away—how in the nine days she had been on his island her mind-set had already altered.

He raised his hands and pulled a face to indicate his nonchalance about such matters. What did he care if she played with the music in front of her or not? All he cared was that she played it.

'I'll play without the accompaniment.'

'Stop stalling and *play*.'

She swallowed and nodded, then closed her eyes.

Her bow struck the first note.

And bounced off the string.

He watched her closely. The hand holding the violin—the hand with the short nails, which he suddenly realised were kept that length to stop them inadvertently hitting the strings when playing—was holding the instrument in a death grip. The hand holding the bow was shaking. It came to him in flash why her nails seemed so familiar. His grandmother had kept her nails in the same fashion.

'Take some deep breaths,' he instructed, hooking an ankle over his knee, making sure to keep his tone low and unthreatening.

She gave a sharp nod and, eyes still closed, inhaled deeply through her nose.

It made no difference. The bow bounced off the strings again.

She breathed in again.

The same thing happened.

'What are you thinking of right now?' he asked after a few minutes had passed, the only sound the intermittent bounce of her bow on the strings whenever she made another attempt to play. Her distress was palpable. 'What's in your head?'

'That I feel naked.'

Her eyes opened and blinked a couple of times before fixing on him. Even with Amalie at the other end of the room he could see the starkness in her stare.

'Do you ever have that dream where you go somewhere and are surrounded by people doing ordinary things, and you look down and discover you have *nothing* on?'

'I am aware of people having those dreams,' he conceded, although it wasn't one he'd personally experienced.

No, *his* dreams—nightmares—were infinitely darker, his own powerlessness represented by having to relive that last evening with his parents, when he'd jumped onto his father's back and pounded at him with his little fists.

His father had bucked him off with such force that he'd clattered to the floor and hit his head on the corner of their bed. In his dreams he had to relive his mother holding him in her arms, soothing him, kissing his sore, bleeding head and wiping away his tears which had mingled with her own.

It was the last time he'd seen them.

He hadn't been allowed to see them when they'd lain in state. The condition of their bodies had been so bad that closed caskets had been deemed the only option.

And that was the worst of his nightmares—when he would walk into the family chapel and lift the lids of their coffins to see the ravages the car crash had wreaked on them. His imagination in those nightmares was limitless…

'Try and imagine it, because it's the closest I can come to explaining how I feel right now,' she said, her voice as stark as the panic in her eyes.

For the first time he believed—*truly* believed—that her fear was genuine. He'd always believed it was real, but had assumed she'd been exaggerating for effect.

This was no exaggeration.

'You feel naked?' he asked evenly. He, more than anyone, knew how the imagination could run amok, the fear of the unknown so much worse than reality. He also knew how he could help her take the first step to overcome it.

'Yes,' she whispered.

The strange distance Amalie had seen settling over him had dissipated, and his attention on her was focused and strong.

'Then there is only one solution. You must *be* naked.'

'What…?'

But her solitary word hardly made it past her vocal cords. Talos had leant forward and was pulling his shoes and socks off.

What was he doing?

His hands went to his shirt. Before she could comprehend what she was seeing he'd deftly undone all the buttons.

'What are you doing?'

He got to his feet.

If she hadn't already pressed herself against the wall she would have taken a step back. She would have turned and run.

But there was nowhere for her to run *to*—not without getting past him first.

'The only way you're going to overcome your fear of nakedness is to *play* naked.'

His tone was calm, at complete odds with the panic careering through her.

She could not dislodge her tongue from the roof of her mouth.

He shrugged his arms out of his shirt and hung it on the back of a dining chair.

His torso was magnificent, broad and muscular, his skin a golden bronze. A light smattering of black hair covered his defined pecs, somehow tempering the muscularity.

As nonchalant as if he were undressing alone for a shower, he tugged at the belt of his trousers, then undid the button and pulled the zip down.

'Please, stop,' she beseeched him.

He fixed her with a stare that spoke no nonsense, then pulled his trousers down, taking his underwear with them. Stepping out of them, he folded and placed them over his shirt, then propped himself against the wall, his full attention back on her.

'I am not going to force you to take your clothes off,' he said, in that same deep, calm tone. 'But if you play naked for me now you will have lived out your worst fear and in the process you will have overcome it. I would not have you at the disadvantage of being naked alone so I have removed my clothes to put us on an equal footing. I will stay here, where I stand. You have my word that I will not take a step closer to you. Unless,' he added with the wolf-ish grin she was becoming familiar with, 'you ask me to.'

All she could do was shake her head mutely, but not with the terror he was reading in her, but because she'd been rendered speechless.

She'd known Talos naked would be a sight to behold, but she had never dreamed how magnificent he would be.

Why him? she wondered desperately.

Why did her body choose *this* man to respond to?

Why did it have to respond at all?

She knew what desire looked like, had seen her mother in its grip so many times, then seen her heart broken as her most recent lover tired of the incessant diva demands and ended things, shattering her mother's heart and fragile ego.

Passion and its companion desire were dangerous things she wanted no part of, had shied away from since early adolescence. Hearts were made to be broken, and it was desire that pulled you into its clutches.

All those protections she'd placed around her libido and sense of self were crumbling.

Talos's grin dropped. 'I said I would help you, little songbird, but you have to help yourself too. You have to take the first step.'

Her breaths were coming so hard she could feel the air expanding her lungs.

She thought frantically. She hadn't ever shown her naked body to a man before. Her few boyfriends had never put pressure on her, respecting her need to wait, the lie she'd told them in order to defer any kind of physicality. Kind men. *Safe* men.

Was it the safety she'd sought that had kept alive her fear of performing?

One of her psychiatrists—the most astute of them all—had once said he didn't believe she *wanted* to be fixed.

She'd denied it but now, looking back, she considered the possibility that he'd been partly right.

Her life was *safe*. Maybe a little boring, but she'd found her niche and she never wanted to leave it or the emotional protection it gave her.

But she had to. She couldn't stay there any longer. If she didn't step out she would lose that little niche anyway—for good. Her job would be gone. Her income would be gone. Her independence would be gone. All her friends' lives would be destroyed too.

'We are more alike than you think, you and I,' Talos said.

His voice was deeper and lower than she had ever heard it, every syllable full of meaning. He still hadn't made a move towards her.

'We have both chosen solitary pursuits. I focus on my boxing, you have your violin. No one can pull my punches for me and no one can play that violin for you. Think of the emotions you get when you're kickboxing, the adrenaline you feel through your veins. *That* is how you must imagine your fear—as something to be channelled and fought. You are on Agon, the land of warriors. We fight. And so must you. *Fight*, little songbird. Loosen your hold and *fly*.'

She gripped onto the piano for support and closed her eyes, his words resonating through her.

Was it time to confront all the fear?

If not now, then when?

If not here, then where?

'Will you turn around when I undress?'

'I will, but when you play I will watch you. I cannot guarantee I will stop my thoughts roaming to inappropriate places, but I *can* guarantee I will not act on them.'

I wish I could guarantee the same.

'If you can get through this you can get through anything. I give you my word.'

Strike her down, but she believed him.

'Right here and now it is you and me—no one else.

If you make mistakes then keep going. You can do this, Amalie.'

Whether it was the calm sincerity in his voice or the confidence emanating from him—God, he was *naked*—something worked, turning the panic inside her down low enough for her to get a grip on herself.

'Please turn around,' she said shakily.

He did as she asked, standing so his back was to her. His back was every bit as beautiful as his front, his body a mass of taut muscle and sinew. He was not professional-body-builder big, but big enough that you would trust him to pull a car off a helpless victim and then carry them over his shoulder to safety without breaking a sweat.

With fingers that fumbled she pulled off her pretty blue top and shrugged her skirt down. Her legs already bare, all that was left was her underwear. She tried to undo her bra, but what was second nature suddenly became the hardest job in the world.

'I *can't*,' she said, suddenly panic-stricken all over again.

Talos turned his head a touch before twisting his whole body round. Arms folded across his chest, he gazed at her, the look on his face something she'd never seen before. It looked as if it hurt him to breathe.

'That is enough,' he said quietly. 'Now, please—play for me.'

This time she allowed her eyes to dart down and look at what she'd tried to keep as a haze, skimming around the area as if it were pixilated.

The heat that rushed through her at one glance almost knocked her off her feet.

The knowing look that came into his eyes had the same effect.

Talos was in proportion in *every* way.

Suddenly she yanked her violin off the piano, put it under chin and began to play.

The bow swept across the strings, bouncing gently because of her less than graceful start, but then it did what it had been made to do, whilst her fingers flew up and down the strings. It was probably the worst start to a performance she'd ever given, but she wouldn't have known either way as at that moment she wasn't hearing the music, but simply relishing the fact that she was winning this fight. She was doing it. She was playing in front of someone.

God, she was virtually *naked*.

And Talos was as naked as the day he'd been born.

Somehow she settled into the music, embraced it, letting it become her. Far from closing her eyes, she kept her gaze on him, felt the heat of his returning stare.

By the time she played the last note the tension in the room had merged with the vibrato of her violin, a tangible, pulsating chemistry she felt all the way through to her core.

For long, long moments nothing was said. Not verbally.

The connection between their gazes spoke a thousand words.

'You brought my skin up in bumps,' he finally said, his voice raspy.

She gave a helpless shrug.

'You didn't play my grandmother's composition.'

She shook her head. She had played the final movement of one of Vivaldi's *Four Seasons* concertos—'Summer'. The movement that evoked a thunderstorm and perfectly fitted the storm raging beneath her skin.

'I didn't want you to hear it when I knew I wouldn't be able to do it justice. Not the first time.'

'The first time should be special, yes.'

She breathed deeply, sensing he wasn't talking about the music any more.

He made no move towards her. The look in his eyes was clear. He'd made her a promise not to get any closer to her. Not unless she invited him to.

Her blood had never felt so thick, as if she'd had hot treacle injected into her veins.

She wanted him. Desperately. Passionately…

No!

The warning shout in her head rang out loud and clear, breaking through the chemistry buffeting them, shattering it with one unsaid syllable.

Without a word she grabbed her top and pulled it back on, smoothing it over her belly as she darted a glance to see his reaction.

He inclined his head, an amused yet pained smile on his lips, then turned to his clothes and stepped back into his underwear and trousers before slipping his powerful arms into his shirt.

'You played beautifully, little songbird. And now it is time for me to leave.'

'Already?' The word escaped before she could catch it.

He dropped his stare down to his undone trousers. 'Unless you want me to break my promise?'

He cocked his head, waiting for an answer that wouldn't form.

'I thought not.' His eyes flashed. 'But we both know it's only a matter of time.'

She swallowed the moisture that had filled in her mouth, pushing it past the tightness in her throat.

'A car will collect you tomorrow at seven.'

'Seven?' she asked stupidly, her mind turning blank at his abrupt turn of conversation.

'Helios's ball,' he reminded her, fastening the last of his buttons. 'Did you receive the official invitation?'

She nodded. Her invitation had been hand delivered by a palace official, the envelope containing it a thick, creamy material, sealed with a wax insignia. Receiving it had made her feel like a princess from a bygone age.

'Keep it safe—you'll need to present it when you arrive. I'll be staying at my apartment in the palace for the weekend, so I'll send a car for you.'

She'd assumed they would travel there together, and

was unnerved by the twinge of disappointment she felt at learning differently.

'Okay,' she answered, determined to mask the emotion.

It wasn't as if they were going on a proper date or anything, she reminded herself. She was simply his 'plus one' for the evening.

'Are you happy with your dress?' he asked.

On Monday Amalie had been driven by a member of Talos's staff to a pretty beachside house and introduced to an elegant elderly woman called Natalia. Natalia had measured every inch of her, clearly seizing her up as she did so. Then she had sat at her desk and sketched, spending less time than it took for Amalie to finish a coffee before she'd ripped the piece of paper off the pad and held out the rough but strangely intricate design to her.

'This is your dress,' she had said, with calm authority.

Amalie had left the house twenty minutes later with more excitement running through her veins than she had ever experienced before. She'd been to plenty of high-society parties in her lifetime, but never to a royal ball. And she was to wear a dress like *nothing* she had worn in her life. Natalia's vision had been so compelling and assured that she had rolled along with it, swept up in the designer's vision.

It was strange and unnerving to think she was to be the guest of a prince. She no longer thought of Talos in that light. Only as a man…

'Natalia is bringing it tomorrow so she can help me into it.' The dress fastening was definitely a two-person job. If the designer hadn't been coming to her Amalie would have had to find someone else to help her fasten it. She might have had to ask Talos to hook it for her…

He nodded his approval.

Dressed, Talos ran his fingers through his hair in what looked to Amalie like a futile attempt on his behalf to tame it.

There was nothing tameable about this man.

'Until tomorrow, little songbird,' he said, before letting himself out of the cottage.

Only when all the energy that followed him like a cloud had dissipated from the room did Amalie dare breathe properly.

With shaky legs she sat on the piano bench and pressed her face to the cool wood.

Maybe if she sat there for long enough the compulsion to chase after him and throw herself at him would dissipate too.

CHAPTER EIGHT

THE BLACK LIMOUSINE drove over a bridge and through a
long archway before coming to a stop in a vast courtyard
at the front of the palace.

Her heart fluttering madly beneath her ribs, Amalie
stared in awe, just as she'd been gaping since she'd caught
her first glimpse of it, magnificent and gleaming under the
last red embers of the setting sun.

The driver opened the door for her and held out an arm,
which she accepted gratefully. She had never worn heels
so high. She had never felt so...*elegant.*

*That's what wearing the most beautiful bespoke dress
in creation does for you.*

Still gaping, she stared up. The palace was so vast she
had to make one-hundred-and-eighty-degree turns to see
from one side to the next. Although vastly different in style,
its romanticism rivalled France's beautiful Baroque palaces.
Its architecture was a mixture of styles she'd seen throughout Europe and North Africa, forming its own unique and
deeply beautiful style that resembled a great sultan's palace with gothic undertones.

Two dozen wide curved steps led up to a high-arched
ornate entrance, where two footmen dressed in purple-
and-gold livery with yellow sashes stood. She climbed the
steps towards them, thinking that this was surely what Cin-
derella had felt like. After studiously checking her official
invitation, another footman stepped forward to escort her
into the palace itself.

First they entered a reception room so vast her entire

cottage would fit inside it—roof and all, with room to spare—then walked through to another room where a group of footmen were being given last-minute instructions by a man who wore a red sash over his livery.

'Am I the first to arrive?' she asked her escort, who unfortunately spoke as much French and English as she spoke Greek—none at all.

It wasn't just the footmen being given instructions or the lack of other guests that made her think she was the first. Scores of waiting staff were also being given a last-minute briefing, many straightening clothing and smoothing down hair. She could feel their eyes on her, and their muted curiosity over the strange woman who had clearly arrived too early.

As she was led into another room—narrower, but much longer than the first reception room—staff carrying trays of champagne were lining up along the walls, beneath a gallery of portraits. At the far end were three tall figures dressed in black, deep in conversation.

Amalie's heart gave a funny jump, then set off at an alarming rate that increased with every step she took towards them. Her escort by her side, she concentrated on keeping her feet moving, one in front of the other.

Suddenly Talos turned his head and met her gaze, his eyes widening with such dumbstruck appreciation that her pulse couldn't help but soar. It was a look men so often threw at her beautiful mother, but never at her. But then, Amalie had never *felt* beautiful before. Tonight, thanks to the hairstylist and beautician Natalia had brought along with her when she'd arrived at the cottage to dress her, she did. She felt like a princess.

And Talos...

Talos looked every inch the Prince.

Like the two men beside him, who matched him in height and colouring, he wore a black tuxedo with a purple bowtie and sash that matched the livery of the palace footmen, and black shoes that gleamed in the same manner as his eyes. For the first time since she'd met him she saw him freshly shaved.

She'd thought the rugged Talos, the man she was getting to know, was as sexy a man as she could ever meet. The princely Talos had lost none of his edge and the wolfish predatory air was still very much there. Not even the expensive dinner jacket could diminish his essential masculinity. He still looked like a man capable of throwing a woman over his huge shoulder and carrying her to a large nomad-style tent to pleasure her in a dozen different ways before she had time to draw breath.

Amalie drew in her own breath as molten heat pooled low inside her at the thought of Talos pleasuring *her*...

Judging from the look in his eyes, something similar was running through his mind.

He strode over to greet her, enveloping her hand in his before leaning down to kiss her on each cheek.

Suddenly she couldn't breathe, her senses completely filled with his scent and the feel of his lips against her skin.

'Little songbird, you are beautiful,' he whispered into her ear, his deep, gravelly voice sending her heart beating so fast it felt as if it would jump out of her chest. 'Let me introduce you to my brothers,' he said while she strove valiantly for composure. 'Helios, Theseus—this is my guest for the evening: Amalie Cartwright.'

Theseus nodded and smiled. 'A pleasure to meet you.'

'And you,' she murmured in reply.

Helios extended his hand to her, his dark eyes studying her. 'I understand you are playing our grandmother's composition at the gala?'

Her cheeks flushing, she nodded and accepted his hand. Suddenly she realised that this was the heir to the throne she was standing before, and bent her knees in a clumsy form of curtsy.

Helios laughed, but not unkindly, before putting his

hands on her shoulders and kissing her on each cheek. 'You are my brother's guest—please, do not stand on ceremony.'

'I'm surprised she even tried,' Talos drawled, slipping an arm around her waist and placing a giant hand on her hip.

Dear God, he was *touching* her. Even through the heavy cloqué material of her dress she could feel the weight of his touch.

'The last time Amalie and I discussed matters of ceremony she reminded me that the French chopped all their royal family's heads off.'

Mortified, she reflexively elbowed him in the stomach, only to elicit more deep laughter from the three Princes that was so contagious her nerves vanished and she found herself laughing along with them.

Although of similar height and colouring, the differences between the brothers were noticeable up close. Theseus, maybe an inch or two shorter than Talos, had a more wiry build and an edgy weariness about him. Helios was as tall as Talos and had a real air of irreverence about him; a man who enjoyed life and was comfortable in his skin.

An officious courtier appeared at their sides and addressed the Princes in Greek.

'We must take our positions,' Talos said quietly.

'Where shall I go?' she asked.

'With me…to greet our guests. Tonight you will stay by my side.'

The gleam in his eyes conveyed a multitude of meanings behind his words. A shivery thrill ran through her, and when he linked his arm through hers she accepted the warmth that followed.

'Where are your brothers' dates?' she asked in a low voice.

'That is the whole purpose of the evening,' he answered enigmatically as they stepped into a cavernous room with a medieval feel, draped with purple sashes. Long dark wood tables formed an enormous horseshoe, laid with gleaming cutlery and crystal glasses that bounced the light from the chandeliers.

She gasped, totally losing track of her interest in his brothers' lack of dates. 'How many people are eating?'

'One hundred and eighty,' Talos answered, grinning.

The Banquet Room never failed to elicit a reaction. And neither, it seemed, did Amalie ever fail to make his senses react. One look and he wanted nothing more than to whisk her away somewhere private and feast on *her*.

With his brothers at the main door, greeting the guests, his role was to welcome them into the Banquet Room and act as host until all the guests had arrived.

Scores of waiting staff were stationing themselves with trays of champagne in hand. Talos helped himself to a glass for them both and passed one to Amalie.

'Drink it in one,' he advised. 'It will relieve the tedium of the next half hour.'

He laughed as she did as he suggested—with enthusiasm and without spilling a single drop.

He could not get over how ravishing she looked. If she hadn't already been there as his guest he would have spent the evening pursuing her, determined to learn everything there was to know about this enchanting stranger in their midst. He would have rearranged the table settings to be seated next to her—would have done everything in his power to keep her as close to him as he could.

But he didn't need to do any of that. For this evening this stunning woman was already his.

'You look amazing,' he said. 'Natalia has outdone herself.'

Strapless, Amalie's gown showed only the slightest hint of cleavage, cinched in at the waist before spreading out and down to her feet, forming a train at the back. It wasn't just the shape of the dress and the way it showcased her slight form that made it so unique, but the heavy material and the colour too—black, with tiny gold sequins threaded throughout into swirling leaves, glimmering under the lights.

The dramatic effect was accentuated by a gold choker around her slender throat, and her dark hair was held in an elegant knot at the base of her neck. She wore large hooped earrings and her eyes were darkly defined, her lips the most ravishing of reds.

Her eyes, wide with obvious awe up until this point, narrowed. 'Has Natalia dressed many of your dates?'

There was a definite hint of tartness in her tone. He eyed her contemplatively. Was that tartness a sign of jealousy?

Jealousy was an emotion he had no time for. He neither cared about his lovers' past bedmates nor felt any pangs of regret when their time was over and they found someone new. If during their time together any sign of possessiveness reared its head, he would end the relationship there and then. Jealousy was dangerous—as dangerous as love itself—driving men and women to lose control of themselves with unimaginable consequences.

And yet hearing that tinge of jealousy filled his chest in a manner he didn't even want to begin contemplating. Not when he couldn't take his eyes from her…couldn't stop his imagination running wild about what lay beneath that stunning dress.

His imagination had run riot since the day before, when she'd played for him semi-naked.

In his head he'd imagined she would wear practical underwear—not the matching lacy black numbers that set off the porcelain of her skin. As slender as he'd imagined, her womanly curves were soft, her breasts high and surprisingly full. What lay beneath those pretty knickers? he'd wondered, over and over. Had she taken the route so many women seemed to favour nowadays? Or had she left herself as nature intended…?

Halfway through her playing he'd smothered a groan, thinking it would be a damn sight better if she were fully naked, as his wild imaginings were utter torture. The expression in her eyes had only added to his torment.

For the first time in his life he'd come close to breaking a promise. He'd known that if he'd taken her into his arms she would have been his. But it hadn't only been his promise that had kept him propped against the cottage wall. It had been the shyness he'd seen when she'd first stood before him wearing only her underwear—a shyness he'd not seen since his lusty teenage years. An innocence that made him certain Amalie had minimal experience with men.

That innocence had acted like an alarm. A warning. Alas, it had done nothing to diminish the ache, which hadn't abated a touch, not in his groin or in his chest. All day, helping his brothers with the evening's arrangements, his mind had been elsewhere—in the cottage, with her.

'Natalia was my grandmother's official dressmaker,' he said softly. 'She made her wedding dress and my mother's wedding dress. She's mostly retired now, but as a favour to me agreed to make your ball gown. I've never sent another woman to her.'

Dark colour stained her cheeks—almost as dark as the wide dilation of her eyes. Was that what her eyes would look like when she was in the throes of passion...?

The thought was broken when the first guests were led into the Banquet Room. Two footmen stood at the door, handing out the evening's booklets—a guide for each guest that was adorned with purple ribbon. Each booklet contained a full guest list, the menu, wine list and a seating plan, along with a list of the music to be played throughout the evening by the Agon Orchestra. The orchestra's role tonight should go some way towards mitigating any underlying resentment that a French orchestra would be playing at the official gala.

As his brothers had already given the official welcome, Talos's job was to keep the guests entertained until everyone had arrived.

He would have preferred to be at the main entrance, shaking hands. He hadn't been joking when he'd described the tedium of what was about to ensue. Almost two hundred guests filed into the Banquet Room, the majority of whom were, at the most, distant acquaintances but all of whom expected to be remembered personally and made to feel like the most important guest there.

Normally Theseus would take this role, and Talos would line up with Helios to do the official greeting. If there was one thing Talos couldn't abide, it was small talk, having to feign interest in interminably dull people. Tonight, though, he wanted to keep Amalie at his side—not wanting her to have to deal with scores of strangers alone. Palace protocol meant only members of the royal family could make the first greeting.

To his surprise, she was a natural at small talk; moving easily between people with Talos by her side, taking an interest in who they were and what they did that wasn't feigned, her smiles as warm for those from the higher echelons of society as for those much further down the social ladder.

If she was aware of all the appreciative gazes being thrown her way by men and women alike she did a good job of pretending not to be.

When the gong rang out, signalling for everyone to take their seats, Talos looked at his watch and saw over half an hour had passed since the first guests had stepped into the Banquet Room. The time had flown by.

'You mastered the room like a pro,' he said in an undertone as they found their seats on what had been designated the top table.

She cast puzzled eyes on him.

'The way you handled our welcome job,' he explained. 'Most people would be overwhelmed when faced with one hundred and eighty people wanting to make small talk.'

She shrugged with a bemused expression. 'My parents

were always throwing parties. I think I mastered the art of small talk before I learned how to walk.'

'You attended their parties?'

'I was the main party piece.'

Before he could ask what she meant another gong sounded out and a courtier bade them all into silence as Helios and Theseus strode regally into the room.

No one took a seat until Helios, the highest-ranked member of the family in attendance, had taken his.

A footman pulled Amalie's chair out for her, while Talos gathered the base of the train of her dress so she could sit down with ease. He caught a glimpse of delicate white ankle and had to resist the urge to run his fingers over it, to feel for himself the texture of her skin.

'Thank you,' she murmured, her eyes sparkling.

'You're welcome.'

Taking his own seat, he opened his booklet to peruse the menu. As Helios had directed, the four-course meal had an international flavour rather than one specifically Greek or Agonite.

White wine was poured into the appropriate glasses, the starter of dressed crab with an accompanying crab timbale, crayfish and prawns was brought out by the army of serving staff, and the banquet began.

'Is your grandfather not attending?' Amalie whispered before taking a sip of her wine.

'He is unwell.'

'Nothing serious, I hope?' she asked with concern.

He forced a smile. 'A touch of flu, that's all.'

'It must be a worry for you,' she said, clearly seeing through his brevity.

'My grandfather is eighty-seven and as tough as a horse,' he deflected artfully.

She laughed. 'My English grandfather is eighty-five and tough as a horse too. They'll outlive the lot of us!'

How he wished that was the case, he thought, his heart

turning to lead as he envisaged a life without his grandfather, a steady if often aloof presence, but someone who had always been there.

For the first time he felt the compulsion to confide, to tell the truth of his grandfather's condition. It was there, right on the tip of his tongue. And he was the man who confided in *no one*. Not even his brothers.

The thought was unsettling.

Talos had learned the art of self-containment at the age of seven. The only person able to give him enough comfort to sleep when the nightmares had become too much to bear had died five years ago.

Yet for all the solace his grandmother had given him she'd never been able to give him peace. No one could give him that. He would sit stiffly in her arms, refusing to return the physical comfort she gave him. It had been a battle of wills with himself, something he could control and that no one could ever take away.

He'd been wise not to return the affection. How much greater would his pain have been if he had? He'd loved his mother with the whole of his heart. Her death had come close to destroying him.

The pain of his grandmother's death had still hit him like one of the punches he received in the boxing ring, but it had been survivable. If he'd allowed himself to love her the way he'd loved his mother, he didn't like to think how he would have reacted. Would the control he'd spent most of his lifetime perfecting have snapped? Would he have returned to those awful adolescent days when his fists had lashed out so many times he'd been on the verge of expulsion?

He was saved from having to respond by a young waiter asking if he would like his wine topped up.

If Amalie noticed his changed demeanour she gave no sign of it, craning her neck to follow their wine server's progress out of the room. 'Doesn't that boy work at your gym?'

He was impressed that she'd recognised him. Workout gear was markedly different from the fitted black-and-white waiter's uniform, with the purple ribbon stitched into the sides of the trousers.

'And she's from your gym too,' Amalie whispered, nodding at a young girl in the far corner.

'Most of the kids who work at the gym are working here tonight—it's extra money for them and good experience.'

He had to admit to feeling an inordinate amount of pride, watching them performing their jobs so well. He'd fought the protocol battle a number of years ago, to allow 'his' kids to work at the palace whenever the opportunity arose.

'Do you make a point of employing teenagers?'

'It was one of the reasons I decided to build my own gym—I wanted to employ disaffected teenagers and make them feel a sense of worth in themselves. The kids who work there are free to spar and train whenever they're off duty for no charge.'

'These kids are allowed to *box*?'

'You disapprove?'

'It's one thing for a fully grown adult to choose to get into a boxing ring and have his face battered, but quite another when it's a developing teenager.'

'Teenagers are full of hormones they have to navigate their way through. It's a minefield for many of them.'

'I agree, but…'

'Agon is a wealthy island, but that doesn't mean it's problem-free,' he said, wanting her to understand. 'Our teenagers have the same problems as other Western teenagers. We give jobs and training to the ones living on the edge—the ones in danger of dropping out of society, the ones who, for whatever reason, have a problem controlling their anger. Boxing teaches them to control and channel that anger.'

Hadn't he said something similar to her just the day before, in her cottage? Amalie wondered, thinking hard about the conversation they'd shared. The problem was her own hormones and fear had played such havoc that much of their conversation was blurred in her memory.

'Is that why *you* got into boxing?'

His jaw clenched for the beat of a moment before relaxing. 'I had anger issues. My way of coping with life was using my fists.'

'Was that because of your parents?' she asked carefully, aware she was treading on dangerous ground.

He jerked a nod. 'Things came to a head when I was fourteen and punched my roommate at my English boarding school. I shattered his cheekbone. I would have been expelled if the Head of Sport hadn't intervened.'

'They wanted to expel you? But you're a *prince*.'

His eyes met hers, a troubled look in them. 'Expulsion was a rare event at my school—who wants to be the one to tell a member of a royal family or the president of a country that their child is to be permanently excluded? But it wasn't a first offence—I'd been fighting my way through school since I was eight. The incident with my roommate was the final straw.'

He couldn't read what was in her eyes, but thought he detected some kind of pity—or was it empathy?

She tilted her head, elongating the swan of her neck. 'How did your Head of Sport get them to change their mind?'

'Mr Sherman said he would personally take me under his wing and asked for three months to prove he could tame my nature.'

'He did that through boxing?' Now she thought about it, Amalie could see the sense in it. Hadn't the kickboxing workouts Talos had forced her into doing created a new equilibrium within her? Already she knew that when she returned to Paris she would join a gym that gave the same classes and carry on with it.

'At my school you had to be sixteen to join the boxing team, but he persuaded them—with the consent of my grandparents—to allow me to join.' He laughed, his face relaxing as he did so. 'Apart from my brothers, I was the biggest boy in the school. There was a lot of power behind my punches, which was what had got me into so much trouble in the first place. Mr Sherman taught me everything we now teach the kids who use our gym—the most important being how to channel and control my anger.'

'Did it work?'

'I haven't thrown a punch in anger since.'

'That is really something.'

Self-awareness nagged at her—an acknowledgement that while Talos had handled his rage through using his fists, she'd retreated from her own fears and buried them. But while he'd confronted and tamed his demons she'd continued hiding away, building a *faux* life for herself that was nothing like her early childhood dreams—those early days when she'd *wanted* to be a virtuoso on the violin, just like her father.

She'd been five years old when she'd watched old footage of him at Carnegie Hall—the same night he'd played on stage with Talos's grandmother—and she'd said, with all the authority of a small child, 'When I'm growed up I'll play there with you, Papa.'

She'd let those dreams die.

CHAPTER NINE

I T TOOK A FEW beats for Amalie to regain her composure. 'Did you get to take part in proper boxing matches?'

'I was school champion for four years in a row—a record that has never been broken.' He placed a finger to the scar on his eyebrow. 'That was my most serious injury.'

She winced. 'Did you want to take it up professionally?'

'I'm a prince, so it was never an option—royal protocol.' He gave a rueful shake of his head, then flashed another grin that didn't quite meet his eyes. 'I *did* win every amateur heavyweight boxing award going, though, including an international heavyweight title.'

'No!' she gasped. 'Really?'

'It was six years ago.'

'That is incredible.'

'It was the best day of my life,' he admitted. 'Receiving the winner's belt with the Agon National Anthem playing… Yes, the best day of my life.'

She shook her head in awe, a thrill running through her as she saw a vision of Talos, standing in the centre of a boxing ring, perspiration dripping from his magnificent body, the epitome of masculinity…

'Truly, that's incredible. Do you still compete?'

'I haven't boxed in a competitive match since. I knew if I couldn't fight professionally I wanted to retire on a high.'

'You must miss it, though.'

She tried to imagine having to stop playing her violin and felt nothing but coldness. Her earliest concrete memory was receiving her first violin at the age of four. Yes, it had partly been forced on her, but she'd loved it, had adored making the same kind of music as her papa, revelled in her parents' excitement when she'd taken to it with such an affinity that they couldn't resist showing her off to the world. She'd loved pleasing her parents but before she'd reached double digits the resulting attention from the outside world had turned into her personal horror story. She might have inherited her parents' musicality, but their showmanship had skipped a generation.

He shrugged. 'I still spar regularly, but in truth I knew it was time to focus my attention on the business my brothers and I founded. Theseus had gone off on his sabbatical, so Helios was running it almost single-handedly along with dealing with his royal duties. It wasn't fair on him.'

'I don't understand why you all put so much into the business when you have so much wealth.'

He eyed her meditatively. 'How much do you think it costs to run a palace this size? The running costs, the maintenance, the staff?'

'A lot?'

'Yes. A lot. And that's just for one palace. Factor in the rest of our estates—my villa, for example—travelling costs, security...'

'I can imagine,' she cut in, feeling slightly dizzy now he was explaining it.

'My family has always had personal wealth,' Talos explained, 'but a considerable portion of our income came from taxes.'

'Came?'

He nodded. 'My brothers and I were determined to make our family self-sufficient, and three years ago we succeeded. Our islanders no longer pay a cent towards our upkeep. I might not compete any more, but I get all the intellectual stimulation I need.'

Amalie swallowed, guilt replacing the dizziness. She'd been so dismissive of his wealth.

Talos Kalliakis might be unscrupulous at getting his own way but he had a flip side—a side that was loyal, decent and thoughtful. He clearly loved his island and his people.

'What about the physical stimulation you got from competitive boxing?' she asked. 'Have you found a replacement for that?'

His eyes glistened, a lazy smile tugging at his lips. 'There is a physical pastime I partake in regularly that I find *very* stimulating...'

The breath in her lungs rushed out in a whoosh.

When he looked at her like that and spoke in that meaningful tone all her senses seemed to collide, making her tongue-tied, unable to come up with any riposte—witty or otherwise.

For the first time she asked herself why she should. Why make a joke out of something that made her blood and belly feel as warm and thick as melted chocolate? Why continue to deny herself something that could take her places she'd locked away?

Hadn't she punished herself enough?

That thought seemed to come from nowhere, making her blink sharply.

Punished herself enough?

But there was something in that. Her fear was wrapped in so many layers, with her guilt over her role in her parents' divorce bound tightly in the middle of it.

Talos had confronted his fears and mastered them. Wasn't it time she allowed herself the same? She didn't have to suppress her basic biological needs and be a virgin for ever out of fear. Or guilt.

She wasn't her mother. Allowing herself to be with Talos and experience the pleasure she just *knew* she would receive at his willing giant hands wouldn't be a prelude to falling in love. A man holding one hundred musicians' livelihoods to ransom for the sake of a *gala* could pose no risk to her heart.

She cleared her throat and dropped her voice to a murmur. 'Would you care to elucidate on this stimulation you speak of?'

She would swear his eyes darkened to match the melting chocolate in her veins.

He leaned his head forward and spoke into her exposed ear. 'I can do much better than that…'

The chocolate heated and pooled down low, right in the apex of her thighs…the feeling powerful enough to make her lips part and a silent moan escape her throat.

Just when she was certain he was going to kiss her—or, worse, *she* was going to kiss *him*—activity around them brought her to her senses.

They were in the Banquet Room of the royal palace, surrounded by almost two hundred people, the heir to the throne sitting only six seats to her right. And she was bubbling up with lust.

During the rest of the banquet she made a studious effort to speak to the gentleman on her right, a prince from the UK. Through it all, though, her mind, her senses, her *everything* were consumed by Talos, deep in conversation with the woman to his left, a duchess from Spain.

Somehow their chairs had edged closer so his thigh brushed against hers, and when their dessert of *loukoumades*—a delicious Greek doughnut, drizzled with honey, cinnamon and walnuts—was cleared away, and they were awaiting the final course of fresh fruit, a shock ran through her when his hand came to rest on her thigh.

She wished she'd tried to talk Natalia into a different material for the dress; something lighter. The heavy fabric suited the theatricality of the dress beautifully, but while she could feel the weight of Talos's hand there was none of the heat her body craved.

It wasn't enough.

She wanted to *feel* him.

Sucking in a sharp breath to tame the thundering of her heart, she casually straightened, then moved her hand under the table to rest on his. As she threaded her fingers through his he gave the gentlest of squeezes, and that one simple action sent tiny darts of sensation rippling through her abdomen.

Strong coffee and glasses of port were poured, whilst the British Prince chattered on about one of the charities he was patron of. Amalie tried hard to keep her attention fixed on him, smiling in all the right places, laughing when appropriate, all the while wishing every guest there would magically disappear and leave her alone with Talos.

She hadn't drunk much wine—a couple of glasses at most—but felt as if she'd finished a whole bottle, because at that moment she felt giddily out of control.

Talos still had hold of her thigh, his thumb making circular motions on the material so torturously barricading him from her skin.

She had no idea where her nerve came from—maybe her fingers had a life of their own, because they moved away from his hand to tentatively brush his thigh. He stiffened at her touch, his own hand tightening its hold on her.

The British Prince chattered on, clearly oblivious to the undercurrents playing out beside him.

Slowly her fingers crept over Talos's thigh until her whole hand rested on it. The fabric of his trousers felt silken to her fingers, contrasting with the taut muscularity they covered. She could *feel* him.

He sat as stiff as a statue, making no attempt to move when, with a flush of heat she realised her little finger was right at the crevice of his thigh, the line of the V that connected it to his groin...

A feeling of recklessness overtook her and she swiped the little finger up a little further—deeper into his heat, closer to the source of his masculinity.

The statue came to life.

Talos swept his hand away from her thigh to reach for his port, which he swilled down before putting the glass back on the table. Not that she saw him do any of those things, rather she felt them, her attention still, to anyone interested enough to be watching, fixed on the British Prince.

Then Talos's hand was back under the table and clasping hers, which was slowly stroking his thigh, her little finger brushing the V of his groin. Twisting it so he could hold it tightly, he entwined his fingers in hers.

'Are you okay?' the British Prince asked, pausing in his talk on water sanitation in developing countries. 'You look flushed.'

She felt her neck and cheeks flame. 'I think I need some air, that's all,' she said to the Prince, hoping she didn't sound as flustered as she felt inside.

A warm arm slipped behind her back and round her waist and Talos was there, pressing against her, ostensibly having abandoned his conversation with the Duchess to join in with theirs.

'Don't worry, little songbird,' he said, his deep voice sending reverberating thrills racing through her. 'The banquet will soon be over.'

Talos felt as if he needed air too...

If her hand had moved any higher and actually touched the hardness that was causing him such aching pain he would have come undone on the spot.

Never in his life had he been so aroused, not even yesterday in the cottage where, despite their lack of clothing, it had been a different arousal.

He sensed no fear in Amalie now.

No, this was a special kind of sweet torture and in front of all Helios's guests he was unable to do a damn thing about it.

So long as he kept her hand away from his crotch he would master it. The most sensible option would be to stop touching her altogether, but sensible didn't count for anything—not when it was Amalie Cartwright he was touching.

He let out a breath of relief when the palace quartet entered the Banquet Room, mandolins and banjos playing out the guests with the folk music beloved of all Agonites.

The Agon royal party rose first. Keeping her hand firmly clasped in his, Talos led Amalie through to the adjoining ballroom, delighting in her gasp of pleasure.

The ballroom was by far the most majestic of all the palace rooms, both in size and stature. With high ceilings and a black-and-white checked floor, even Talos experienced a thrill of stepping into a bygone age whenever he entered it.

As soon as the royal party entered, the orchestra, situated in a corner, began to play.

Most of the guests took seats at the highly decorated round tables lining the walls, free to choose where they wanted to sit. The two ornate thrones at the top of the room shone under the swooping chandeliers. Looking at them sent a pang through him. They would remain empty for the duration of the evening.

He wondered how his grandfather was, his stomach twisting at the remembrance of the vomiting episode he had witnessed just a few short hours ago. He consoled himself with the knowledge that should his grandfather take a turn for the worse he and his brothers would be notified immediately.

Talos guided Amalie to a table and poured them both a glass of wine. Theseus joined them and, as was his nature, soon had Amalie giggling as he regaled her with tales of their childhood.

A strange tightening spread across his chest to see her so clearly enthralled, and with a start he realised the cause. Jealousy. *His* jealousy. She'd never laughed so freely for him.

This was becoming dangerous.

Desire was one thing, but jealousy… That was one emotion too far and too ugly.

That was what you got for spending so much time with a beautiful woman without bedding her. If he'd bedded her from the start her allure would have vanished already and he would now be focussing on getting her performance-fit without wasting energy wondering how she looked naked or whether she moaned loudly when she came.

For all his words about 'partaking' regularly, he hadn't been with a woman in months—not since his grandfather's diagnosis. It was as if his libido had gone into stasis.

And now his libido had gone into hyperdrive.

Forget noble thoughts about not taking advantage of her position on the island, or that she was there because of his blackmail. The chemistry between them had gone off the charts. All they needed was one night to detonate it. One night. Come the morning, their chemistry would be spent. If not, they still had three weeks to expel it completely, but they would have tamed the worst of it. They would be able to concentrate on nothing but her gala performance.

At that moment the orchestra broke into a waltz, indicating the start of the evening's dancing. Talos watched Helios take a deep breath, fix a smile to his face and cross the ballroom to tap a princess from the old Greek royal family on the shoulder. She was on her feet like a shot, allowing him to lead her onto the dance floor. It was the cue for the other guests who fancied trying their hands at traditional ballroom dancing to get to their feet.

'Shouldn't you find a lady to dance with?' Talos pointedly asked his brother in Greek.

Theseus's smile dropped. He grimaced, his eyes darting around the room as if he were searching for someone. 'I'll have a drink first. But don't let me stop you—you two make a beautiful couple.'

Talos narrowed his eyes and fixed Theseus with his 'stare'. Theseus pulled a face and swigged his wine.

'Would you like to dance?' he asked Amalie. Talos might loathe dancing, but the thought of having her in his arms was a temptation not to be resisted.

'I've never waltzed,' she said dubiously.

'Most of our guests have never waltzed. I will lead you.' That was if he could remember. He hadn't waltzed since the Debutantes Ball in Vienna, which his grandfather had forced him to attend when he was twenty-one. If his brothers hadn't already been forced into attendance at the same age he would have put up more than an obligatory protest.

She allowed him to help her to her feet and guide her onto the dance floor.

Facing her, he dropped her hand, took a step back and bowed. 'You must curtsy,' he instructed.

Her luscious lips spread into a smile. 'Certainly, Your Highness.'

He returned the smile and reached for her right hand with his left and held it out to the side. 'Now, place your other hand on my bicep.'

'There's enough of it for me to hold on to,' she answered, that same smile still playing on her lips, her eyes glimmering with a private message to him—a message he understood and that made his blood pressure rise so high his heart felt in danger of thudding out of his ribs.

To hell with the traditional hold, he thought, placing his right hand on her back and resting his fingers on the bare flesh above the lining of the dress.

She felt exquisite.

Soon they were swirling around the room, the enchantment on her face making all the ridiculous ballroom-dancing lessons he and his brothers had been subjected to in their teenage years worthwhile—something he had *never* thought would happen.

Amalie felt as if she'd stepped into heaven. She'd never waltzed before but it didn't matter; Talos guided her around the dance floor with a tenderness and grace that was as unexpected as it was heavenly.

She had never felt so feminine before either, the security of his arms something she would savour and relish.

The original gap between them when they'd started dancing had closed, and suddenly she was very much aware their bodies were pressed together.

Releasing her grip on his bicep, she smoothed her hand up to clasp the nape of his neck, glad a slower waltz was now being played, one that allowed her time to do nothing but gaze up into his eyes. Her legs followed his lead with no thought.

The heels she wore elevated her enough that her breasts pressed against his chest, his abdomen against the base of her stomach, but to her intense frustration she couldn't *feel* him anywhere other than on her back, where his hand rested, his heat scorching her skin in the most wonderful way imaginable.

'Your brothers seem nice,' she said, frantic to cut through the tension between them before she was forced into something drastic—like dragging him away.

'They're good men,' he agreed, his gaze not dropping from hers.

'What did you mean earlier, when I asked if they had dates and you said that was the whole purpose of the evening?'

He laughed lightly. 'It is time for Helios to end his bachelor days. He is hoping that tonight he will meet someone suitable.'

'Someone suitable? For marriage?'

'Yes. A woman of royal blood.'

'That sounds clinical.'

'He is heir to the throne.'

His fingers were making the same circles on her back that he'd made on her thigh, but this time she could actually feel it. And it felt wonderful.

'It is traditional for the heir to marry a woman of royal descent.'

'Is there a reason why he's looking for a bride now?' She thought of their absent grandfather, the King, and wondered if there was more to his illness than Talos was letting on.

'He's of the right age.'

She felt his muscles ripple as he lifted a shoulder in a shrug.

'He wants to be young enough to enjoy his children.'

'If you marry, will it have to be someone of royal descent too?' As she asked the question a strange clenching gripped her heart.

'No.'

'So if you marry it will be for love?'

His lips twisted into a mocking grin. 'If I marry it will be because someone has placed a gun to my head.'

'Marriage is a piece of paper. It doesn't mean anything.'

Love was the state she'd always feared—not a commitment so easily broken it wasn't worth the paper it was signed on. It was passionate love that made fools of people. A piece of paper could dissolve a marriage into nothing, but a severed heart never fully healed.

'It means a lot if you're a member of the Kalliakis royal family. Divorce is forbidden.'

That's fine, she thought. *I don't want to marry you. All I want is to touch you. Everywhere.*

That was why she would be safe from the threat of a severed heart. Her passion for Talos was purely physical. When she returned to Paris her heart wouldn't feel a thing, would only skip at memories of being with him.

'Is divorce forbidden for everyone on your island?'

'Only members of the royal family,' he murmured.

'And are you allowed lovers? Before you marry?' she added, dropping her voice even lower.

His eyes were a blaze of molten lava, his strong nose

flaring, his jaw clenched. 'If I want a lover no decree is going to stop me.'

Nothing and no one could stop this man doing *anything* he wanted.

The thought should appal her, but it didn't—not when the thought of allowing him to do whatever he wanted was so strong she dug her nails into his neck to stop her fingers yanking at her dress so she could press her bare skin to him. Her desperation to feel him was matched only by her desperation for him to feel *her*.

A finger tapped her shoulder. It was the British Prince. 'May I have the next dance?'

'No,' Talos growled, not looking at him, but tightening his hold on her back and his grip on her hand.

'You can't blame a chap for trying,' the Prince said, laughing ruefully before striding off to find another dance partner.

Talos stopped dancing. The clenching of his jaw was even more pronounced. 'I have an apartment here in the palace.'

She didn't miss a beat or fake coyness. 'Is it far?'

'It's closer than my villa or your cottage.'

A spark passed between them, so real and powerful she felt it in every atom of her being.

He brought her hand to his lips. 'Follow me,' he murmured.

CHAPTER TEN

HER HAND CLASPED tightly in his, Amalie followed Talos's lead, weaving through the waltzing couples, yearning to run but keeping her pace steady, avoiding eye contact lest anyone wanted to talk.

She could see the door he was leading her to, in the left-hand corner of the great room. The closer they got, the longer his strides became, until they were nodding at the footmen posted there and then slipping out into a corridor she didn't recognise. Judging by the strong scent of food, she figured they had to be close to the palace kitchens.

They took a left into another long corridor, then another and another. Staff were everywhere, all bowing as they passed.

It wasn't until they reached a fifth corridor, this one dimly lit, that they were completely alone.

Talos had her pinned to the wall so quickly there was no chance to draw breath.

His hands clasped her cheeks and his mouth crashed onto hers with a passion her starving body responded to immediately. His tongue swept across her lips, forcing them to part, then darted into her mouth, his resulting groan stoking the heat consuming her.

She responded with fire, cradling his head, returning the kiss with all the hunger that burned inside her for him.

No sooner had it started than he broke the kiss, keeping her pinned to the wall with his strength, his thumbs running in swirls over her cheeks, his brown eyes dark with intensity.

'I have never been closer to ripping a woman's dress off and taking her in public than I was in that ballroom,' he said roughly.

A pulse ran through her, deliciously powerful. In answer, she nuzzled into his hand and kissed his palm.

He stepped back, trailing his fingers down her neck to the edge of her dress, his breathing heavy. 'We're almost at my apartment.'

They set off again to the end of the corridor, walking at a speed only a tiny rate below a run, until they came to a spiralling marble staircase with a heavy rope barrier across the base of it. Talos moved it swiftly, indicating for her to go up. At the top was a small passage with a door at the end and a small security box by the side. He punched in the code and the door swung open.

Lights came on with the motion and Amalie found herself in an enormous masculine living space, richly furnished with plump charcoal-coloured sofas against a backdrop of muted blues and creams. The room's walls were covered in huge colourful paintings.

There was no time for looking with depth. Talos threw his jacket, sash and bow tie on the floor and guided her through the living area and into a bedroom dominated by the largest bed she'd ever seen—an enormous sleigh bed with intricate carvings.

On the wall opposite the door stood a floor-length mirror, edged with the same intricately carved wood. Catching sight of her reflection, she came to a stop.

Was that woman staring back at her with the flushed cheeks and wild eyes really her? Amalie? The woman who had formed a cosy life for herself while shying away from everything this man—this gorgeous man—was offering her? The man staring at her with a hunger she had only ever seen in films.

Transfixed, she watched as he stepped behind her, not touching her other than to place his hands on the tops of her arms. A small moan escaped her throat when he dropped a kiss in the arch of her neck.

Swaying lightly, she let her eyes flutter closed and sighed as his fingers swept across her shoulder blades and down her spine to rest at the top her dress.

Bending his head to kiss her ear and brush his lips lightly against her temple, he found and unfastened the hidden hook, then pinched the concealed zipper and slowly pulled it down, all the way to the base of her spine. His hands slid back up the exposed flesh to the top of the dress, then skimmed it assuredly down to her hips, exposing her bare breasts. When he released his hold on it the dress fell in a lazy whoosh to her feet, leaving her naked bar skimpy black knickers and gold shoes.

He wrapped an arm around her middle and held her against him, so she could lift her feet one at a time and step out of the vast amount of material. Talos kicked the dress away, then met her eyes in the reflection of the mirror, a dangerous, lustful glimmer in his stare.

Her chest thrust forward, almost begging for his touch.

The hand holding her so protectively brushed over her stomach and up her side, circling round her breasts to trace along her collarbone and up her neck to the base of her head. Slowly he worked at the elegant knot of her hair until he freed it, gently pulling it down to sprawl across her shoulders.

'Have you had many lovers, little songbird?' he asked, inhaling the scent of her hair.

Speech had deserted her; all she was capable of doing was shaking her head.

'Have you had *any* lovers?'

The second shake of her head had more force behind it, but inside she reeled.

Was her virginity *that* obvious?

He must have read the question in her expression. 'I am an expert at reading between lines,' he said enigmatically, before twisting her round to face him. He ran his thumb over her bottom lip. 'Why don't we even things up and you undress me?'

With hands that trembled, she reached for the top button of his shirt, fumbled with it, then found some dexterity and undid it, then the next. Working quickly, aware of the heaviness of his breathing, she undid them all, then spread the shirt open. Not even conscious of what she was about to do, she pressed her lips to his chest and breathed him in, inhaling the muskiness that evoked thoughts of dark forests and adrenaline-filled danger.

His chest rose and swelled, his hand reaching into her hair and gathering it in his fingers.

Her fingers trailed down the thickening black hair to his abdomen and found the hook fastening his hand-stitched trousers. She swallowed as the palm of her hand felt the heat beneath. She unhooked it, but then her nerve deserted her. Suddenly a burst of sanity crashed through the lustful haze she'd been entranced in.

She'd never touched a man intimately before.

She wanted to touch Talos with a need bordering on desperation, but for the first time her virginity was something she was wholly aware of.

How could she be anything but a disappointment to him? A man as rampantly masculine as Talos would have had scores of lovers, all confident in their bodies and sexuality.

Talos felt Amalie's hesitation, felt the fear creep through her.

His suspicions about her being a virgin had been right. He would have been more surprised to learn she'd had *any* lovers.

He didn't care about her reasons for never having had a lover; cared only that at this moment she was here, with him, and that the crazy chemistry between them could be acted upon. Amalie wasn't on the hunt for a relationship any more than he was; her comment about marriage only being a piece of paper had concurred with his own thoughts entirely.

But confirmation of her virginity *did* force him to take a deep breath and try to cool his ardour. All prior thoughts of simply discarding their clothes and falling into bed were gone. He needed to take it slow. He didn't want to hurt her. By the time he made her his he wanted her so turned on but also relaxed, he could enter her without causing any pain.

Gently he twisted her back to face the mirror, placing an arm around her belly. Her eyes closed and her head rolled back to rest on his shoulder, her breath coming in tiny hitches. He could feel her heartbeat hammering with an identical rhythm to his own.

Moving quickly, he unzipped his trousers with his free hand and worked them off, deliberately keeping his boxers on so the temptation to plunge himself straight into her could be more easily denied.

Done, he pressed himself into the small of her back, felt her tremble, saw her lips part in a silent moan.

'Open your eyes,' he commanded quietly into her ear.

They fluttered open and met his gaze in the reflection of the mirror.

His fingers played on the lace of her knickers and then tugged them down, delighting to find the dark silky hair below. He dipped a finger into her heat and groaned when he found her moist and swollen.

Keeping the pressure there light and rhythmical, he splayed his other hand upwards and captured a raised breast. It fitted perfectly into his hand. He could hardly wait to taste it, to taste every part of her but before he could take her into his arms and carry her to his bed her back arched, her groin pressed hard against his finger and she stiffened. He watched in awe at their reflection. Her eyes were tightly closed, her lips parted, her cheeks flushed. Then she shuddered and became limp in his arms. If she hadn't been secure against him, he had no doubt she would have fallen to the floor.

He'd never seen or felt anything like it—such a primal, animalistic response. It filled him with something he couldn't name...could only feel, gripping his chest.

Keeping her pressed tight against him, he turned her enough to lift her into his arms.

There was no resistance; her eyes gazed into his, dazed bewilderment ringing out. When she reached a hand to press a palm to his cheek he swallowed, his heart beating so fast it had become a painful thrum.

He laid her down on the bed and shrugged his open shirt off, discarding it on the floor.

She'd covered her breasts. He took hold of her hands and carefully parted them, exposing her full nakedness to him.

To his eyes, Amalie was perfect—her arms and legs toned and smooth, her skin soft, her breasts high, ripe peaches, begging to be tasted.

Bringing his head down to hers, he captured her lips. She returned his kiss with passion, her tongue sweeping into his mouth, her hot, sweet breath flowing into his senses. Her hands reached for his head and razed through his hair.

As he deepened the kiss he stroked his fingers down her body, exploring the soft skin, delighting in the mews escaping her throat.

Breaking the kiss, he ran his lips down her throat and lower, to her breasts, capturing one in his mouth...

Theos.

For the first time since his teenage years he was on the verge of losing control already. He had never felt so constricted by his boxer shorts, the tight cotton material as tight a barrier as steel.

But she tasted so *good*, of a sweet, feminine essence his senses reacted to. Not just his senses. Every part of him reacted to it.

'Is something wrong?' she whispered, uncertainty in her voice.

'No,' he promised, dragging his mouth back up to her lips and kissing her again. 'Everything is perfect.'

Her hands grabbed at his face, her fingers kneading his cheeks before sweeping over his neck and chest and down to his abdomen. This time she didn't hesitate, pushing under the cotton to lightly touch the head of his erection.

Her kisses stopped and she sucked in a breath.

'It doesn't bite,' he teased, smoothing her hair off her forehead.

Her lips twitched into a shy smile and she burrowed her face into his neck before her tongue darted out to lick his skin. She rubbed her leg against him, all the while slowly trailing her fingers down his length, which throbbed madly under her gentle ministrations. She made no attempt to take hold of it, seemingly content simply to stroke and explore. That this only made him harder than ever—something he had not thought possible—only added to his painful ardour. If he didn't find some release soon he feared he might actually combust.

'I don't use birth control,' she whispered into his neck.

'I didn't think you did,' he assured her, moving her hand away so he could lean over to his bedside table, where he dimly remembered throwing a packet of condoms into a drawer. They were still there. He pulled one out and ripped the foil off, all the time keeping his focus on Amalie, who had sat up and was now exploring his chest with her fingers, the expression on her face something close to rapture.

Kissing her first, he got off the bed and tugged his boxers down.

She met his eyes and swallowed.

'Don't be scared,' he murmured, kneeling back on the bed and gently pushing her flat, so her head rested on the pillow and she was laid out beneath him.

Her smile was dazzling. 'I'm not.'

He kissed her again, then disentangled her arms, which had hooked around his neck at the first press of his lips.

Working swiftly, he securely rolled the condom on, then knelt between her parted thighs. He brushed his hands over her beautiful downy hair, a thrill racing through him to feel her damp heat all over again, his arousal increasing when she bucked upwards to meet his touch.

Then, moving slowly, he laid himself on top of her, taking care not to put his full weight on her. Moving even slower, he guided his erection to the welcome warmth of her opening.

Her hands gripped his shoulders, her nails digging into his flesh.

Her eyes were screwed tight shut.

'Look at me, little songbird,' he said, stroking her cheek.

She opened her eyes. That dazed look had returned to them.

He pushed forward a little more, clenching his teeth as he stopped himself from driving in any deeper. Amalie had never done this before. If he were to do what he so desperately wanted and simply plunge deep inside her he would hurt her, no matter how hot and wet she was for him.

Theos, she felt so *tight*.

He inched forward some more, giving her time to adjust before pressing a little further. Each new push forward elicited the same gasp from her lips: a hitch of surprised pleasure.

As he continued to inch slowly into her he brushed his lips against hers, relishing the short, ragged breaths she breathed back into him.

When he was fully sheathed inside her he paused to catch his own breath and closed his eyes, forcing his mind to think of something—*anything*—other than what they were doing at that moment.

But no matter how hard he tried, even with his eyes firmly shut, all he could see was Amalie.

She shifted slightly beneath him, her hands moving from his shoulders to trail down his back, causing thrills of shivers racing down his spine.

Only when he was sure he had control of himself did he withdraw—not all the way, but enough so that when he pushed back he had to grit his teeth more to retain his control.

This was *torture*. The most divine torture he had ever known.

For the first time in his life he truly wished he could make love without the barrier of a condom, to experience every single aspect of it.

He withdrew a little further, pressed back a little deeper.

Once he was certain Amalie had adjusted to this whole new experience, and that there was no discomfort for her, he allowed himself to settle into a rhythm, all the while telling himself to be gentle, to make this special for her.

He'd never experienced anything like it. Every thrust felt as if he were diving deeper into some unknown abyss, one filled with beautiful, dream-evoking colour.

There was something so *pure* about her responses. Nothing was for effect; everything—all her touches, all her kisses, all her soft moans—was an expression of how she was feeling at that moment and the pleasure she was taking from their lovemaking.

When he gripped her bottom and raised it, just enough to let him penetrate a little deeper, her cry into his mouth was the most beautiful sound he'd ever heard. Even though he was desperate for his own relief he held on, keeping the rhythm that had her tossing her head from left to right and made her breath shallow. Then he felt her thicken around him, felt her pulsing at the same moment she breathed out his name and clung to him, burying her face in his neck as her orgasm made her whole body vibrate and shudder.

He held on, waiting until her climax was spent, then raised himself onto his knees and spread her thighs further apart. He wanted to look at her, to drown in those emerald eyes. Placing one hand on her shoulder and the other on her breasts, he upped the tempo, thrusting in and out, gazing at her beautiful face, her wide eyes, her red-kissed lips, revelling in the little pulses that still came from within her, until he took one final, long thrust and his world exploded in colour.

When the jolts racketing through him finally abated his face was buried in Amalie's hair, which was sprawled over the pillow like a fan. Her arms were locked tightly round him; the only sound was the heavy thudding beat of their hearts.

Lethargy spread through him and he eased himself off her, something dim in the back of his sluggish mind reminding him he had the condom to dispose of. Dragging himself off the bed, he could feel her eyes on him as he padded to the bathroom.

He returned a few moments later, his chest tightening to see she'd slipped under the silk sheets. A shy smile played on her lips.

He hadn't thought this through. As a rule, he didn't bring women to his palace apartment, preferring to conduct his affairs in the privacy of his villa, or wherever in the world he happened to be.

It suddenly dawned on him that not only had he broken his unwritten rule of not conducting an affair within the palace walls, but he'd also run from Helios's ball. It was inconceivable that his absence would go unnoticed.

He couldn't bring himself to care. His grandfather was in bed and his brothers would understand. They'd both had their heads turned by beautiful women over the years. The ball was for Helios, and to a lesser extent for Theseus—not for him. He would never need to marry. The burden of continuing the Kalliakis dynasty was in his brothers' hands.

Now that the flush of lust had been satisfied he should

get dressed, get a chauffeur to take Amalie back to the cottage. Except…

She stretched under the covers, that smile still playing on her lips. 'Can we do that again?'

Amalie pulled Talos's shirt, discarded on the floor the evening before, closer around her, catching a wonderful whiff of his woody scent. She sighed dreamily.

That had to count as the most wonderful night of her life.

It amazed her to think she'd spent so long denying this sensual side of herself, marvelled that it had ever scared her. What had she been so frightened of? How could such pleasure be terrifying?

She gazed at Talos sleeping, from her vantage point of the bay window, where she'd settled herself earlier. She'd woken with the sun, the buzz in her blood from their passionate night still alive in her veins, zinging too loudly for her to fall back into sleep. Usually she did everything she could to eke out as much sleep as she could muster. But not today.

The view from his bedroom window was stunning, over-looking the palace maze. In the distance lay the open-air theatre the gala was to be held in—an enormous round dome, cut into the ground like something from Middle Earth. Judging by the view, and the fact that if she craned her neck she could see turrets in the distance, she figured his apartment must be in the far left tower of the palace.

The view from the window was nothing compared to the vision on the bed, curled on his side, one arm splayed out where she had been sleeping, as if he'd been seeking her. She wanted nothing more than to crawl back under the covers, but was determined to hold back and let him sleep. After all their lovemaking he would be exhausted.

She smiled. In sleep he looked curiously vulnerable.

For the first time in her life she felt complete. Like a

woman. Like she'd discovered a glorious secret. And at that moment she was happy to savour it and hold it close.

Talos stirred, his hand groping. He lifted his head.

'*Bonjour,*' she said softly, resting her chin on her knee.

He stretched onto his back and smiled lazily. '*Kalimera*, little songbird. Did you sleep well?'

She gave him a coy smile. 'No.'

'You should come back to bed, then.'

'I should,' she agreed, adopting the same mock serious tone.

He threw the sheets off him, unabashedly displaying his large erection.

Moisture filled her mouth and pooled down low. Sliding off the ledge of the bay window, she padded over to the bed. No sooner had she climbed on than Talos's huge hands were at her waist, pulling her over to straddle him.

He stared into her eyes, trailing a hand down the valley between her breasts. 'No regrets?'

She shook her head and sighed as his fingers found her nipple. 'No regrets.'

'Then make love to me, you sexy woman, and prove it.'

Sexy? *Her?* Sexy was a word she'd never associated with herself before.

Yet as she sheathed him, then sank down onto him, taking the whole of him inside her, she realised she'd never felt as sexy and as alive in her life.

And, dear heaven, it felt amazing.

CHAPTER ELEVEN

WAS IT TRULY possible to become addicted to sex?

The question played happily in Amalie's mind as she sat beside Talos in his Maserati, making polite noises as he pointed out a pile of stones he assured her had once been a monastery. Because there was no doubt about it—she was in lust. Glorious, incredible, beautifully reciprocated *desire*. It was basic biology at its finest. And it didn't frighten her in the slightest.

He'd taken her out for lunch in Resina, the main town on the island, and now they were driving back to her cottage, taking the scenic route through Agon's verdant mountains, avoiding wandering sheep and goats who seemingly had no sense of the danger posed by moving vehicles.

The view on this blue, cloudless day was spectacular, the Mediterranean was gleaming in the distance, and the temperature was sitting comfortably in the mid-twenties. She was mostly oblivious to it, too busy anticipating the moment they'd return to the privacy of the cottage to concentrate on nothing so mundane as *scenery*.

In the two weeks since the ball they hadn't spent a night apart. They'd returned to her cottage on the Sunday, leaving through Talos's private exit so at least she'd been spared the embarrassment of bumping into his brothers, and had more or less lived there since.

Amalie would work on the score during the day, while he went to his villa or the palace to do his own work. In the evening he would collect her and take her to the gym, then they would return to the cottage and make love, and would often still be awake when the sun came up.

She could now play her violin for him with hardly any nerves at all, although she still didn't feel ready to play his grandmother's piece. She wanted to be note-perfect for that. Her orchestra would arrive on Agon tomorrow morning; her first scheduled rehearsal with them was in the afternoon. They would know then if she had truly made progress.

For today, Talos had insisted on taking her out and showing her Agon, arguing that it was a Saturday and that in the three and a half weeks she'd been on his island she'd hardly seen any of it. She would have been happy to stay at the cottage and make love, but he'd brushed her arguments aside with his usual authority, claiming her lips to whisper, 'We'll only be gone a few hours.'

'What are you thinking about?' he asked now, casting a quick sideways glance at her.

Her gaze drifted to his hands, holding the steering wheel with deft assuredness in much the same manner as he handled her.

'Sex,' she answered, tingles racing through her at the thought of their imminent return to privacy and all the things they would do...

He burst into deep laughter. 'Do you ever think about anything else?'

She pretended to think about it before shaking her head. 'No.'

'I am tempted to ask *exactly* what you're thinking about in connection to sex, but if I crash the car it will take us longer to get back,' he said drily. 'You can tell me in graphic detail exactly what you're thinking later.'

'I will,' she murmured, her eyes drifting to his muscular thighs, barely contained in his chinos.

'Can I ask you a personal question?'

His voice had taken on a serious hue that made her

twist on the seat to face him properly. 'What do you want to know?'

'Why did you wait until you were twenty-five before having sex for the first time?'

It was the question she'd been waiting a fortnight for him to ask. She was still no more prepared with an answer.

She pressed her cheek to the back of the seat. If she couldn't touch him she could at least look at him.

'I never set out to stay a virgin, but I avoided relationships where lust and desire were the driving forces—I've seen my mother's heart broken too many times to have any faith in passionate *love*. The flame is too bright and burns to ashes too quickly. I didn't understand it was possible to have a passion for someone that is purely about sex.'

'Is that all this is to you?' he asked, a surprising edge to his voice. 'Sex?'

'Isn't that all it is to *you*?' she asked right back, momentarily confused.

He was quiet for a moment, before laughing. 'You're right—what we are sharing is just sex. I admit I find it disconcerting to hear that coming from a woman, and even more disconcerting to actually believe it.'

'Do all your lovers say it's just sex?'

'I set out the ground rules from the beginning. I make it clear I only want a physical relationship and they all agree.' He pulled a mocking face. 'It never takes them long to change their minds and think they can be the one to tame me.'

'I don't think anyone could tame you,' she commented idly, and swallowed away the strange acrid taste that had formed in her throat. It was no secret he'd enjoyed numerous lovers before her, and would enjoy more when she returned to Paris in little more than a week. 'You're as tameable as a fully grown wolf with territory problems.'

Now his laughter came in great booming ricochets. 'I enjoy my life. I have no wish to be tamed.'

She eyed him shrewdly, wondering why she didn't quite believe him. She believed his words, but there was a part of Talos he kept closed off. Physically, he was the most generous and giving lover she could have dreamt of, but he had demons inside him she couldn't reach—demons she caught glimpses of when he would shout out in his sleep, cries in Greek she didn't understand.

She'd asked him about it and he'd affected ignorance, saying he didn't remember his dreams. She didn't believe him but hadn't pushed the subject. If he wanted to open up to her, he would. And, really, she was hardly in a position to demand to learn all his secrets when their whole relationship was based on sex and getting her performance-ready for the gala.

'So you've never had a relationship of any kind?' he asked.

'I've had boyfriends,' she corrected him, 'Quite a few of them.'

'And they didn't try to get you into bed? Were they gay?'

She gave a bark of surprised laughter. 'I suppose it's possible, but the relationships weren't like that. It was more about a meeting of minds than physical chemistry.'

'Isn't that what normal friends are for?'

'Probably.' She swallowed. 'We would kiss… But my boyfriends were the type of men who were happier to spend an evening discussing Mozart's eccentricities and how it affected his music rather than trying to get me into bed.'

He flashed her a grin. 'I don't pretend to know anything about Mozart, but if I did I can assure you I would be happy to discuss him with you—provided I could be stripping you naked at the same time.'

'But that's what I was hiding from,' she confessed.

'You liked those men because they made you feel safe?' he asked.

For such a physically imposing man Talos was incredibly perceptive—something she was coming to understand more on a daily basis.

'I…' She stopped to gather her thoughts. 'Yes. You're right. After my parents divorced my mother fell head over heels for so many different men that I lost count, but she couldn't hold on to any of them. Her heart was broken so many times it was painful for me to watch.'

'Why couldn't she hold on to them?'

She shook her head and inhaled deeply. 'I don't know. I *think* it was because my father spoilt her during their marriage. He adored her, you see—worshipped her. He treated her like his queen for fifteen years. It was what she was used to and what she expected. And I think it's what pushed her lovers away—they would fall for her beauty and fame, but as soon as they found the needy woman inside they would run a mile. It hurt her very badly. She would smile and sing to the world, pretend nothing was wrong, but behind closed doors she would wail like a child.'

'And you witnessed this?'

She nodded.

'I can understand why that must have been painful for you,' he said quietly.

Hadn't he witnessed his own mother's pain enough times to know how damaging it could be? Especially to a child? The helplessness of being too small and insignificant to offer any protection—either an emotional or a physical sort.

'I know you must think my mother is a brat, and she *is*. But she's also funny and loving and I adore her,' she added with defiance.

'I can tell,' he said wryly, turning the car into the road marking the start of Kalliakis land. 'But you have to admit that it isn't fair of her to place all her emotional problems on *your* shoulders.'

'She can't help the way she is. And, fair or not, it's no less than I deserve.'

'What do you mean by that?'

She didn't answer, turning her face away from him to look out of the window.

'Amalie?'

She placed a hand to her throat, her words coming out in a whisper. 'Her misery is all my fault. If it wasn't for me, my father would never have divorced her.'

A lump formed in his throat at the raw emotion behind her words. 'I don't believe that for a minute.' How could a child influence its parents' marriage? 'But I am surprised to learn that your father divorced her. From what you've said, I assumed your mother had divorced *him*.'

'My father worshipped the ground she walked on but to protect me from her ego he divorced her when I was twelve.'

The pieces were coming together. 'Which was around the time you were pulled from the spotlight. I assume the two things are connected?'

'Yes,' she admitted hoarsely, before closing her mouth with a snap.

He brought the car to a stop outside her cottage and reached out to stroke the beautiful hair that felt like silk between his fingers. He wanted to gather her in his arms, not just to devour her body but to give her comfort. It was a feeling so alien to him that the lump in his throat solidified.

Giving comfort implied a form of caring, and if there was one thing Talos avoided with the zeal of a medic avoiding the plague it was caring. Sex wasn't meant to be anything but fun; it was an itch to be scratched. Nothing more.

Before he could withdraw she turned her face back to him and raised her hand to palm his cheek. Helpless to resist, he brought his mouth down to hers and breathed her in, his heart thundering as he felt her own inhalation and knew she was breathing *him* in in turn.

Being with her was like living in a fugue of desire—a constant state of arousal that needed no encouragement.

It struck him that touching her and being touched in return was becoming as necessary to him as breathing.

Theos.

He *had* to keep his mind focussed on the bigger picture.

No matter how good the sex was between them it didn't change the fact that Amalie was in Agon for the gala and that it was his job to get her on the stage and performing for his grandfather. She had come on enormously in the past fortnight, but still she wouldn't play his grandmother's composition for him, although she would perform other pieces. She swore she knew it by heart and only wanted to perfect it, and he believed her, but the clock was ticking painfully. The gala was only a week away.

Where had the time gone?

He could sense she was close to unbuttoning the secrets she clutched so tightly, and knew it was the key to unlocking what she kept hidden—the thing at the very centre of her stage fright.

A creamy envelope lay on the welcome mat of the cottage, the sight of which made him blink rapidly. It was an official royal envelope.

Amalie opened it as she walked into the living room. 'I've been invited for dinner with your grandfather,' she said, passing it to him.

His heart accelerating, he read the invitation, which was for dinner that coming Wednesday.

'Did you know about this?' she asked.

'No.'

He hadn't been told a thing. Naturally his grandfather's permission had been sought before Talos began his quest to find a soloist, his only wish concurring with Talos's—that the soloist had to be special. Other than that, his grandfather had been content to leave all the organisation for the gala in his grandsons' capable hands, his energy reserves too limited for him to want any part in it.

Talos shouldn't be surprised that he had sought out

Amalie before the gala, and made a mental note to tell his grandfather he would be attending too. Astraeus Kalliakis still grieved the love of his life, and would want to meet the woman chosen to step into her footsteps on the stage.

He knew he should take the opportunity to tell Amalie the truth about his grandfather's condition. Prepare her. But the words stuck in his throat, a cold, clammy feeling spreading through his skin as it always did whenever he thought of what the coming months would bring.

The death of the man who had raised him from the age of seven. The man who had come into Talos's bedroom and woken the small boy from his sleep, had taken him into his arms and told him in a voice filled with despair but also with an underlying strength that Talos's parents wouldn't be coming home. That they were dead—killed in a road crash on their way to an event at the Greek Embassy.

It was the only time his grandfather had ever held him in such an informal manner. He'd then left Talos in the care of his Queen, Talos's grandmother, and flown to England so he could personally tell his two other grandsons at their boarding school.

Talos thought back to how it must have been for his grandfather, having to break such tragic news while grieving the loss of his own child. His quiet strength had been something for Talos to lean on in those dark few moments when he'd learned his whole world had been turned upside down and inside out. It had been the last time Talos had ever allowed himself to lean on anyone.

And now his grandfather was nearing the end of his own life.

And there wasn't a damn thing Talos could do about it.

He could no more protect his grandfather from death than he'd been able to protect his mother from his father's fists and infidelities.

'Is something wrong?' Amalie asked, peering at him closely. 'You look a little pale.'

He swallowed and returned her stare, suddenly wishing he could throw his arms around her waist and rest his head on those soft breasts, feel her gentle fingers running through his hair, soothing all the pain away.

He wrenched his thoughts from such useless wishes.

To vocalise it…to reveal the truth about his grandfather…*Theos*, he couldn't even speak of it to his brothers. They skirted around it in conversation, none of them prepared to be the one to speak up, as if saying it would make it true.

He ignored her question, reaching out to stroke her cheek, to have one quick touch of that beautifully textured skin before he continued the conversation they'd started in the car. Except Amalie leaned in and hooked her arms around his neck, her breath on his skin as she razed his throat with her mouth before stepping onto her toes to claim his lips.

Her tongue swept into his mouth, her warm breath seeping into his senses. Wrapping his arms around her, he selfishly took the solace of her kisses, the place where all thought could be eradicated in the balm of her mouth and the softness of her willing body.

The last coherent thought to go through his mind as he carried her up the stairs to the bedroom was that he was nothing but putty in her hands.

Amalie stretched luxuriantly, then turned onto her side to run her fingers over Talos's chest, tugging gently at the dark hair that covered it, brushing the brown nipples, pressing her palm down to feel the heavy beat of his heart.

He grabbed her hand and brought it to his mouth, planting a kiss to her knuckles.

She stared into his eyes, those irresistible brown depths, and a feeling of the utmost contentment swept through her. She could stare at him and lie in his arms for ever…

His hand made circular motions in the small of her back.

She raised her leg a touch, pressing her pelvis into his thigh. It didn't matter how deep her orgasms were, still she wanted more. And more…

'You're insatiable,' he growled.

'That's your fault for being so sexy,' she protested with a grin, moving her hand lower.

His eyes gleamed, but he grabbed her hand and brought it back up to rest at his chest. '*You*, my little songbird, are the most desirable woman alive.'

My little songbird?

The possessive pronoun made her heart jolt and soar in a motion so powerful it reverberated through her whole body, right down to the tips of her toes.

My little songbird.

And in that moment came a flash of recognition of such clarity that her heart stuttered to a stop before stammering back into throbbing motion.

This wasn't about lust and desire.

She loved him.

Loved him. *Loved him.*

CHAPTER TWELVE

STRUGGLING TO COMPREHEND, Amalie detached herself from his arms and sat up, crossing her legs to stare down at the face she had, without knowing how or when, fallen in love with.

'Is something the matter?' he asked, his eyes crinkling in question. 'You look as if you've seen a ghost.'

She shook her head, partly to refute his question and partly in wonder that this could have happened to her. She waited for self-recrimination to strike, but the wonder of the moment was too great, her mind a jumble.

Shaking her head again, she said, 'You forcing me here…that horrible contract you forced me to sign…the threats you made…'

He winced and she was glad. She *wanted* him to be ashamed of his behaviour. It meant he had a conscience. And if he had a conscience that meant he was the flesh-and-blood man she'd got to know these past few weeks and not the terrifying ogre she'd first met. It meant they had a chance. A small chance, she knew. Tiny. But a chance all the same.

She rubbed her thumb over his bottom lip and said softly, 'Just because I think you're the sexiest man alive, it doesn't mean I've forgotten what you did to get me here and the abhorrent threats you made.'

But did it mean she'd forgiven him? Talos wanted to know. He opened his mouth to ask, but then closed it.

What if she said no? What if she said she could never forgive him for how he'd got her here and the threats he'd made?

Why did he even *want* her forgiveness? He'd never sought forgiveness before.

Recalling the intimidation he'd put her under to get her acquiescence made him feel tight and compressed inside, and his skin felt as if claws were digging into it. Ruthless behaviour when necessary was nothing new to him, but it had a different taste when you had spent the previous night in bed with the recipient of that behaviour. It tasted different when you knew you would maim anyone who would dare even dream of hurting a hair on the head of that person.

It suddenly struck him that he would give his life to protect this woman.

And as the shock of that revelation filtered through him she continued to speak, cross-legged beside him, naked, the sheet twisted on her lap.

'Whatever the initial circumstances, I can't help thinking coming here is the best thing that could ever have happened to me.'

'Why?' His voice sounded distant and his head was spinning, his pulse racing so hard nausea gripped the lining of his stomach.

'Because being here has given me the time and space to see things clearly.' She dipped her head and gnawed at her bottom lip before speaking again. 'One of my psychiatrists told me outright that he thought I didn't want to be fixed. He was wrong. I…' Her voice caught. When she looked at him her eyes were glassy. 'It's not that I didn't want to be fixed…it's that I didn't think I *deserved* to be fixed.'

Talos ran a hand over his jaw, at a loss as to what he could say. She was unbuttoning herself to him, ready to spill her secrets, and all he wanted to do was shout out and beg her to stop.

He didn't want to hear them. He didn't want to feel anything else for her. Not pity, not empathy. He would take his guilt like a man, but nothing more.

'Maybe you can understand the early part of my life,' she said, oblivious to the turmoil going on within him. 'You've always been public property too. Before I'd reached the age of ten I'd played for the President of France, had taken part in a celebrity-led anti-poverty concert that was beamed around the world to a billion people...'

All of these facts were things he'd learned when he'd first discovered her in that practice room and known she was 'the one'. It had made her refusal to perform at the gala all the more ridiculous to his mind.

'I was a household name, a child prodigy, and it was easy for me.' She shook her head ruefully. 'I loved performing and I loved the applause. But then I turned ten. I found the reviews my parents had kept of my performances and re-alised that people had *opinions* about my music—that they weren't just enjoying it but dissecting everything about it. They were dissecting *me*. All the joy I'd experienced on stage evaporated.'

She snapped her fingers.

'Gone. I'd never experienced fear once, and all of a sudden I was crippled by it. What if they found me wanting? What if the way I interpreted a particular piece compared unfavourably to another violinist? So many thoughts and fears, when before there had been nothing but the joy of playing. It all came to a head on my mother's birthday, when I was twelve.'

She broke away and reached for the glass of water on the bedside table.

'What happened?' he asked, once she'd placed the glass back. She'd stopped talking, clearly gathering her thoughts together.

'She had a party at our holiday home in Provence. I'd spent two years begging not to play in public any more, begging to go to school and make friends, begging for a normal life—but she wouldn't allow it. I was *special*, you see, and, in my mother's eyes I belonged on the stage, receiving the plaudits she took for granted in her own career.'

Her voice dropped.

'I love my *maman*, but she can be very manipulative. She was not ashamed to use emotional blackmail to get me to play. She'd had a stage built at the bottom of the garden. I remember standing on it and seeing all those eyes upon me—there were at least a hundred guests, most of them international household names—and I froze. And then...'

'And then?'

Her eyes were huge on his. 'I wet myself. In front of all those people. They all saw it. All of them. They stopped talking amongst themselves and stared at me—and, God, the *horror* in their eyes. The humiliation was excruciating.'

Talos's throat had closed completely. He thought back to the clip he'd found on the internet, of her at her last public performance, before she'd retreated from the limelight. It could only have been months before the party she'd described. She'd been a scrap of a girl at twelve, without any of the knowing precociousness of preadolescence, and small for her age. She'd been a *child*.

Amalie sighed and visibly gathered herself together, tucking her hair behind her ears.

'Maman was mortified, but she swore it was just a blip. I was booked to play at the Royal Albert Hall a week later, as part of a Christmas celebration, and she insisted I still play. My father tried to get her to see reason but she couldn't— really, she *couldn't*. I was her protégée; she'd created me. Minutes before I was due to go on stage I had a panic attack, bad enough that a stagehand called an ambulance. When I was released from hospital my father collected me alone. Maman had refused to listen to reason so he felt he had no choice but to leave her and take me with him for my own protection.'

She blew out a long puff of air and gave a laugh that was full of bitterness rather than humour.

'He loved her, but he knew that by staying with her he would be condoning her treatment of me. Since then I've watched my mother rebound from relationship to relationship, knowing that if I'd been stronger they would still be together—'

'No,' he cut in, finally finding his voice. 'No, it was your mother—not you. You were a child.'

Her eyes caught his and she jerked her head in a nod, relief spreading over her features that he understood.

'That's what I mean about it being good for me here in Agon,' she said. 'It's given me the space and perspective to see reason and the time to think. You see, even though my father was awarded custody of me, given sole responsibility for my welfare, I still spent holidays and weekends with her. He never stopped me seeing her. He never stopped loving her but he felt he had to put my well-being first and take any decisions about my welfare out of her hands. I watched them both suffer apart and all I could see was that it was *my* fault. I felt as if I'd destroyed their lives. I've been punishing myself because subconsciously I didn't think I deserved to have the future I'd dreamed about. I created a nice, safe life for myself and thought it was enough.'

'And now?' he asked. 'You've come so far already. You've played for me, which in itself was a huge hurdle to overcome. Your orchestra will be here tomorrow, so we will see how successful we have been, but I have faith. You can do this, my little songbird. But you need to want this for yourself, regardless of any repercussions.'

Her head tilted. 'Do those repercussions still exist?'

'I don't know,' he said honestly. 'I would prefer not to find out.'

'So would I.' A sad smile spread over her face. 'It is hard

for me to reconcile the man I'm sharing a bed with with the brute who forced his way into my home.'

'They're one and the same. I make no apologies for being the man I was raised to be. When it comes to my family and my country I fight—and when necessary I fight dirty.'

'That you certainly do,' she said with a sigh, before reaching for his hand and threading her fingers through his. 'Why is this gala so important to you? I understand a nation's pride in half a century of successful and prosperous rule by one monarch, but I can't help thinking it means more to you than that.'

'You don't think that's enough?' he deflected. 'Fifty years of rule is no easy feat. In Agon most monarchs abdicate when their heir reaches forty, allowing them to enjoy their retirement. My grandfather's heir died before he reached that age, so he was left with no choice but to carry on—which he has done with dignity and pride, for his people. Helios will be forty in four years.'

Before she could ask another question he pulled her down to him and rolled her onto her back. Devouring her mouth, he allowed the sweetness of her touch, the sweetness of *her*, to encompass him and drive away the tightness pinching his skin to his bones.

And as he moved in her, her soft moans dancing in his ear and the short nails of her left hand scratching and gripping his back and buttocks with as much need as the long nails of her right, his mind emptied of everything but the ecstasy he experienced in her arms.

Talos had dozed off. Amalie lightly traced the bow of his full top lip, resisting the urge to replace her finger with her mouth. He looked at peace, all that latent energy in hibernation.

She'd told him everything. About all the shame she carried, the shame she hadn't even known she was carrying—

not just what had occurred at her mother's birthday party but the knock-on effects. Talking about it, admitting it— not just to Talos but to herself—she'd felt cleansed. Purged. He was right. She'd been a child.

Her heart felt so full, and it was all because of him. He'd stolen her heart and it astounded her how willing she'd been in allowing him to take it. But then he'd marked her with that first look. She'd stood no chance, not once she was on his island. Not once he'd shown her his human face. Even that damnable contract didn't make her fists clench any longer. She loved that he was prepared to fight for what he believed in.

What would it be like, she thought wistfully, to have this great man's love? To be enveloped under the protection he extended to his family and his people?

She couldn't allow herself to think like that. She was not her mother. Accepting that she'd fallen in love with him did not give her any illusions that he would have fallen for her in return. Only a few hours ago he'd made it clear it was all about sex.

But hadn't she said exactly the same thing? And hadn't she meant it too?

No. She would not allow herself the futility of hope. While she was on Agon she would cherish the time she spent with him. When it was time for her to leave she would go with her head held high and slip back into her old life.

She blinked.

Did she even *want* to go back to her nice, cosy existence?

Prickles spread out over her skin as she thought about what the future could hold for her. The future she'd once dreamt about.

She'd been terrified of passion and love. With Talos she had found both and she was still standing. Not only standing, but with an energy fizzing in her veins that made her feel more alive than she'd ever known.

All the walls she'd built—in part to protect herself, in part to punish herself—had been dismantled, revealing a future that could be hers if only she had the courage to reach out and take it.

Talos was a fighter. He wore his courage in his skin. He'd forced her to fight too, had found a way to bring out her own inner warrior. Now she needed to hold that inner warrior close and never let it go.

Slipping out of the covers, she helped herself to his discarded black T-shirt and tugged it over her head as she made her way down the stairs and into the living room. There, she opened her case, tightened and slid resin over her bow, tuned her violin. Then she took one final deep breath and went back up to the bedroom.

Talos still slept, but he'd shifted position in the few minutes she'd been gone. The moment she sat on the edge of the bed he opened his eyes.

Heart thundering, she smiled shyly at him, then closed her eyes, tucked her violin under her chin and positioned the bow.

The first note rang out with a high sweetness that hit Talos like a punch in his gut, waking him fully in an instant.

She didn't need to tell him. He knew.

This was his grandmother's piece. Her final composition, never before played to a living soul.

And as he listened, watched Amalie play, the punches continued to rain down on him, throwing him back a quarter of a century to his childhood, to the time when his whole world had been ripped apart.

Whereas before he'd been eager to hear her play it, now he wanted to wrestle the violin from her hands and smash it out of the window. But he was powerless to move, to stop the music from ringing around the bedroom, to stop the memories from flooding him. He was as powerless as he'd been when he was seven years old, unable to stop his father throwing blows upon his mother.

As he was assailed by all those torrid memories something else stole through him—a balm that slowly crept through his veins to soothe his turmoil, forcing the memories from his mind and filling him with nothing but the sweet music pouring from Amalie's delicate fingers.

It was like listening to a loving ghost. If he closed his stinging eyes he could see his grandmother. But she wasn't there. It was Amalie, who had interpreted the music with love and sympathy and such raw emotion it was as if Rhea Kalliakis had pointed a finger down at her from heaven and said, *She's the one.*

To watch her play felt like a precious gift in itself—a gift to love and cherish for ever.

It wasn't until she played the final note that she opened her eyes. He read the apprehension in them, but saw something else there too—an emotion so powerful his heart seemed to explode under the weight of it.

He dragged a hand down his face and inhaled through his nostrils, trying to restore an equilibrium that was now so disjointed he couldn't find the markers to right it.

'When my parents died I suffered from terrible nightmares.' His words were hoarse from the dryness in his throat. 'My grandmother would sit on my bed, as you are now, and she would play for me until the nightmares had gone and I had fallen back to sleep.'

Amalie didn't answer; her eyes wide and brimming with emotion.

'You've brought her music to life,' he said simply.

She hugged her violin to her chest. 'It's the most beautiful piece of music I've ever been privileged enough to play, and I promise you I will fight as if I were Agon-born to play it at your grandfather's gala.'

His heart twisted to see the fierceness on her face. He knew it was directed at herself, knew the battle wasn't yet won, but also that she would fight with everything she had to overcome half a lifetime of fear. There was something about the way she looked at him that made him think she wouldn't be fighting solely for the sake of the contract and the repercussions that would come from failure, but for *him*.

And the thought of her fighting for him made his disjointed equilibrium do a full spinning rotation.

CHAPTER THIRTEEN

TALOS GOT INTO his car and turned on the ignition. He'd barely cleared his villa before he turned the car back and turned the engine off.

He imagined her cottage, in the distance, hidden from where he sat by dense trees. He imagined her waiting by the door for him, dressed in the tight-fitting sweats that showed off her slender curves. Imagined the welcoming kiss she would give him, her enthusiasm, as if they'd been parted for weeks rather than a few hours.

Since she'd played for him in the bedroom she'd had no problem with him being around while she practised his grandmother's piece. The problem was that her orchestra had arrived a couple of days ago and proper rehearsals for the gala had begun. Amalie had taken to the stage for the first rehearsal and frozen.

Today he'd been there to witness it for himself—and this time she'd played it to the end, but only by keeping her terror-filled eyes on him. She'd visibly trembled throughout, and the notes she'd played had been tense and short—nothing like the flowing, dreamlike melody she achieved when they were alone.

Her obvious distress felt like sharpened barbs in his heart.

It was too soon for her. Maybe if the gala were in a couple of months, or even weeks, there would be time but it was only four days away. She knew her part perfectly, and the orchestra knew theirs, but what use was that when she couldn't get her fingers to work?

And he, arrogant bastard that he was, had forced this nightmare on her, believing that some fighting spirit could cure half a lifetime of severe stage fright.

There was no way to fix it in time, not without putting her through an enormous amount of distress.

Tomorrow she would dine with his grandfather. Talos had invited himself along as well and hadn't liked the look in his grandfather's eyes when he'd suggested he come. It had been far too knowing.

Amalie's solo was the one performance of the whole gala that his grandfather was looking forward to. He might have to miss large chunks of the ceremony, but he had told Talos only yesterday that he would sooner be in his coffin than miss her performance.

Swallowing the acrid bile in his throat, Talos dug his phone out of his pocket and called her. 'I'm going to have to give tonight a miss,' he said, speaking quickly. 'Something's come up.'

'Are you all right?' The concern in her voice was plain.

He didn't want her concern. He didn't deserve it. The only thing he deserved was a dozen punches to his gut for forcing this nightmare on her.

'I'm busy with work, that's all. I'll try and catch up with you later.'

He blew out a breath of stale air as he disconnected his phone and tried to clamp down on the emotions raging through him, the feeling that his whole life was converging in a tipping point over which he had no control.

Amalie stepped through the trees surrounding her cottage and gazed at the villa in the distance. The moonless night was dark, but the white building glowed brilliantly under the stars.

It took her ten minutes to cross the land and reach it, and by the time she knocked on the front door her heart was thundering at a rate of knots, her hands clammy. She'd never been inside Talos's villa before. It occurred to her that she'd never been invited. His villa was very much his private sanctuary. Kept apart from her.

All evening she'd been waiting for another call from him or a knock on the cottage door. Something was wrong, and had been for the past couple of days. There was an unbreachable distance between them.

She knew he was worried about the gala. She was too. Terrified about it. They'd both had such confidence that she was ready to play in public, but that confidence had been a deception. Her nerves were winning the war. She'd just about managed to scrape through the rehearsal earlier, when she'd had his face to focus on, but her shaking fingers had prevented any hint of musicality.

Was that the reason for his distance?

Frustration and disappointment with her?

The maid who opened the door recognised her and welcomed her in with a smile. As neither spoke the other's language, the maid beckoned Amalie to follow her.

The interior of the villa was as fresh and modern as the palace was old and medieval, but with a definite nod to Agon's Minoan ancestry; Greek sculptures and artwork adorned the walls.

After leading her down a wide flight of marble stairs and through a large door the maid stopped and pointed at another closed door, gave a quick bow, and disappeared back up the stairs, leaving Amalie on her own.

Heart in her mouth, she tapped on the door. When there was no answer she rapped again, louder, pressing her ear to it. She heard nothing. She chewed her lips before deciding to turn the handle. She pushed the door ajar and peered through the crack, pushing it wide open when she realised this was Talos's personal gym.

Weight-lifting equipment, a treadmill and a rowing machine—items she wouldn't have known one from the other a month ago—were lined up against the mirrored wall opposite the doorway. Through the same mirror she caught sight of a blur and turned to the left.

There he was, oblivious to her presence, thrashing the living daylights out of a punching bag.

She knew she should call out to him, let him know she was there, but she was captivated by what she saw.

All he wore was a pair of black shorts. His feet were bare, his hands gloveless. She winced to imagine the damage he could be doing to his fingers, her chest constricting as she realised something must be seriously wrong for him to forgo the gloves he always insisted on. Only the week before she'd seen him admonish a teenager for daring to hit a basic pad without gloves. A punching bag was a much harder target.

All the same, she was mesmerised by the energy he exuded.

This was Talos stripped back, in all his graceful, powerful glory.

Sweat dripped off him, his muscles rippled, his punches were hard and merciless—as if he were imagining the punching bag as a living target, a foe to be destroyed.

He was in pain. She knew that as surely as she knew her own name. His pain was in every one of his punches.

He must have caught sight of her in the mirror, for he suddenly stopped and spun around. Breathing heavily, he stared at her disbelievingly, his throat moving, his jaw clenched.

Her lips parted to apologise for the intrusion—and it *was* an intrusion—but the words stuck in her throat.

Not taking his eyes off her, Talos reached for a towel and wiped his face and chest, then dropped it to the floor and prowled over to stand before her.

His chest was rising and falling in rapid motion, and his nostrils flared before his mouth came crashing down on hers and she was pushed back against the wall.

His kisses were hungry, the kisses of a starving man.

His powerful strength was something she'd always been hugely aware of, but until that moment she'd never appreciated the restraint he displayed around her. Now, holding her upright against the wall with one arm, he gripped her hip with his free hand and pulled her tight against him, before loosening his grip to slide his hand down her thigh to the hem of her short skirt and rip her knickers off. Manipulating her thighs to wrap around him, he freed himself from his shorts and plunged into her with a groan that spoke as much of pain as it did of pleasure.

Amalie held him tight, breathing in his salty, woody scent, cradling his scalp, wanting only to take away his pain.

As far as lovemaking went this was fierce, primal, but she embraced every carnal thrust, felt the pulsations building in her core as she clung to him. He gave a roar and buried his face in her hair, his whole body shaking, and his final thrust pushed her over the edge as the pulsations exploded with a shocking power that took all the life from her bones and left her limp in his arms.

Time lost any meaning.

It was only when he gently placed her back on her feet, tugged her skirt down from around her waist and stepped back, that she saw the red mark on the top of his shoulder and realised she had made it with her mouth.

Talos spotted it too and gave a ragged grin. 'My first love bite,' he said, in an attempt at humour that didn't fool her for a second.

She waited for him to ask why she was there, but all he did was cup her cheeks and kiss her with something close to desperation, then pull her to him.

'I'm sorry,' he said, his voice husky. 'That was incredibly selfish of me.'

'I'm not,' she murmured, tilting her head to look up at him.

His eyes closed and he muttered an oath. 'I didn't use protection.'

That made her blink. She hadn't been in the right frame of mind to think of protection either.

'We should be okay. I'm due on tomorrow.'

'*Should* be okay?' He gave a savage shake of his head.

'I'm not an expert, but I'm certain I'm way past the ovulation stage of my cycle. And I'm always regular,' she added, trying to reassure him even while the image of a dark-haired baby wrapped in vine leaves filtered into her mind. 'I'll know within a couple of days if we have a problem.'

The pulse in his jaw was working overtime. 'Make sure to tell me the minute you know.'

'I promise.' She hesitated before asking, 'Talos, what's wrong? You've become so distant.'

He gazed back down at her, and for a moment she was certain he was about to talk. Instead, he pulled his arms away and took a step back.

'Nothing's wrong. I'm a little stressed about the gala, I have a few minor problems with work, a lack of sleep… the usual.'

'I'm sure the rehearsals tomorrow will go better,' she said, trying to inject positivity into her tone. 'At least I was able to play it today.'

Even if it *had* sounded like a cats' chorus ringing out, and even if the members of her orchestra *had* been gazing at her with something close to horror.

He raised his eyes to the ceiling and shook his head, before jerking it into a nod. 'I'm sure you're right.'

And in that moment she knew he was lying.

He wasn't merely *concerned*.

He didn't believe she could do it.

Panic took hold in her chest.

Up until that point Talos's conviction that he could fix her had taken root in her head, allowing her to believe that she could overcome her fear in time. But if her warrior prince had lost faith, what did *that* say? Where did that leave her? Where did that leave *them*?

'I need to go to Athens first thing in the morning,' he said, rubbing the back of his neck. 'I'll collect you at seven for dinner with my grandfather.'

Was this his way of dismissing her?

'Okay…' she answered uncertainly. 'Are you certain it's informal dress?'

'My grandfather insists. He wants it to be a relaxed occasion, where you can both talk without formality.'

'That sounds good,' she said. 'Are you coming back to the cottage with me?'

Instinct had already told her his answer, but she had to ask. She wouldn't presume to invite herself to stay here at the villa with him—even if it wasn't so obvious he wished her gone.

'Not tonight. I've an early start. I'll only disturb you if I stay over, and you need a good night's sleep as much as I do. I'll walk you back.'

His words made sense. That didn't stop them feeling like a knife plunging into her heart.

She forced a smile to her face and leaned up to kiss him, pretending that nothing was wrong when it was blindingly obvious that he was steeling himself to end their relationship.

Not that what they shared was a relationship, she scolded herself on their silent walk back to the cottage. It had always had an end date attached to it; she had accepted that. She just hadn't considered that he would tire of her before the end date. She hadn't considered that he would lose faith in her.

Amalie strove to hide the shock that meeting King Astraeus Kalliakis evoked.

With Talos's hand in the small of her back, they had

been escorted by a courtier to the King's private dining room—a space a fraction of the size of the Banquet Room but every bit as sumptuous.

The pictures she'd seen of the King had depicted a tall, handsome man. Even at his eightieth birthday celebrations, with his ebony hair having thinned and turned white, he'd exuded vitality. That was the man she had prepared herself to meet.

'Forgive me for not rising to greet you,' he said, his voice weak. 'If I could get up I would kiss your hand.'

She had no idea what possessed her, but when she took the unsteady hand he offered she was the one to place a kiss on the paper-thin skin, rather than giving the curtsy she'd practised earlier.

He smiled warmly, then indicated for his nurse to wheel him to the table.

Amalie tried to catch Talos's eye but he was avoiding her gaze, just as he'd avoided any conversation other than the usual pleasantries on their drive to the palace. He hadn't even mentioned her phone call early that morning confirming that her period had started.

As masochistic as she knew it to be, she'd felt a definite twinge of disappointment when she'd spotted the telltale signs of her period. She'd never even *thought* of having children before. Not once. But for less than twelve hours there had been the smallest of chances that she might have conceived and her imagination had taken root. Any initial concerns about what a disaster it would be, seeing as she was in anything *but* a loving relationship, and it would affect the career she longed to reclaim, had fallen by the wayside as she'd imagined what it would be like to have Talos's child.

It had felt almost dreamlike.

She had no idea if she would be any good as a mother, but instinct told her he would make a fantastic father. She sighed. It was something she would never know, and it was pointless to allow her thoughts to run in such wayward directions, not when there were so many other things occupying her mind.

When she'd given Talos the news his response had been a distant, 'That's one less thing to worry about.'

And now she knew why he'd been so distant. He had been thinking of his grandfather.

Why hadn't he told her his grandfather was ill? And not just ill, but clearly dying. It was there in the gauntness of his features—he must have lost half his body weight since those pictures had been taken at his eightieth. And it was there in the sallow yellow complexion of his skin, the hollowness of his eyes… It was everywhere. She could feel it.

'You must be curious as to why I wanted to meet you,' the King rasped, once their first course of tomato and basil soup had been served.

'I assumed you wanted to meet the woman who will play your wife's final composition.'

As she spoke, her skin chilled. Today's rehearsal had been a step backwards.

It had started well enough. Christophe, the orchestra's conductor for the gala, had found a screen for her to hide behind, so she could actually play in time with the orchestra. It had worked beautifully. Then the screen had been removed and she'd found herself breathing in and out of a paper bag in an effort to stem the panic attack clawing at her.

Christophe was on the verge of his own nervous breakdown, freaking out so much he'd contracted a hypnotist to fly over to Agon for her.

She'd searched in vain for Talos, waiting for him to step through the practice room's door and give her confidence with a simple smile. But he'd been in Athens. If he was by her side she would be able to get through it; they'd already proved that. With more practice, and with Talos and his calming presence, she might be able to do the score the justice she gave it when they were alone.

'Indeed.' Watery brown eyes held hers. 'Tell me about yourself, *despinis*.'

'My career?'

That would be a very short conversation.

He waved a hand. 'I want to know about *you*. The music you enjoy, the books you read, the films you watch.'

And so they fell into easy conversation, Amalie doing most of the talking and the King making the odd encouraging comment. She was thankful for her childhood spent surrounded by powerful people, otherwise she would have been completely overwhelmed to be dining with a king.

He ate very little: a few spoonfuls of soup…a couple of bites of the main course of red snapper.

Talos stayed silent, following the conversation without contributing, his gaze on his grandfather. He didn't once meet her eyes.

When the dessert was brought in—light pistachio cakes with an accompanying chocolate mousse—the King finally asked her something in connection with the violin.

'Do you find it hard, learning new music?'

She considered the question, aware that Talos was finally looking at her. 'It's like reading a book where the words are notes and all the adjectives are replaced with tempos and dynamics.'

Astraeus gave a wheezy laugh. 'I'm sure that makes sense to you.'

She couldn't help but laugh too. 'I've probably overcomplicated it. I should have just said I read music the way you read a book.'

'And how did you find learning my wife's music?'

'I found it the most fulfilling experience of my entire musical life,' she answered with honesty, trying to tune out Talos's stare. 'To know I am the first person to play it publicly… Can I ask you a question?'

The King nodded.

'Did she ever play it for you?'

'No.' His eyes dimmed. 'She never spoke of her music when she was composing. When she finished a piece, only then would she tell me about it and play it for me.' His shoulders slumped. 'She contracted pneumonia shortly before she completed this one. She struggled to finish it, but my wife was a very determined woman. She died two days later.'

'I'm very sorry.'

'I still miss her. All the time.'

Forgetting protocol—not that she even knew what the protocol for an audience with the King *was*, as Talos hadn't seen fit to fill her in—she leaned over and placed her hand on his.

Shock flared in his eyes but he made no effort to relinquish her hold, tilting his frail body a little closer to her.

'What your wife created,' Amalie said gently, 'was a concerto about love. It's a tribute to *you*.'

'How do you know this?' he whispered, leaning even closer.

'It's all there in the music. I can't explain how I know, but I feel it. She wrote this score with love in her heart—not maternal love, but romantic love.'

The King's eyes closed. For a moment she allowed her glance to dart at Talos. He sat rigid, his jaw set, his eyes filled with something she couldn't comprehend.

When Astraeus opened his eyes he stared at her with great concentration, before turning his head to the courtier standing to his right and nodding at him. The courtier left the dining room, returning almost immediately with a violin case. He laid it on the table before the King.

Astraeus gestured for Amalie to open it.

Apprehensive, certain he was going to ask her to play for him, she obeyed. The gorgeous scent of wood and resin puffed out and she inhaled it greedily, as she had done since toddlerhood, when her father would open *his* violin case.

She made to lift the violin out but the King stopped her, placing his hand on the instrument and stroking it.

'This belonged to Rhea,' he said. 'It was hand-crafted for her by Massimo Cinelli. It was my wedding present to her.'

Massimo Cinelli was one of the foremost twentieth-century luthiers, a man who made string instruments of such tonal quality it was argued that they rivalled Stradivarius. His had been a life cut tragically short, and when he'd died at the age of fifty-three he had been known to have made around three hundred string instruments, a quarter of which were violins. In recent months an auction for one of his violas had fetched a value of half a million pounds.

Amalie could only imagine what a violin made for a queen would fetch—especially a queen who'd left such a huge legacy to the classical music world. It made her joyful and sad all at the same time to know this would have been the violin Rhea had used at Carnegie Hall, when she'd played with Amalie's father all those years ago.

'I am bequeathing it to you,' the King said.

'What do you mean?'

Surely he had to be talking about her using it for the gala?

'It is yours, child.'

'Mine...?'

His smile was sad. 'It's sat in darkness for five years. It needs to be played. I know you will treasure it and I know you will honour Rhea's memory. Take it, child—it's yours.'

Amalie was truly lost for words. She knew this was no joke, but all the same... The King of Agon had just given her one of his wife's most prized possessions—a gift beyond value.

'Thank you,' she said, shrugging her shoulders with helplessness at her inability to come up with anything more meaningful.

'No. Thank *you*,' he answered enigmatically, then beckoned his nurse over and spoke to her in Greek.

The nurse took hold of his wheelchair.

'And now I bid you a good night,' Astraeus said. 'It has been a pleasure meeting you, *despinis*.'

'It has been an honour, Your Majesty.'

Talos had risen to his feet, so she followed suit, only to have the King take her hand and tug her down so he could speak in her ear. 'I'm glad my grandson has found you. Please look after him for me when I'm gone.'

In another breach of protocol she kissed his cold cheek and whispered, 'I promise I'll try.'

It was the best she could do. She doubted Talos would ever give her the chance.

CHAPTER FOURTEEN

A DRIVER RETURNED them to Talos's estate. They'd been sitting in the back, the partition up, for a few minutes before he spoke.

'What did my grandfather say to you?'

That was what he was concerned about? Not that she'd been given a family heirloom? The heirloom that now sat on her lap, where she held it tightly.

'I think he whispered it to me because he didn't want you to hear,' she answered, striving for lightness.

'Don't be absurd. I'm his grandson. We have no secrets.'

She finally found the courage to look at him. '*You* hold on to your secrets extremely well. You must have inherited that from somewhere.'

'Are you deliberately talking in riddles?'

'Why didn't you tell me he was ill?'

His jaw set in the clenched fashion it had been fixed in throughout the evening. Her heart ached to see it and she wished she could breach the wall he'd erected between them. Even before they'd become lovers she'd never felt as if she couldn't touch him, but right then she was certain that if she reached out he would recoil from her.

'My grandfather's illness is not a subject for idle gossip.'

'I appreciate that.'

She took a breath. It wasn't so much his answer that had cut, but the dismissive tone in which he'd said it. As if she were no one.

'But if you'd told me the truth about his health from the beginning...'

'Then *what*?' he asked bitingly. 'You would have agreed to perform for him *without* having to be blackmailed into it?'

'I don't know.' She tightened her grip on the violin case, soothing her fingers on the velvety material. It was the only part of her she could soothe. 'I don't know if things would have been different—my point is you never gave me the chance to find out if I would have reacted differently.'

'You wouldn't have,' he said, with tight assurance.

'We'll never know.' Now she clenched her own teeth, before loosening them. 'What I don't understand is why you haven't told me since. We've shared a bed for over a fortnight.'

There had been plenty of opportunities for him to tell her. Times when she'd asked him if there was something wrong. The time she'd asked him outright if the gala held more importance to him than the reason he'd shared with her.

'Do not presume that sharing a bed means I owe you anything.'

She had never known him to be this cold. She'd never known him to be cold at all. When something angered him Talos *burned*.

This coldness chilled her to the bone.

The car came to a stop. The driver opened her door.

Not another word was exchanged as she got out and entered the cottage. Not a word of goodnight. Not a kiss. Not a touch. Not a look.

She flinched to hear the engine spark back to life and the car driving off, taking Talos to his villa.

Feeling as if lead weights had been inserted into her limbs, she kicked off her shoes and placed Rhea Kalliakis's violin on the piano. If she didn't feel so numb she would already have it out of the case and be tuning it. This was a *Cinelli*. Any other violinist in the world would likely have passed out with shock to be given it. It was the classical violinist's version of winning the lottery.

But the weight of the gift lay heavily on her. And Talos's parting words lay even heavier.

'Do not presume that sharing a bed means I owe you anything.'

He'd really said that. He'd hardly said a word all night but he'd said *that*. And as the full weight of those words filtered through her brain the numbness disappeared, pain lanced through her, and something even more powerful filled her.

Anger. Unadulterated rage.

How *dared* he talk to her as if she were nothing more than a notch on his bedpost?

Consumed with a fury she only partly understood, she flung open the front door and ran out into the night. Cutting through the trees, she saw the lights of the villa in the distance, along with the lights of the car just approaching it.

The lead in her limbs had gone. Her legs were now seemingly made of air as she flew over the fields, running faster than she'd ever known she could, the wind rippling against her face, the skirt of her blue summer dress billowing out behind her.

It seemed as if no time had passed before she set the security lights ablaze. In the time it had taken her to race there the car had dropped Talos off and begun its return journey to the palace.

As she banged on the front door with her fist, then punched the doorbell, she was assailed with memories of that morning a month before, when Talos had knocked on her own front door and turned her world on its axis.

The door was wrenched open.

Talos stood there, staring at her as if she'd just appeared from the moon.

'Sharing your bed doesn't mean I *presume* you owe me anything—let alone know what's going on in your head,' she spat from her place on the doorstep, before he could utter a word. 'But we've shared more than just a bed. Or at least *I* have.'

He looked murderous. He looked as if he wanted nothing more than to wrap his hands around her throat.

'Have you run all the way here from the cottage *in the dark*? Are you *insane*? It's the middle of the night—there could be anyone out there!'

'You didn't worry about that the other night when I walked here in the dark.'

Suddenly the exertion of her run hit her and she bent over, grabbing her knees as she fought desperately to breathe. God, but her lungs burned.

'Amalie?'

She lifted her head to look at him, puffing in air until she felt able to straighten again.

He stared at her with eyes now curiously vacant. His detachment ratcheted her fury up another notch.

She straightened. 'Do not treat me as if I'm some nothing you had sex with just because it was available. It was more than that and you know it—and you owe me more than to treat me like that.'

'I do not owe you anything. If you think your being a virgin before we became lovers means I have to treat you—'

'It's nothing to do with me being a virgin!' she yelled, punching him in the shoulder.

He didn't so much as jolt.

'This is to do with me sharing everything with you. I spilled my guts about my childhood and my life to you. I gave you *everything*! I didn't expect a marriage proposal, or declarations of love, but I *did* expect some respect.'

'It was never my intention to be disrespectful.'

'Then what *was* your intention? Tell me, damn you. Why have you closed yourself off? I thought you were frustrated because I'm still struggling to play with the orchestra, but now I'm wondering if you're just bored with me. Is that it?

Are you too gutless to tell me that you don't want me any more and rather than come out and say it you're taking the coward's way of withdrawing, hoping I'll get the hint?'

Her voice had risen to a shout. No doubt half the live-in staff had been woken.

Suddenly he jerked forward and grabbed her forearm. 'Come with me,' he said through gritted teeth, marching her through the reception room, down a wide corridor and through a door that revealed what at first glance appeared to be an office, filled with plush masculine furniture.

He slammed the door shut and loomed over her, his arms folded over his chest. His eyes had darkened to a point of blackness.

'First of all, do *not* presume to tell me what I think.'

'I have to make assumptions because you don't tell me anything!'

'What do you want me to say? Do you want me to *apologise* because my grandfather is dying?'

'No!' She clamped her teeth together and blinked back the sudden stinging tears welling in the backs of her eyes. 'Of course not. I didn't mean—'

Before she knew what was happening Talos's control shattered before her eyes.

He punched the wall, blackness seeping out of him. 'I know what you meant. You think because you have shared confidences with me that I must do the same in return.'

'No!' She shook her head over and over, terrified not for herself but for him. She'd never seen such pain before, etched on every line of his face and in every movement of his powerful body.

He seemed not to hear her, kicking the solid wood desk with such force he put a dent in it. 'Do you want me to pour my heart out about my childhood? To understand where my nightmares come from and why I went so off the rails in my adolescence? Is that what you want?'

'I—'

'Do you want to hear about the day I watched my father punch my mother not once but a dozen times in the stomach? Do you want to hear how I jumped on his back to protect her and how he threw me off with such force my head split open on their bedframe? That my lasting memory of my mother is her holding me and her tears falling on my bleeding head? Is *that* what you want? To know that I couldn't protect her then and that my vow to always protect her in the future came to nothing, because two hours later both my parents were dead? And now my grandfather is dying too. And I have to accept that as a fact of life and accept there is nothing I can do about it. You want me to share how I feel? Well, it feels as if my stomach and heart have been shredded into nothing. Is that enough for you? Is that what you wanted to hear?'

His eyes suddenly found hers, and he threw his hands in the air and stalked towards her.

'So now you know all my dirty little secrets and I know yours, is there anything else you want from me or feel I should tell you, seeing as we're having such a *wonderful* time trading confidences?'

If it hadn't been for the wildness radiating from his eyes she would have hated him for his contempt. But she couldn't. All she felt was horror.

'No?' He leaned down so his face was right against hers. 'In that case, seeing as you've got what you wanted from me, you can leave.'

Abruptly he turned away and lifted the phone on the sprawling desk, rasping words in Greek to whoever was on the receiving end.

'Talos…' she said hesitantly when he'd replaced the receiver.

She didn't know what she wanted to say. Couldn't think of anything *to* say. What she did want was to take him in her arms and hold him close, but she knew without having to be told he didn't want that. He didn't want her or the solace she yearned to give him.

'We have nothing more to say to each other.' He seemed to have regained his composure, but his focus on her was stark. 'We've enjoyed each other's company but this is as far as we go.'

A knock on the door made her start.

Talos pulled it open and indicated for her to leave. 'Kostas will take you back to the cottage. I hope for everyone's sake the hypnotist your conductor has arranged for you works, because there is nothing more *I* can do to help you.'

With as much dignity as she could summon Amalie walked past him to Kostas, who had already set off to the front door.

Talos kicked the covers off and got out of bed. A large glass of single malt should help him sleep.

He glanced out of the window. Three o'clock in the morning and all was in darkness, but in the downward sloping distance he could see the dim lights of the cottage.

Amalie was awake.

He closed his eyes. He would bet every last cent he owned that at that very minute she was playing his grandmother's violin, taking the only comfort she could. In his mind's eye he watched her fingers flying over the strings, imagined the purity of the sound she produced. Knew that to hear it would tear his soul in half. That was if any part of his soul remained. After the way he'd spoken to her the other night whatever had been left of it had been ripped out.

He'd treated her abominably. He still didn't know where all that rage had come from, knew only that she'd been getting too close. He'd been trying to protect himself. Squashing anything that resembled an emotion down into a tight little ball that could be hidden away and forgotten about.

Somehow Amalie had unpicked the edges of that ball and it had exploded back into life, making him feel more than a man could bear.

Theos, had he ever felt more wretched?

He'd been heartsick before—of course he had; the loss of his parents had devastated him. His father had been a brute, but Talos had still loved him…with the blind faith with which all small children loved their parents.

This felt different, as if the weight of a thousand bass drums had compressed inside him, beating their solemn sound through his aching bones.

He was wasted, physically and emotionally.

He closed his eyes, imagined Amalie padding into his room and settling on the corner of his bed to play for him, her music soothing him enough to drive all the demons from his head.

He hadn't known his grandfather intended to give her the violin, but he couldn't think of a better person to have it. What good would it do sitting in a glass cabinet in the Kalliakis palace museum, nothing but a tourist attraction? At least Amalie would love and care for it. When she played it she would play with her heart.

He'd spent the day deliberately avoiding anyone connected with the orchestra. But palace whispers ran more quickly than the tide, and his avoidance hadn't stopped rumours about the solo violinist having to play behind a screen for the third day in a row reaching his ears.

He imagined her standing there, shaking, her face white and pinched, terror in those beautiful green eyes, her breath coming in increasingly shallow jerks.

What was he *doing* to her?

It would be kinder to strip her naked and stand her on display. The humiliation would be less.

She'd come so far—been so incredibly brave. To force her to go ahead with the gala now would surely ensure his damnation to hell. Forget any potential ruination of the gala—forcing Amalie to go ahead would completely destroy her.

He couldn't do it to her.

He would rather rip his own heart out than let her suffer any more.

Amalie rubbed her sleep-deprived eyes, then picked up her knife and chopped the melon into small chunks, the action making her think of Talos and the knife he carried everywhere with him.

Do not think of him, she ordered herself. *Not today.*

There would be plenty of time to mourn what had happened between them when she returned to Paris, but for now she had to get through today. That was all she should focus on.

The scent of the melon was as fragrant as all the fruit she'd had since her arrival on the island, but her stomach stubbornly refused to react to it other than to gurgle with nausea.

Please, stomach, she begged, *accept some form of nourishment*.

At the rate she was going, even if she managed to get on to the outdoor stage that evening, she would likely fall into a faint when the heat of the spotlight fell upon her and her starved belly reacted to it.

Hearing movement, she cut through to the entrance hall and found a letter had been pushed through the door.

A heavy cream-coloured A4 envelope with *'Amalie Cartwright'* written on it with a penmanship that resembled a slash.

Her heart thundering erratically, it was clear her body knew who the sender was before she'd torn it open.

In the top right-hand corner was Talos's full name, including his royal title and the palace address.

Dear Mademoiselle Cartwright
This letter is written to confirm the cancellation of
the contract between us dated tenth March. All pen-
alties stipulated in the contract are hereby revoked,
and the Orchestre National de Paris shall continue
in its current form.
Sincerely,
Talos Kalliakis

Her head swimming, Amalie read it a number of times before the words sank in.

Her stomach dived, nausea clutching her throat.

One hand over her mouth, the other pressed against her heavy, thundering heart, she swayed into a table, fighting to stop the deluge of misery knocking her from her feet.

He didn't believe she could do it.

He really had given up on her.

It was over.

Everything.

His belief in her.

Her reignited dreams of playing on a stage.

All gone.

But before the despair could crush her in its entirety, a thought struck her.

Why now, on the day of the gala—the day they'd spent a month preparing for…?

She rubbed her eyes, frantically trying to stem the tears pouring out of them, and read it one more time.

It didn't make any sense.

She looked at her watch. Nine a.m. The gala would be starting in six hours. She was due onstage to perform the solo and close the gala in eleven hours. The schedule had been released to the media, who were crawling all over the island in preparation for the day's events. At that moment heads of state were preparing to descend on the island.

And Talos was allowing her to leave.

No, it really did not make any sense.

Since their last encounter she'd done nothing but think of him and his words. She'd known from the beginning that her playing his grandmother's final composition was important to him—you didn't blackmail and threaten someone for something trivial. Dining with his grandfather had brought the true importance of the gala to life for her. This was King Astraeus's swansong. This was the final celebration of his life.

And now Talos was prepared to scrap what he'd fought so hard to attain.

His grandparents had raised him and his brothers since he was seven. His family meant everything to him. This piece of music meant everything to his entire family. Of all the things the gala represented, *this* was the performance that meant the most. It wasn't just the icing on the cake; it was the sponge and filling too.

She thought back to that evening three days ago, and the contempt in his voice when he'd ordered her to leave his villa. She'd thought then that the contempt was directed at *her*, but suddenly she realised it had been directed inwards, at himself.

And suddenly she realised something else.

For Talos to release her from the contract now meant he was putting her emotional well-being above *everything*.

Talos Kalliakis was a warrior. He would fight to the bitter end, even if it meant frogmarching her onto the stage and holding her upright while she played. Their time together had proved she could play when she was with him— something he would use as a weapon in his arsenal He would carry on their affair until she'd outlived her use. He wouldn't have lost faith in her because faith didn't exist in his vocabulary. For Talos it was all about spirit and belief.

She thought back to the rehearsal earlier in the week, when his presence had enabled her to play the whole piece without having to hide behind a screen. There had been pride in his brown eyes, but mingled with it had been something troubled. Now she understood what that had meant—her distress had troubled him on a *personal* level.

She scrambled for her phone and scrolled through her contacts until she found the gala coordinator's name. She pressed the call button.

'Has the schedule been changed?' Amalie asked without preamble.

'I was told an hour ago that the final orchestral piece has been changed,' the coordinator replied. 'I'm still waiting to hear what it's been changed *to*.'

'But my orchestra will still be performing the final piece?'

'Yes.'

'Thank you.'

Disconnecting the call, Amalie rubbed a hand over her mouth, then dialled Melina's number. The kickboxing instructor's *froideur* towards her had thawed over time—enough so that she'd given Amalie her number.

'Melina? I need your help...'

CHAPTER FIFTEEN

THE GALA WAS proving to be a huge success. The open-air theatre was filled; not a single seat was free. The day had started with Helios announcing his engagement to Princess Catalina of Monte Cleure, and then the guests had been treated to a variety of acts—from a children's choir to a world-famous circus troupe—and each in turn had been given rapturous applause.

Talos was too keyed up to enjoy it.

He'd sat down with his grandfather that morning and explained that Amalie would not be performing after all. He'd told him that the orchestra had rehearsed in Paris with another violinist before flying over, and how that violinist was prepared to take the role.

His grandfather had looked him straight in the eye and replied, 'An understudy won't do. We both know Amalie is the one.'

Talos had responded with a sharp nod, refusing to think of the undertone in his grandfather's words or the expression in his eyes as he'd said them.

The penultimate act was on stage now; Agon's Royal Ballet School, performing a condensed version of the *Nutcracker Suite* with the accompaniment of Agon's Royal Orchestra. Ballet bored him at the best of times, but tonight he didn't notice a single thing about it. As hard as he tried to concentrate, his mind was with Amalie.

His grandfather, sitting to his left with a blanket snug over his lap, was thoroughly enjoying it all, nodding along to the more upbeat performances and snoozing his way through those that failed to capture his attention.

If Helios and his new fiancée were enjoying it they were doing a fine job of pretending otherwise, the atmosphere between them decidedly frosty. And Theseus… He might as well not be there, for all the attention he was paying to the acts.

Finally the ballet finished and the curtains closed so that the Orchestre National de Paris could set up with privacy. Talos could not care less what piece they chose to play as a replacement. His only stipulation was that it must not be the 'Méditation' from *Thaïs*.

The compère, a famous American comedian, came on-stage and told some jokes to keep the crowd entertained. They'd been sitting in the amphitheatre for over five hours but showed no sign of restlessness.

The audience burst into a roar of laughter at a joke the compère had told but Talos hadn't heard a word of it.

Grinning hugely, the compère pressed a finger to his ear, listening to his earpiece, then raised a hand for silence.

'It is now time for the final performance,' he said, becoming solemn. 'As this is such a special occasion only the most special performance can be allowed to finish it. Ladies and gentlemen, performing the final composition of this beautiful island's Queen Rhea, I give you the Orchestre National de Paris and their celebrated violinist, Amalie Cartwright.'

What…?

Loud applause broke out, and the curtains were drawn back to reveal the orchestra already seated.

Heart thumping, Talos's first thought was that someone had forgotten to tell the compère about the change. It had been too late to alter the programmes, so they'd agreed that the compère would inform the audience that Amalie had been taken ill.

He got to his feet, ready to find out what had gone wrong.

Then he spotted the figure standing at the front left-hand side of the stage.

His heart twisted into a clenched fist. He couldn't move; his feet seemed rooted to the floor until his grandfather took hold of his wrist and gently tugged it.

Unable to move his eyes away from her, he sat back down, breathing heavily.

Amalie looked beautiful. Divine. She wore a snug-fitting mid-thigh-length dress, with a scooped neckline and short sleeves. Its red wine colour set her apart from her orchestra, who all wore black. It highlighted the paleness of her skin, and with her hair swept up in an elegant knot she looked fragile. Incredibly fragile. And scared—like the rabbit caught in the headlights he'd found in the Parisian practice room all those long weeks ago.

Her eyes searched his side of the crowd until she found the royal box. It was too dark for her to pick him out but he swore that she found him.

The conductor stood before the orchestra and silence fell. The first pluck from the string section echoed out, then the whisper of the flutes.

Amalie's teeth bit into her lip before she placed her violin under her chin and put her bow in position. She straightened, visibly strengthening. Then she closed her eyes, listened for her cue and played the first note.

Talos held his breath. Beside him, he heard his brothers and grandfather hold their breaths too. It had been an open secret around the palace that the star soloist was suffering from a severe case of stage fright.

Their worry was unfounded.

Her eyes scrunched tightly shut, Amalie began to play.

When she'd played the piece for him in the bedroom the beauty of the underlying melody had made his heart expand. Coupled with the accompanying orchestral arrangement it was taken to a whole new level of beauty, heightening the sensation he'd experienced that first time, pulling him into a swell of emotion.

Watching her, the sway of her hips as she played with the whole of her body, the marvel of her finger-work, the purity of her vibrato…

The child prodigy was reborn—a virtuoso of such melodic stature that he was certain there couldn't be a dry eye in the amphitheatre.

As she approached the climax of the piece—the part that tore his heart into shreds—her eyes flew open and found the royal box. She was crying, he realised, huge tears falling down her cheeks.

His grandfather tugged at his sleeve for attention.

Blinking away the burn at the back of his eyes, Talos felt his chest constrict to see his grandfather's face also swimming with tears.

'Surely my fighter of a grandson isn't so scared of a woman's love that he would throw away his one chance of true happiness?' he asked in a choked voice.

It was as if his grandfather had stared right into his heart and read what was there. And in that moment the truth hit him with full force.

Suddenly it was there, as if he'd always known. There in his head. In his heart.

He'd fallen in love with her.

As epiphanies went, it beat them all.

He loved her.

Gazing back at the beautiful woman who held the thousands in the audience in silent captivation, he had never felt so full; as if his heart and chest had expanded so much they could explode out of him.

Theos, she was magnificent…holding her composure right until the final note played out.

The applause was instantaneous.

Everybody got to their feet, orchestra and crowd alike.

Wiping her face with shaking hands, Amalie bowed to the royal box, then bowed again to the audience at large. The conductor strode over to her, clapping hard, then put his hands on her shoulders and kissed her cheeks, then bowed to her. She laughed and put a hand over her mouth, so clearly overwhelmed at the reaction that Talos wanted to run on to the stage and scoop her into his arms.

But this was her moment, and she needed to cherish it.

She found the royal box again, kissed her hand, then pointed it at his grandfather, more tears falling down her cheeks.

The crowd were calling for an encore.

Amalie, the rest of the Orchestre National de Paris and all the other performers were whisked back inside the palace for the after-gala do.

She took the offered champagne and drank it with gratitude, still dazed at what she had accomplished.

She had done it.

Her parents had both messaged her.

Her father's message had read: I'm very proud of you, sweetheart—maybe the old dream of playing together at Carnegie Hall might one day come true xxx, while her mother's had been much longer and more rambling, but filled with just as much pride.

On impulse, she'd messaged them both back, suggesting the two of them celebrate together. Life was too short to be miserable, and far too short to be alone. They'd been divorced from each other almost as long as they'd been married, and still neither of them was happy without the other. If there was one thing Amalie had learned during her time on Agon it was that it was time to forgive the past. They needed to forgive it too.

A gong rang out, which brought everyone in the ballroom to attention. A courtier entered the room and announced the arrival of His Majesty King Astraeus and the Princes Helios, Theseus and Talos.

Her stomach somersaulted as a different courtier approached to lead her over to the royal family. She'd been warned that she would be the first one to be addressed by them.

Taking a deep breath, she finished her champagne and followed him to where the royal family were lined up, awaiting her. The other guests were forming an orderly queue, and she was taken to the head of it.

The King, frail in his wheelchair, broke into a smile to see her and grabbed her hands with surprising strength to tug her down to him. A tear trailed down his cheek. 'Thank you, *despinis*. Thank you from the bottom of my heart.'

Her own eyes filled. Hadn't she cried enough for one evening? Having not cried in years, her life being too safe for anything emotional to pierce her, it was as if her tear ducts were now making up for it.

'It was an honour,' she whispered.

This time it was the King who breached protocol, planting a kiss to her cheek, and then he indicated for his nurse to wheel him out, leaving the queue of people behind her staring in disbelief as the King left his own party.

Theseus was next in line, and surprised her by ignoring her hand and clumsy curtsy to kiss her on both cheeks. His eyes were a darker brown than Talos's, and rang with a strong emotion he didn't have to put into words.

Helios was even more demonstrative, pulling her into his arms for a tight embrace and whispering in her ear, 'My family honours you—our island is your home for as long as you want it to be.'

And then it was Talos's turn.

Jaw clenched, he shook her hand formally—his own had a bandage wrapped tightly around its forefinger and index finger—and bowed as she made her curtsy.

She met his eyes. 'You've hurt your hand…' She thought

back to the punch he'd given the wall of his office, and to the time she'd found him thumping that punching bag without protective gloves on.

'It'll heal.' A pulse throbbed beneath his ear, the black pupils of his eyes thick and dilating as he gazed at her without speaking any further.

She didn't know what to say. She knew he cared for her, but that didn't mean anything had changed. No matter how his feelings for her had developed, it didn't change the fact that he was a lone wolf.

Did lone wolves ever pair up?

Aware of the other performers jostling next to her, eager to have their audience with him, she turned to walk away but a huge arm hooked around her waist.

'Where do you think you're going?' he said roughly, pulling her away from the line.

Joy filled her so rapidly she felt her toes lifting with the extra air it generated. 'I was letting the others have their audience with you.'

'I don't want an audience with anyone but you.' He steered her further away from the line approaching the Princes, now a good two hundred people deep.

'Shouldn't you stay with your brothers?'

His massive shoulders lifted into a nonchalant shrug. 'They can handle it.'

She couldn't prevent the smile that broadened across her face so widely she felt it pull at every muscle in her face.

Talos wanted privacy for them. This was not a conversation he wanted to have with his brothers and hundreds of guests watching.

Gripping her hand firmly, he steered her out of the ballroom and through all the corridors they'd travelled together three weeks before. He hadn't expected her to agree so readily to his request to talk. After the way he'd spoken to her the other night he hadn't expected much more from her than a possible slap around the face.

He also hadn't expected that she would hold his hand as tightly as he held hers—so tightly it was as if she didn't want to let it go...

Punching in the security code for his private apartment, he led her inside. Dropping his hold on her hand, he strode to the high window of his living area, braced himself, and then turned around to face her properly.

'Before I say anything further I need to apologise for forcing you to come here to my island. The contract I made you sign and the pressure I put you under was unforgivable.'

She smiled. 'Thank you.'

What was she smiling for? 'There is no excuse.'

'Maybe not, but I forgave you ages ago.'

'I treated you abysmally. I refused to take you or your fears seriously because I am an arrogant bastard who thinks only of himself.'

'The arrogant bit is true...' She nodded, her eyes ringing with what looked startlingly like compassion. 'But the rest of your self-assessment is wrong. If you had blackmailed me for your own needs I would never have forgiven you, but it wasn't for selfish reasons. You did it for your grand-father...because you love him.'

He sucked in a breath and swallowed. 'I must also apologise for the way I spoke to you the other night. I lashed out at you, which is also unforgivable.'

'You were in pain.' She closed the gap he'd created between them and placed her hand on his arm. 'I should never have forced the issue with you.'

How could she keep forgiving him and making excuses? He didn't deserve it. He didn't deserve *her*.

'You were right to force it. You were right that what we shared was more than sex. But I was in denial. I lashed out because I find it hard to talk about how I feel, and at the time I was struggling to understand how I felt.'

Those compassionate green eyes held steady on his. 'And how do you feel now?'

How to put into words what was in his heart? He didn't know—knew only that he must.

He took a deep breath.

'All my life I have tried to protect those I…I feel deeply for. I wanted to protect my mother from my father. The night they died I heard them argue. My mother had discovered he was having another affair. She begged him to end it.'

He took another breath.

'My father was an only child and very spoiled. He was never denied anything he wanted. Their marriage was arranged and he wanted it to be one of duty, not love and to be able to continue having his needs met by whatever woman took his eye. But my mother loved him despite all his faults and couldn't accept that. Whenever she found evidence of his affairs her jealousy would get the better of her. That night their argument escalated and he turned on her with his fists—just as I had heard him do before. This time I summoned up the courage to try and protect her, but I was too small and clumsy. I made a vow to myself that from that moment I would do everything I could to protect her, but I never got the chance.'

Talos stared at the woman he knew he had to open himself to if he had any chance of winning her love. Her eyes were tugged down into crinkles at the corners, her teeth gnawing at her lips, but she kept her silence, letting him speak of the demons in his heart.

'You're the only woman I've met who brings that same compulsion out in me. I wanted to protect you—no, I *want* to protect you. Always.'

'Is that why you released me from the contract?' she asked softly.

'Yes.'

Remembering how magnificently she'd played made him shake his head in awe. Never mind that she'd played as if she were a *Mousai*, a Muse, one of those beautiful goddesses of music and song—she'd displayed the greatest act of bravery he'd ever witnessed in his life.

'I knew you could do it—believe that—but I couldn't put you through the emotional damage it would bring. Your distress…it cuts me.' He shook his head again. 'How did you get up on that stage?'

'I got Melina to come to the palace and put me through the workout of my life. With all those endorphins racing through my blood I imagined I was an Agonite—a born warrior. I imagined your voice in my head, telling me to fight.'

'But *why*? I gave you a free pass to leave.'

'And it was that freedom which gave me the choice. Do you remember what you said to me? You told me to loosen my hold and fly, and you were right—and the only person who could cut that hold was me. I *wanted* to fly. I *wanted* to throw off the past, stand on that stage and play that beautiful score. And I wanted to do it for you and your grandfather as much as I wanted to do it for me.'

'You wanted to do it for *me*?' How he had hoped…

'I knew how much it meant to you and how much you love your grandmother.'

A painful lump formed in his throat. 'My grandmother died without ever hearing me say those words. When my parents died I became lost, out of control. I didn't want to let people get close to me—not on an emotional level. I have friends…I've had lovers…but I kept them all at an emotional distance. And then you…'

'Me?' she prompted gently, her fingers digging into his arms.

'You…' He swallowed. 'I let you in. I had no choice in it. You crept into my heart.'

Something sparked in her eyes. 'Say it,' she urged. 'Please. Even if you only say it once I won't care, once will be enough. *Say it.*'

'I…'

'Shall I say it first?' Reaching up to palm his face with her hand, she stepped flush against him. 'I love you. You're ferocious and loyal and you've taught me to fly. I will love you until I take my dying breath.'

All the air rushed from his lungs.

'Say it,' she beseeched.

'I love you.' And as he said the words more tumbled out with them. 'I love you and I want to protect and honour you until I take my dying breath.' He kissed her hard. 'I love you.'

Raining kisses all over her face and neck, he kept repeating those words, letting them sink into every part of him until he was enveloped in the love that bound them so tightly he knew it would never let them go.

'Will you let me love and worship you for ever?' he asked, his hands buried in her silky hair.

'Only if you let me love and worship *you* for ever too.'

'If we marry you'll have no choice. Divorce is forbidden for me, remember...?' He pulled back to look deep into her eyes. *'Will* you marry me?'

'It's only a piece of paper, but I'll sign my heart on it because it belongs to you now. I'm trusting you to take care of it for me.'

'I'll protect it with my life.'

And with those words his hungry mouth moulded to hers.

He felt cleansed. Whole. Loved.

He loved her. And she loved him.

He would say the words to her every day for the rest of his life.

EPILOGUE

AMALIE STEPPED ONTO the sunny balcony of the New York hotel in time to catch Talos hastily turning the page of the newspaper he was reading.

'Stop reading my reviews,' she chided him, settling herself gently onto his lap and nuzzling his neck. Even after two years of marriage she liked nothing more than to bury herself into him and smell his gorgeous, woody scent.

He laughed. 'Do you want me to tell you what it says?'

'No.'

It was a standing joke between them.

Talos trawled the media for any review and snippet about her career he could find, getting any paper versions couriered to wherever they happened to be in the world. Although his pride in her touched her deeply, she preferred to live in blissful ignorance of the critics' voices.

The past couple of years had been a whirl. It made her dizzy to think back on it. After the gala she'd been inundated with offers to perform and record all over the world. Talos had encouraged her to follow her dreams, had been by her side every step of the way. It had been hard—especially the live performing side, which she chose selectively—but the nerves she'd lived with for so long had almost been banished. *Almost*.

He placed a hand to her swollen belly. 'Did you manage to get any sleep?'

'Some.' She kissed his neck. 'Junior gave up playing football in my belly when the sun came up.'

Seven months pregnant with their first child, she already resembled a watermelon. It was a look Talos assured her suited her. She was so excited about the pregnancy she wouldn't have cared if she looked like a bus.

'And how are you feeling about tonight?'

'Sick! But excited too,' she hastened to add.

Being so heavily pregnant meant that she couldn't do the vigorous kickboxing workout that usually served her so well before a performance. And tonight would be the performance she'd spent her whole life waiting for.

Tonight she and her father would be performing onstage together at Carnegie Hall.

'As long as you're there I'll be fine.'

He rubbed a big hand over her back. 'I want you to be more than fine—I want you to enjoy it.'

'Seeing as this is likely my last performance for a very long time, I intend to make the most of every moment.'

He'd started to say something—no doubt about to offer more reassurance—when the suite's buzzer went off.

Talos groaned. 'I bet that's your mother.'

Amalie's parents, who had remarried to great fanfare six months after Amalie and Talos's own nuptials, were staying in the same hotel. Her mother was enjoying the trip enormously, dragging her husband here, there and everywhere as she threw her weight around.

'Let's pretend we're not in,' Amalie murmured.

'She has unnatural senses.'

'We'll pretend to be asleep.'

Grinning, she slipped a hand down to the waistband of his shorts and undid the button.

'Come on, my Prince, take me to bed.'

Brown eyes gleaming, he pressed a kiss to her neck. 'Nothing would give me greater pleasure.'

Smothering their laughter, in case Colette had her ear

to the door, they tiptoed into the master bedroom of their suite, sneaked under the bedcovers and pretended to be asleep for a very long time.

* * * * *

If you enjoyed this book, look out for the next instalment of THE KALLIAKIS CROWN *trilogy:*

THESEUS DISCOVERS HIS HEIR
Coming next month.

And look out for the concluding story:

HELIOS CROWNS HIS MISTRESS
Coming in February.

MILLS & BOON®

**If you enjoyed this story,
you'll love the the full *Revenge Collection*!**

1115_MB517

MILLS & BOON®

Why shop at millsandboon.co.uk?

Each year, thousands of romance readers find their perfect read at millsandboon.co.uk. That's because we're passionate about bringing you the very best romantic fiction. Here are some of the advantages of shopping at www.millsandboon.co.uk:

* **Get new books first**—you'll be able to buy your favourite books one month before they hit the shops

* **Get exclusive discounts**—you'll also be able to buy our specially created monthly collections, with up to 50% off the RRP

* **Find your favourite authors**—latest news, interviews and new releases for all your favourite authors and series on our website, plus ideas for what to try next

* **Join in**—once you've bought your favourite books, don't forget to register with us to rate, review and join in the discussions

Visit **www.millsandboon.co.uk**
for all this and more today!